Praise for Lorelei James's
Cowgirls Don't Cry

"...turn on the air conditioner, get the fan out and grab some ice cubes because not only is this a good story, it's also a hot one...even with all that strife there is still a great romance to be written and Ms. James does it with pure abandonment, reminding us that even in times of great stress there is happiness to be found..."
~ *Fallen Angel Reviews*

"...This book is for lovers of romance, family drama, hot sex and delicious cowboys. Prepare to be swept away as a little boy, a cowboy and a widow climb right into your heart."
~ *Romance Reviews*

"...one of the best parts of these books is the hot cowboys and fantastic sex...but wrapped throughout this amazing story is some of the best erotica that you can read. It's real, it's raw and it's all out there."
~ *Night Owl Reviews*

"The 10th book in the Rough Riders series just totally blew me away...this story kept me captivated and entertained as I raced through the pages to see two people who deserve their own happily ever after as much as Brandt and Jessie...regardless of the many hurdles that they face along the way."
~ *Maldivian Book Reviews*

Look for these titles by
Lorelei James

Now Available:

Rough Riders
Long Hard Ride
Rode Hard, Put Up Wet
Cowgirl Up and Ride
Tied Up, Tied Down
Rough, Raw, and Ready
Branded As Trouble
Shoulda Been A Cowboy
All Jacked Up
Raising Kane
Slow Ride
Chasin' Eight

Wild West Boys
Mistress Christmas
Miss Firecracker

Print Anthologies and Collections
Wild Ride: Strong, Silent Type
Three's Company: Wicked Garden
Wild West Boys
Wild Ride

Running With the Devil
Dirty Deeds
Babe in the Woods

Cowgirls Don't Cry

Lorelei James

SAMHAIN
PUBLISHING

Samhain Publishing, Ltd.
11821 Mason Montgomery Rd., 4B
Cincinnati, OH 45249
www.samhainpublishing.com

Cowgirls Don't Cry
Copyright © 2011 by Lorelei James
Print ISBN: 978-1-60928-291-2
Digital ISBN: 978-1-60928-256-1

Editing by Lindsey Faber
Cover by Scott Carpenter

First Samhain Publishing, Ltd. electronic publication: November 2010
First Samhain Publishing, Ltd. print publication: September 2011

Dedication

For readers who were worried about Brandt and Jessie forever being star-crossed lovers...this one is for you.

Prologue

"Who's up for a threesome?"

Whoops and catcalls echoed around the campfire while Brandt McKay seethed in the shadows of the pine trees.

"And I mean *anyone*," Mike, that little fucking prick, emphasized with a drunken leer. "Guys, gals. Hell, it don't matter if it's more than three. In fact, the more the merrier! Me'n Jessica here—" he whacked Jessie's bikini-clad butt hard, "—are up for a good fuckin' time tonight."

"Or a good time fucking," someone shouted.

"You got that right," Mike shot back to additional wolf whistles.

Jessica. The little fucking prick didn't even know Jessie's name, for Christsake. What the hell was she doing with him?

Ain't that why you're spying on her like some lovesick peeping Tom? To figure out why she turned you down but she's hooked up with a loser worse than you?

Brandt ignored his sarcastic internal voice that resembled his father's. He remained as still as a hunter tracking prey as he spied on his brother's widow. The woman he'd purposely stayed away from for the last six months. Sweet Jesus, sweet Jessie looked good. Better than good and it didn't have a damn thing to do with the skimpy string bikini she wore. He'd always suspected a knockout body lurked beneath the frumpy western clothes she'd favored, but holy shit. She was perfect—all long, lean muscles with a few well-placed curves.

"Any takers?" Mike prompted the motley group of drunks.

"Hell yeah!"

"But Mike—"

Mike ground his mouth into Jessie's, cutting off her protest.

Encouraging whoops rang out when Mike wrapped his arms around Jessie's bare thighs. He clumsily threw her over his shoulder, half-stumbling past the fire pit as he headed toward the campsites.

Since Jessie was hanging upside down, Brandt couldn't tell how she felt about Mike's invitation for a sexual free for all.

He scowled and picked his way around rocks and shrubs, trying to keep the couple within his line of sight. But his damn flip-flops slipped on the pine needles. Tree branches scraped his bare chest and legs since he only wore board shorts. His fishin' buddies, Rob and Brent, had already packed up their tackle boxes. He should've gone home an hour ago, after his less-than-productive chat with Jessie...except he didn't trust these douchebags, and his gut instinct had been dead on. He doubted Jessie had turned into a party girl, indulging in random fucks with strange guys.

Maybe she's changed. Maybe she wants to experience every sexual scenario Luke had indulged in.

Highly unlikely. But he wanted to keep her from doing something she'd regret.

Mike stopped in front of a mid-sized camper. He let Jessie slide down his body and pushed her against the side of the camper as he opened the door.

Was she that drunk Mike had to hold her up?

Nope. Jessie walked into the camper on her own accord.

Fuck.

A couple minutes later, two guys, talking loudly about blowjobs and double penetration, wandered up from the bonfire.

Brandt was out of the darkness, blocking them before either reached the door.

"Hey, man." A sunburned, shirtless blond guy waved a bottle of vodka in Brandt's face. "You here to fuck that skinny chick too?"

"I don't wanna fuck her. I'm gonna ram my dick so far into her mouth she'll feel my balls on her chin," boasted the second guy, who sported an ape-like chest.

Brandt crossed his arms over his chest. "We've got enough

players, so take off."

"Fuck that, man," the blond spat. "We were invited."

"Yeah," the hairy one chimed in, "move it."

"Make me." No way was he letting these guys past him. No. Fucking. Way.

"You think you're tough," hairy guy sneered. "There's two of us and only one of you. I'd say the odds are in our favor."

"Yeah? Then bring it, motherfucker, 'cause I ain't goin' nowhere."

The blond dude squinted at Brandt. "Hold up a sec."

"What? We can take him."

"You're that cowboy asshole from the bar fight at Rockin' R last month." The blond guy spoke to his friend. "He's the one who punched Troy."

"Is that the guy whose ribs I broke?" Brandt asked, hoping the lie sounded credible.

"No. You busted Troy's tooth. Fucked up his face good too."

Brandt shrugged. "Huh. I guess it must've been the other guy who wanted a piece of me—right after I handed your buddy his ass. Or should I say after I handed him his tooth."

The two guys exchanged a look.

"To be honest, I don't remember a helluva lot from that night except I was pissed off, shitfaced and spoilin' for a fight." He flashed his teeth in a feral grin. "Unlike now. I'm pissed off, spoilin' for a fight, but I'm completely sober."

"Shit."

"So we doin' this? Or are you two walkin' the fuck away?"

Both guys held up their hands and backed off. "No problem, man. We're going."

"Good. And feel free to pass along the message that Mike's invitation for an orgy has been canceled."

They nodded and stumbled back toward the party.

Brandt waited another couple of minutes, but no one else appeared.

His deep inhalation didn't provide a sense of calm. Chances were high his temper would still get the best of him tonight, but it couldn't possibly be worse than his imagination. He opened the door.

The older model camper smelled musty and was dark except for a light shining from the back. He passed a cramped

11

living area and froze by the miniscule cook top when he noticed two naked forms. One standing. One...not.

Jessie was on her knees. Her strawberry blonde waves hung down her spine, brushing the dimples above her bare ass when she bobbed her head. Mike's hands were twisted in her hair as he bumped his pelvis into Jessie's face. His chorus of "That's it, baby" and "Suck it harder" bounced off the fake paneling.

Brandt had been ready—eager even—to jump in and pummel that little fucking prick Mike if he'd taken advantage of Jessie. But it appeared Jessie...was enjoying giving Mike a blowjob. Brandt must've made a noise, because Mike looked up with a drunken leer.

"I was beginning to wonder if anyone was gonna take me up on my offer. Go ahead and get nekkid. I'm about finished." Mike's hold on Jessie's head tightened as he rammed his cock into her mouth. "Almost there. That's good, baby. Get ready to swallow."

Jessie vehemently shook her head no.

Mike's braying donkey laughter grated. "No swallowing on the first date, huh? I'll come on your tits. But you hafta do the work."

She pushed back, dislodging his cock from her mouth with a soft pop. Her arm moved up and started moving fast as she jacked him off.

Mike shut his eyes, not watching as Jessie finished him.

Brandt should've been turned off. He should've walked off.

So why was he having the exact opposite reaction? Why had his dick leapt to attention as if it were next in line?

"That was fantastic." Mike pulled up his trunks as Jessie got to her feet.

"Can I get a drink?" Jessie asked, wiping off her chest with a beach towel.

"I've got something right here." Mike handed her a nearly empty bottle of Southern Comfort.

Jessie grabbed it, chugging until Mike snatched it out of her hand, warning, "Hey, leave some for me."

"I thought you wanted me drunk so we could get our freak on."

Another donkey like laugh erupted. "You need to be drunk

to do that?"

"Probably."

He swatted her ass. "Hop up on the bed. I'll be right back."

Jessie face-planted in the center of the mattress.

Before Brandt moved, Mike blocked him and whispered, "Don't do nothin' to her until I get back."

"Where are you goin'?"

"Ah. I left a joint in my truck. I'd offer to share, but there's really only like half left, so..."

Man, Jessie really knew how to pick 'em. This fucker had no problem sharing her with another guy or two, but he had an issue sharing his pot?

Unbelievable.

Mike pointed at Brandt's swimming trunks. "Might as well strip them off so we can get right to it when I get back."

Brandt shook his head. "I'll be leavin' them on."

A slimy smile distorted Mike's face. "You sly motherfucker. You like to watch, eh?"

I'd like to watch my fist connect with your face. But Brandt merely shrugged.

"Suit yourself." The camper door slammed behind Mike.

Brandt paused by Jessie's side, unsure what to do. He swept her silky hair from her face, which caused her to emit a disgruntled sound and turn her head away from him.

Awesome.

Brandt sat on the edge of the bed. "Jessie?"

Her body went rigid, but she didn't move.

He tried again. "Jessie? It's me."

"Luke?"

Holy hell that hurt. Like a hoof to the solar plexus that knocked the breath from his lungs kind of pain. "No, it's not—"

"Go away, Luke, you're not real."

Was she slurring her words? "Are you drunk?"

"Sorta, but I won't let you make me feel guilty after all the times you were drunk. After all you did to me, you bastard."

Her voice cracked, creating another chink in Brandt's armor.

A beat of silence passed. And another. Finally Brandt spoke. "Jessie. Listen—"

"No. I'm done listening to my dead husband's phantom voice. So go away, get outta my head."

"Goddammit, Jessie, look at me."

Miracle of miracles, she rolled over, angrily pushed her tangled hair from her face and squinted at him.

Brandt didn't let his gaze fall below her chin.

Jessie had that glassy-eyed look from too much alcohol, and her reaction time was slower, but she didn't react like he'd expected. No embarrassment. No trying to cover her naked body. Hell, she didn't even shriek with surprise. She just stared at him.

He stared back.

"I forgot how much you and Luke sound alike."

"I wasn't tryin' to pretend to be him," Brandt said softly.

That comment brought her sad smile. "I know. There's no comparison."

There was that kicked-in-the-heart sensation again.

"Why did you stick around? I wasn't very nice to you."

His thoughts skipped back to Jessie's bored appraisal of him and her insulting parting shot. "I intended to take off. B-but..." Goddammit. Why was he such a stammering freakin' idiot around her?

"But you didn't because you were worried about me." She held his gaze. "Why? Luke would have left me."

"I'm not Luke." Like he needed to remind her of that fact, after she'd already done such a bang up job of reminding him.

"I know that too, Brandt."

Do you? Do you really?

She frowned, almost as if she'd heard his internal thoughts.

"Come on. Get dressed and I'll take you home."

Jessie shook her head. "I'm staying here with Mike."

"Why in the hell would you do that?" he demanded.

"Because he treats me like I'm sexy."

"Christ, Jessie. He almost *treated* you to a gang bang."

"Maybe that's what I want."

"Huh-uh. I know you and that's not you talkin'." Brandt pointed to the bottle of Southern Comfort. "That's the booze talkin'."

The camper door slammed.

She tossed her head. "Maybe you don't know me as well as you think you do, *McKay.*"

The emphasis on McKay, as if it were some sort of disease, had Brandt seeing red.

The instant Mike swayed into the doorway, Jessie scooted to the end of the bed, cooing, "What took you so long?"

"Why? Didja miss me?"

"Yep. Let's get this party started."

Enough. Brandt pushed to his feet. "I'm outta here."

Mike shot Brandt a stoned look. "I thought you were gonna watch us fuck? You know. Like live porn."

When phrased that way? Jesus. It made him sound like a loser who couldn't score his own woman. He looked at Jessie—just as she started to slide off the bed.

Brandt dove for her, snaking his arm around her waist, bringing her naked back against his chest as he anchored himself.

"Dude." Mike blinked at him. "Talk about Superman reflexes."

"That's Brandt. A superhero in the flesh. A boy scout. A real trooper. The ultimate gentleman cowboy, always willing to lend a hand."

They'd known each other for four years and that's how Jessie saw him? A damn do-gooder? While some guys might like those comparisons, he didn't. Not at all. Especially not from Jessie. Especially not tonight when he was skating so close to the edge of disproving that gentleman cowboy remark to her in explicit detail.

But she wasn't done taunting him. "He's the guy who always does the right thing. Which is why he'll skip out, even if he wants to stay."

And with that smartass comment...Jessie had pushed him too far.

"You know, on second thought, I do believe I will stick around and *lend a hand.*"

Jessie gasped when Brandt brought them down on the edge of the mattress. He hooked her legs over the tops of his thighs, then moved her body forward so her ass hung off the bed. After circling her wrists with his fingers, he rested on his elbows and placed her palms flat on the mattress and nestled his groin against her back.

"You hold her and I'll go first. Then it'll be your turn," Mike promised.

She squirmed, sliding her smooth shoulders against Brandt's bare chest. The friction of his swimming trunks rubbing against his cock as her body writhed on his instantly turned his cock into granite.

Brandt allowed his gaze to drop to the Mike's groin after he ditched his cutoffs.

What the hell? Mike's dick hung between his scrawny thighs like a limp worm. Seeing Jessie's naked body spread out for him like a feast didn't affect him at all? Jesus. How would that make Jessie feel?

Maybe she's so drunk she won't notice.

For the first time, Brandt hoped that was true.

Will you step in and show her how she affects you *if this douche fucker can't get it up?*

No. But that didn't mean he couldn't distract her. Brandt angled his head and spoke quietly. "Jessie, is this really what you want?"

"I-I d-don't... Yes," she reiterated firmly, "it's what I want."

"Then close your eyes."

"But you—"

"Do it," he said harshly. Then he softened toward her, in mind and body, nuzzling the tender, fragrant skin behind her ear. "Just close your eyes. I've got you."

A heartbeat or two later, Jessie relaxed into him, turning her head so her rapid breaths drifted across his chest.

In that moment he wanted her with an ache that defied reason. It went beyond sex. It went beyond anything he'd ever felt before.

Brandt tore his attention away from Jessie and looked up at Mike—who frowned at the state of his non-responsive dick. Mike knocked back a slug of Southern Comfort and set the bottle aside. His fingers traced the inside of Jessie's thighs as he leaned over to suck her right nipple into his mouth.

Jessie arched and she tried to move her hands to touch Mike, but Brandt held her firmly. She wiggled, moaning as Mike kissed down her belly and staggered to his knees. Brandt knew the instant Mike's mouth connected with Jessie's sex. Her back bowed as if she'd been touched by a defibrillator.

Goddammit. This was so fucking bizarre, but also almost...erotic, holding her, feeling her body's response as another man pleasured her.

She whimpered, "Yes. Please. More."

Mike kept a slurred dialogue, extolling the virtues of Jessie's pussy in outdated porn terms, which he probably believed turned her on. But the idiot didn't notice Jessie reacted most strongly when he quit flapping his gums and put his mouth on her.

Finally, Mike got to it, spiking Brandt's jealousy to epic proportions to hear Mike's slurping, sucking noises from between Jessie's quivering thighs. *He* wanted to be the one eking out her feminine sighs and moans. *He* wanted to be the one tasting her. *He* wanted to be the one driving her to the brink of ecstasy.

Sweat broke out on his brow. On the back of his neck. Moisture coated his balls. And it didn't help that Jessie's sexy, slippery body was sliding all over his. Specifically against his impatient cock.

A loud thud sounded and Jessie's thrashing stopped abruptly. Brandt released her wrists to see what the hell the noise was.

Jessie maneuvered her body away from Brandt's. They peered over the edge of the bed.

Holy shit. Mike had passed out cold on the floor.

In the middle of going down on Jessie.

Unfuckingbelievable.

She whispered, "You think he had a heart attack or something?"

But she wasn't frantically checking him over, which meant she wasn't so out of it she couldn't see the truth. She nudged his leg. "Mike?"

Mike let out a soft snore.

Once again Brandt's heart broke when Jessie made a soft sob. She scampered away from him quickly, like a crab sinking back into the sand. "Jessie—"

"Just go away."

"No. I'm takin' you home. Where are your clothes?"

No answer.

Focusing on his anger on her behalf kept him from pitying her. "Fine." Brandt tossed the comforter over her, rolled her like a sausage, and lifted her into his arms.

She gasped, "What're you doing?"

"Takin' you home."

"But I'm naked!"

"Wasn't like that swimsuit covered up much anyway." And yeah, when Brandt stepped over Mike's sprawled form, he might've kicked the guy's ribs. The idiot wouldn't have noticed if he'd been kicked in his numb nuts.

"Put me down, Brandt. I mean it."

"No way in hell."

The walk from the camper to his truck was mighty long and mighty quiet. He deposited her in the passenger side of his pickup before he climbed in. After he started backing out, she said, "Wait."

"What? You feel like you're gonna barf?"

"No. I forgot my purse."

"Where?"

She bit her lip. "I'm pretty sure it's still in the cab of Mike's pickup."

Brandt whipped a U-turn and followed the bumpy trail from the public parking area back to the campsites. He pulled up behind Mike's camper and shut off his truck, pocketing the keys. He issued a stern, "Don't go nowhere, Jessie, I mean it," and bailed out.

The pungent scent of pot smoke wafted out of Mike's truck as Brandt opened the door. A roach clip dangled from the rearview mirror, weighted with feathers and skinny strips of leather. He pushed aside food wrappers and empty beer cans until he found a small bright orange fanny pack. Since he'd forgotten to ask specifics about size and color, he unzipped the main compartment. His hand froze.

It wasn't the unopened package of condoms that snared his interest, but the hand-tooled leather wallet. The wallet he'd made Jessie for Christmas—in what turned out to be the only Christmas they'd spent together.

The ragged edge of Brandt's thumb traced the row of flowers he'd so painstakingly pounded out in the supple leather above the metal clasp. After he'd tanned the row a rich brown and finished the rough edges with a leather whipstitch, he'd painted each tiny flower a different color.

He couldn't believe Jessie had kept the wallet. She'd seemed embarrassed when she'd opened his present. Too late Brandt learned such a labor-intensive gift was appropriate for a girlfriend. Or a lover. Or a wife. None of which Jessie was to him. Luke had been a real prick about it, too, teasing him mercilessly. Ragging on Jessie. They'd both ignored Luke, and Brandt figured Jessie had probably thrown it out to keep the peace with her husband. Warmth expanded in his chest even as he called himself ten kinds of fool for feeling that spark of pleasure.

He scrutinized the inside of the truck cab for anything else that might belong to her before he zipped up the purse and jogged back to his pickup.

Jessie had wedged herself in the corner. Relief swept over her when he tossed the purse in her lap. "Thank you."

"You wanna check to see if anything is missing?"

"No. Just take me home."

He let her be, even when he wanted to assure her that Mike's reaction was a result of booze and pot, not a reaction to her. They'd barely driven two miles when he heard Jessie sniffle. Brandt glanced over at her. "Jess. Baby. Please. Don't cry. I swear to God you're killin' me here."

Her voice was a raw rasp. "Chin up, buck up, right? Be strong, be tough. Don't snivel. No man likes a crybaby. Yeah. I know. I've heard that a time or fifty."

That wasn't what he'd meant and her response jabbed that raw wound in his gut again. Before he could explain, Jessie said, "Do you wanna know something? Tonight was supposed to be 'the night' when I'd finally..." She sniffled again. "God. How pathetic is it that I had to build up my courage to do it and this is how it turned out? How fucking pathetic that I'm twenty-seven years old and I haven't been with any man besides Luke?"

"Ever?" spewed out of his mouth before he could stop it. Brandt knew Jessie hadn't dated at all during the year they grieved together over Luke. But he hadn't expected she'd stayed celibate during the months he hadn't seen her, especially since he'd heard she'd been out, hitting the local honky-tonks.

It burned his ass to think her experience with that little fucking prick Mike was her first foray into reclaiming a sexual part of herself.

Her soft sigh tempered his anger. "Yes, Luke was my first, my only, but we *were* married for two years. So I'm not...inexperienced as much as I'm out of practice."

Brandt wanted to tell her to shut up as much as he wanted her to keep talking.

"I miss sex. A lot."

She intended to torture him all right.

"Does it make me sound like a horny widow if I admit I want that body-to-body connection? I can get myself off with my vibrator a dozen times a day if I want. But it's not the same, is it?"

I can demonstrate the difference, if you want.

She was quiet for a minute or so, and Brandt thought she'd fallen asleep. But her voice broke into his thoughts.

"When was the last time you had sex?"

It'd been a few weeks, which didn't compare to the two years she'd gone without.

"So out there in the dating world, does oral sex count as real sex? Because I'm thinking if I didn't get off, even if he did, then it shouldn't count as sex."

"I cannot believe we're havin' this conversation." He sensed her studying him, but he kept his eyes on the road.

"Well, it is a pretty one-sided conversation, Brandt." She paused again. "Think Mike will tell everyone we did the nasty?"

Brandt snarled, "If he opens his goddamn mouth and says anything to anyone about you, I will track that little fucking prick down and cut his tongue out."

"Oh. That's sweet. Okay, maybe not sweet, and wow, I never imagined you had such a violent streak, Brandt. It's kinda scary."

You have no idea.

Jessie made a noise that sounded like a choked laugh.

"What?"

"Then again, maybe you'd be doing a service to womankind, cutting out his tongue. Because, man, he really did not know how to use it."

Jesus, Mary and Joseph give him strength to survive this discussion with Jessie about oral sex, vibrators, tongues, abstinence and...nope. The devil had taken over his thoughts and was conjuring up some smokin' hot scenarios, adding in rope for fun.

When she thrashed to get more comfortable, Brandt looked over to double check she hadn't wiggled too close to the door handle. He hit the automatic locks as a precaution.

Always looking out for her, aren't you?

Somebody has to.

The rest of the drive might've been awkward if she's kept peppering him with questions about sex and freely offering her own insight. But she either drifted off or pretended to, and Brandt was grateful for the reprieve. Didn't keep his brain from offering advice in case she suddenly became chatty again.

At the turnoff to her trailer, Jessie stirred. After he parked by her front porch steps, she faced him. Not with a sheepish look, as he expected, but with a resigned look. "Thank you. I'm sorry you had to..." She gestured wildly. "Be party to my humiliation tonight."

"It wasn't—"

She held up her hand. "It was. And you don't have to be nice about it. So thank you. Please...now that I've had time to think about what an idiot I was, I never want to talk about it again, okay?"

Brandt bit back, *No, it's not okay, goddammit, what the hell were you thinking tonight?*

"In fact, I don't want any kind of reminder of tonight."

Like he'd ever forget this night.

"Get rid of it. Burn it, use it as a rag, I don't care."

He refocused on her. "Get rid of what?"

"This." She unwrapped the comforter from around her body and shoved it between them.

Then Jessie was as naked as a newborn babe, in the front seat of his truck.

Oh no. No, no, no.

Brandt was so pole-axed he couldn't make his mouth work when Jessie bounced out of his truck and strolled to her house, wearing nothing but her birthday suit.

If he hadn't been so busy gawking at her perfectly pear-shaped ass, or if he hadn't become mesmerized by the sassy way her hair teased the dimples above that perfectly pear-shaped ass, or if he hadn't been drooling over the way her long-legged strides made that perfectly pear-shaped ass shake so jauntily, he might've remembered Jessie had warned him that he didn't know her as well as he thought he did.

When she turned in the doorway and blew him a kiss, Brandt realized he should've listened to her.

He also understood some things hadn't changed, namely Jessie's brotherly feelings toward him. So he'd do as she asked, pretend this night never happened, and continue to stay away from her, as hard as that would be.

Chapter One

Four months later...

Talk about being a total chickenshit. Here she was, twenty-seven years old, doing her best wallflower imitation again.

Story of your life, Jessie McKay.

At least she'd had the foresight to bring along a couple of beers for company. Or solace. Or courage.

Jessie swigged from the bottle of Corona as she watched the newlyweds swaying to an old George Strait tune. Keely and Jack fit the love song they'd chosen for their first dance as husband and wife. The happy couple only had eyes for each other, despite repeated attempts from Keely's assorted male family members to cut in. Although Jack used a charming smile to dissuade interruption, a possessive male lurked beneath his polished demeanor.

Keely deserved a man so perfectly suited for her. A man who worshipped her as a strong-willed cowgirl, but clearly was fierce enough to stand up to her—and her family. Because when you married one McKay, somehow you ended up with them all.

So it wasn't a surprise that Jessie was still considered part of the McKay family. Well, most of the McKays. They'd been supportive after Luke's death, especially during the first month of shock and grief. She'd been forced from her home. Forced to find a job. Forced to stand on her own. If it hadn't been for Luke's brother Brandt, she might've taken the easy way out and driven her truck off a cliff.

But Brandt became her pillar of support. He helped her, no matter if her problem was big or small. He was there for her like a brother would be. Except one night, a year into her widowhood, Brandt had confessed his feelings for her weren't merely brotherly.

At the time, she'd been shocked. She'd never looked at Brandt in that light. In her heart, in her mind, she would always be Luke's wife. She hadn't known how to explain it without sounding delusional.

After that night, everything changed between them. Brandt stopped coming over. He'd quit answering her calls. In a moment of clarity a month or so later, she realized it was time to let go.

In those soul-searching moments, she'd faced a lot of truths, half-truths and untruths. About herself. About Luke. About their marriage. Then she'd taken three steps that helped her move on for good.

One: she'd stopped wearing her wedding ring.

Two: she'd had the McKay "brand" tattoo above her ankle reworked into a butterfly emerging from a cocoon.

Three: she'd decided to have a one-night stand with a complete stranger.

The last step had been a biggie. Not only had Luke McKay been her first and only lover, Luke also hadn't been faithful during their marriage. So she'd needed to prove—if only to herself—that she could attract a lover.

Which was how she'd ended up at the lake last summer when she'd run into Brandt. She hadn't recognized him at first. She'd never seen Brandt McKay without all his cowboy regalia— boots, jeans, hat. She'd definitely never seen him shirtless, barefoot, wearing funky board shorts, looking tanned, fit and unbelievably sexy.

Upon closer inspection, the baby fat Luke had always teased Brandt about was gone, replaced with muscle. Lots of muscle. He'd hacked off his dark, wavy hair in a military buzz cut style. Goatee? Gone. Soul patch? Gone. Despite the leaner appearance, Brandt's angular face was still too rugged looking to be considered handsome in the classical sense, like Luke's had been.

What hadn't changed about Brandt? His captivating smile that managed to be both cocky and shy. The stunning blueness of his eyes. His overprotective instinct. The first thing he'd done after seeing her for the first time in months was lecture her on hooking up with a douchebag like Mike.

At that point, Jessie had told Brandt she was predestined to wind up with douchebags like Mike and Luke, and if he were smart, he'd continue to stay away from her.

He'd started to argue and she'd glimpsed something dangerous in Brandt's eyes she'd never noticed. But true to form, he'd walked away.

Or so she'd thought.

She'd been so eager to convince Mike and his friends she was good-time Jessie the party girl, not a mousy widow with a pathetic past, that she ended up drinking way more than was healthy or smart.

The details were hazy through the veil of alcohol. Except for the humiliation of not holding Mike's sexual interest even when she was naked and willing. Chivalrous Brandt had taken her home. She hadn't seen or heard from him until today.

Jessie slumped against the wall. So far she'd been able to avoid talking to him.

Or maybe he's avoiding talking to you.

She heard, "Miss Jessie!" and saw her boss's twin daughters racing toward her.

Peyton exclaimed, "There you are," and attached herself to Jessie's hip. "We've been looking *everywhere* for you."

Not to be outdone, Shannie hugged the other leg and added, "Yeah, *everywhere.*"

"I've been here the whole time." Jessie whistled. "You look like princesses in those dresses."

Both girls beamed and twirled in a flurry of ribbons, ruffles and frills that adorned their pink and lavender dresses. Not matching dresses. Peyton and Shannie were fraternal twins, but they'd exerted their individuality early on. Since Jessie ran the daycare at Sky Blue, she'd watched these girls over the last two years, always amazed by how different they were from each other, and from their older sister, Eliza.

Eliza, who was trying to keep up with her dozen or so boy cousins.

"Will you dance with us?" Shannie asked.

"Please?" Peyton begged.

"Where are your mom and dad?"

Shannie rattled off, "Mama is right over there, see? She's helpin' Aunt Ginger with her little babies since Daddy and

Uncle Buck hadta take Hayden's grandpa home."

Jessie wasn't surprised Kane and Ginger McKay had brought their twins, Madelyn and Paulson, to Keely's wedding. Babies abounded at McKay gatherings because there were plenty of hands to help out harried mothers and fathers.

"Miss Jessie, can we ask you something?"

"Sure, Peyton."

"How come we don't call you Aunt Jessie? You're a McKay, just like us, right?"

Boy howdy. How long had these precocious three-year-olds been waiting for a chance to ask her? She snagged a chair and sat. The girls scrambled onto her lap. "I became a McKay after I married your dad's cousin Luke."

"But he's in heaven, huh?" Shannie said.

"Yep. Right after he...went to heaven, I started working for your mom at Sky Blue. We decided it'd be too confusing for the other kids in daycare if you two and Eliza called me Aunt Jessie, so we thought it'd be best if everyone called me Miss Jessie."

Shannie exchanged a sly look with Peyton before she said, "So if you don't got a husband hogging all your time, then you *can* dance with us."

She smiled at their logic. "I suppose so."

"Yay!" The girls hopped down, each grabbed a hand and tugged her onto the dance floor.

Jessie spun the girls through two songs. When a slow number started, she started to herd them off the dance floor, but Calvin McKay intercepted, scooping both his giggling granddaughters into his arms for a dance.

Before she reached her table, a firm grip circled her waist and she was towed back to the dance floor. Brandt slipped his arms around her—at a proper distance naturally—and said, "Thanks for dancin' with me."

"Like you gave me a choice."

"You would've said no if I asked, so I didn't ask."

She couldn't help it; she smiled.

Brandt's gaze wandered over her face. "You look beautiful tonight, Jess."

She blushed. "Thank you. You clean up pretty good yourself." No lie. Brandt wore a black suit with a silver vest. The same silver vest all Keely's male McKay relatives wore, but he somehow wore it better...which was really saying something.

"How have you been?"

Lonely. "Busy. How about you?"

"The same."

The song shifted tempo and he slowed them to a gentle sway.

"It was a beautiful wedding. I've never seen Keely so happy," Jessie murmured.

"Me either."

They stayed quiet in the moment, just dancing. The song ended and another one began. "I should go," she said, trying to slip from his embrace.

But Brandt's grip tightened. "Stay. We need to talk."

The last thing she wanted was to talk about the fiasco at the lake. "If in my drunken idiocy I forgot to say thank you for...what you did for me that night—"

"You said thank you," he replied tersely, "repeatedly, and that's not why I wanna talk to you."

"Well, thank heaven for that. Because God knows I haven't relived the most embarrassing night of my life in my nightmares enough times in the last four months."

"You're not the one who oughta be embarrassed."

"Can we please stop talking about this?"

"No."

She took a step back.

He jerked her forward again.

"Knock it off, Brandt."

"No. We are gonna talk about this now that *you* brought it up. Did Mike call you the next day?"

She knew he wouldn't let it go. "Yes. He didn't remember anything, okay? Not a single thing."

"That little fucking prick. Do you remember anything?"

Heat rose in her cheeks. "Some."

"What did he say when he called?"

"He asked me out again."

"Did you go?" Brandt demanded.

She glared at him. "What the hell do you think?"

He stared back, pulling that silent accusing crap he did so

well. Once again she tried to get away from him, once again he didn't let her.

"Let me go."

Before Brandt answered, Dalton appeared. "Hey, guys. Mind if I cut in?"

"Get the fuck away, Dalton," Brandt snarled.

"Look, people are watching. Dad especially. I ain't gonna let either of you fuck up Keely's wedding reception by givin' Dad the chance to cause a scene. Which we all know he'd love to do. So back the fuck off, Brandt, and let me dance with Jessie."

"Fine." Brandt leaned in and kissed Jessie's cheek. Then he whispered, "This ain't over. Mark my words, Jessie. We will talk, even if I have to hogtie you to make it happen." He gave them both a feral smile and ambled off the dance floor toward the bar.

Without missing a beat, Dalton brought her into his arms. "I ain't gonna ask what the hell that was about."

"Smart choice, Dalton."

"I may be slow, but I ain't dumb."

She relaxed and let him lead. Her relationship with Dalton was more sibling-like than her relationship with Brandt. Dalton still called her every couple of weeks just to shoot the breeze. Last month he'd come over and helped her fix fence, regaling her with tales of his dating life, which always made her laugh.

"So, sister, you're lookin' good."

"You're looking dapper yourself, young McKay. Did you bring a date to the wedding?"

"Are you kiddin'? Bring a woman to a wedding and they immediately start hearin' wedding bells. And I ain't close to ready to settle down."

"The wild McKay boys are still goin' strong?"

"You know it." He danced them toward the stage. "Although, lately, Tell seems to be takin' a page from Brandt's book, actin' like a freakin' monk."

Jessie's pulse jumped. Dalton never talked about Brandt around her. "Oh really? A few months back someone mentioned Brandt seeing a woman from Hulett."

"Lydia? She's old news. They've been on-again, off-again for the last ten months."

Her immediate burst of jealousy was ridiculous.

"Something is goin' on with him. He's been a real dickhead the last month. I thought maybe he was pissy because he wasn't getting laid, but I ain't sure that's what's been bugging him. I wondered if he'd said something to you, 'cause he sure as hell ain't talkin' to me or Tell."

"I'm sorry, but Brandt hasn't been around much the last year."

A blush stole across Dalton's cheeks.

"What?"

"Nothin'. I just ain't surprised."

And then Jessie knew. Brandt must've told his brothers that she'd turned him down. No wonder Dalton never talked about Brandt around her. In fact, with their Three Musketeers mentality, she was surprised Dalton and Tell stayed in contact with her at all and they hadn't taken Brandt's side.

Tell approached, elbowing Dalton aside. "My turn. Your girlfriend is lookin' for you anyway."

"What girlfriend?"

He whispered something to Dalton that had him blushing beet red.

"Fuck off. I'd punch you in the mouth for even sayin' that, but Dad would love to see us mixin' it up, so I'm bein' the bigger man and walkin' away." Dalton made it two steps before he tossed, "Asshole," over his shoulder.

"Such a loving family," Jessie muttered as Tell took her hands.

"Miss us, doncha?"

She smiled. "Not touching that one."

He laughed. "So what's new?"

"You'd know if you ever bothered to call me." At his guilty look, she whapped him on the shoulder. "Tell. I'm kidding. Since my life is incredibly boring, why don't you tell me what you've been up to?"

"I've been hittin' as many local rodeos as possible, tryin' to complete my PRCA judges course."

Tell had been talking about doing that since the first time they'd met. "You actually followed through with it?"

"Yep. I got tired of waiting for the right time to get certified and they accepted me as a candidate because of my past rodeo experience. I've been studying DVDs and scoring the rides.

Then they match how I scored them to the real scores to see how I did."

"It hasn't interfered with your ranch work?"

Tell scowled. "To hear Dad talk, I've all but abandoned the ranch. Hell. I'm gone one day, two at the most in a month. Brandt and Dalton ain't complaining. And since Brandt's pretty much in charge, he's the one I'm the most concerned with. The season's almost over. Dad's just pissy because I'm headin' to the NFR in December for a week's worth of hands-on classes."

Casper had always condemned any activity that took his sons away from the ranch. She remembered Luke saying that Tell could've gone pro in saddle bronc or bareback riding, but Casper wouldn't allow it. Of all Casper's sons, Tell was the peacemaker. So this new direction in his life, against his father's wishes, surprised her and she said as much.

"After Luke died, I realized that Dad wouldn't ever be happy again about anything any of us did. I decided to do what I want and he can deal with it."

Jessie studied him. Tell resembled Luke more than either Brandt or Dalton, but he had the same world-weary look she'd seen on Brandt. "Are things any better between you guys and your dad?"

He shook his head. "Worse, actually."

"I'm sorry."

"I know you are." Tell smiled. "So let's look like we're havin' a blast out here on the dance floor, eh? That oughta really piss Casper off good."

She laughed.

As soon as the dance ended, she booked it to the women's bathroom. Halfway down the hall, she felt a hand on her shoulder. She didn't have to turn around to know it was Brandt.

Why wouldn't he just leave her alone?

"Jessie. Wait."

She spun to face him, shrugging out of his hold. "What do you want now?"

"We need to talk."

"I'm talked out." She wheeled back around...and found herself pushed against the wall with Brandt in her face.

"Goddammit, this is really important."

"So is the fact I was on my way to the bathroom."

His eyes darkened and his grip on her biceps increased. "I'm serious."

"Fine. Spit out what is so important that I'm not even allowed to pee first."

He stared at her with that wordless threat.

She'd had enough of his tough guy attitude. "Let me go...or I'll punch you in the stomach."

His shock gave way to a smarmy grin. "Punch me? You? Sweet Jessie? I'll bet you've never hit another person in your life."

Mistake.

Jessie released a fast, hard uppercut to his solar plexus that immediately had him falling back to clutch his gut. She leaned closer and hissed, "I might not've hit a person, but I own a punching bag now, so back off."

A gasp echoed and she looked up to see Keely and AJ McKay staring at them in openmouthed horror.

Shit. "Sorry, Keely. I didn't mean..."

"To punch Brandt in the stomach? That was an accident?"

"Umm. No. I meant to do that. I didn't mean to cause a scene and I...really have to wash my hands."

Keely's gaze darted between them. "Okay. Don't be too long. I'm about to throw the bouquet."

Like that was an incentive not to run out of here screaming. Jessie watched Keely and AJ disappear into a dressing room and hightailed it to the ladies room, not sparing Brandt a second glance.

She hid out as long as she could—or at least until all the wedding guests were occupied with the tossing of the bouquet.

As soon as the coast was clear, she snuck out the back door and drove straight home.

Take that, Brandt McKay. I won't talk to you if I don't want to and there's not a damn thing you can do about it.

Chapter Two

Brandt couldn't believe Jessie had snuck out.

He really couldn't believe she'd sucker punched him.

Not a sucker punch if she warned you.

True.

Fifteen minutes after she'd socked him a good one, he'd noticed she hadn't returned to the reception. He checked the parking lot and saw her pickup was gone.

Brandt had left immediately.

The drive to her place had been little more than a blur. He knew when he'd cut the truck's headlights and pulled into her driveway that she hadn't gone to bed yet. Even if her trailer had been completely dark he'd still be standing on her porch, ready to rip the damn door off the hinges if she didn't answer his knock.

A knock, which she'd ignored for the fifth time.

Screw it. Jessie already thought he was heavy handed, so he used that heavy hand to beat on the aluminum siding. "I ain't leavin' Jessie, so open up."

Lexie barked inside and Jessie shushed her as the door swung inward.

His braced himself, half-expecting she'd be aiming a shotgun at him.

Why that thought heated his blood just proved how twisted he was when it came to his conflicted feelings about his former sister-in-law.

But Jessie wasn't packing heat. She crossed her arms over her chest and glared at him through the screen door. "Did you bring the ropes to hogtie me with?"

"Funny. I'm comin' in."

She muttered, "Typical McKay macho bullshit," and unlocked the screen door.

Any relief that she'd relented to listen to him vanished when he remembered what he had to tell her.

Inside, he absentmindedly patted Lexie's head and watched Jessie grab two beers out of the fridge. She passed him a bottle on her way to sit on the couch.

She'd changed out of the slinky gray cocktail dress and into baggy red sweatpants and a black sports bra that molded to her upper torso, emphasizing the slenderness of her shoulders, the gentle curve of her breasts and the flatness of her belly. Damn woman looked good no matter what she wore.

Or didn't wear. The image of her naked in his arms had been permanently burned into his memory banks, but oddly, that wasn't the first thing that popped into his head whenever he saw her. Usually the word *mine* flashed behind his eyes in big red letters, and that was just all kinds of fucked up.

By the time she faced him, he'd managed a bland expression.

Jessie's gaze dropped to his stomach. "Sorry for punching you."

"No, you're not."

Her smile was there and gone. "Why are you here?"

"Because I need to tell you something." At her uncomfortable look, he held up his hand. "I promise it doesn't have nothin' to do with the embarrassing way I threw myself at your feet last year."

She frowned.

"You don't remember?"

"Of course I remember. I just...didn't see it that way."

"Thank God for that," he muttered, swigging his beer.

"What's up, that you had to chase me down at eleven o'clock on a Saturday night?"

Blurt it out.

No, break it to her gently.

"Brandt?"

"It's..." Fuck. This was gonna suck ass.

"What? You're scaring me."

"I came across some information... Well, that ain't exactly true. I wasn't the one who made initial contact... Ah hell. I'm doin' this all wrong." He chugged another drink of beer. "Last month a woman called me. She said she knew Luke."

Jessie didn't speak. She just blinked those amazing baby blues at him.

"She said she knew Luke intimately, so intimately in fact, that he'd knocked her up."

"What?"

"This woman claimed she'd been sleepin' with Luke and didn't know she was pregnant until after he died."

Every bit of color drained from Jessie's face.

"She said she broke it off with him a week before his accident. When she discovered she was pregnant...somehow she'd heard you got kicked off the ranch. She figured she'd get the same treatment from Luke's family, and get nothin' but grief from you, so she didn't tell anyone Luke was the father."

"Bullshit," Jessie spat. "She knew carrying the baby of a dead man was worth something."

Brandt shook his head. "I honestly don't think she did."

"But she knew Luke was a married man when she slept with him?"

"Yes. There's no excuse for that. But I will tell you, she's young, Jessie."

"How young?"

"She just turned twenty-one."

Her mouth tightened. "That bastard Luke was fucking a nineteen-year-old *girl*?"

Hearing such crude words from Jessie caused Brandt to flinch. "Apparently."

"How old is the kid now?"

"Sixteen months."

"It's pretty damn convenient, if you ask me. Luke's been dead for two years. There's no way to prove..." Jessie's sharp gaze pierced right through him. "You have a guilty look on your face, Brandt McKay."

"Because I did demand proof. Right away. I contacted Dr. Monroe and she put me in contact with a place that specializes in fast paternity tests. Long story short, Landon is Luke's child. But really, all I had to do was look at the kid and I knew."

Jessie's tough shell cracked and her face crumpled. "Oh God. No. This is not happening."

Brandt was beside her in an instant. He wanted so badly to pull her into his arms, offer her comfort, but he wasn't entirely sure she wouldn't slap and claw at him, taking her rage out on the messenger since she couldn't take it out on the person who deserved it.

Goddamn you, Luke. What the fuck were you thinking?

He hadn't been. As usual his brother thought of himself first.

Jessie hugged her knees to her chest, hiding her face beneath her tangle of hair. Her shoulders shook as she rocked on the couch.

Brandt was helpless to do anything but watch her fall apart.

Lexie came over, whining at her mistress's distress, but even the dog seemed at a loss.

He drained his beer. Then he got up and grabbed another. Staring out the window, his thoughts as jumbled now, as when Samantha Johnston had contacted him six weeks ago.

Brandt hadn't told anyone in his family about meeting Samantha and Landon. It'd been ripping him up inside to the point he was pretty sure he'd given himself an ulcer.

He lifted the bottle to his lips only to come up empty. He'd sucked down the whole damn thing without thinking about it, without tasting it—which was why he hadn't been drinking the last month. It'd be too easy to wind up drunk every damn night, without intending to.

"Am I the last one to know about Luke's secret love child?" Jessie asked.

Her tear-choked voice startled him. "No. Hell no. I wouldn't do that to you." He crossed the room and sat next to her. "You're the first one I've told. You're the *only* one I've told."

"Why me first? Why not Tell or Dalton or your folks?"

How did he phrase this?

You've gone too far to worry about sparing her feelings now.

"Because this isn't happy news for you, Jess."

Her mouth trembled and he watched as she fought to stop it. She inhaled. Exhaled. "But it will be happy news for them."

Brandt nodded.

"Jesus. This is a nightmare. Just when I think it can't get worse, it does. Just when I think Luke McKay can't possibly hurt me any more than he already has, he does."

He didn't dispute it, which forced her to meet his gaze.

She paled further, if that were possible. "It gets worse, doesn't it?"

"Afraid so. Look, Samantha has had a rough go of it. She's young, a single parent with no one to turn to, so she's made some mistakes."

"What kind of mistakes?"

"She got a DUI when Landon was six months old. She managed mostly to stay on the straight and narrow...until two months ago."

"What did she do?"

"Got a second DUI."

Jessie's mouth dropped open. "Are you joking?"

He shook his head.

"Is that why she contacted you? To bail her out of jail?"

"No. She contacted me after the arrest because she knew she'd be sent to jail. She moved away from the guy she'd shacked up with and moved back in with her aunt. But the aunt can't take care of Landon. So she needs..."

"Oh no. Please tell me you didn't volunteer to—"

"What choice do I have?" He stood and paced to the door and back. "If one of Landon's blood relatives doesn't take him, her aunt will turn the child over to Protective Services."

"It sounds like the kid will be a helluva lot better off with a child protection agency than with her," Jessie snapped.

Brandt froze. "You don't mean that."

"Yes, I do. She's a perfect example of why there are these types of agencies, Brandt. Let them deal with her and with the kid. They're more qualified to make a rational decision about—"

"The only living link I'll ever have to my dead brother? I'm just supposed to say, *oh well, not my problem*? Not care? He's little more than a baby, Jess. None of this is his fault. Don't you see that? I'm sorry, but I can't walk away. I won't."

"Fine. You can't. I get that. But I don't understand what any of this has to do with me."

Here was the moment of truth. He knelt in front of her. "Because I can't do this by myself. I need your help."

"No."

"Just hear me out."

"No. God. No. Stop. Brandt. Please. Just stop."

The look on her face was killing him, but somehow he soldiered on. "It's a temporary situation. Just a few months."

"You can't be serious. You really aren't asking me to help you take care of my dead husband's illegitimate child."

"That's exactly what I'm asking."

"Oh God, I'm gonna be sick." She shoved him aside so hard he fell on his ass and she raced to the kitchen sink.

Her retching sounds, mixed with her heartbreaking sobs, made his eyes burn and his throat tighten.

He was asking the impossible of her. He knew that. But he also knew that Jessie had the kindest soul and the purest heart of anyone he'd ever known. That's why he hated how his brother had treated her. And it pissed him off that Luke still had the power to hurt her—to hurt both of them—from beyond the grave.

Brandt wasn't a religious man, but maybe there was a reason this child had happened and a reason why Samantha had come to him for help. He had to believe this shitty situation would mean something good in the end. Because if he thought too hard about the cruelty of it, he'd go stark raving mad. Hell. He was almost there.

He picked himself up off the floor and went to her. Jessie didn't shrink away when he wrapped his arms around her. She turned and burrowed into his chest, sobbing.

Brandt held her and let his tears fall along right with hers.

Finally, she whispered, "I can't do it."

"You don't know that," he soothed. "I'm only askin' you to try."

"How? By forcing me?"

He tipped her chin up. "I'd never force you. You know me better than that."

Again, she looked away. Again, Brandt lifted her chin and studied her eyes. The misery was still there, but something else was too. Something that resembled anger. "What?"

"Why me, Brandt? Why am I the first person you thought of?"

Because you're the most caring person I know.

"Is this some sort of punishment?"

Confused, he frowned. "Punishment? Why would you ask that?"

"Because I hurt you. Then you cut me out of your life completely. And you can deny it all you want—"

"I'm not denyin' that you hurt me, Jessie. But *I* was the one outta line, not you. I was mad at myself, not at you."

Jessie's entire face held an expression of disbelief.

"So you think I'm usin' this as an opportunity to get back at you? To hurt you?"

"That's what I'm asking," she said softly.

"Christ, just bringing the goddamn thing to your attention is hurting you. I can see that. You think I like the way you're lookin' at me right now? No. But I remember you looked at me the same way right after Luke died. I remember how we helped each other through it. One day at a time. How bein' together somehow made it...bearable at times." He closed his eyes against the pain in hers. "Do you remember the night you told me you wouldn't have survived that first year if it hadn't been for me? How you owed me and if I ever needed anything from you, all I had to do was ask? Well, Jess, right now, I'm askin' you. I'm begging you. Please. I need you to help me do this."

After a minute or so of hellish silence, she burrowed into him again. Her tears soaked his shirt. "I don't know if I can do it. I need some time, Brandt."

"I hate to say it, but that's the one thing I can't give you. I'm picking Landon up tomorrow."

"And you're just telling me now? This is going way too fast."

"I hadn't intended to spring this on you. But Samantha's sentencing was moved up last week. She went to the women's correctional facility in Lusk on Wednesday. Her aunt agreed to keep Landon only for a few days. If I don't go get him tomorrow..."

Jessie jerked back. "Why is her aunt being so difficult?"

His hand shook as he brushed baby-fine strands of hair from her tear-stained face. "She's actually her great aunt, who's nearly eighty and is almost legally blind. It was easier takin' care of baby contained in a crib. But now that Landon is walking, she literally cannot keep an eye on him." That wasn't all, but Brandt wasn't about to put the cart before the horse.

So he shouldn't have been surprised Jessie connected the dots.

"The aunt is afraid this isn't a temporary arrangement. She's worried she'll get stuck with the kid permanently."

Brandt didn't bother to lie. "I'm assuming so. Like I said, Samantha has made some mistakes, but I'm not writing her off completely."

"You should. God. Why couldn't she have given him up for adoption?"

He couldn't say he felt the same, because he didn't. Even as much as it hurt Jessie, Brandt was glad Samantha had contacted him. He dropped his hands and stepped back. "Look. I know this is a lot to process. But it doesn't change the fact I need your help."

"And if I refuse? What then?"

"Then I'll..." He blew out an exasperated breath. "Have no choice except to ask my parents to pitch in."

There was Jessie's horror-filled look. "But Casper—"

"Is the worst possible choice, yeah, trust me, I know. My mother would be fine takin' care of Landon, but she won't stand up to my father, which means I'd have to leave Landon at their house. Every goddamn day. And I don't trust my dad not to go around me."

"Go around you how?"

"Given Samantha's circumstances, he'll try for full custody of Landon, and the court would award them guardianship, even temporarily, over me. I don't want it to come to that. Ever."

"When did you plan on telling them about him?"

"Tomorrow. I'd hoped to have a firm plan in place first, but if I don't, I'll wing it. Tell and Dalton will back me up, no matter what happens."

In the unbearably long, brutal silence, Brandt felt his hope drying up. Felt her pulling away.

Shivering, Jessie wrapped her arms around herself. "It's late. And I'm..."

In shock. Heartbroken. Angry.

Every emotion was written on her face. "Do you want me to go?"

She said, "Yes," then amended, "unless you're too tired to

drive home. You can crash on the couch. But you won't get much sleep. It's the last thing on my mind right about now."

When Jessie was upset, she cleaned house like a maniac. He'd rather sleep in his damn truck than surround himself with her strange compulsion and the smell of bleach. He snagged his suit coat off the back of the chair. "I'll go. Think about it, okay?"

She looked him dead in the eye and said, "I doubt I'll think of anything else."

Jessie didn't sleep. She paced to the point it annoyed her dog. She drank two shots of whiskey and the booze stopped the shaking in her hands, but didn't blot out the surrealness of the situation.

Luke had a child.

With someone else.

That alone would've been bad enough, if not for the fact she'd lost a baby. Every problem they'd ever had stemmed from that unintended pregnancy, which had forced them to get married. She'd miscarried at four months, after getting thrown off her horse. Luke hadn't been devastated at the loss of the child as much as she had.

No, his devastation came from being trapped in a shotgun marriage.

The doctor's suggestion that she remain at home to heal gave Luke an excuse to go out. While he'd been carousing in honkytonks in four counties, she'd been the dutiful wife.

He'd been so sweet and loving to her at times she wondered if she'd exaggerated his surliness when he wasn't around. She'd wanted to try for another baby right away, but the doctor suggested she wait a year and put her on birth control pills. Which had re-ignited their sex life for a while. But she hadn't been enough for him. He'd gone elsewhere to satisfy his sexual needs.

She'd stumbled upon evidence of the first affair by accident. She hadn't confronted him about it. She just tried harder to satisfy him—in bed and out—hoping it'd keep him home.

It hadn't. As the months wore on, it was almost as if Luke wanted to get caught. He wanted Jessie to know he'd been with other women. He hadn't tried to hide it from anyone, including his family. Casper McKay had been snide about it. Joan looked at her with pity. Dalton and Tell skirted the subject. But Brandt had seethed.

One afternoon Brandt had yelled at Luke for screwing around on her. Luke told Brandt to mind his own goddamn business and he could screw whoever he wanted. When Brandt insisted Jessie deserved better, Luke had laughed, warning Brandt that he wasn't the better man, and if Brandt ever touched Jessie, Luke would kill him. Neither man knew Jessie watched in misery from the shadows of the barn.

She'd never understood why Brandt had stood up for her. It wasn't like they'd known each other before she'd married Luke. She'd never understood why Luke had threatened Brandt over her, because she wasn't the type to turn heads or inspire fierce loyalty. Or fidelity.

So the question on her mind now: Would he have left her for this Samantha girl once he'd found out she carried his child?

No. Luke would've bucked up to his responsibility for the kid, but he wouldn't put himself in a repeat situation of being stuck in a relationship because of a child.

What a mess.

Imagining her husband in bed with another woman was bad enough. But seeing the proof of his passion? Of seeing the physical embodiment of what he'd denied her but he'd given to someone else?

She felt hollow. Totally eviscerated.

How could she look at the child with anything but loathing?

Brandt's words, *He's little more than a baby, Jess, none of this is his fault,* rang in her head and slashed at her heartstrings.

She would not feel guilty. She owed this Samantha girl nothing. She owed Luke nothing.

But she owed Brandt McKay everything.

Didn't she?

She'd just gotten her life back on track on her own terms. She owed it to *herself* not to suffer through the heartbreak of wishing the little boy was hers. Of getting pissed off because he should've been hers. Of resenting Luke because he should've left her pregnant, not some strange teenager.

So when Brandt called tomorrow, she'd tell him no.

She'd scream no if she had to.

But she would say no.

Chapter Three

When Brandt pulled up to Jessie's place late the next morning, she didn't immediately exit the house. He waited in his truck, listening to Landon's soft snuffles drifting from the rear cab. The boy had screamed from the time he'd left his aunt's house until ten minutes ago when he'd conked out.

Thank God.

He hoped the kid would be on his best behavior, all cute smiles and big blue eyes, because Brandt didn't want to give Jessie a reason to say no.

She couldn't say no. She was the key to everything.

Brandt unbuckled Landon and lifted him out of the car seat. He adjusted the hood covering Landon's head and cuddled him against his body to block the wind. At the last second he remembered the diaper bag. Kids came with a lot of stuff.

Fine flakes of snow pelted him in the face as he climbed the stairs. He stood in front of the door, figuring he'd use his foot to knock on the bottom aluminum panel if need be.

But the door opened and Jessie stared at him through the screen. Her eyes never left his, never strayed to the sleeping child on Brandt's shoulder. "So much for not forcing me, huh Brandt? You just show up on my doorstep?"

This did not bode well.

After glaring at him, she held the door open and shushed Lexie's excited barks.

He put Landon onto the couch, wedging him against the middle couch cushion facing out. He unzipped the tiny winter coat and tried to rearrange the hood, but the kid didn't seem to mind it, so he left it as is rather than risk waking him. Turning around, he expected to see Jessie behind him, but she'd shooed

Lexie outside and retreated to the kitchen.

Brandt ditched his coat and followed her.

"Coffee?" she asked softly.

"That'd be great."

After she poured his cup, she leaned against the counter, keeping her back to the living room. Keeping her back to Landon.

He searched her face. Dark circles hung beneath her eyes, the only color on her too pale skin. Her lips were drawn in a tight line, as were her eyebrows. She looked like one wrong word would shatter her. "Did you sleep at all?"

Jessie shrugged. "I think I dozed off around dawn, but then I had to get up and feed the animals." She blew across her coffee. "What about you?"

"About the same." He'd lain in his bed, staring at the ceiling, trying to make plans for the next few months—a pointless endeavor, when everything was up in the air.

"What time are you meeting your parents?"

"I don't know."

She frowned. "You're just gonna spring this on them too?"

He felt his face heat. "Not an ideal situation, but I'm in limbo until you..."

"This decision shouldn't be on my shoulders," she snapped.

"It's not. But your answer does have an affect on what I do next."

Her chin dropped to her chest and she gazed into her coffee mug. "I'm sorry."

Disappointment lodged in his gut like a stone. "Jessie—"

"I'm sorry, Brandt. I can't do it. I can't help you—"

The remainder of her sentence was lost in Landon's cry.

He set aside his mug and crossed to the couch. Landon had already pushed himself upright and was looking around with confusion. Brandt dropped to his haunches, keeping the kid from scrambling down. "Hey, buddy. Didja have a nice nap?"

Those somber blue eyes studied him as Brandt removed the little guy's coat.

"I brought some of your toys."

But Landon held up his arms.

"Okay. I guess you'd rather be picked up." Brandt settled the boy on his hip and turned around.

Jessie had her back to him as she faced out the front window.

Disappointment warred with panic. If she wouldn't even look at the kid, there was no way she'd help him. No way.

Lexie scratched at the door and Brandt automatically let her in, like he'd done a hundred times when he used to visit Jessie. The dog jumped and yipped at seeing Landon.

Landon clapped his hands and laughed—a pure, innocent burst of joy that made Brandt grin. "A boy who likes dogs, imagine that." Brandt sat in the easy chair with Landon on his lap. He patted his leg. "Come on over and say hello, Lexie."

The dog slunk over to sniff Landon's toes. He giggled again and reached for Lexie's ears.

"Whoa there, partner. Gotta be gentle. Play nice. Touch her like this, see?" Brandt kept one arm wrapped around Landon's middle as he petted Lexie's back. He took Landon's hand and slowly moved it across Lexie's fur. "She likes that."

Landon's whole body wiggled, he was so excited.

So Brandt kept helping the boy pet the dog, keeping Lexie's head and teeth away from Landon's poking fingers. He shot a glance toward Jessie, but she hadn't moved.

Come on, Jess. You can do this. I know you can.

Three things happened while he was silently begging Jessie to look at them. His cell phone rang in his back pocket. As he shifted to reach for it, he stepped on Lexie's tail. She yipped and scampered away, heading toward Jessie. When he loosened his hold on Landon, the monkey kid jumped down and raced after the dog.

But Lexie had wormed her way between Jessie and the kitchen cabinet. Before Brandt could catch Landon, he smacked into the back of Jessie's calves, squealing, determined to get a hold of the dog.

Startled, Jessie spun around and knocked Landon to the floor. He landed with a thud on his diapered butt and cried out.

The rest of it happened in slow motion.

Jessie instinctively picked him up, with a reassuring, "You're okay," and smoothed her hand over his dark head.

Brandt watched, not breathing, as Jessie realized what she'd done.

A tiny gasp escaped. Her hand froze, as if the kid had

suddenly become radioactive, but her gaze tracked every inch of Landon's face.

"My God. I can't believe how much he looks like Luke."

"It's a little spooky." He took another step closer. "I'll take him, if you want."

She swallowed with difficulty. "No. It's okay. I've got him."

"You sure you're all right?"

"No, not really."

Tell her she doing great.

The words stuck in his throat. An excruciatingly long minute passed before he said, "I didn't mean—"

"I said I'm working on it, Brandt. Just give me a second."

He nodded. He'd give her all the time she needed.

Jessie hiked Landon higher on her hip. He seemed to be studying Jessie as closely as she was studying him.

Then Landon pointed to a package of crackers on the counter and grunted.

"Has he eaten anything?"

"Not since I've picked him up."

"Does he have food allergies?"

Brandt scratched his chin. "Not that she mentioned."

"Maybe she left instructions." She wandered into the living room and rummaged in the diaper bag. Landon started to fuss when she pulled out an empty bottle. She frowned. "He's still on a bottle?"

"I guess. Is that bad?"

"Most kids I've dealt with have been weaned by this age. But I'll be the first to admit all kids develop differently, so I'm not sure." She dug out a can of baby formula and studied it. "This is a special formula for underweight toddlers. It has more nutrients than regular formula." When Jessie realized she'd been babbling, she backtracked, "I only know this because one of the kids at Sky Blue was on this formula until she turned two."

"Good to know," Brandt murmured.

"Here." She passed Landon to him. "Entertain him while I fix his bottle."

Lexie decided to give Landon another chance and let herself be petted, patted and pulled on. By the time Jessie brought the full bottle over, Landon was antsy for it.

Brandt held Landon while the kid sucked down his bottle, keeping an eye on Jessie.

She sat in the couch, knees drawn to her chest. Her gaze hadn't wandered from Landon for several long minutes. "You knew once I saw him I wouldn't say no, didn't you?"

He shook his head. "I'd hoped."

"So what now?"

"Now I need to know if you're really on board with this."

"It's temporary, right?"

"Right. Samantha was sentenced to two months in jail in Lusk and two months in a halfway house in Casper. Which might actually end up less time if she exhibits good behavior."

"So we're looking at four months before she's out and can take him back."

"Roughly."

She tipped her head back and sighed. "I can't believe I'm saying this...but okay. I'll help you."

Brandt nearly shouted with relief. "You are an amazing woman, Jess. Thank you, for doin' this."

"Before you sing my praises, I have a couple of conditions that we can talk about after I hear the plan you've sketched out with me on board."

"What makes you think I've got more than one plan?"

Jessie gave him a wry look. "Because I know you, Brandt McKay. You prepare for every possibility."

"I'm not exactly a go with the flow kind of guy."

"That's not a bad thing. In fact, it's a better trait than impulsiveness."

"You always say that." He smiled. "I figured since you work in a daycare, and if Skylar was okay with it, you could take Landon to work with you. Not every day. Three days a week." Brandt suspected it'd be harder to convince Jessie than her boss Skylar, married to Brandt's cousin Kade, to agree to the arrangement.

"It'll be good for him to be around other kids. I'm no expert, but he seems to be behind in stuff, like...talking."

Her eyebrows rose. "He doesn't talk at all?"

"I've heard him say *no* and *mama* and *goggie*, which means doggie as far as I can tell. That's it."

"When I take Landon to daycare with me, I won't be

spending all my time with him teaching him to talk. In fact, it'll present a conflict."

"How so?"

"After Sky hired me, she changed the daycare structure. Before, because each employee had kids, they had to rotate into the daycare for a week. But since I don't have kids and wasn't trained for factory work, she made me fulltime in the daycare. I won't put Sky in the position of assuring her employees—who are also my friends—that Landon won't be getting all my attention."

"Anyone who knows you, Jess, understands you won't play favorites."

"No need to flatter me. I already said yes." She ran an agitated hand through her hair. "What happens after the five o'clock whistle blows?"

"After I'm done workin' on the ranch during the week, I'll be at your place."

"Every night?"

Was that alarm in her tone? "Yes. Why?"

"You didn't say a dang thing about moving in with me, Brandt."

"Well, I didn't say I *wasn't* movin' in with you either." He gave her his most charming grin.

She didn't even crack a smile.

"To be blunt, my place is too far away. It doesn't make sense for us to drive back and forth a couple times a day. I'll be here after you get off work to take care of him, including anything he needs at night. In the morning you guys will go to Sky Blue, I'll head to the ranch."

"There's some other reason you're insisting on this happening here at my place, so spill it."

Brandt sighed. "It'd be easier for everyone if I wasn't livin' so close to my folks while he's under my guardianship."

"Oh, yeah, I can see where it'd be so much better if you tell Casper you're living with *me*."

"Guess I didn't think that one through, did I?"

"No." Jessie's eyes kept wandering to Landon. "I just want you to make sure they both understand that this was not *my* idea, Brandt."

"I promise."

"And as long as we're heading down this road, I have a few conditions. First, I will not have any contact with Landon's mother. Period. You will deal with her. I don't want to hear about how she's doing in jail or any of her problems. Ever."

"That sounds reasonable."

"Second, I will not have any contact with Casper. Your mom? Fine. Casper. No way."

"Understood. Which is why it'll be best that I stay here for the most part."

"Third, I'm done in four months. Regardless of what Landon's mother does, or what you've promised her beyond that, my part in helping you is finished." Brandt started to speak, but she cut him off. "I'm not kidding about this. Four months. That's it."

"Fine."

"I know I won't have to spell it out to you that I won't be doing everything myself for this kid, like feeding him, changing him, entertaining him, plus all the regular household stuff I already do."

"And why don't you have to spell it out for me?"

Jessie looked away. "Because you're not like Luke. For the record, that's a compliment. You'd never ask me to help you and then abandon me."

Yeah, Luke had been awesome at that. He'd called it *delegating*. Everyone else called it bullshit.

"Anything else?" he asked.

"Last thing. You won't bring women into my house and no expecting me to baby-sit while you're out on the town."

Brandt looked at her sharply but kept his voice down. "Jesus, Jessie, you really think I'd bring another woman into your home? You think I'm that heartless I wouldn't give a damn about your feelings just so I could get my rocks off? Wrong, especially now that I'm—" He snapped his mouth shut, just in time. Dammit, he'd almost been goaded into admitting that he was exactly where he wanted to be.

"What Brandt? Now that…?"

"Now that I'm forced to pick up the pieces of Luke's stupidity once again. The thought of me causin' more shit for you to deal with rips me apart, Jess. What don't you understand about that?"

By her startled look, she hadn't foreseen that answer. Then again, he hadn't expected Jessie to make demands of her own. And he had a sneaking suspicion she wasn't done making demands.

Evidently Brandt hadn't been successful in keeping his voice down. Landon's eyes popped open and he wiggled until he was sitting on Brandt's lap.

Jessie stood. "I've said my piece, you've said yours. Can we just move onto the next thing? Because there's plenty of other stuff we have to deal with today."

"Yeah." He squinted at the clock. "I need to get goin'. I'm supposed to meet my brothers at my place in an hour."

"I'll call Skylar and give her a heads up, but it'd probably be best if I drove out there and talked to her."

"True." He reached for Landon's coat. "Come on buddy. Let's ride."

Jessie insisted on meeting Skylar face to face because she had the overwhelming urge to put distance between herself and Brandt.

Don't you mean between you and Landon?

What'd happened to her backbone? She'd sworn last night she'd say no. She'd said it out loud. Hell, she'd screamed it. No one in the world would blame her for washing her hands of the situation. In fact, now she'd have the exact opposite problem. People in the community would think she was a masochist or a martyr.

But when she'd seen that sweet little innocent face...something shifted inside her. Something big. Something beyond pity or a sense of duty. Something she was afraid to put a name to.

She turned off the highway and bypassed the Sky Blue manufacturing plant. Seemed strange to drive past it and through the gate that divided the manufacturing plant from Kade and Skylar McKay's private residence. As handy as it was for Skylar to have her business so close to her home, she kept the two buildings separated.

Girls and dogs raced up as soon as Jessie parked.

"Miss Jessie," Peyton exclaimed. "Mama said you were

comin' here." She stood on tiptoe and peered around Jessie.

"Someone else you're looking for, Peyton?"

"She's checkin' to see if you brought the llamas, which is just stupid," Eliza drawled.

"I'm tellin' Mama you called me stupid," Peyton shot back.

"Go ahead."

Shannie stepped between her warring sisters. "Stop or Daddy won't take us ridin'."

"'Cause you'll tattle," Eliza said.

"Yeah," Peyton added. "You got us all in trouble last night."

Three dogs sniffed Jessie as three girls argued.

The screen door slammed and Skylar started down the steps, followed by Kade.

The girls' fighting ended immediately and they lined up, all sweet smiles, the pictures of innocence.

Jessie bit her cheek to keep from laughing.

"Hey, Jess. It's good to see you, but you didn't have to drive out here."

Maybe she was interrupting some family thing. "Oh, if this is a bad time, I can go."

"No," Skylar assured her, "it's fine. Actually, I'm happy to see you."

Kade set his hands on Skylar's shoulders and spoke to his daughters. "You girls get the tack ready for the horses and I'll be right there."

"'Kay. Bye!" All three girls took off, boots clomping on the gravel, pigtails flying as they raced each other to the barn.

Before Jessie uttered a word, Kade demanded, "What's this I hear about Luke havin' a kid?"

"Kade," Skylar murmured.

"No sense in beatin' around the bush, Sky."

Jessie jammed her hands in the pockets of her vest. "Obviously it was news to me too, but Brandt has been dealing with the boy's mother for the last month." She relayed the story, knowing she'd better get used to telling it, even when the news would spread through the McKay family like wildfire.

Both Kade and Skylar were quiet, yet Jessie could sense some silent communication between them.

Kade sighed. "Hell, Jessie. I don't even know what to say. I'm sorry none of us can kick Luke's ass for what he done. But

I'd be lyin' if I didn't tell you I wanna kick Brandt's butt for even suggesting that you be a party to takin' care of this kid."

"I'm pretty sure you'd have to get in line. Not to mention how Casper…"

"Casper can shut his big goddamn mouth, as far as I'm concerned. He's never—"

"Kade," Skylar said, stopping his tirade. "This isn't helping. Go hit the trail with the girls. They're waiting for you."

"All right." Kade held Jessie eyes with a sympathetic look from beneath his gray cowboy hat. "If you need anything at all, just ask."

"Thanks, Kade. I appreciate it."

Kade kissed his wife and sauntered off.

Skylar grabbed Jessie's shirtsleeve. "I made iced tea. Or maybe you'd prefer something stronger?"

Jessie shook her head. "Tea would be fine. I think if I start drinking I won't stop and that won't help anyone."

After they settled in wicker rockers in the three-season porch, Skylar sighed. "I thought the girls would sleep in this morning after their late night at the wedding reception, but they were up at the crack of dawn, as usual. They definitely take after their father in that respect."

How would Landon take after Luke? Just in looks? Or in temperament?

Jessie braced herself for more questions because Skylar wouldn't pull any punches.

"I hope you don't think I'm taking advantage of the situation, but there's something else I needed to talk to you about anyway."

That didn't sound very good. "Am I in trouble?"

"No. Not even close. Despite the circumstances that brought you to Sky Blue, Jessie, I'm thrilled to have you working for me."

"But?" she prompted.

"But it seems the dynamic in the daycare has changed in the last year. I've always had the daycare for just my employee's children, but with those kids growing up we've got vacancies. Even my girls aren't around fulltime anymore."

"You thinking of opening up the daycare for non-employees?"

"Just family. You, naturally, for as long as Landon needs it. I know India has been dropping Hudson off occasionally and taking Ellison with her to the shop. Ginger needs to go back to work soon, but she doesn't want to put the burden of caring for twins on Kade and Kane's mother Kimi, although Kimi has volunteered." Skylar smiled. "Grama Kimi loves her grandbabies. She'd happily take all three of our girls and all three of Kane and Ginger's kids every day."

Kimi McKay was the mother-in-law Jessie wished she'd had. Vivacious, caring, fun, fiercely protective of her family, yet the blonde spitfire didn't take any crap from either of her twin sons or her husband or the rest of the McKay clan.

"Ginger and I talked last night at Keely's wedding reception, she weighed her options, and I sort of volunteered the daycare at Sky Blue."

"Of course you did, she's your family. And it's your business Sky, you can do whatever you want."

"True. I just don't want to take advantage of the situation, or you, especially now that Landon will be part of the mix."

Jessie was quiet for a minute or so while she considered the options. "To be honest, it'd be easiest for everyone if we could arrange it so the twins and Landon weren't there the same days."

"Ginger plans to work four days a week. Have you given any thought to what Landon's schedule will be?"

"Brandt and I discussed having Landon come on Monday, Wednesday and Friday."

"So it's okay if I tell Ginger Tuesdays and Thursdays work best? The babies won't start coming for another two weeks."

"Sure. Thanks, Sky, you have no idea how much..." *Don't cry because once you start you won't be able to stop.* Jessie sipped her tea and tried to swallow the lump in her throat.

"Okay, now that we're done with the business portion of this conversation, Jess, tell me how you're really doing."

"I'm..." *A mess.* "Handling it. Yes, I'm in shock. Yes, I'm pissed off. Really pissed off at Luke on so many levels I don't think I've even discovered them all yet. And this probably will sound horrible, but right after Brandt told me about this kid, I wanted to hate him. Before I ever laid eyes on him. I thought I could look at him and not feel a goddamned thing.

"But when I saw him? I didn't see a dead ringer for Luke, or

53

a kid who should've been my son. I saw a lost little boy. A kid who wouldn't have anyone to see to his basic needs if not for Brandt stepping up to the plate. But Brandt is smart enough to admit he can't do it alone. He's also smart enough to know that if he left Landon's future in his father's hands, Casper would take legal action to ensure the boy's mother never saw her son again. Landon doesn't need that. None of us needs that. What Landon needs is the stability Brandt and I can provide until his mother cleans up her act."

When Jessie looked up because Skylar hadn't made a peep, her gut constricted at the tears rolling down Sky's face.

Shit.

"I promised myself I wouldn't do this." Skylar swept her fingertips under her eyes. "And I agree with Kade. I was tempted to track Brandt down, grab a two by four and beat him over the head for acting so much like his father." She shook her head. "But between your call and you showing up here, I've had time to rethink my original response, and Brandt's head is safe."

"Because you've come to the same conclusion everyone else will?" she asked tightly. "That I'm a spineless twit?"

Skylar's eyes filled with shock. "God no. I think you're closer to a saint."

Jessie scowled. "I'm far from that, Sky, trust me."

"Listen, I understand why Brandt asked you. Not because you're spineless. Not because you're a sucker. But because you've got the biggest heart of anyone I know,"

She was highly unnerved with the conversation. It was disconcerting to be praised for something she hadn't yet done, when she knew it'd be a miracle if she made it through the next four hours, let alone the next four months.

"And now that I've made you uncomfortable, let's talk about something else." Ice rattled as Skylar fiddled with her tea glass. "Why didn't you stick around for the bouquet toss last night at Keely's wedding?"

"It would've been awkward since it was Luke's family's event. Plus, I'm not eager to get married again. Especially not after being blindsided with proof of my husband's infidelity." And she'd been doing so well keeping a lid on the whining. "Who caught the bouquet? Ramona West? I think she might've actually brought a catcher's mitt."

"No. Some family friend from down by Casper's section of

the ranch. She seemed to know Dalton. I've never seen her before. Sorry, but I don't remember her name."

"That's okay." Jessie stood. "I should be going. I appreciate you taking time out of your day off to talk to me, Sky."

"Like I said, anytime. Kade meant it too. Anything you need, just ask us. Not because I'm your boss but because you're family."

Chapter Four

Now that Brandt was waiting on his brothers to show up, he'd begun to have doubts. Maybe Tell and Dalton wouldn't want to help out with Landon. God knew they were scarce as soon as the workday ended and they spent most Monday mornings sharing the down and dirty details of their wild weekends.

You ain't exactly a saint. You've ripped it up plenty. Especially in the last ten months.

Landon's face turned red, he grunted and the odor chased the air from Brandt's living room. Sighing, Brandt grabbed a diaper and had just finished changing Landon when his brothers burst in.

Tell and Dalton stopped inside the door, noses wrinkled. "I don't know what the hell you've been eatin', bro, but it's nasty…" Dalton's voice trailed away when Landon scampered off the couch.

Before the little devil could make a break for the open door, Brandt snatched the back of his overalls. "Whoa, not so fast there, partner." To Tell, he said, "Would you please shut the damn door?"

"Ah. Sure." Once the latch clicked, Brandt released Landon.

But the boy stopped, apparently scared by the two bigger men. Tell and Dalton topped Brandt's five feet ten by a good four inches, and while he'd hated being the shortest of his brothers, he'd never considered their height imposing. But then again everything probably seemed enormous when you were only two feet tall.

They stared at one another in silence, but Dalton or Tell were focused solely on Landon.

Dalton cleared his throat. "Uh, Brandt, you wanna tell us what's goin' on? Why you've got a kid here that looks exactly like—"

"Luke," Tell finished.

"No, I was gonna say like a mini-version of Brandt."

Tell strode over and crouched in front of Landon. "Hey, buddy. You don't gotta be scared."

Landon blinked those McKay blue eyes at Tell and shrank against Brandt's leg.

Brandt rubbed his hand over Landon's head. "This is Landon. He's Luke's son."

"For sure?" Tell asked.

"Yeah. Did the paternity test and everything."

Dalton whistled. "I'll be damned."

"How long have you known about him?" This from Tell.

"A month."

Both sets of his brothers' eyes zoomed to him.

"Look. Samantha, Landon's mother, contacted me. Fed me this story about her and Luke...which turned out to be completely true. But I didn't believe her, not at first, which is why I insisted on a paternity test before I told you guys."

"Jesus. You've worked with us every goddamn day for a freakin' month and you couldn't let us know this was goin' on?"

Brandt held Dalton's angry gaze. "No. First of all, it's been a rough month anyway, with Dad bein' a first class jackass about how bad we—I—fucked up by lettin' the north pasture stay fallow this year. I didn't want to get anyone's hopes up about Landon in case it was bullshit. Second, because Samantha asked me not to."

"I don't think she gets a say in nothin' since she's kept Luke's kid a secret from us," Dalton shot back.

"Chill out, Dalton," Tell said. He pinned Brandt with a hard look. "Start from the beginning."

By the time he'd finished, Dalton had plopped in the easy chair and Tell had coaxed Landon into sitting on the floor with him.

"Well, Mom and Dad are gonna shit bricks."

"Ya think? That's why I need you guys to go over there with me when we break the news about their first grandchild."

"Oh hell no. I ain't gonna pretend I knew anything about

this. You know how dad is, Brandt."

"Which is exactly my point. We've gotta show him we're united on this, on doin' what's best for Landon."

"Given the fact Luke is dead, if this Samantha chick is goin' to jail, then Dad will wanna sue for permanent guardianship," Tell pointed out.

"I won't allow that to happen. Before you argue that turnin' Landon over to Mom and Dad is the best option, I'll remind you this is a temporary situation. And if we show Samantha we want Landon to be part of our lives, without the threat of takin' him away from her, the better it'll be for everybody in the long run." Brandt glanced down at Landon, surprised the rambunctious kid was sitting still.

"You so sure Samantha will want her kid back when she gets outta jail?"

No. Brandt wasn't surprised his brothers had voiced the same question Jessie had. "I've got no choice but to believe it."

Dalton and Tell traded a skeptical look before Tell spoke. "Fine. We're with you on this. But how in the hell do you plan to baby-sit this kid for the next four months? We've got a ranch to run. I'll remind you the workload has increased since Luke died and Dad ain't doin' diddly anymore."

"It'd be really shitty if you expect Mom to watch Landon all the time and then in four months just snatch him away from her like he didn't exist," Dalton added.

That option wasn't any better for Jessie, either. "I know. Which is why I'm gonna suggest Mom watches him one weekday, and then the three of us could rotate and take over on the other weekday and I'd have him on weekends."

Tell frowned. "And what about the three other days during the workweek?"

Brandt said, "Jessie has agreed to take Landon to Sky Blue daycare those three days," and braced himself for their reaction.

"Jessie knows about this?"

"I told her last night after the wedding reception."

Dalton launched himself out of the chair. "You've gotta be fuckin' kiddin' me! You not only blabbed to Jessie about Luke's bastard child, you asked her to help you take care of him?" He stomped closer and loomed over his older brother. "Is this your way of makin' sure she hates you so you can stay the hell away from her for good?"

Tell didn't jump to Brandt's defense either. "I'm with Dalton on this. It's goddamn selfish of you to expect anything from Jessie except a knee to the balls."

"Yeah? Then how come Jessie agreed to help out?" Brandt demanded. "If I'm such a flaming fucking asshole who doesn't give a good goddamn about how she feels then why did she call Skylar and explain the situation? Why did she agree with me that it'd be better if I stayed overnight with her during the week instead of us dragging Landon back and forth between our places? Why did she—"

"I don't know!" Dalton bellowed. "Was she drunk?"

"Fuck off, Dalton."

Tell said, "Guys—"

"This is why we wanted you to stay away from Jessie, Brandt. You two keep hurting each other over and over and neither of you even realizes you're doin' it! Goddammit, do you know what it's like for us to have to watch you both miserable—"

Landon started to wail, scared by the raised voices. Before Brandt could pick him up, Tell pulled the boy onto his lap. "Hey, it's okay. We're just a little freaked out by you and this whole situation. But we're gonna do everything we can to make sure your needs are met above anyone else's."

No surprise Tell looked right at Brandt when he said the last part.

Tell said, "I don't know if you've got some warped version of happily ever after floating in your head, bro, but even if you and Jessie do spend all this time together in close quarters taking care of Luke's kid, you do know she ain't gonna fall in love with you, right?"

Hurt, resentment, denial swelled up inside Brandt to the point he thought he might explode. But he tamped it down; refusing to lash out at Tell or give into the hair trigger temper he'd inherited from their father.

"More likely than not, when it's all over, she'll hate your guts for forcing her hand."

The thought of Jessie hating him had bile crawling up Brandt's throat.

Dalton added, "Hate to agree with Tell, but I don't see it endin' up any other way, Brandt."

Silence.

Then Tell, the peacemaker, said, "What was up with Uncle Carson givin' Keely and Jack some land as a wedding gift?"

"Think Dad knew about it?" Dalton said.

"Probably. Typical that he didn't tell us. But it doesn't fit that he ain't throwing a shit fit about it. He's always insisted the McKay land trust won't allow for pieces just to be handed out. Not even to the next generation. It has to be a unanimous decision."

"Yeah, if I thought we could get part of our land parceled out to us and away from Dad's control..." Brandt snorted. "It'll never happen. Dad's gotta have something to lord over us."

Dalton looked at both his brothers. "Think he'll see Landon as something you're tryin' to lord over him?"

Brandt hadn't considered that. God. He wasn't like his father. Not everything he did was some sort of power play.

"We'd better get goin', if we're takin' Landon over to Mom and Dad's," Tell said.

"The carseat is in my truck." Brandt pushed to his feet. "Look, you guys can call me names, think I'm the biggest asshole on the planet, question my end game, but I'm askin' that we at least pretend we're on the same page in front of Dad."

"Yeah, Dad will definitely home in on any weakness."

"Do we let him know about Jessie helping out?"

"We have to. There'll be hell to pay if he hears about it from someone else."

"True."

Brandt swung Landon into his arms. "Let's get this over with."

The meeting with his parents went about like Brandt expected. Rage on his father's part, mostly directed at the woman who'd dared to keep Luke's child a secret from his family. His mother cried a lot while she carted Landon around, enticing him to eat, then chasing him through the house. She looked happier than he'd seen her in years.

When Brandt relayed Landon's childcare arrangements during the months he'd have guardianship, his father accused Jessie of trying to keep the boy from his real family out of spite.

That was the last straw for the visit. Brandt pried Landon out of his mother's arms amidst his father's threats for legal action.

Dalton and Tell were quiet on the way back to Brandt's place. They kept the boy entertained while Brandt loaded up Landon's things and double-checked everything since he'd be gone for five days. After they agreed to meet at Dalton's house to figure out the week's work, Brandt made the forty-five minute drive to Jessie's.

Something stirred in him when he saw Jessie sitting on the front steps with Lexie by her side. The afternoon had warmed up from the bouts of snow flurries earlier in the day and the wind blew random strands of her reddish blonde hair across her appled cheeks. She looked young, fresh and wholesome. Which made him feel guilty as sin for the direction of his impure thoughts.

Landon kicked his feet to be let out of his seat. Brandt set him on the ground and the kid took off toward Lexie with a squeal of delight. When the dog cowered beneath the deck, Brandt plucked a plastic ball from one of the bins of toys in the back of his truck and tossed it into the yard. Landon held the ball, dropped it, threw it, moving as fast as his legs could carry him.

"Looks like he's got some pent-up energy," Jessie remarked.

"I figure it'll be good for him to run around, get some fresh air, maybe he'll sleep better tonight, bein's he's in a strange place."

She scooted over, making room for him to sit beside her.

"How did it go with Skylar?"

"She's one hundred percent on board with it. Probably more so than I am."

Brandt said nothing.

"Sorry. It's just... God, it's really freakin' weird, okay? I'm sitting here watching Luke's kid run around, and I had such a close connection to Luke, but I also feel like I didn't know him at all. I look at the kid and I don't know what I feel. It didn't help Skylar started saying all these things about how I should be nominated for sainthood for opening my heart and home to Landon, and I couldn't take it. I had to leave. And then, your mom called about a half hour ago."

"What'd she say?"

"That she was sorry about how everything played out after

Luke died, but she had no say in the matter since she had nothing to do with the McKay Ranch." Jessie turned her head to look at him; Brandt had no choice but to meet her gaze. "Joan cried, Brandt. She broke down and basically said she can't imagine how hard this is for me, but at the same time she feels like she's been given a miracle."

Dammit. "If she said—"

"No. That's it. She said she wouldn't fight her husband when it came to ranch matters, but when it came to matters involving her sons, she'd fight that mean bastard tooth and nail."

Brandt knew neither he nor his brothers would've grown up to be half the men they were if not for their mother. She gave them the love and affection their father wouldn't, even if she had to hide that affection from her husband. "Mom said that?"

"Yeah. Said she'd do anything to help out, including taking Landon another day of the week to save you boys the hassle. She volunteered to drive here. Told me she'd lie to Casper if she had to, but she doubted he'd notice she was gone unless it was mealtime."

"What did you say?"

"I reminded her the decision wasn't up to me, that you're Landon's guardian, but we'd talk about it and you'd call her."

"Is this a good idea, my mom takin' care of Landon two days?"

Jessie sighed. "Yes, it'd be good for both of them. Besides, I've never had a problem with Joan. We weren't best buddies, but I chalked it up to the fact she doesn't have many female friends. Or your dad didn't want us to be friends."

Lexie had inched her way to the edge of the yard and seemed fascinated by Landon and his ball.

"I never understood why my dad was so mean to you, Jess. Well, besides the fact he's an asshole and he pretty much acts like that toward everyone."

She managed a wan smile. "Probably because Luke felt trapped and I'm the evil sorceress responsible for that entrapment. One time Luke told me Casper said..." Her mouth snapped shut. "Shit. Sorry. Never mind."

"Tell me."

"It serves no purpose, Brandt."

"Wrong. Tell me."

"Evidently Casper suggested I'd faked the pregnancy because I knew Luke would never marry someone like me without being forced into it."

Brandt's jaw tightened and he barely gritted out, "Luke just *said* this to you?"

"We'd had a fight and he'd been drinking and he said a buncha stuff that was just downright nasty. The next morning he'd realized what he'd done, he hated himself for acting like his dad, and he apologized over and over. But it wasn't like he could take any of it back. It wasn't like he could pretend he'd just made it up, because we both knew it was true."

He didn't say a word. He couldn't speak around the ball of rage clogging his throat.

Finally, Jessie put her hand on his arm. "Brandt? You okay?"

"No. It's...I hate that I don't realize what an assholish thing I've done until it's too late."

She frowned. "Like what?"

Like am I acting just like my dad? Forcing you into doing things my way and following my plan regarding Landon because I know your weak spots and know just how to exploit them?

Before he could give her a less honest, less painful answer, Landon face-planted and commenced to wailing. Brandt was off the steps in an instant, but he didn't beat Jessie to Landon's side.

She cocked the boy on her hip and murmured, "You're okay," and brushed the dried grass from his hair.

Landon stared at Jessie and then squirmed toward Brandt.

"Think he's hungry?"

"Maybe. Come to think of it, I'm hungry."

"Your Uncle Brandt is always hungry so I know you won't starve when he's taking care of you."

Brandt grinned. "As long as the kid likes meat, potatoes and veggies, we'll get along fine."

"What? No super spicy chicken wings? No cheesy nachos with jalapenos?"

"Nope. I gave most of that kinda stuff up."

"Well, whatever you've been eating, keep it up. If I haven't mentioned it, you look great." Jessie headed for her house, leaving Brandt staring after her, dumbfounded.

A compliment? From Jessie? Out of the freakin' blue?

What did she want?

Not everything is a power play. Maybe she was just being nice.

While Brandt unloaded the truck and set up the crib in the spare bedroom, Jessie cooked hamburgers and macaroni and cheese. Landon ate a pile of food and almost fell asleep in his high chair. Brandt probably would've just put the kid in his jammies and tucked him in bed, but Jessie suggested a bath.

Turned out Landon was a kid who didn't enjoy baths. It was like wrestling a wet worm—an angry, screaming wet worm. Once he had Landon cleaned up, dried off, freshly diapered and wearing pajamas, Brandt was ready to nod off. But he prepared Landon's bedtime bottle and settled in the recliner.

Landon made short work of the bottle and was out. Brandt placed him on his back in his crib, tucking the covers around the sleeping boy.

Jessie glanced up from the kitchen table when he returned to the living room. "Is he down?"

"Yeah. I didn't think it'd be that easy. Quinn is always complaining about how hard it is to get Adam to go to bed."

"Adam's a little older and it is harder when a kid is past the 'bottle before bed' age."

He sank into the couch. "That's the second time you've mentioned the bottle thing. Like Landon's somehow...too old to have a bottle."

She dropped the pen to the table and rubbed the skin between her eyes. "I was just sharing my experience—my limited experience. It's up to his mother to decide when to wean him."

"So you don't think getting him off the bottle is something I oughta tackle while I'm takin' care of him?"

"God no." Then Jessie didn't say anything else.

Brandt didn't relish spending the next four months waiting for Jessie to converse with him. He snagged the remote and turned the TV on, keeping the sound low, happy that Jessie still had satellite.

After catching up on the latest football games, he hunkered down to watch a western.

As soon as Jessie finished whatever she'd been doing at the table, she joined him on the couch. Might make him selfish, but Brandt wouldn't mind if this was how the nights for the next four months played out.

Once the movie ended, Jessie stood. "You need anything before I turn in?"

"Nah." He pointed at the baby monitor. "I've got it handled if Landon wakes up."

"How early are you heading to the ranch tomorrow?"

"I figured I'd leave around six."

"I get up at five thirty to feed the animals, so that oughta work out. Since it only takes fifteen minutes to get to Sky Blue, I don't leave until six forty-five."

"If it'd be easier, havin' me stay until then—"

Jessie got a strange look on her face. "Don't trust me alone with him?"

"For Christsake, Jess, what the hell is that supposed to mean? Of course I trust you with him or I wouldn't've asked for your help."

"That's good to know."

Say something.

"Goodnight, Brandt."

"Night, Jessie."

He stretched out on the couch and flipped through channels. Fighting a wave of sleepiness, he pulled his ball cap down over his forehead. He'd just rest his eyes for a minute.

Soft cries roused him. Groggy, he pushed up from the couch and fiddled with the volume on the baby monitor and heard the noise again.

Not Landon. Jessie.

Brandt tiptoed down the hallway to Jessie's bedroom. Her door was open and he listened just outside the jamb. Sure enough, another soft sob echoed. Without thinking, Brandt entered her room.

She'd curled into a ball in the middle of her bed, resting her forehead to her knees. Her shoulders shook with each sob.

His heart fell straight to his toes. "Jessie."

"Go away."

"No. Let me help you."

"Help me do what? Fall apart even more?"

He stared at the snarled hair shadowing her face.

Jessie slowly raised her head, burning him with a look of pure venom. "I hate you for doing this to me."

His breath stalled.

"And when Landon is back with his mother? I never want to see your face again. Now get the hell out of my room."

Suffocation and dizziness set in. Jessie's image wavered and everything went black.

Brandt sat straight up, gasping for air. It took him a second to get his bearings. He was at Jessie's house. Not slumped in her doorway but sprawled on the couch, TV droning in the background. Squinting at the clock, he realized only a half hour had passed since he'd closed his eyes.

Except it hadn't felt like a bad dream; it felt more like a premonition.

Chapter Five

Jessie wished she'd taken Brandt up on his offer to come to Sky Blue and help with Landon on his first day because the kid was a holy terror.

The other kids scared him, so he cried and screamed, "No!"

The other adults scared him, so he cried and screamed, "No!"

At first Landon didn't want anything to do with Jessie. Then he refused to let go of her leg. He clung to her, crying like his heart was breaking.

I know how you feel, kid.

Lunchtime was a disaster. She'd buckled Landon in the high chair while she readied the other kids' lunches. He beat his hands on the tray, arched his back, and tried to throw himself out of the chair, all while screaming.

Spitting mad, his face was bright red and covered in a mix of tears, drool and snot. She wiped him up and let him out of the chair. The poor little boy didn't know whether to run off or stick by her. When she walked to the refrigerator, he followed. She took a bottle from the top shelf and held it out to him. Landon snatched it out of her hands, like a wild animal afraid his meal would be stolen, and scampered off.

She glanced at the clock. Only five hours to go. Yay.

He calmed down for about ten minutes while he cowered in the corner, watching with those big blue McKay eyes. When Jessie approached him and tried to take away his empty bottle, he returned to shrieking. And he added hitting, just to make things interesting.

For about three seconds Jessie considered setting him in a playpen and leaving him in one of the empty offices upstairs until he screamed himself to sleep.

Buck up and deal with it.

She crouched down in front of him. "No hitting, Landon. Ever. Do you understand me?"

He swatted at her and she grabbed his wrist. "No hitting."

He wailed.

Since none of the other kids could nap through his screaming, Jessie let them take their blankets and pillows and watch a movie in the separate play room.

The main door to the daycare opened and Skylar walked in, cringing at Landon's ear piercing shrieks. She motioned Jessie aside.

Jessie blurted, "I'm sorry if he's disturbing you, but I've tried everything and nothing is working."

Skylar placed her hand on Jessie's arm. "I'm not blaming you. It'll probably take a couple of days for him to get used to this place and the other kids, so I'm going to suggest we ease him into it. A few hours at a time this week, okay?"

Jessie knew that was the smart thing to do, but she still felt like she'd failed with him. "Okay."

"Also, I know you'd intended to take Landon over to Joan's tomorrow, but it'd be better if he got used to coming here all week. Take him to Joan's or whatever at night, but he needs to get acclimated here first."

"Agreed. I'll call Brandt and have him pick Landon up right away, but it'll probably be at least an hour before he can get here from the ranch."

"No offense, Jess, but you should take Landon back to your place now. Have Brandt meet you there." Sky shot the still screaming kid a quick glance. "With a six pack and a bottle of aspirin."

Jessie managed a smile. "Thanks. Who's filling in for me for the rest of today?"

Two raps sounded on the glass part of the door and Kade sauntered in, wearing his usual workday clothes; jeans, boots, hat and flannel shirt.

Immediately Landon stopped wailing.

Jessie and Sky exchanged a *what the hell?* look and then looked at Kade.

Kade shrugged. "It's probably the hat." He crouched down,

facing Landon, far enough away not to scare him. "You sure got a set of lungs on ya. And I thought Miz Eliza was loud."

Landon raced to Kade and threw himself at the cowboy with a sob.

Logically, Jessie knew Landon went to Kade because he reminded him of Brandt. But emotionally, it made her feel like she was lacking a maternal instinct.

You're not the boy's mother. You shouldn't have that instinct.

The last thing she needed was more self-doubt. She backed away to get their belongings and to call Brandt.

Kade was such a good guy he put on Landon's coat. Then he carried Landon to her truck and buckled him in his car seat. Jessie braced herself for the frustrated cries to start again, but Landon was silent. He'd fallen asleep.

Thank God.

So Jessie drove. Past her house and into Moorcroft. She killed almost an hour, reluctant to rouse Landon. While she drove, she compiled a list of reasons why this wouldn't work.

Her stepfather's mantra echoed in her mind—*winners never quit and quitters never win.*

But this was different. This was a losing situation all around.

She saw Brandt climbing out of his truck when she pulled into her driveway. She motioned him over and rolled down the window.

He said, "What's up?"

"Get in. Fast. Landon's asleep and I don't wanna wake the little beast up."

"That bad, huh?"

"You have no idea."

Brandt climbed in the passenger side. "Look, Jess, I'm sorry—"

She held up her hand. "I just want to enjoy the silence for a little while longer."

He nodded and relaxed in the seat.

But Jessie could feel him looking at her. And for the first time, maybe ever, she didn't mind.

After about ten minutes, Brandt asked, "What happened today?"

"Landon melted down. Completely. Skylar has suggested I

only take him to daycare in the morning until he gets used to it. She even suggested we skip taking him to your mom this week until he's more settled." Her hands tightened on the wheel. "I'm gonna let you handle that with Joan. And I want you to make sure she knows I'm not trying to keep Landon away from her."

"Hey, Jess, I'd never do that to you."

She expected him to say "I'm not like Luke" but he didn't.

Brandt stretched his arm along the back of the seat. "So if Landon's only gonna be there part time this week, where do I come in?"

"You'll have to pick him up at noon, because I can't afford to take every afternoon off."

"Understood. It shouldn't be a problem. I'll let Tell and Dalton know it'll be a short work week for me."

"So Casper won't chew your ass for not being around?"

"Probably. But nothin' I ever do makes him happy anyway, so he'll just pile on more shit work for when I am there. Threatening to..."

"Threatening to what?"

"Same old tune, him remindin' me I gotta 'prove' to him that I'm dedicated enough to take over the ranch. He's been hangin' that over my head since Luke died."

If that irked her, Jessie couldn't imagine how Brandt felt. "Would Casper really do that?"

"What? Cut me out of ownership of our part of the ranch? If he decided he had a good enough reason, absolutely."

Silence filled the cab—not comfortable silence.

Brandt gently said, "Talk to me."

"I don't know if I can do this, Brandt."

He paused a second. "Okay. I appreciate your honesty."

"But?"

"But I don't know if a few hours is enough to make a decision. Especially if all you've had with him are a few bad hours."

"How long did it take you to decide to ask me to help you with Landon's care?"

He mumbled something.

"Say what?"

"Three days. Three very long days when I second and third guessed this from every possible angle and...I still ain't sure I did the right thing."

That admission surprised her.

"Every one of my McKay cousins showed up this morning and that's a rare thing, trust me."

Jessie frowned. "Why? Is there something going on with the ranch?"

"There's always something goin' on, but I usually hear about it long after it's happened. Dad ain't real good about keepin' me informed, which pisses me off because I've been doin' every damn thing he's ever asked and he still has all the control and never lets me forget it." He inhaled. Exhaled. "Sorry. That's twice I've gone off about it today. For once my cousins showing up didn't have nothin' to do with the ranch. They came because of Landon. But mostly because of you."

Her gut clenched. "Me? Why?"

"They asked why I didn't come to them first and ask for help."

No surprise the McKay's circled the wagons around one of their own. "What'd you say?"

Brandt sighed, pushing his hat back to rub his forehead. "I didn't know what to say. It pissed me off a little, to be honest. Because of the...family dynamic between my dad and his brothers, it'd make things ten times worse for everyone if I'd asked one of Uncle Carson's, or Uncle Cal's, or Uncle Charlie's sons or daughters-in-law to help."

She weighed aspects of this situation she hadn't considered. "Is it a family pride thing?"

"Jess—"

"It's not a nosy question. Maybe for the first time I understand why you involved me—because I'm neutral. The lesser of two evils. You knew your dad would prefer to have me, who he's never liked, helping out with Landon, rather than taking his brothers' or his nephews' charity." Another thing occurred to her. "And you don't want your McKay relatives knowing you don't think your father would be a fit guardian for Landon, even temporarily."

"But it's more about how they view my mom and not my dad."

Logical, sweet Brandt. Sparing his mother's feelings. Figuring out every contingency before he made a single move. It used to drive Luke crazy, since Luke was the impulsive one.

And look what happened to him.

"Yeah. I'm a bastard."

"No. You're just a good guy who's been put in a no win situation and you're trying to make everyone happy." Jessie had circled back to her house. She braked and turned into her driveway.

Brandt said nothing until after she'd parked. Then he faced her with such a look of misery her breath caught. "You're wrong about me, Jessie. I'm not a good guy. I'm selfish. You were always my first choice. *Always.* Even when I knew this would hurt you like nothin' else, I still went ahead and demanded this of you anyway. And I have to live with knowing when this is done, you'll probably hate me and I'll deserve it."

He jumped out and hefted a still sleeping Landon into his arms before she could formulate a response.

Three hours later, Jessie couldn't believe the change in Landon. He played quietly with his toys on the floor, although he never ventured very far from Brandt. Happy as she was that he wasn't screaming, she worried his adjustment at the daycare would take longer if was subjected to continual quiet instead of chaos. After she popped the casserole in the oven, she returned to the living room where Brandt was working on his laptop.

He glanced up and smiled.

Mercy. That smile of his could knock her for a loop.

Since when? Her practical side demanded.

Since always, her feminine side countered.

When she didn't respond, that roguish smile died. "What?"

"Nothing. You just look so studious. I'm not used to it."

Landon pushed to his feet and ran to Brandt, possessively wrapping his arm around Brandt's thigh.

Jessie shook her head. "He's really afraid I'm gonna take him away from you, isn't he?"

"He'll get used to you. I'm just the only familiar thing in his world right now."

"How many times did you see him before his mother went to jail?"

He shrugged and continued looking at Landon. "I stopped by about twice a week. Sometimes Samantha needed a break from bein' a single parent and I'd take him off her hands for a couple of hours. Other times she just needed someone to talk to. Either way, I ended up hangin' out with him."

An unfamiliar, sharp pang arose. For the first time Jessie wondered if Brandt might've developed feelings for Landon's mother.

"Jessie. Look at me."

She met his gaze.

"You're not doin' anything wrong with him. Give him more than a day to get used to you."

She was relieved Brandt hadn't picked up on the real reason for her worry. Especially since she didn't understand why it'd caused a spark of jealousy. "I'm going out to feed the horses and the llamas."

"Do you need help?"

"Nah. I'm used to doing everything myself."

A guilty look flashed in his eyes. "How are the llamas?"

"Lucy and Ethel are great. But they'd like male attention. They miss their mates. And their babies." Jessie hated selling her male llamas and Lucy and Ethel's last babies. But they'd been raised specifically to work cattle and were easily bored and got into trouble if they didn't have a herd to protect. A bored llama was a dangerous llama. Luckily Lucy and Ethel had half a dozen horses to run with, but they had escaped a few times, probably looking for intimate male companionship.

You'd like some intimate male companionship too.

What the hell was wrong with her today?

"Those baby llamas were awful cute," Brandt said.

"Someday I'll have babies, but not now. The timing is all wrong."

Brandt frowned.

"I'll be back in a bit."

Jessie slipped on her coveralls, her ratty old Carhartt coat, her leather gloves, and her ridiculous looking, but very warm, Elmer Fudd hat. She tugged on the waterproof work boots, whistled for Lexie and was out the door.

I'm used to doing everything myself.

It wasn't a shot at him, but Brandt still felt guilty. In the

73

six months before Luke died, he'd passed a lot of his ranch responsibilities to Jessie. Jessie already had her hands full taking care of the horses, Luke expected she'd learn every aspect of being a ranch wife and worked her to the bone.

Which was why Brandt, Tell and Dalton had become so enraged when his father kicked Jessie out of the home she and Luke shared. After Jessie turned down Brandt's offer to live in his house, which he owned free and clear, he'd scrambled to find Jessie a place where she could bring her horses and llamas. It pained him to think she'd still had to give up some of them up.

When he didn't feel Landon clinging to his leg, he glanced at the boy standing by the door. The kid only cared about the dog, and running free outside as he chased the dog, so maybe fresh air would do him good. "Wanna go outside and see the llamas?"

Landon just stared at him.

"It'd be nice if you could talk. Or at least try to talk."

But when Brandt grabbed his coat off the peg, Landon seemed to grasp Brandt's intention. He didn't fuss at all when Brandt bundled him up. But his winter wear options were sorely lacking and the kid needed snow boots and snow pants.

No snow covered the ground today, although it was cold and the wind blew like a bitch. He blocked the worst of the wind from Landon's face as he carried him to the fence.

Jessie was in the pasture with the llamas. They were intent on whatever she was talking to them about, until they noticed Brandt and Landon.

Given the way Landon was scared of everything, it surprised him that the boy reached over the fence to touch the animals. "Whoa, buddy, wait a second. Let's make sure it's okay." Brandt looked at Jessie.

She said, "As long as you hold him, it should be all right." She spoke to the llamas in a lilting tone, and Brandt had a moment of jealousy. What would it be like to have Jessie murmuring to him like that?

Pure heaven.

Landon shrieked, "Goggie!" and Lexie bounded away, her doggie body language said, *Ha ha, you can't catch me now, sucker.*

Brandt laughed. For some reason Brandt's laughter made

Landon giggle.

Jessie grinned. "This is much better than earlier today."

"No doubt."

She wrapped her arm around a llama's neck and urged her closer. "This is Lucy. She is far too curious for her own good." She looked at Landon and held out her hand, palm up.

He blinked at her and frowned. But he watched her.

She reached in her pocket and pulled out a chunk of carrot. She opened her palm, put the carrot in the center and held it out to Lucy.

Lucy sniffed and lowered her head over the carrot, bringing it into her mouth.

"See? You wanna feed Ethel? You've gotta do the same thing. Just like this." She explained the whole process again. Landon held his hand out, exactly the way Jessie instructed.

Brandt was blown away by her patience, showing Landon every step, speaking to him softly, but not in a baby-talk voice.

When Ethel gobbled the carrot chunk from Landon's hand, he shrieked with happiness.

Both he and Jessie winced. "We've gotta find a better way for him to communicate."

"Agreed. I'm almost finished."

"With all the animals?"

"No, just the llamas. See? Here come the horses."

The six horses trotted in from the pasture, tossing their manes, as if eating the hay Jessie had spread out was of no consequence. That if they truly wanted something better, they could've gotten it themselves. Temperamental damn things. He preferred cows. They ate. They bred. They calved. They either went through the cycle again or went away. Simple.

You used to like horses. You used to want to implement a breeding program.

But it'd become just another thing Casper McKay had ridiculed and Brandt let that idea go.

Landon squirmed to be let down. Brandt crouched beside him next to the fence and gave him a play by play of what Jessie was doing. The kid actually seemed to be listening.

Maybe that's because someone is taking the time to talk to him.

Samantha hadn't been forthcoming about her parenting

skills, probably because they were lacking.

As Brandt was about to hoist Landon onto his hip, the gate opened and Lexie tore out. Landon gave chase before Brandt could grab onto his hood and stop him. Damn. The kid was fast.

"Hey, wait a second. Come back here."

"Let him run."

He'd known the instant Jessie came up behind him, even before she spoke. It might've been the scent of her cherry Chapstick carried on the wind. Or it might've been the sound her coveralls made as she walked closer. A sound he'd heard a lot in the year they spent together doing chores. He faced her. "Need me to do anything?"

"No. Unless you wanna stay out here and watch Landon run his legs off while I shower."

"You thinking what I'm thinking?"

She smiled. "I can wash my own back, but thanks for offering."

Holy hell. That wasn't what he'd been thinking at all. But now that she'd brought it up, Brandt couldn't get the image of her wet, nekkid body out of his mind. Watching the water sluice over her curves through a cloud of steam surrounding her. Steam that hung heavy and damp with the sweet scent of her soap. Or with the musky aroma from her...

"Brandt?"

Dammit. He looked toward Landon to hide his blush. "The offer stands. Any time. However, I was thinkin' along the lines of the longer I keep him out here, the earlier he'll hit the hay tonight."

"Good plan. Come in whenever you guys are ready."

Brandt commended his willpower in not turning around and watching her hips sway as she headed to the house.

Snap out of it, man. This is the first day. If she catches you eyeballing her ass, she'll kick yours right out the door.

True. But that pesky feeling of hope arose, that feeling he'd all but stomped out when she'd shot him down last year. Given months to reflect, he understood how lousy his timing had been.

Landon started to fall asleep during supper. While Brandt bathed him, Jessie washed the dishes. She'd changed into sweat pants after her shower, and when he returned to the living room after putting Landon down for the night, he had to stop and grip the back of the reclining chair.

How many nights had they spent just like this? Jessie sitting cross-legged on the couch, engrossed in her knitting. Him watching TV, or pretending to watch TV when it was far more interesting to covertly watch her.

They'd spent dozens of nights together. Revisiting those nights gave him the same sharp ache of want he'd felt back then.

Jessie looked up. Her gaze flicked over him and she smiled. "Nice jammies."

Brandt glanced down at the camo fleece pants and camo tank top. Okay, maybe they didn't match, but they didn't look *that* bad. "Hey, at least I'm wearin' jammies. Normally I sleep commando."

"Must be a family thing. Luke did too."

A perfectly natural comment, but for some reason it rubbed him wrong. He plopped right beside her. He leaned over and peered at the twisted ball of yarn on her lap. "Whatcha makin'?"

She held up a brown blob. "A mess. It's supposed to be a hat for my mom's husband for Christmas. It sort of looks like a cowpie right now, huh?"

"Maybe. But it don't smell like one."

"You're so sweet."

Brandt held his breath, expecting her to say something about Luke being sweet, too, but she just sighed.

"You wanna watch *X-Files* reruns? This is pointless tonight." She set aside her knitting. "I'm too wound up."

"I'm sorry you had a rough morning. Think tomorrow will be easier?"

"I hope so. I don't know if I can stand being the kid's last choice for the next four months." She expelled a soft, bitter laugh. "Although I should be used to it. Like father like son, right?"

That crack about Luke didn't sit any better with Brandt than the first one did.

Jessie sighed again. "Sorry. I should probably haul my cranky self to bed."

He reached for her hand. "Stay. Drink a beer with me. We'll

heckle the bizarre plot line and wonder why in the hell Mulder and Scully don't just get it on already. Jesus. How long can they drag out the sexual tension when it's obvious the two of them belong together?"

She faced him and frowned. "It takes them a while, but they do end up together. We watched the last season, last year, remember?"

Not really. As usual, he'd been more interested in gawking at Jessie. "I must've forgot."

"You forgot that Mulder and Scully drove off toward a happy future?"

"Yeah. It's easier to believe in monsters because happily ever after doesn't happen in real life."

Jessie gave him a curious look before she tossed him the remote. "One episode. Then I'm going to bed."

Landon's behavior Tuesday at daycare was marginally better than Monday.

Landon's behavior Wednesday at daycare was markedly better than Tuesday.

Landon's behavior Thursday at daycare was good enough he stayed the entire day.

Brandt and Jessie had fallen into an easy evening routine—too easy. The three of them fed the animals together. They ate supper together. Brandt bathed Landon and tucked him in bed. Then he and Jessie watched TV together until one of them or both of them fell asleep. If she conked out first, he'd watch her like a fucking perv, but he couldn't keep his eyes off her. Something about seeing her so unguarded in sleep reinforced the idea she was vulnerable and strengthened his resolve to protect her at all costs.

Even if he was the one most dangerous to her.

So when they were offered a break in the routine, Brandt grabbed it, telling Jessie his mother wanted to have Landon for an hour or so after supper. But first on their to-do list was outfitting Landon for winter weather.

As far as shopping went, Brandt didn't mind the farm supply store. Tisdale's carried everything essential to ranching and he usually ran into someone he knew. It hadn't occurred to him that might not be a good thing until it happened.

He and Jessie were in the boot section of Tisdale's, trying to figure out if rubber boots worn over shoes were a better choice than simple snow boots. Since neither he nor Jessie had shoe shopped for a toddler, getting Landon to sit still proved a major obstacle.

"No. Put those back. We don't want anything with laces."

Brandt held up the camouflage boots. "But they have drawstrings on the top. They'll stay tied."

Landon reached for them with a possessive grunt.

"See? He loves them. They're hip. And manly."

Jessie grumbled and let go of Landon for two seconds. The kid was off like an antelope.

"Dammit, Landon, get back here." Shit. He wasn't supposed to swear. He snagged the boy by the waist and hung him upside down on the trip back to the boot department. Landon shrieked, the good kind of shrieks, but still, he was awful damn loud.

"Now sit on Jessie's lap and be a good boy so we can get this over with, okay?"

Landon nodded and Brandt grinned. The kid was already getting better at communicating and it'd only been a few days.

"Brandt?"

He whirled around and looked into the beady eyes of Margene Hieb. Margene and her husband Larry lived up the road from his folks. They'd been friendly neighbors for years until their oldest daughter, Pandora, became the walking wounded due to Luke's heartbreaking ways. Consequently, Margene took every opportunity to run her mouth off about anything less than flattering about the McKay family—and there always seemed to be plenty to talk about.

"Margene." Brandt peered over Margene's shoulder. "Where's Larry?"

"At home." She sidestepped Brandt and stood in front of Jessie. "Oh my. It is true. I wasn't sure, you know how rumors are, never know how they get started."

Usually by people like you.

"He really looks like his father, doesn't he?"

Jessie said not a word.

Margene sighed. "Such a shame that Luke won't be around

to watch him grow up. It's an even bigger shame..." She shook her head at Jessie. "I don't know how on earth you're just sitting there, holding him, like he was your own. Granted, he is a cute little boy, and you *were* married to his father, but I don't see how you can overlook the fact he was born on the wrong side of the sheets."

"She can overlook that fact, Mom, because Jessie was used to Luke cheating on her, like he cheated on everyone before her." Pandora, mean, nasty Pandora, tossed her fat head and Brandt thought he might've seen a snake or two trying to slither out of her hair. "Honestly, the only thing that surprises me? That more of his secret spawn haven't shown up. The man couldn't keep his pants zipped to save his life."

Brandt looked back and forth between mother and daughter, mentally trying to slap a lid on his temper before his mouth opened and he said something he'd regret. But it didn't work. "Did that crack about Luke's character make you feel better, Pandora? You're still bitter that Luke dumped you...what? Ten years ago?"

"There is no time limit on the effects of infidelity, Brandt, as Jessie well knows," Pandora sneered.

"But there is a time limit on my patience and you've reached it. Now get out of here before I tell Pastor Jones you both need a personal sermon on learning and practicing forgiveness." Brandt looked over his shoulder. "I saw him around here someplace."

"You wouldn't."

"I would happily relay everything you just said and then some."

Huffing and whispering, they took off.

Brandt looked at Jessie. He started to say *I'm sorry*, but she shook her head.

"That's the first, Brandt, but it won't be the last." She pointed to the boots, the pair of snow pants and the University of Wyoming tasseled hat. "We're done."

After they'd paid and loaded Landon in his carseat, Jessie said, "I should've driven into town because after that fun time, I'm ready to go home. And no offense, but I can't stomach the thought of riding out to your folks' house with you."

"Okay. But my mom is expecting him—"

"Just take me to Dewey's. I'll grab something to eat while

I'm waiting."

He started to reach for her hand, but stopped himself. "I'll keep it a short visit. But it'll be at least an hour."

"I can entertain myself, Brandt. I've gotten used to it in the last two years."

He pulled up in front of the Sandstone Building and she bailed out with a mumbled, "Later."

Landon was fairly good at his parents' place, considering his mother insisted on holding him all the time. And from what Brandt had seen of Landon, he wasn't the snuggliest kid. Brandt cut the visit short when his dad started in on him about prepping for calving season, which was still several months away.

Plus, he was anxious to get back to Jessie.

He texted her: *You ready 2 go?*

Her response was fast: *Already gone. Walking home.*

What the fuck?

Panicked, Brandt called her. "Jess? What do you mean you're walkin' home?"

"I couldn't stay in there another second. So I left. I figured you'd catch up with me."

Do not yell at her. "Where are you?"

"By the Shell station."

"Stay put. I mean it. I'll be there in ten minutes."

It took him eight minutes to reach her.

Jessie climbed in his truck without a word. She didn't turn around to check on Landon, who was asleep. She stared straight ahead. He was so freaked out about her fucking *walking* when it was fifteen degrees out, that he didn't say anything for fear of saying the wrong thing.

They'd gone about three miles in brutal silence, when she said, "Stop. I feel sick."

He eased the truck to the shoulder and she practically jumped out. He gave her a minute before he cut the headlights and checked on her.

With no moon, city lights or sodium glow from the interstate, everything was pure black—the sky, the ground, the hillside on the left, the sweeping valley on the right. The cold bit into him with sharp teeth.

No, the chill in his bones was from something else entirely.

Fear.

Jessie teetered on the edge of the road, arms wrapped herself, nearly lost in that dark void.

Brandt moved in behind her. Close enough if she needed him, far enough away to offer the illusion of space.

"Get back in the truck and leave me alone, Brandt."

"Like hell. What happened?"

"The same thing that happened in Tisdale's. Not once, but ten times. I had ten different people, people I barely know, come up to me and tell me how fucking sorry they were for me. Sorry! For me. Like I'm some pathetic excuse of a woman that can't keep a man or birth a child. They're sorry that my husband ran around on me. They're sorry that Landon exists. It was horrible."

"Jess." He set his hands on her shoulders.

She flinched and shook off his show of sympathy. "Don't touch me. I'm so mad right now I just want to scream!"

Brandt could take it if she lashed out at him—physically or verbally. Instead of heeding her warning, he enfolded her in his arms, hugging her against his chest. Just as he suspected, she didn't fight him at all.

A minute or so passed and he whispered, "Still wanna do it?"

"What? Scream?"

"There's no one here but us. No one would hear but me and maybe a few mule deer."

Her body tensed.

"Come on. Let it out."

And she did. She screamed and screamed and it absolutely ripped his heart from his chest. Brandt closed his eyes and listened while she let that anger go. Let the frustration go. The hurt, she'd hang onto. He held her until the screams tapered off into sobs. She ended up facing him, her face buried in his neck.

"Oh God, it hurts."

"I know it does."

"I loved him. I loved him like crazy, so how can I hate him so much now?"

"You hate the position he put you in, not him."

She hiccupped. "This is so fucked up. Here I am telling you that I loved your brother, but I hate him, and you're trying to make me feel better about having those conflicting feelings, even when you can't possibly understand because you loved him."

"Yes, I did. But that doesn't mean I can't hate some of the things Luke did, Jess."

She tipped her head back and blinked away her tears. "Will this get easier?"

"The situation with Landon? I wish I could say yes, but I don't know."

"At least you didn't bullshit me."

"Honesty is always the best policy in my book." Brandt smiled and pecked her on the forehead. "I'm here for you. Anything you need."

Jessie shivered. "Thank you. We'd better get going."

"Good. And after hearing those excellent screams, I'm suddenly in the mood for a horror flick."

She actually laughed and shoved him. "Fine. But this time you're making the popcorn."

Chapter Six

Friday afternoon Brandt came into Sky Blue daycare to pick Landon up for the weekend. They'd already loaded Landon's paltry amount of stuff in Brandt's truck before they started their respective workdays, so the kid handoff was all that remained.

"Is there anything else?"

She snagged the last bottle out of the fridge and jammed it in the diaper bag. "No. That's it."

"We'll get outta your hair then." He hefted Landon onto his hip and slung the diaper bag over his shoulder.

"What are your plans?" she asked. How was it that Brandt looked masculine even carrying a quilted diaper bag printed with yellow duckies?

"Nothin' big. Dalton suggested we test Landon's rodeo skills on the back of a bull first thing in the morning. Tell thinks Landon is built more like a saddle bronc rider. While I'm leanin' toward blowin' off all them rough stock events and teachin' him bulldoggin'. Naturally the afternoon will be devoted to getting Landon used to his very own dirt bike."

Jessie laughed. "I'll bet Landon would look cute in teeny tiny chaps and a little hat." She reached down and snapped the bottom button on Landon's coat. "Tell and Dalton are spending the night?"

"Yeah. Chores don't stop because it's the weekend. Thought we'd do the minimum tomorrow and take Landon with us."

"Sounds like you guys will have fun."

"What are your weekend plans?"

"Depends on the weather. Might work the horses. I'll probably just stay home." Like usual. She used to go out with

Keely at least one Saturday night of the month, but after Keely and Jack got engaged, Cowgirls' Night Out stopped.

"If you get bored or need anything, or just wanna hang out with us guys, call me, or just show up, okay?"

Brandt was so damn sweet. She couldn't help reaching out and running her hand up his arm to let him know she appreciated his offer. "Okay."

How did Brandt respond to her show of affection? By brushing his lips over her cheek. "See you Sunday night, Jess."

About thirty seconds after Brandt exited the main door, Simone barreled into the empty daycare room. "Omigod. How did I miss cowboy hottie *again*?"

"Gotta be quicker."

All five feet eleven inches of Simone perched on a mini plastic chair. Long arms and longer legs akimbo, she resembled a praying mantis about to strike. "So, is cowboy hottie quick on the trigger too?"

Jessie rolled her eyes. "I wouldn't know." But it wasn't like she hadn't been thinking about it. Nonstop. In vivid detail.

"I hate it when you get all quiet and introspective. We need to go out and get you loud and rowdy. Get you riled up, dishing on the slim pickins on men around here." Simone held up her hand when Jessie started to decline. "No arguing, no excuse. Because I saw cowboy hottie sneak out with the young'un."

"The cowboy hottie has a name," Jessie retorted. She faced the wall, wiping off the letters from the white board.

"Oh. So you're not denying he's hot?"

"Hell no. I've got eyes. Brandt is unbelievably hot. That body..." Jessie whistled and winked over her shoulder. "World class, my friend."

"How do you know?" Simone asked with a lifted brow. "Has he been running around your place buck-assed naked?"

"No. But last summer? I saw him wearing a pair of board shorts and a really great tan."

Since Simone had started at Sky Blue six months ago, she wasn't aware of Jessie's history with the McKays, Brandt in particular. Which hadn't been all bad, because Simone saw her as Jessie, her work pal, her sometime barhopping buddy. Not as that-poor-young-widow-Jessie-and-isn't-it-a-shame-her-husband-ran-around-on-her-all-the-time phrase the locals used to describe her. She shuddered to think what other description had been added since Landon's appearance.

"That's it? No shirt?"

"No shirt. And if you think he's drool-worthy in Wranglers? You oughta see that perfect butt and those muscled legs in the flesh. Not to mention how awesomely buff his chest is. Totally lickable. I've known him for four years and I had no idea the man had pipes like that." This was the fun part hanging with Simone; she could say whatever popped into her head and Simone didn't judge her for it. Simone didn't consider Jessie too sweet or too innocent looking to have such lewd thoughts or call bullshit on Jessie's opinion.

Not that what she'd just said about Brandt McKay's slamming body was bullshit. It was all too real and all too close.

"I oughta slap some sense into you, Jessie girl."

"Why?"

"Because to hear you talk about cowboy hottie, you've been paying very close attention to him a lot longer than you'll admit to. Which means you want him."

Duh. But she couldn't have him.

Why not?

Because I fear he's a package deal and he wants more than I'm willing to give him.

Two raps sounded on the door. She and Simone whirled around to see...Brandt McKay lounging in the doorway.

Holy freakin' crap. Had he heard their raunchy girl talk, with him starring front and center?

"Hey, cowboy hottie. We were just talking about—ow! Jessie, what the hell?"

She'd pelted Simone with a marker to shut her up. "Sorry. It must've slipped." She ignored the wash of humiliation and focused on cowboy hottie. Dammit. Now Simone even had her calling him that. "Brandt. I thought you left?"

"So I gathered," he said dryly.

So he *had* heard them. "What's wrong?"

"Nothin'. I realized I forgot Landon's snow boots."

"Oh. They're in his cubby. I'll grab them."

"I know where his cubby is." He crouched and pulled the boots from the bottom shelf. "I figured he might get a little muddy this weekend."

"With all that rodeoin' and wild McKay man time."

He stared at her quizzically, which made her curious about which part of the conversation he'd overheard.

"What?" she asked, a little testily.

"Just wondering where you ladies were headed to tonight?"

Simone shrugged. "Wherever, whenever and whatever."

"Which is Simone's way of telling you she doesn't have a freakin' clue what we're doing."

"Well, wherever you end up, if you have a little too much liquid fun and need a ride, just call. I'd be happy to pick you up and take you home."

She knew Brandt meant both of them, but he didn't look at Simone even once. "Thanks, but—"

"We'll keep it in mind," Simone inserted smoothly. "It's always good to have a man on standby."

Brandt's intense gaze never strayed from hers. "That's something I'm very familiar with, isn't it, Jessie? Bein' on standby."

Her mouth became desert dry and her tongue useless.

"Later, ladies." And he was gone.

She sagged against the wall. Another reminder that everything had changed last night. Not only when he'd held her tightly and told her to scream her frustration into the wind and darkness. After returning to her house and tucking Landon in bed, they'd sat on the couch, heckling some stupid horror movie. At some point, she'd curled into him and had fallen asleep. Then she was in Brandt's arms. He hadn't done more than tenderly brush her hair from her face after depositing her on the bed fully clothed, but it'd felt intimate. It'd left her unsettled. Mostly because it'd left her wanting more of him.

"Earth to Jessie."

Her gaze zoomed to Simone's. "Sorry. What did you say?"

"I said we're hitting the pizza and beer joint. And you're gonna tell me everything about your past with the cowboy hottie."

"Simone—"

"No arguing. And if you're lucky, I won't rail on you too hard for being a complete idiot."

"Why am I an idiot?"

"For not snapping that man up. I swear I've never seen any

man look so ready to lick a woman up one side and down the other as he was when he was eating you up with his eyes."

"Or given his family history, he might chew me up and spit me out," she shot back.

"Don't be a fool. Pride and fear are best left in the past when it's obvious he wants to be part of your future."

Well, hell. How was she supposed to respond to that? Especially when she suspected Simone would retract that statement after she heard the sordid truth about the situation?

Jessie's house was way too quiet. Sad, how quickly she'd gotten used to Brandt and Landon's presence in the last five days—which would make it ten times harder when they were both gone for good.

Rather than dwell on what she couldn't change, or spend a perfectly beautiful Saturday moping, she took action. She whipped up a spice cake with rum frosting. Then she loaded Lexie and the cake in the truck and drove to Sky Blue for a box of stuff she'd intended to donate to the women's shelter.

How would Brandt take her unexpected appearance at his place? More importantly, what did it mean that she was making the first move?

After talking to Simone last night, Jessie was beginning to see Brandt in a different light. But she wasn't sure what to do about it, or if Brandt would ever agree to her new condition. Or if she had the guts to actually broach the subject with him.

As soon as she'd parked at Brandt's place, McKay men surrounded her truck.

Maybe they'd smelled food.

She started to open the door when Brandt elbowed Dalton aside to get there first. "Jess! Hey, I'm glad to see you."

Damn he looked good. Relaxed. And honestly happy she'd showed up.

Dalton sniffed. "Is that...cake?"

"What are you? Part bloodhound?" Tell shoved him and grinned at her. "But please tell me it's cake."

"Yes, it's cake. Spice cake."

"What's the occasion?" Brandt asked.

"It's Saturday?"

"Good enough for me. I'll put it inside so these two don't eat it all." He grabbed the pan and said, "Be right back," as Dalton followed him inside.

She said, "Where's Landon?" to Tell.

"There." He pointed to a dirt mound. Landon sat in the midst of a pile of small shovels and Tonka trucks of every size and shape.

"Are those new?"

"Yeah, me'n Dalton were at the feed store so we got some boy toys for Landon."

That was so cute, and heartening, they were taking an interest in their nephew.

"Besides, we all loved playin' in the dirt. He's a McKay. Figured he would too."

"Yes, the true test of a McKay male is seeing how dirty he can get his damn clothes on a daily basis." Funny how she'd forgotten how filthy Luke's clothes were after he finished up on the ranch. Funny how she'd forgotten how much of her life had been devoted to putting Luke's needs first. Still, she couldn't help but smile at the dirt-covered urchin lost in muddy playtime. "Landon looks like he's having a ball."

"He is now. But he was damn cranky when he woke up. I think he was missin' you, Jess."

She gave Tell a droll look. "Such a suck up. I already said you could have some cake."

He laughed. "You're just in time because we were about to play football. And I'm draftin' you to my team because I don't think Landon is gonna be much help in the tackling department."

"You're playing tackle football?"

"Flag football is for pussies." Tell bumped her with his hip. "Come on. It'll be fun."

"Fun. Right. It's all fun and games until someone breaks an arm or gets a concussion."

But Tell wasn't listening to her. He waved to Dalton and Brandt as they ambled closer. "Guess who's on my team, *suckas*?"

Dalton loomed over her. "If you think we're goin' easy on you since you're a girl, Jessie—"

"You'd be exactly right," Brandt said. "Because she is not

playin' football with us."

What? Not that Jessie had a burning desire to chase around a pigskin, but who was Brandt to decide what she could and couldn't do?

Tell said, "Oh shit. Now you did it, bro."

Jessie got in Brandt's face. "Don't make decisions for me. Don't made assumptions about me. And you sure as hell better never speak for me, Brandt McKay. Understood?"

Everyone froze.

Brandt said, "Understood."

"Good." Jessie placed her hands on Brandt's chest and playfully shoved him. "You are goin' down, buddy. Me'n Tell are gonna whup your sorry butts."

He smiled. "Bring it. No cryin' for mercy when I've got you pinned down."

When Brandt grinned at her like that? Sexy and mischievous? Her heart went into free fall.

Tell tugged on her arm. "Come on, killer, let's devise a strategy."

Unfortunately Tell's strategy consisted of handing Jessie the ball damn near every time, while he tried to tackle both his brothers at the same time. Which never worked. Which meant Jessie spent a lot of time hitting the ground. She did score one touchdown, but she suspected they'd let her score out of pity.

As she waited for the next play, she realized it'd been ages since she'd goofed around outside with no real purpose. Likewise, Brandt, Tell and Dalton worked in the great outdoors every day, no matter what the weather did, so they tended to stay indoors when they finished for the day.

Maybe the sunshine and crisp air had brought out her melancholy. But it bolstered her spirits to see these three banding together outside of the hours they spent working on the ranch. It hadn't always been that way, due to Casper's tendency to pit his sons against each other, so at least one good thing had come out of Luke's death.

"Stop chasin' butterflies, Jess, and pay attention," Tell shouted right before he threw her the ball.

She yelled, "Crap!" but somehow managed to catch the football. Then she took off.

Behind her came a loud *oof* as her teammate tackled one of

his brothers, but she didn't stop to see which one, because guaranteed, the other one was chasing her.

She'd almost reached the goal line—a stick jammed in a dirt pile—when she was brought down. Hard. Hitting the ground on her side with a bone-jarring *thud* knocked the wind right out of her.

She couldn't move. She couldn't breathe.

"Jess? God, I'm sorry." Brandt rolled her on her back. "Are you okay?"

No air had entered her lungs yet. Her eyelids seemed glued shut.

"Fuck." Gentle hands swept the hair from her face. "Come on, sweetheart. Wake up."

Footsteps stopped by her head.

"Jesus, Brandt. How fucking hard did you hit her?"

"I—I didn't think it was that hard."

"Did you knock her unconscious?" Dalton asked.

"I don't know. She hasn't moved."

Tell said, "Maybe you oughta give her mouth-to-mouth or something."

Jessie gasped and her eyes flew open.

Brandt was in her face, blocking her view of anything but him. Panic darkened his eyes. Distress lined his forehead. "I'm so sorry. I didn't mean—"

"You just knocked the wind out of me."

"*Just?*" he repeated. "Where else are you hurt?"

"Nowhere."

He didn't believe her. He unzipped her coat and curled his hands around her ribs beneath her breasts. "What about here? Does this hurt?"

She shook her head. She really wasn't hurt, but having Brandt so concerned about her and putting those rough hands of his all over her? Well, there was the upside to getting tackled.

His palms slowly slid down her belly. "Here?"

Again, she shook her head.

His big hands slid further down to circle her hips. "Feel like anything is bruised or out of joint?"

"Not really."

"Hey, bro, why don't you just cut the shit and volunteer to kiss her all over and make it better," Dalton taunted, adding kissing noises.

Tell smacked him in the arm. "Shut it, asshole."

Her gaze winged between Dalton and Tell, kneeling beside Brandt. "You saw me pass the goal line, right? That counted as a touchdown."

"You didn't pass the goal line," Dalton scoffed. "See? You dropped the football well short of the goal."

They all turned and looked at where Dalton was pointing, which was why they didn't see Landon barreling toward them until he landed on Brandt's back with a happy shriek.

Luckily Tell and Dalton pulled the boy free, but not before Brandt fell forward, blocking Jessie's body with his.

Tell laughed. "Seems like someone wants to play football. Maybe you are good at tackling after all. Come on, squirt." He stood, tucking Landon under his arm like a football and Dalton gave chase—much to Landon's delight.

"I'm glad to see you're smilin'. You scared me."

"I scared you? You're the one who hit me like this was the last four seconds in the Superbowl."

Brandt pushed to his feet and held out his hands. "Come on. Up you go."

As soon as she was upright, she grabbed his biceps to steady herself, which brought them close. Very close.

When Jessie looked into Brandt's eyes, he wore the oddest expression. So when he touched her cheek, almost reverently, with a hoarse, "Christ, you're so pretty," she wondered if maybe *he* hadn't hit his head at some point.

"You guys playin' or what?" Dalton yelled.

She stepped back. "I think I'll sit this one out."

"Good plan."

"I'll just go inside and cut the cake."

"Sounds good."

"And take some aspirin."

"Good idea."

But her feet wouldn't budge. Neither would Brandt's. They stared at one another and something just...clicked.

"Come on guys," Tell shouted.

Brandt smiled before he turned and jogged to his brothers.

Grateful for the time to regroup, she sliced the cake and carried in the boxes from the daycare. By then the boys'd had enough football and were starving.

They demolished the cake in one sitting.

Brandt bathed a dirt-covered Landon, leaving her with Tell and Dalton, listening to their Saturday night plans.

"There's a great band playin' at Ziggy's tonight," Dalton suggested.

"Yeah, but it always gets so damn crowded on Saturday nights," Tell said. "What else is goin' on?"

"I heard Busby is havin' a party at his place."

Tell shook his head.

"Why not?"

"Remember his last party? Hell, most of those 'hot' girls he promised us were jailbait."

"True." Dalton repeatedly tossed a tennis ball into the air. "I wish we could go to that strip club in Wheatland. That's always a good time."

"Also true," Tell said. He looked at Jessie. "Brandt said you were goin' out on the town last night. What did you end up doin'?"

"Simone and I went to the Pizza Barn for pizza and beer."

"That's it?"

"Yeah. Why?"

Tell rolled his eyes. "Brandt made it sound like you were goin' out, getting wild and getting laid."

"Brandt said that? About me?"

"Hell no, I didn't say that," Brandt retorted. "I said you had plans. That's it." He sat Landon on the couch next to Jessie.

"You are such a liar," Dalton said. "I remember exactly—"

"Forget it. Let's just go." Tell grabbed his coat. "Thanks for the cake, Jess."

"Yeah, it was good," Dalton said.

Brandt frowned at his brothers. "You guys comin' back here tonight?"

"No. Hopefully we'll be getting wild and getting laid." They sailed out the door.

Jessie watched Landon scramble off the couch and head to the boxes she'd brought in.

"What're those?" Brandt asked.

"Some stuff we don't use at Sky Blue I thought Landon might like."

"Cool. Do you mind keepin' an eye on him while I shower?"

Do you mind if I keep an eye on you while you shower?

"Jess?"

"Umm. Sure. No problem."

Her mom called and they chatted about Thanksgiving plans since Jessie had promised to spend the holiday in Riverton. She watched Landon while she talked. He'd thrown the toys from both boxes all over the floor, but he'd stopped tossing things when he reached the stack of books. He'd stayed in one place and flipped through them slowly, mesmerized, as if he'd never seen a book before.

The truth hit her and she felt like she'd had the wind knocked out of her again. She studied Landon so closely she was barely aware when Brandt sat beside her.

"What's wrong?"

She pointed at Landon, who hadn't noticed Brandt entering the room either, which was a first.

Brandt whispered, "What? You're surprised he's bein' good?"

"No. Look at him. It's like he's never seen a book before. I can't believe..." She closed her eyes and dropped her chin to her chest.

"Hey." Brandt brought her face toward his. "Look at me."

She opened her eyes, hating that once again Brandt would witness her tears. "What kind of mother doesn't read to her child? Or at least give him books to look at himself? My God. Do you know how much my heart aches for him..." Her voice cracked. She tried to turn away, but Brandt pulled her into his arms.

"You're changing that for him. See? Can you imagine how excited he's gonna be when you sit down with him and read those books to him?"

Jessie's pulse raced when she felt Brandt's warm lips brush her forehead, above her eyebrow, her temple, her damp cheek.

"This is why I asked for your help. Because you're cryin' for a little boy who's never had what another child would take for granted. And I know this heart of yours, Jessie. I suspect by next week Landon will have more books in his possession than any other kid in the state of Wyoming."

She laughed against his neck.

Brandt kissed her temple. "It's gonna be okay."

But she wasn't so sure. It was getting harder to stick to her original plan of thinking as Landon only as another long-term daycare assignment. With each day, he was becoming less an obligation, more a joy. That scared her to death. Because guaranteed, even though he was small, he still was just another McKay male who would eventually break her heart.

She wiggled out of Brandt's embrace and put some distance between them. "I'd better be getting home."

"I wish you'd stay. Me'n Landon are gonna have a gourmet meal tonight and you're welcome to share it with us."

"Gourmet meal?"

He grinned. "Spaghettios. And canned peaches for dessert."

"Tempting, but I wouldn't want to intrude." She crouched down by Landon and straightened the seam on his footie pajamas. "So, I'll leave the books here, but tomorrow night, I'm thinking we'll start having story time before bed. Does that sound good?" When she smoothed his damp hair from his brow, he looked at her with those enormous blue eyes. Then he crawled closer and held his arms out for her to pick him up.

Definitely gonna break my heart, kid.

She planted a kiss on his sweet-smelling cheek before handing him to Brandt and going home.

Jessie was surprised to see Brandt's truck pull in the next day around noon. She hung the bucket on the fence and walked to his rig as he finished carting Landon's stuff into the house.

"What's going on?"

"My mom's cousin died yesterday. Of course, my dad has refused to take her to the funeral in Nebraska. And since she doesn't want to go by herself—"

"You volunteered."

He rubbed his gloved hand across his forehead, knocking his hat askew. "Yes. I'm sorry. I know I seem to be sayin' that to you a lot lately, but short of takin' Landon with me—"

"No. We're trying to set a routine for him, so it's best if he stays with me."

"You're sure?"

"Positive. Plus it's not like you have any other choices besides me."

He frowned.

"How long will you be gone?"

"The funeral is Tuesday afternoon. We'll leave right after and be home late Tuesday night, so Mom wants to go to the family memorial tonight. We're takin' off in about an hour."

How was it that after only spending a week together she already knew she was going to miss him? She reached up and fixed his hat, which pleased him, by the way his eyes softened.

"Jessie—"

"Brandt. It's okay." She skirted him and released Landon from his carseat, propping him on her hip. She forced a smile and said, "Drive safe."

Chapter Seven

Day two of Landon screaming was more than Jessie could take. She knew it wasn't Brandt's fault that he'd had to leave, but it was little comfort when she'd been up half the damn night with a cranky toddler. All Landon wanted was to be held. But not held while she was sitting down. No, she'd paced the floor with him in her arms because constant movement was the only thing that soothed him. She'd begun to suspect he was cutting molars, the way he constantly gnawed on his blanket.

She'd had no choice but to bring him to work with her. The other kids in the daycare didn't seem to mind that Landon clung to Jessie like a monkey and screeched like one if she set him down. Everyone would've been better off if she'd been able to stay home. But that wasn't an option. How did single mothers handle all this by themselves? Juggling work and a sick kid?

Around noon Skylar came in to have lunch with her girls and she kept stealing glances at Landon. What if Landon really was sick? And by bringing him here she'd somehow infected all the other kids? Flu and colds spread like wildfire in daycare. They took every precaution to prevent it, but kids' immune systems weren't fully developed. No matter how much bleach, hand sanitizer and Lysol they used, regardless of how many times hands were washed after runny noses were wiped, there was bound to be germs passed around.

So how was she supposed to know when it was something serious and not just the effects of teething or a cranky toddler?

She didn't. Despite the fact she spent her days taking care of kids, this child health stuff was a mystery. Parents told *her* when their kid was sick. She rarely had to make that determination on her own, which made her feel even more helpless when she looked at Landon and couldn't figure out what was wrong with the poor little boy.

After Skylar finished lunch, she took Jessie aside. "I thought we were through his adjustment phase."

"I'm sorry. He started getting fussy Sunday night and I thought maybe it was because Brandt wasn't around. But yesterday it got a little worse. He was fussier than normal. Last night after I took him home? He was awful. Upset. Crying all the time. I think he's teething. He hardly slept. I hardly slept."

"Brandt didn't get up and help you?"

"He wasn't there. He had to take his mom to a funeral in Nebraska. He got back at three in the morning and he's trying to play catch up at the ranch today. He'll be around to help me tonight. If I survive that long."

Skylar frowned and placed her hand on Landon's forehead. He didn't jerk away. "Have you taken his temp?"

"Not since this morning. It was around ninety-nine point four, which is not that far from normal."

"He feels hot to me. How long has he been tugging on his ear like that?"

Jessie glanced down. Sure enough, Landon had a chunk of the blanket jammed in his mouth, but he also had his finger hooked just inside his ear. "I don't know." She looked at Skylar with utter confusion. "Should I know?"

"Probably not. I doubt you could see it. I watched him from the lunch room and noticed it." Skylar smoothed her hand over Landon's hair. "It might be teething. It might be an ear infection. But I definitely think it's worth a trip to the doctor to find out."

Jessie must've appeared dazed because Skylar said, "Call Brandt. He's been in contact with Landon's mother, he'll have the information on what doctor to take him to."

Would they give him a shot? Take blood? How could she watch them poking him when he was already in so much misery?

"Out here in the wilds of Wyoming it'll probably take the rest of the day, once you actually get an appointment at the clinic."

"But I can't be gone from here—"

"Jess. Go. I'll handle the daycare."

She stared at Skylar, feeling mountains of regret as well as gratitude. "I'm sorry."

"Don't be. Kids get sick. You know that. And while I'm on the subject...if Landon does have an ear infection, it wouldn't be from something you've done or not done regarding his care. You know that, right?"

"I do now." She set her chin on top of Landon's head. The poor kid was burning up. "Thank you. Not only for being so understanding, but for the advice."

"None of this parenting stuff comes naturally, no matter what anyone tells you. It's live and learn. And usually, the first baby ends up being the guinea pig. Poor Eliza, huh?" She smiled. "Go call Brandt. Let me know what you find out from the doctor."

For some reason it made Jessie feel better that Brandt exhibited the same initial panicked reaction she had. He called Dr. Monroe and set up an appointment, then called Jessie back, promising he'd meet her at the doctor's office in Sundance after he cleaned up.

By the time she finished a couple things, got Landon loaded, and traveled the less than ideal road conditions, she figured Brandt would beat her to the doctor's office.

Sure enough, he jumped out of his truck the second he saw her. He didn't look in the rear cab, at Landon. He cupped his hand over Jessie's cheek. His eyes roamed her face. "Honey, no offense, but you look like hell."

Jessie gave him equal scrutiny. "You don't look one hundred percent rested yourself, Brandt."

"I'm not."

She sensed something else was bothering him. "What happened?"

"Funerals suck. I didn't know my mom's cousin, but she was really close to him at one time. It was weird, bein' around those people, who are just as much my relatives as the McKays, and I know nothin' about any of them."

"Did it make you sad?"

"No. It made me aware."

"Of?"

"What it might be like for Landon in the future with us."

Jessie bit back the next question—how far Brandt would go to ensure Landon wouldn't be a stranger in the McKay family.

Brandt's thumb arced over her cheekbone, beneath her eye, in such a loving move she had no idea how she resisted the temptation to lean into his gentle touch. It'd been so long since she'd been touched. So very long.

"Jess—"

Landon cried out and the moment ended.

The three of them trooped into the doctor's office. Which was completely full. Completely full of people she knew.

Great.

She held Landon on her lap while Brandt filled out the paperwork. Finally Brandt gave up on deciphering the Title IXX forms and agreed to pay cash for the visit, since Landon didn't have health insurance.

Brandt tried to take Landon from her, to give her arms a break from constantly holding him, but Landon shrieked and wouldn't let go of her.

This brought the attention of the whole room their way. Whatever buzz their appearance generated that'd kept people gossiping amongst themselves for twenty minutes ended.

A woman Jessie recognized as one of the local bar rats with half a dozen kids from half a dozen husbands sidled in front of them. Her gaze flicked from Landon to Brandt. She smiled. "Brandt McKay."

"Francie."

"I haven't seen you in Ziggy's for a while."

"Been busy. You know how that goes."

Her gaze zeroed in on Landon. "I guess you have been busy. I didn't know you had a kid."

The way she cooed it, as if she was considering him as father material for her kids, set Jessie's teeth on edge.

"I don't. This is my nephew. He's sick."

Most people would've gotten the hint and left. Not this woman. She switched her curiosity to Jessie. "I know you. You used to come in to Ziggy's once in a while with—"

"Keely McKay? We hung around for a while during dart league season last year."

When the woman's eyes took on a mean glint, Jessie realized this bar wench probably knew more about Luke's nocturnal activities than she did. "No. You used to come in with your husband. Luke, right? Although I'll admit he came in by himself frequently."

"Yeah, well, I doubt he's been in recently since he's dead."

Brandt stilled next to her, shocked by her smartass response.

Jessie was sick of feigning ignorance about Luke's blatant infidelity. Better to go on the offensive than to cower in the corner because she'd done that for years and she was finished with the timid routine.

But Francie kept digging for dirt. "So is this your son?" she asked sweetly.

"No. But he is Luke's son. My dead husband's secret love child, who I had no idea existed until recently. And yes, I am taking care of him while his mother cleans up her act in jail."

Francie was dumbfounded, not only by Jessie's tart response, but by the biting edge to her tone.

"Any more ridiculously invasive questions? No? Good. But you're more than welcome to fling this really juicy piece of gossip around the bar tonight to get your fair share of free drinks."

Dismissed, Francie stomped off.

A solid minute passed before Brandt drawled, "Have I mentioned how much I like your new 'screw you' attitude? I didn't think you had it in you, Jess."

His opinion meant more than she wanted to admit. "I didn't think I had it in me either. I wouldn't have done that a year ago. I wouldn't have wanted to draw attention to myself."

"You've definitely got my attention."

"Really?"

"But then again, you've always had it."

Jessie faced him. Her pulse spiked when she realized how close their heads were. She could make out every one of his absurdly long black eyelashes. She could see the imperceptible flecks of green in Brandt's deep blue eyes. She noticed the bump in his nose where it'd been broken in his younger years. She could feel his every quick exhale teasing her lips. She wanted so badly to drop her gaze and leisurely take in the full measure of his mouth, but she didn't dare. Because for some crazy, mixed-up reason, probably due to lack of sleep, she doubted she'd be satisfied with just a peek at his lips. She'd want a taste. A full taste.

"Jess?" he murmured.

"What's happening between us?"

"I don't know, but it's twisting me in knots."

"Me too."

"But unless you wanna add more fuel to Francie's fire, you'd better stop lookin' at me like that."

"Like what?"

"Like you want...well, mostly like you don't hate me."

"Brandt, I don't hate you. I've never hated you. It'd be easier if I could. But I can't. Not by a long shot."

Whispering to him while staring into his eyes created an odd sort of intimacy.

When he didn't say anything, just continued gazing at her with those compelling eyes, she felt that pull between them get stronger.

"Landon McKay?" the nurse said from the doorway.

Another untimely interruption, but Jessie didn't dwell on it, nor did she bother seeing where all the curious looks were coming from in the waiting room. She stood, wincing when she shifted Landon to her left side. She thought she'd built up a strong set muscles from working with horses and hauling hay bales, but holding a toddler for hours on end used a whole different muscle group.

Brandt noticed. "What's wrong?"

"I've been holding Landon nonstop since Sunday. My arms are sore. My back is sore."

"I'm sorry. I wish—"

"It couldn't be helped."

"Let me take him." Landon was so exhausted he went into Brandt's arms without fussing.

The wait for Doctor Monroe to appear was remarkably short. She bustled into the room. Frowned. "Has the nurse been in yet for a height and weight check?"

"No."

"Gotta do that first. Strip him down and Fiona will be right in." Then she left.

Landon hated getting naked. So by the time they'd undressed him down to his diaper, he was screaming mad. He wouldn't stand so the nurse could measure him. They ended up using the baby scale to weigh him. He was fighting Brandt at every turn, giving Jessie such pitiful eyes, that she had to look away.

Which made him madder yet.

Doctor Monroe bustled into the room. Brandt gave up and let Landon run to Jessie, screaming, "Mama, mama, mama," throwing himself at her.

Jessie froze. The tension in the room doubled. "That's the first time he's called me that."

"I'm surprised it hasn't happened before. To some extent, given the circumstances, the women in his life are interchangeable," Doctor Monroe said.

"Like father like son," slipped out before Jessie could stop it.

Doc Monroe ignored her, but she felt Brandt's probing gaze.

Once Landon was seated on Jessie's lap, he was fairly docile. He let the doctor poke and prod him, all the while she kept up a light chattering tone that soothed him. When the doc checked his ears, she sucked in a sharp breath. "Kid's got an ear infection all right. Poor thing." She rubbed his bare back before she rolled away to jot down notes. She addressed Brandt. "Did Landon's mother tell you if he's allergic to penicillin?"

"No clue."

Doc Monroe looked at Jessie. "Was Luke allergic to penicillin? The allergy tends to have genetic properties."

"No, far as I know Luke wasn't allergic."

"In that case, I suggest a shot of penicillin. Sometimes I treat this type of infection with amoxycillin but the shot works faster. Plus, you won't have to mess with trying to get him to take his medicine, since he seems a little strong willed."

"No surprise—he is a McKay," Jessie muttered.

Doctor Monroe shut the file folder. She smiled at both of them, but it was strained. "Kids heal quickly. He'll have to stick around for twenty minutes or so after the shot to see if he has an allergic reaction. If he's not better after forty-eight hours, bring him in right away."

"Will do."

Jessie got the feeling that Doctor Monroe disapproved of this situation with Landon and she gave them both an odd look before she left the room.

"I see what you're thinkin'," Brandt said. "And yes, she argued with me about askin' for your help with Landon."

She frowned at him. "How did she know you intended to ask me?"

"I told her. I brought Landon in for a checkup after hours the week Samantha went to jail. She grilled me on how I planned to take care of him so I asked her opinion. She said I was self-serving and stormed out of the room after she signed off on the physical documentation for temporary guardianship."

Doctor Monroe had performed the D&C after Jessie's miscarriage. She'd recommended the yearlong wait before they attempted another pregnancy, and by that time, she and Luke were having problems, so she'd stayed on the pill. But the doc knew how devastated Jessie had been about losing that baby. It gave her a rush of gratitude that the doctor knew losing another child, albeit not one from her womb, might cause her sorrow.

Would it? Or will you be glad to hand this boy back to his mother?

The nurse came in. "He gets this one in the butt, so you'll need to take his diaper off."

Brandt plucked Landon from Jessie's lap, turned the kid over his knee as he pulled back the diaper tape, exposing Landon's left buttock. He held the squirming boy firmly as the nurse swooped in with—holy crap—a really big needle and jabbed Landon's tiny butt cheek.

Landon screamed bloody murder.

The nurse was fast. She pressed on a Spider-Man bandage on the spot and Brandt had the diaper refastened in a hurry.

Landon practically jumped into Jessie's arms. Her stomach clenched, seeing him so scared. She slipped his clothes on, trying to calm him. When she looked up, Brandt had the oddest expression. "What?"

"Don't get mad, okay? But you're good with him. Better than I thought you'd be."

Jessie didn't snap off a smart comment, it'd serve no purpose. She hefted him up onto her hip. She winced.

"I'll get him, Jessie."

"I'm fine. I'll wait here with him. Just pay the bill and I'll meet you back at my house."

Chapter Eight

"No, Mom. I understand you wanna see him, but he won't be much fun with an ear infection. Okay. I'll ask her. Yes, I promise. Bye."

Brandt tossed his cell on the seat and rubbed his eyes. Jesus, he was tired. It'd been a long couple of days. Traveling, a funeral, the guilt of leaving Jessie alone with Landon. He wanted to drink a couple of beers, watch TV and crash. But that probably wasn't in the cards tonight.

Plus, he had a surprise for Jessie. Things had been going great between them today, up until the point she pushed him out of the doctor's office. Her text requesting items they needed from the store had been curt, but texts often were, so he wondered what kind of mood she'd be in. He grabbed the grocery bags and headed inside her trailer to find out.

First thing he noticed was the quiet. And the heavenly smell.

Jessie tossed a quick glance over her shoulder. "How were the roads?"

"Shitty."

"Need a beer?"

"Like you wouldn't believe." He set the bags on the kitchen table. "Landon sleeping?"

"Finally."

Brandt moved in behind her and placed his hands on her shoulders, which were hunched up by her ears. She immediately relaxed a little. "I'm sorry I wasn't here the last couple days. Especially since Landon has been sick." She hadn't shrugged him off, so he kept his hands right where they were. "Tell me something, Jess. Have you thought about backing out of this deal?"

"Maybe last night when I was up walking the floor with him at four a.m. I considered loading Landon up and driving to your house."

"I can imagine."

While she struggled—Brandt sensed she wanted to say something—just for a second, he closed his eyes and pretended this was a normal night in his life. A sweet, sexy wife to come home to. Supper on the stove. A cold beer nearby. As the phantom life teased him, he inhaled slowly. The scent of her shampoo drifted into his nose, filled his lungs. The scent was hard to place—a mix of fruit and honey. But beneath that aroma was the undeniable heady scent of Jessie. Which was better than any perfume in the world.

"Brandt."

"Mmm?" He let his thumbs sweep across the muscles between her shoulder blades.

"You said 'backing out of this deal'."

"And?"

"And what am I getting out of this deal?"

That snapped him out of his fantasy lickety-split. "What do you want?"

"I don't know yet. But I'm thinking about...some things."

Brandt angled just a little closer. "Anything you want, Jessie, all you have to do is name it and it's yours. Anything." Before Brandt felt cocky or relieved, or hell, even hopeful she'd wrap herself around him and kiss him, she bolted.

"I'd better get these groceries put away, huh?"

He'd didn't push it, not now anyway.

Landon woke up about halfway through Brandt's first beer. The kid started out cranky, but that morphed into sweetness after Brandt dosed him with grape-flavored Tylenol. Landon dragged his blanket with him and curled into Brandt as he sat on the couch, watching the news.

Even Lexie sensed something was wrong with her tormentor. She sniffed his feet and put her head on Brandt's lap so she could lick Landon's hand.

Landon wasn't interested in eating Jessie's beef and noodle casserole. He didn't suck down his bottle like a junkie, either. Brandt hated to watch Jessie eating alone, but he couldn't move now that Landon had finally settled down.

After about an hour, Jessie said, "Why don't you tuck him in bed? I don't think he'll wake up. He's had a rough couple of days."

"So have you." Brandt grinned at her. "Want me to tuck you in bed too?"

Jessie blinked. Blushed. Then a sneaky smile stole across her face. "We'll see."

When Brandt returned from putting Landon down, Jessie was washing dishes. He rolled up his sleeves, snagged an embroidered dishtowel and stood beside her. Right beside her.

She gave him a strange look. "What are you doing?"

"Helpin'. Doesn't seem fair that you cooked supper and have to wash the dirty dishes too." He rinsed a plate and began to dry it, still feeling her eyes on him. "What?"

She smiled. "Thank you."

"At your service."

They chatted easily, although Brandt was surprised by how long it took to wash dishes with two people...until he realized, Jessie was dragging out their time together as much as he was.

Don't hope, man. You've done this before and it nearly destroyed you.

When she began to rub the back of her arm, Brandt took a chance. "Want me to do that?"

"Nah. It'll probably be fine by tomorrow."

"You sure? Because after I left the doctor's office today I stopped by Healing Touch Massage and talked to AJ. I told her you'd been carting Landon around nonstop for three days, and she gave me some specific pointers on how to loosen up those muscles."

Jessie's eyes went wide. "Seriously? You did that? For me?"

"Yeah. I don't think you understand how bad I felt leavin' you here with him, when I promised that wouldn't happen. So I'd like to make it up to you."

"By giving me a massage?"

Brandt held up his hands in the face of her obvious skepticism. "No biggie if you don't want it."

"Would my clothes be on? Or off?"

Think with your head, not your dick. Do not blow this. "I believe AJ said the part of your body bein' massaged needed to be uncovered. So since it'd be an arm and back massage, probably I could work around a...short-sleeved T-shirt or something."

A thoughtful look crossed her face. "How about if I wore a sports bra?"

Hell yes. And maybe some of those ass-hugging boy shorts. "Ah sure. I suppose that'd be okay."

"Where we doing this?"

"In your bedroom," slipped out right away. Dammit.

"Okay. Give me about five minutes?"

"Sure." That'd allow him time to brush his teeth, shave, see if he'd brought four or five condoms... No. He had to be a perfect gentleman. Just a massage. Nothing else.

That sucked.

He drank the rest of his beer in the kitchen. At the five minute and thirteen second mark, he knocked on her bedroom door. "Jess? You ready?"

"Uh-huh."

Brandt stepped over the threshold and the first thing he noticed was her butt. She hadn't worn sweats, but ass-hugging workout shorts.

Do not do a celebratory fist pump, man. Act casual.

His gaze leisurely followed the curve of her back, the very sexy, very feminine curve of her back, stopping when his eyes reached the wide band of her black sports bra. It criss-crossed between her shoulder blades and the straps separated and disappeared down her front.

He'd forgotten what all that creamy, mouthwatering flesh looked like in the flesh.

Jessie looked at him strangely. "What's wrong?"

"I just realized I forgot to ask AJ one thing. Where am I supposed to sit when I'm givin' you a massage?"

"Good point. How about if we both sit on the bed. You can sit behind me."

"I guess that'll work."

She sat in the middle and crossed her legs.

Okay. Brandt had to keep his groin from touching her backside because then she'd know he had a hard-on, which had popped up the instant it'd gotten wind he'd be putting his hands all over her.

"Brandt?"

"Hang on." He scooted behind her, trying to spread his legs out, but damn, he wasn't very flexible. Maybe he could reach her from here. When he brushed his fingers across the slope of her shoulder, she jumped.

"You sure you wanna do this?" Killed him to say it, but he did anyway.

"Yes. It's just...I've never had a massage before and it's awkward to sit like this when I can't see you. It just startled me." She stopped babbling and sighed. "The truth is, no man's hands have touched me in a really long time, and I think I forgot how to act when it's anyone's hands but my own on my body."

"This is supposed to be relaxing you, not makin' you nervous."

"I know. Let's try again."

Thank God. "Close your eyes." This time when Brandt put his hands on her, she didn't flinch. Her skin was so warm. So soft. So pale, compared to his rough knuckles and sun-soaked flesh. When he dug his thumb into the base of her neck, she moaned.

"Did that hurt?"

"No. It feels good. Really good. Keep going."

He thoroughly massaged up and down both sides of her neck. Then he moved to arc of her shoulders, concentrating on the section between her shoulder blades. After that he branched out to her arms, earning another series of soft grunts and groans.

No matter how hard he tried, Brandt couldn't help but wonder if Jessie would make the same throaty sounds if he used his thumb on the sweet spot between her thighs.

"God, Brandt. If this whole ranching gig doesn't work out for you, I'm thinking you could give massages for a living."

"I'll take that as a compliment, although I wouldn't enjoy givin' someone like Bart Clarkson a rubdown." Brandt shivered, imagining the crotchety old timer's wrinkled skin and flabby ass. "And I'd hate to be accused of bein' sexist, because I'd only wanna put my hands on ladies. Young ladies. Definitely would scar me for life to see some of the senior citizen set spread out on a massage table."

"But having a hot, young, studly cowboy rubbing them

down?"

Jessie had just called him hot and studly.

"You'd make a ton of money, and I bet your tips would be outta this world."

"Now you've gone too far." Brandt smoothed his hands down her sides, somehow just knowing how ticklish she was.

She screamed, "Brandt!" and tried to squirm away from him.

He held fast, keeping hold of her ribs as she rolled, taking him with her. She wiggled to the other side of the bed, and Brandt released her, letting her think she'd won.

Wrong.

Once she let down her guard, he pounced, she shrieked again, and he pressed her back into the mattress, squeezing her thighs together with his knees as he pinned her arms over her head. He leaned forward. "I oughta tickle you until you cry for mercy for puttin' thoughts of nekkid octogenarians in my head right before I go to bed."

"Hey, some octogenarians are sexy."

"Name one."

"Raquel Welch?"

"She ain't eighty. Besides, even if she is, she's the exception, not the rule."

Simultaneously they realized the intimacy of their position. Brandt stretched out over her, holding her down...and why wasn't Jessie trying to get away?

They stared at each other, but neither made a move to get closer or to break apart.

Brandt let go of her arms. "I suppose any relaxation you had is gone."

"My muscles are still singing your praises. Thank you. It was an awesome massage."

He thought she'd leap up and throw him out of her room, but Jessie studied him. "What?"

"I suppose you'd like me to return the favor?"

He couldn't stop himself from sweeping her hair from her face, then gently running the back of his knuckles from her temple to her chin. This woman who'd given so much, wanted to give more. "No. This was for you. I did it because I wanted to, Jessie. I enjoyed it, but I don't expect anything in return."

Her eyes softened. So did her body.

As much as he wanted to stay...That was his cue to leave.

Brandt scooted backward on his hands and his knees until he was off the bed and his feet touched the floor. "I'll get up with Landon tonight if need be."

"Thank you."

"Get some sleep. See you in the morning."

He made it to the door before she said anything.

"Brandt?"

"Mmm?"

"How did you know my ticklish spots?"

"I didn't. But I sure do know them all now."

She laughed, a little huskily, and said, "Oh, you don't know all of them."

Damn. Was that...suggestive?

"Goodnight."

As Brandt tossed and turned on the couch, he replayed every second of their interaction. Twice. At the end of the third dissection, he'd determined Jessie probably wouldn't rebuff his sexual advances this time.

While that possibility caused a gnawing feeling of anticipation in his gut and made his dick stir with interest, it also served as a warning. He'd have to wait for Jessie to approach *him* about making a change in their relationship. Not because he intended to punish her for turning him down previously, nor did he want her to beg, but he had to be one hundred percent certain it was a change *she* initiated—not a change she was reacting to if he suggested they become lovers.

It'd be hard as hell to wait. But he would, because he knew taking that next step, a permanent one in his mind, would definitely be worth the wait.

"I think your best option is just to walk up to him, stark naked and say, *Ride me, cowboy hottie.*"

Jessie glanced up from tying a bag of garbage. "You cannot be serious, Simone."

"What's the problem? It's direct."

"A little too direct."

"Girlfriend, ain't no man gonna turn and run when faced

with a sexy, naked, willing woman such as yourself. Trust me on this."

Problem was, Jessie *had* seen a man turn and run when faced with her naked, willing self. Well, in Mike's case it was more like he fell down and passed out, but still, it'd happened.

"Trust Simone on what, Jessie?" Skylar asked.

Crap. She blushed. "Oh, nothing."

Simone harrumphed and said, "Later," leaving her alone with Skylar.

Thanks, Simone.

Jessie spent an extra long time securing a knot in the plastic garbage bag, hoping Skylar would leave.

"I have a confession to make," Skylar said, moving in closer.

"What's that?"

"I overheard your conversation with Simone."

Jessie looked at her boss. "Which part?"

"The *ride me, cowboy hottie* part. I'm assuming she meant Brandt."

"Yes, but it's not what you think." *Liar.*

"So you're not planning on riding him into your bed?"

Don't blush. "I am. It's just..." *A whole new possibility to me and I'm flustered with you grilling me about my plans.* "I imagine you want to talk me out of it."

Skylar shook her head. "Exactly the opposite."

Jessie wasn't expecting that.

"Look, although our situations aren't similar, in some ways they are. I sprang a surprise baby on Kade. He moved in to help me take care of her. I insisted we just be friends and parenting partners, nothing else, meaning absolutely no way, no how, was I having sex with him."

"How long did that last?"

Skylar smirked. "You've seen my husband. So, oh, about two weeks before we were getting naked together at every opportunity. I hope this isn't too much information, but I wanted to let you know, I've been exactly where you are. And I almost let the best thing that ever happened to me get away because I was afraid to take a chance."

Kade and Skylar had a nauseatingly perfect marriage, so Jessie doubted the truth to that statement.

"Like you, I had past relationship issues to work through. Like Brandt, Kade had family issues to work through. I wasn't sure if Kade wanted me, or if he only cared about me because of Eliza."

Okay. So that did sound a little familiar.

"The point I'm trying to make? Brandt is a great guy. He's crazy about you. I know you're crazy about him, too, and well, it wouldn't be the worst thing in the world if you two got to know each other on a whole new level, would it?"

"No. But this...situation with Landon isn't permanent. I don't want it to be permanent. But Brandt wouldn't mind if it was. So can I start something with him knowing I'll have to walk away?"

"The better question is: how can you be willing to walk away from him now and not be willing to take a chance that you might never have to walk away from him?"

For the psychoanalytical slant she used to make her statement, Skylar could've just said, *you'll never know unless you try.* Jessie smiled. "Thanks, Skylar. I appreciate your candor."

"Good." At the door, she turned. "For what it's worth? Simone was dead on. Getting naked always works."

Chapter Nine

"Landon is down for the count."

"Thank God," Brandt muttered. "You have the magic touch. I swear the kid looked like he'd punch me in the face if I so much as touched him."

She rolled her eyes. "He's a little young to start brawling. But he is a McKay, so I wouldn't be surprised."

Brandt took another pull off his beer and gestured to the couch. "Sit down and take a load off."

Jessie paced to the door, peering out the window, cursing her nervous energy. Hah. Who was she trying to kid? She was just plain nervous. This seemed like such an easy idea in the truck on the way home from work. Get naked. But it was two hours later and she still had her clothes on.

"Something on your mind?"

She couldn't un-stick her tongue from the roof of her mouth.

"Jess? You know you can tell me anything," Brandt said.

Yeah, just spit it out. You turned him down once. What's to say he won't do the same to you...just to even the score?

She closed her eyes, trying to slam the door on the self-sabotaging portion of her brain. "This...the way we've got this set up isn't working for me any longer."

He exhaled a frustrated burst of air. "Okay. What's the problem?"

"I'm tired—"

"We both are. That said, I can probably pick Landon up earlier and take him back here until after you get off work so it's not—"

"This isn't about Landon. It's about...us."

"Us?" he repeated.

"Yes, us. Living in the same space. Sharing everything."

Another one of his thoughtful pauses. "I've tried to keep to myself and not cause you extra stress."

Jessie whirled to face him. "That's what's not working, Brandt. I am stressed and it's because you're everywhere. In every part of my life. In every part of my house. We eat together. We do chores together. We take care of Landon together. We watch TV together. You're the first person I see when I get up in the morning and you're the last person I see before I go to bed at night. We're acting like a married couple."

The muscles in his jaw rippled and he gritted out, "And that bothers you?"

"Yes, dammit, because we're doing all the hard day-to-day couple stuff without the benefit of the good couple stuff."

"Such as?"

"We're not sleeping together. And if we're gonna act like a married couple then I want you naked in my bed every night."

Brandt's mouth dropped open so fast Jessie swore she heard his jawbone crack. Then his eyes tapered to fine points and his entire posture changed. "Since when?"

"You want an exact moment? How about last night when you gave me a backrub? I wanted you to stay with me all night and rub more than just my back. I know you're probably thinking I'm crazy since I freaked out last year when you told me you wanted more than friendship."

"What's changed?"

"Honestly? Me." Jessie briefly closed her eyes. "I'm not as emotionally raw as I was even four months ago. I've also realized I don't want to spend my life unwilling to take a chance because I'm scared."

"I scare you?"

"Yes."

Embarrassment flickered on his face.

"You don't scare me physically. There's an intensity to you that is intimidating as hell. There are no half measures in your world, Brandt. It's all or nothing. Being with a man like you would be unlike anything I've ever experienced."

That muscle in his jaw continued to jump in an agitated

manner. "How do you know that?"

Now that she was floundering, she realized getting naked in body was a helluva lot easier than stripping herself emotionally bare in front of him.

"Jessie. Answer me."

"I figured it out last summer when you warned me about Mike, but you didn't pull that highhanded McKay attitude and drag me out of there. Even though that situation ended in my humiliation, the way you forced me to accept the consequences of my rash decision proved you weren't the gentleman I thought you were. But you didn't leave. I know you wanted to finish what Mike couldn't. But I was too—"

"Shitfaced?" he supplied with a soft snarl.

"No, I was too mortified you'd witnessed yet another man who found me as sexually lacking as my husband had," she said without flinching.

But Brandt flinched. "Jessie that's not—"

"True? Yes, it is. Yet, I know you would've tossed me a pity fuck if I'd asked."

That shocked him. But he recovered quickly. "You sure?"

"No. I'm not sure of anything. Except I can't get you out of my head since you've moved in. All that mundane household shit that oughta be boring and I hated doing by myself? I look forward to doing it with you. Even when you're driving me crazy with lust."

"Crazy with lust?" His dark eyebrows winged up. "That's a stretch, ain't it?"

His skepticism might've sent old Jessie scurrying to her room to hide. But new Jessie soldiered on. "Every night after you get out of the shower and the scent of your shaving cream drifts out of the bathroom I fantasize about you rubbing your face and that scent over every inch of my skin."

Surprise and something else like...desire flashed in his eyes, which spurred her to keep going.

"Sometimes when you're talking to me? I'm so busy staring at your mouth, imagining your kiss that I don't hear a single word you say."

With that, his surprise changed to recognition. So Brandt had noticed her attention to his lips whenever they were within kissing distance.

"But know what really twists me into knots? Seeing the way you look at me now."

"And how's that?"

"Like you no longer see me as sweet, innocent Jessie. That if you ever got those big hands of yours on me, the last thing you'd be with me...is sweet. You'd get a thrill pushing past my boundaries, the ones I had before Luke and the ones I've erected since Luke. You'd derive great pleasure in showing me facets of sexual intimacy that I've been denied—or denied myself."

"Fancy talk." Brandt cocked his head, as if he was trying to study her from a new angle. "I'll admit, you've got me pegged better than I ever thought you would. With one exception."

"Which is?"

"If we set this in motion, I'll demand more than just physical intimacy from you. It ain't only gonna be about scratching an itch, Jess, because I can get that any time I want."

How had Brandt picked up on her plan to prove to herself that she could experience sex without the pesky emotional ties?

Because he knows you better than you've ever given him credit for.

"I'll expect a different kind of intimacy than what we've had in the past. A connection between us that has nothin' to do with Luke."

She looked away.

"What?"

"It's a nice thought, but this connection has everything to do with Luke and there's no way we can ever get around that. Besides, you brought Landon into my life, Brandt, and he's connected to Luke. We wouldn't be in this situation if not for him. And maybe Landon's presence has forced us to deal with this—" she gestured to the space between them, "—so I'm done denying the pull is there."

"Is this 'pull' something you recently realized? A proximity thing? I'm a man, I'm here, I'm good enough to fuck for a few months?"

Jessie twisted her fingers together. "It's more than that and you know it. After you made that pass at me, I convinced myself you were exactly like Luke—biding your time until your charm earned an invitation into my bed. You'd get your fill of me, work me out of your system and move on. And no, you can't fault me for that mindset, because of my limited experience with men, and my experience with Luke in particular. Plus, I wasn't so sure you wouldn't be using me to settle a score with Luke."

"You really think that lowly of me?" he bit off.

"You really think I'm a clichéd horny widow desperate to screw the first man who smiles at me?" She didn't bother to bank the anger in her eyes when she met his glare head on. "If that was true, I wouldn't have waited two goddamn years, would I? I wouldn't be asking you to touch me, would I? I could've found another man to scratch that itch in the four months since we last saw each other. But I didn't. Something held me back."

"Again, nice sentiment, but spell it out for me."

"I want no-strings sex for these four months we're together. At the end of those four months, we'll walk away."

"Just like that?"

Be strong, be confident. "Can't we try it and see?"

"What do we tell people? Because you know my family, they're gonna ask."

"We are living together, even if it's temporarily. People are already gonna assume we're sleeping together, especially in the gossipy McKay family."

"So if Skylar comes right out and asks you if you're with me? Will you tell her that we're just fuck buddies?"

She couldn't confess that Skylar encouraged her to get naked with him. "What would you rather I told her? That we're attracted to each other, but we're keeping our hands off each other because it'd be like Luke was in bed with us?"

She'd struck a nerve with that. She hadn't meant to but there was no sense in apologizing now.

"I'm not Luke."

"Then stop acting like him," she snapped. "Quit trying to tell *me* what I'm feeling is wrong. I'm being completely honest with you. I'm telling you this because I realized if we start this, I'd own my sexuality for the first time in my life. I want that. With you. Starting tonight." Jessie took a breath, figuring she'd said enough. Too much probably.

He studied her more intently than she was used to. With an edgy stillness that seemed totally foreign to him.

The longer she stood before him, the more her paranoia built.

Finally, Brandt pushed to his feet. His dark eyes remained on hers as he deftly skirted the coffee table and the pile of Landon's toys. He stopped in front of her, his big hands clenched at his sides. "Starting tonight, but especially this first time, I call the shots. All of them. *I* own your sexuality. We clear?"

Talk about being the big, bad wolf. Jessie nodded.

"Say the word so there's no misunderstanding between us."

She swallowed and said, "Yes."

Brandt slanted his mouth over hers. But he didn't kiss her with lust-fueled passion. He drank her in—with his eyes, with the short, choppy breaths he pulled into his lungs.

Although Jessie was pretty sure he wanted to take a possessive kiss, he didn't, which indicated his monumental control.

His tongue darted out and slid along the plump inside curve of her bottom lip. A leisurely, sensuous glide across the sensitive flesh that caused her mouth to tremble even as her lips parted in invitation. But he didn't dive in for a greedy, openmouthed kiss. He lightly swept his damp lips over hers. Repeatedly. Male hunger and hot breath, tempered with softness that was unlike anything she'd ever experienced.

He gauged her responses and inched closer, but didn't allow their bodies to touch. Heat shimmered between them.

Jessie actually felt dizzy from want. What would he do if she fisted her hands in his T-shirt and just took the kiss she craved? His warning, *This first time, I call the shots,* forced her to truly surrender to him.

And that's when Brandt kissed her.

Holy mother of God did the man lay a kiss on her. His hands framed her face with utmost gentleness as his mouth conquered hers. Dominated. Destroyed. Ignited.

After several minutes of proving his mastery, Brandt changed the angle of his head, taking the kiss from fiery to flirty. Sucking on her tongue. Nibbling on the very edges of her lips. Kissing the corners of her smile.

"Jessie?" he murmured between kisses. "Can you do something for me?"

Her head buzzed. She had no idea how her body remained upright when he'd turned her inside out.

"Jess? Darlin'? Are you listening?"

"Umm. What?"

"Hang on." His hands dropped from her face and he took her arm.

She thought he was taking her to bed, but he detoured to the couch. She blinked at him. "What are we—"

"I'm getting to it." Brandt curled his hand around her jaw, feathering his thumb across her kiss swollen lower lip. "Take your clothes off." Her eyes must've given away her confusion because he clarified, "I don't need a striptease. I need you nekkid."

With shaking fingers, Jessie gripped the edges of her mock turtleneck and tugged it over her head. He'd seen her naked before, but her whole body flushed with color anyway.

Brandt didn't help with her clothing removal, besides the heat in his eyes urging her to hurry.

Next she unhooked her bra, tossing it on the floor. She yanked to release the button on her jeans. Brandt's hand shot out and held her shoulder as she shimmied the denim down her legs. She'd hooked a finger in each side of her black lace panties, when Brandt's rough hand covered hers, forcing her to look at him.

"Those are mine." He gently pushed her onto the couch.

The tweed fabric scratched her skin. Weird to think she'd never sat naked on this couch before now. Leather probably would've been a better furniture choice.

This is not the time to contemplate home furnishing mistakes. Look at Brandt, dummy, not the weaving pattern in the fabric.

"What are you thinkin' about so hard?"

"Not thinking about anything but you, Brandt."

"Such pretty words from such a pretty mouth." He used the tip of his finger to trace the contours of her lips. "Do you have any idea how jealous I was that night at the lake? Seein' you on your knees in front of that little fucking prick, Mike?"

"I don't remember much from that part of the night."

"I do, and I wanna erase that mental image of you with another man's cock in your throat. All I want to remember is the image of *my* cock in your throat. Your mouth on *my* dick." Brandt unbuckled his belt and unzipped his jeans. Eased both to the floor without losing eye contact with her.

What a rush, seeing Brandt's take-charge side. In the last week she'd been thinking a lot about the kind of lover he'd be. And thank God sugarcoating his demands wasn't his style.

She barely got a peek at his cock before he commanded, "Hands on my thighs." He grasped the base of his dick in his right hand and rubbed his cockhead across her lips. "Open."

Jessie let her eyes drift shut in anticipation of tasting him, of pleasing him, of pleasing herself by admitting how much she wanted this, wanted him.

His gentleness during the slow glide across her lips, over her teeth and across her tongue, surprised her. As did the loving way he framed her face in his hands, sweeping his thumbs over her hollowed cheeks up to her temple. "Beautiful."

The musky, salty, utterly masculine flavor filled her mouth and zoomed straight to her core.

His gentleness vanished without warning. He held her head tightly, angled her neck and rammed in fully so the base of his cock rested on her bottom teeth.

She opened her throat against her immediate reaction to gag. She relaxed her jaw and sucked air in through her nose. The circumference of his dick was thick enough that her lips were stretched to the limit. But man, she loved this. Giving in to him. Giving it all to him.

"Look at me."

The only things she could move were her eyes. The satisfaction in Brandt's caused her heart to jackhammer. Caused her pulse to pound between her thighs. In that moment, she knew there was no going back. Anything that happened between them would be so much more than sex.

"I'm gonna want you usin' that mouth more. Swallow."

She did, but it wasn't easy.

"That's it." He withdrew, leaving just the head balanced on the edge of her teeth. "Use your tongue. Good. Oh, yeah, I like that." Then he flexed his hips and buried his length into her throat again, starting the rapid in and out thrusting that told her he was already close to the edge.

Mired in a sexual haze, Jessie listened to his play by play of what he wanted. Of how hot she looked. How sexy she was.

How much he'd wanted her. She lost herself in the deep cadence of his voice. In the heat of his cock driving into the wetness of her mouth. In the feeling of connectedness to him. In his tenacity.

He swore and stopped halfway in her mouth, until the tip rested on the back of her tongue. He said, "Suck. Jesus. Suck hard. Fuck." He grunted and hot semen burst against her soft palate.

She sucked and swallowed, tightening the seal on his spasming cock. Wanting to blow his mind. Wanting to keep this bond as long as he allowed. Those big, wonderful hands went from gripping her head to tenderly caressing her hair to tapping her jaw so he could slide his spent cock free from her mouth.

Before he could get too far away or say anything, Jessie grabbed his butt. She pressed kisses to his left thigh, moving up to kiss his hipbone and over to rub her mouth across the trail of dark hair that started between his pectorals and ended right there. He twisted her hair between his fingers as she nuzzled this sexy part of him.

"Jess."

"Hmm?" He smelled so good in this spot. She nuzzled again.

"Enough. Baby. You're killin' me."

She froze mid-kiss, not daring to look at him. "You don't like it?"

"I love it. But it's my turn now." He stepped back.

Jessie glanced up just as Brandt dropped to his knees. Oh man. He wasn't looking at her face. At all. A delicious curl of heat ebbed through her.

His hands circled her hips. He slid the lower half of her body off the couch cushion, practically ripping off her panties, uttering a terse, "Brace yourself."

She scrambled to lock her arms when Brandt's rough-tipped fingers scraped the top of her thighs as he spread her knees apart.

A half snarl left his throat. He snagged an extra pillow and tapped her butt in a signal for her to raise her hips. The soft velvety fabric brushed her bare ass. Ooh. That felt nice.

But not as nice as Brandt's soft, velvety tongue brushing her sex from bottom to top.

She gasped when he did it again. And again. And again.

His fingers opened her pussy completely, baring every wet inch, allowing Brandt to taste every wet inch. Thoroughly. Burrowing his tongue into her channel, retreating to delicately lick her folds. Using his mouth in ways that caused her body to twitch and tingle. In ways that had her making noises she'd never heard before.

No play by play this time. Brandt's mouth was too busy driving her higher and higher until she feared she'd combust.

Almost embarrassing how short her fuse was. The zip down her spine of impending pleasure was a brief warning—a microsecond later, she exploded. Imploded. Went sailing headlong into bliss. She arched back and gasped. Her legs shook. Her arms shook. Her internal organs shook.

This man had the power to shake her to her very core.

After the trembling stopped, she peered down at him, expecting he'd be gazing at her with a cocky grin, because oh, yeah, he'd rocked her world. But Brandt's dark head was pressed into her lower belly as he fought to level his breathing.

She smoothed her hands over the short hair on his scalp. The stubble on his head felt as funky and cool beneath her palms as it did between her thighs. Just touching him reinforced her feeling of rightness. Of the sense of security and trust he gave her. Yet, he made her feel like a hot-bodied porn star. "You okay?"

"I should be askin' you that," he muttered against her skin.

"I'm excellent. That was—"

Suddenly, he pushed away from her and rolled to his feet. "Ah. I need to get something." He yanked his duster on over his naked body, shoved his feet into his over boots and booked it out the door.

What the hell?

Panic seized her. Had she done something wrong? Why had he just up and left?

They always leave you. Haven't you learned that by now?

This couldn't be happening. Jessie was trying to process Brandt's retreat when the door slammed. A muffled thump echoed to her as boots hit the carpet.

Then he stood in front of her. "Jess? What's wrong?"

Startled, she tore her gaze from her feet. "I thought you

left."

"What? No! No way. I said I'd be right back, didn't I?"

"No, you didn't."

He crouched down and tilted her chin up. "I'd never do that to you. Never up and leave you. And it has nothin' to do with you sitting here nekkid."

He brought her mouth to his for a prolonged kiss that soothed as well as aroused. If he could read her so perfectly now, what would it be like after they really got to know each other intimately?

Paradise.

"So you tired?" he asked in a husky tone that dripped with bedroom prowess.

"Not at all."

"Good." He tugged her to her feet, stalking her with another show of masculine grace, backing her down the hallway with such raw possession she could scarcely breathe. No man had ever looked at her like that.

After he shut the bedroom door, she said, "Where'd you go?"

Brandt shucked off his coat. He tossed a box of condoms and an unopened tube of lube on the bed. "Kept them in my truck. Just in case." He offered her a shy smile. "I never assumed anything, just wanted you to know that."

No, like a true gentleman he wouldn't assume, but like a true boy scout he was prepared. Another little shiver of desire rippled through her. "Oh. Well, we don't have to use the condoms, if you'd rather skip it. I'm on the pill."

"Why? When you haven't…"

"Keeps my cycle regular. But if you're used to using them, then that's okay with me."

"No condoms." He slowly dragged his hungry gaze over her body with a terse, "On the bed on your hands and knees."

When Jessie hesitated, Brandt made the warning growl that meant there was no room for argument.

Okay, the big, bad wolf was back. She faced the headboard. The mattress dipped as Brandt joined her. She flinched when his big hands circled her ankles and widened her stance.

Brandt stilled behind her. "Jess? Am I scaring you?"

"No."

"Why'd you flinch when I touched you?"

"You surprised me."

He draped his body over hers—his chest to her back.

"You're cold."

"It is November and I was just running outside nekkid." He brushed aside her hair and kissed the back of her neck.

She shivered.

"Now that's the kind of shiver I like," he murmured. "I want you. You ready or do I need lube?"

"I'm ready. Are you ready?"

Brandt answered by sliding into her slowly to the hilt. He continued to pepper warm, soft kisses across the slope of her shoulder.

She savored the sensation. Nothing in the world compared to this heat and fullness and connection.

"I love it when you kiss me like that."

"I could spend hours kissing every inch of your skin. Next time, I will."

She turned her head and looked at him when she noticed his body vibrated. "Are you still cold?"

"No."

"Then why are you shaking?"

"Because I'm tryin' not to rut on you. I'm not feelin' real...gentlemanly, if you wanna know the truth." His lips tickled her ear. "I know this is our first time but it doesn't change my body wantin' to fuck you hard."

That admission caused a gush of moisture to flood her sex. She moaned.

He sucked in a swift breath. "The thought of me fucking you hard makes you wet?"

"Everything you've done to me so far makes me wet."

"Reach your arms above your head."

Jessie pressed the side of her face into the mattress as she gripped the rungs on the headboard.

"Look at you, so goddamn sexy stretched out like that." His calluses scraped her skin as he swept his hands down the length of her back to circle her hips. He pulled out and slammed back in quickly.

She hissed, "Yes."

In this position, every time he thrust, the flannel sheet

abraded her nipples. The simple eroticism of Brandt's sure and steady movements as his cock tunneled in and out of her pussy forced a whimpering sigh from her lungs.

"So tight. God that's good. Not gonna last."

She closed her eyes, allowing the sensations to wash over her, sensations exclusive to sex; the rhythmic squeak of the bed, harsh male breathing on her back, rough-skinned hands gripping her hips, the heat, wetness, the sounds of their body parts meeting, the friction of the sheets on her knees, elbows and nipples.

But it was more than that. And she couldn't find the right words to explain it because the push and pull lulled her to a floaty plane where need and satisfaction were in perfect balance.

He plunged faster, muttering, jarring Jessie from her fog of pleasure. As soon as she felt his cock jerking against her inner walls, she bore down on his shaft, earning a *holy fuck* and then another groan. Followed by another louder *holy fuck* and another longer groan.

Then his stillness.

Between panting breaths, he said, "Jess. I know...you didn't..."

Brandt pulled out and flipped her onto her back, imprisoning her arms above her head. He sealed his lips to hers, as he slid his length of his shaft along her cleft, rubbing the rim of his cockhead directly on her clit.

Oh. Wow. This was something new for her, but Brandt knew exactly what he was doing. He skipped the gradual buildup, going straight for the high point. With his relentless attention, she ripped her mouth free from his, unable to breathe or gasp or even whimper as the orgasm pulsed in short, intense bursts and he rode every wave of it with her.

After her brain clicked back on, she peeked at Brandt. "What?"

"I could get very used to watching you come." He kissed her. Sweetly, tenderly, but with the hunger that let her know he wasn't done with her. "Regrets?"

"Not a single one." She twisted her wrists as a hint for him to release her.

"Good." He pushed up. "Are you sore?"

She said, "No," a little too quickly.

His eyes narrowed. "Dammit, if I was too rough on you—"

"I would've said something. I'm not fragile, Brandt, remember that."

"You'd say that even if you were bleeding, Jessie."

Sometimes it surprised her how well he knew her.

"I need a drink," he said rolling off the bed. "You need anything before we go for the round two?"

"Round two?"

"Uh-huh. Because we're just getting started."

Chapter Ten

Brandt gulped two glasses of water in the kitchen and took a minute to grasp the situation.

Holy hell, he'd just had sex with Jessie.

Jessie.

It boggled his mind.

Not only that, she'd initiated sex.

Not only that, she hadn't wanted gentle lovemaking—she wanted to be fucked. Hard.

Not only that, she hadn't balked when he'd called her on her bravado, pushing her to put her money where her mouth was.

Holy hell, talk about a mouth that could own him body and soul. How he'd managed to hold out for more than fifteen seconds when those soft, warm lips circled the base of his cock while she sucked his shaft also boggled his mind.

How he'd managed to keep his cool when he got his first taste of her pussy was another miracle. Because damn, she'd been so wet that he could've stayed buried between her thighs, licking away that sweet juice, feeling her come against his mouth, all damn night.

Brandt's mental play by play fired his blood and he knew he'd have Jessie at least one more time tonight. Maybe in straight missionary position.

Boring. Don't you want to blow her circuits with your sexpertise? Show her every position you've ever tried and some you've only seen in porn?

Hell yeah. No. Hell no. That cocky attitude made him sound like...Luke, actually. He never wanted the comparison, especially not from Jessie. Not ever.

He could admit he'd taken her from behind for their first time because he worried she might whisper Luke's name in his ear during a moment of passion. Maybe he feared he'd see regret or sadness in her eyes. But he'd pushed aside those worries when the primitive side of his brain seized control and he flipped her on her back, just to see the look on her face when he made her come.

A look he couldn't wait to see again.

He refilled the water glass and he walked to the bedroom. For some reason his heart sped up and he lingered in the doorway. Had he left her alone too long? What if she'd fallen asleep?

"Brandt?"

He found her resting on against pillows propped against the headboard with the comforter tucked beneath her armpits. "You want a drink?"

"Sure." She drank half before handing the glass back. "Did you check on Landon?"

"Nah." He set the glass on the dresser. "I thought I might wake him up and he's not included in the plans I have for you."

She smiled. "What plans?"

"That depends on if you think we need to talk about anything that just happened."

"We've done enough talking."

"I agree. Let's go to plan B."

"Which is?"

"It'd be easier to show you." Brandt ripped back the covers and crawled over her body, until he was hanging directly above her. He whipped aside the pillows so she laid flat on the mattress. He angled his head over hers, seeing her eyes spark interest and heat as his lips closed the distance between their mouths.

Jessie released a soft moan, which reverberated in his mouth as he kissed her. Her lips were warm and eager. Her tongue as curious to explore as his was. They kissed, drawing out the pleasure by switching between hungry openmouthed kisses, sweet nibbles, teasing nips and soft smooches.

Brandt gazed down at her.

She caressed the side of his face. "Man, I could kiss you for days."

"I can arrange that. But first..." Brandt let his hands skim over her skin. "I want to touch you. Everywhere. It might take a while, because I've been living for the day I got to put my hands all over you." He stretched out, propping his head on his left hand, figuring it'd take twice as long to acquaint himself with her body if he limited himself to one hand.

"You still trying to figure out all my ticklish spots?"

"No. I wanna figure out which spots make you squirm and which ones make you moan." He let the rough tips of his fingers follow the line of her delicate neck down to the base of her throat. Then his thumb swept across her collarbone to her shoulder. Her skin was pale, he'd expected to see more freckles or moles, but it was just a silky smooth expanse of white.

His palm cupped the ball of her shoulder, traveling down to squeeze her firm biceps. He traced the bend in her elbow, first with his fingers, then with his tongue.

"Oh, I...wow. That feels good."

"Tastes good too." Brandt's fingers drifted down the inside of her forearm to her wrist. He threaded his fingers through hers and brought their joined hands to his mouth, lightly kissing each fingertip. He reversed course back up her arms and did the same thing, bestowing the same diligent treatment to the other side, except he dragged it out a little more.

Jessie's body wilted when he skimmed his fingers up and down her side, in a feather-light caress, from her armpit to the curve of her hip. She managed not to squirm too wildly when he wrapped her fingers on the rungs of the headboard and zigzagged openmouthed kisses down that same tender section of skin. Twice.

Her chest rose and fell rapidly with the marked increase in her breathing. His cock was so hard it pained him to bend over as he moved down the wonders of her body, but Brandt would not be rushed. He'd take his time, even if it damn near killed them both.

He paid no attention to her breasts or her nipples. Instead, his mouth brushed over every rib in her ribcage. Then down the centerline of her belly, past her belly button, to that sensitive span of skin between her narrow hipbones. When he put his mouth on her there, her entire belly rippled. So he did it over and over until she huffed out an impatient breath.

"What are you doing to me?"

"Memorizing you." He pressed kisses around the triangle of strawberry blonde hair at the juncture of her thighs. Again he allowed his fingers to map the muscles in her legs, tease the skin on the inside and smooth his palm over the curve from hip to ankle.

He kissed the tops of her thighs. He lifted her leg to nuzzle the back of her thighs and to trace the bend in her knees with his tongue. He peppered kisses down her shinbones, which were covered in bruises from Landon smacking into her all the time. When he reached the top of her foot, he sucked at the delicate skin and Jessie shot up off the bed so fast she almost kicked him in the face. "Easy there," he murmured.

"I heard that toe sucking was erotic, but this...this is way better. I never knew that would make me..."

"Make you what?"

"Tingle. My God. My whole body is tingling."

He switched feet just to see her come unglued.

"Okay, and now in addition to making me tingle, you're making me wet. Really wet. In fact, I think you should check it out," she purred.

Brandt chuckled. "I believe you. But I'm not finished yet." The same time he lifted her right ankle for a kiss, he noticed the tattoo. He outlined the shape of the butterfly with the pad of his thumb. "When did you get this?"

"The first time a bunch of us went in and India gave us all McKay brands."

He'd heard about his cousin's wives getting inked with the McKay cattle brand, but he'd never seen Jessie's. He'd been too busy noticing other parts of her body.

"But last year, about the time I...quit grieving for Luke so hard and realized our life wasn't as perfect as I'd made it out to be after he was gone, I wanted the symbol of his ownership gone too. So India designed this one, using the original tat, but you'd have to look really hard to see it."

The colorful butterfly emerging from a land cocoon fit Jessie's personal metamorphosis. Yet, it bothered him that she'd had the McKay brand removed. Why not just get a new tattoo? Keep the old one as a reminder of a past life event? If he thought about it too hard, he might take offense to it. Like Jessie no longer wanted to be associated with the McKays. Like she wanted to erase any part of her life with them.

If that's true, why did she keep the McKay name?

"Brandt? What's wrong?"

"Nothin'." He met her gaze and managed to smile before he placed a tender kiss on her tattoo. "But since I'm down by your feet, that means I'm all done exploring. Unless you can think of a spot or two I missed."

He waited for her to remind him he hadn't touched her nipples, and she didn't disappoint him.

Jessie released the headboard to cup her breasts. "Put your mouth on me here."

Brandt centered himself between her thighs and lowered his mouth to her left nipple. The peach colored tip was already hard so he began to draw circles around the quivering flesh on her chest with his fingers and his tongue. If he thought she squirmed before, it was nothing compared to how she reacted when he lavished attention on her breasts. Every part. From the nipples to the upper curve to the lower swell. He could stroke gently or pinch the tips with a little force, or nuzzle or softly suckle and she whimpered, moaned and thrashed.

Okay. Loved nipple play. Check.

He scattered kisses up her neck, stopping at her mouth. He kissed the corner of her smile, nipping and licking the seam until she parted her lips. He dove in for a blistering kiss, feeling her hands moving all over him, on his lower back, pressing down as she tried to connect their hips.

He buried his lips in her hair above her ear. "Jess—"

"If this is another warning to be patient...you oughta know I almost came just from you sucking my nipples. When you went down on me? Just thinking about it now still makes my entire groin throb."

Brandt smiled against her temple. "Throb, huh? So, does that mean you don't want to show me this super vibrator of yours that can get you off a dozen times a day?"

"Huh-uh."

"Why not?"

"Because I'm thinking of throwing it out."

"Why?"

"I'd rather you got me off a dozen times a day."

"Glad to know I'm a step up from a vibrator," he

murmured.

"You're ten stories above a vibrator and you know it." She murmured, "You have a mouth made for sex. When you kiss me it's like my brain goes on overload."

He levered himself over her, watching as her eyes went dark with anticipation. "There's something else you oughta know about me, Jess."

"What's that?"

"I'm a sexual man. I'll push you, but the biggest thing you'll need to get used to with me is that I like sex. I like a lot of sex. Once we start this, there's no backing down. No changing your mind. I will want you morning, noon and night, because you've proven you've got a pretty magical mouth yourself."

"Bring it on, cowboy. I'll have no problem keeping up with your demands. But if you expect I'm gonna be a passive lover, think again."

Her cocksure reply made his dick jump against his belly. "Bring it on, cowgirl."

And Brandt continued to focus on her face as he slipped inside her inch by inch.

Jessie wrapped her feet around the inside of his ankles, holding him in place. Soon as her hands landed on his ass, she arched, driving him deeper.

The slow, steady, easy strokes didn't stay that way for long. She urged him on by canting her pelvis, moaning *yes, yes.* Brandt forced himself to keep the same pace as he greedily watched Jessie unravel. She held him still with a nail digging grip on his ass as her pussy spasmed around his shaft.

As soon as she went limp, his hips pistoned harder, faster. His entire body seemed to boil—blood, skin, balls and bones—when his seed shot out of his dick in a hot wash of pleasure. An eye crossing, leg cramping, sweat pouring, primal grunting, he'd found heaven kind of ecstasy.

When he found his way back to reality, he realized this was true heaven. Not the outstanding orgasm, but seeing Jessie's soft smile. Feeling her soft, sated body beneath his. Having her here, with him. Where she belonged. Because his beautiful, sweet Jessie was his perfect match in every way.

How long before she realized it?

"Brandt?"

"What? Sorry." He smiled a bit sheepishly. "Zoned out."

"I noticed." She rubbed circles on his lower back that sent another wave of tingles dancing up his spine. "That was amazing."

"Uh-huh."

Wow. Got some sexy love talk going on there.

Spent, emotionally and physically, he rolled onto his back.

Immediately Jessie snuggled into him so thoroughly she was practically on top of him.

"Comfy?" he murmured.

"Mmm. Very. You don't mind, do you?"

No. I freakin' love it. "No. But do you, ah...need to go to the bathroom or shower or anything before we call it a night?"

"Nope. I wanna fall asleep like this."

"You do?"

"Yep. I like your scent all over me. I like feeling the stickiness between my thighs and remembering how it got there. Does that sound weird?"

"No." He brushed his lips over her crown. "It's hot as hell." The remnants of his seed would ease the way when he fucked her first thing in the morning.

"I like having you in my bed." She kissed his pectoral. "Thank you."

"For what?"

"For the smokin' hot sex. But also for not being petty and turning me down. I would've deserved your rejection for the way things have gone between us in the past."

Brandt forced her to look at him. "As far as I'm concerned that's where it can stay. In the past. We're movin' forward, right?"

"Right."

He pressed her cheek back down on his chest. "Go to sleep. Mornin' is gonna come awful early."

She snickered. "Already got your wake-up call for me planned out?"

"Definitely."

"Tell me."

"And ruin the surprise? No way."

Chapter Eleven

Jessie and Landon were sitting side by side on the couch watching a Winnie the Pooh DVD when Brandt returned from the ranch. As soon as he'd divested himself of his outerwear, he marched over and cradled Jessie's face in his hands.

The man nearly set her lips aflame with his hungry, and yet unhurried kiss. She tried to pull away, but he breathed, "Not yet," against her mouth and returned to those deceptively lazy kisses. Then he eased back and murmured, "Not nearly enough, but it'll do for now."

Right then, Jessie understood she wasn't prepared for what it meant to be Brandt McKay's lover. Sure, he'd tried to warn her last night about his sexual appetite. About his intent to satisfy that appetite as well as building the same type of appetite in her. Maybe she'd even suspected his declaration was a little too filled with machismo. A little too over the top.

She should've known better. She should've understood after he'd made love to her so thoroughly that last go around. She should've understood when he'd proved his desire for her first thing this morning. Spooned behind her, lifting her top leg over his, fucking her slowly while one hand played with her nipples and the other controlled her clit, whispering in her ear with that made-for-morning-sex voice. She came so hard she'd ripped the sheet off the bed.

"Jess? What's up? You've got a scared rabbit look goin' on."

"Seeing this forceful side of you...is a bit of a shock."

"You'll get used to it." He smooched her mouth again.

Landon made a noise and she saw him watching them with wide-eyed wonder.

"Hey, buddy, how's the ear? Better?"

He blinked at Brandt and refocused on the TV.

Brandt laughed. "Thrown over by a cartoon bear. I'm gonna hit the shower."

Less than a minute later the water kicked on.

Landon pointed at the TV and bounced on the couch cushions when Tigger appeared on the screen. Animation and cartoons were new to him, if his total absorption in them was an indication. Jessie doubted Landon's mother used the TV as a babysitter.

Once she heard the bathroom door open, she headed down the hallway, inhaling the steam that held hints of Irish Spring soap and lime shaving cream.

She stopped in the doorway to her bedroom. Ooh. Naked Brandt. The man had such a hard-toned body. All ropy, bulging muscles and pure masculinity. Virility. Luke had been built more rangy than bulky and she'd never appreciated the differences in the male form as much as she did right then.

"Getting an eyeful, are you?"

She let her gaze drop to his groin. "Definitely got more than a mouthful going on there, Brandt."

"Christ, Jessie," he sputtered, "that's—"

"A great idea?" she supplied. "Or shocking?"

"Both, actually. And if Landon wasn't..." He made a growling noise in his throat. "We'll finish this later."

"Actually, that's why I wanted to talk to you." She watched Brandt slip on a pair of navy colored boxer briefs. Then a pair of faded Wranglers. "Last weekend you took Landon back to your place. Are you sticking around this weekend now that things have changed?"

Brandt didn't miss a beat buttoning his flannel shirt. "Do you want us to stay?"

"Yes. I can't imagine spending the weekend by myself."

Then he was in her face, kissing her almost before she finished the sentence.

She heard a thump in the living room. She broke the liplock to go check on Landon, and as she turned around, the little wild man smacked into her knees. "You afraid we're having fun without you or something?"

He tried to hoist himself up on the bed. Soon as she set him on the mattress, he started jumping in his best Tigger imitation.

"You little monkey. Where'd you learn—" Jessie's head whipped to Brandt when he snickered. "You let him jump on the bed?"

"All kids jump on the bed. Besides, I was there the whole time."

"What happens if you're not there? What happens if he sneaks into a bedroom and starts jumping while you're doing something else? What if he flies off the bed and breaks his neck?"

Brandt snagged Landon around the waist and propped him on his hip, much to Landon's displeasure. "Okay, okay, I get it. Bad uncle. No more jumpin' on the bed. And I'll make sure since I've introduced this bad behavior that all bedrooms doors will be shut from here on out."

"Good." After they trooped back into the living room and Jessie said, "I didn't plan anything for supper because I didn't know if you'd be here."

"I don't expect you to cook for me every night."

"I like to cook. So do you have any requests?"

"I'm feelin' like pizza."

Jessie frowned. "That's the one thing I don't have the stuff for."

"Don't you have frozen pizza in the freezer?"

"Nope."

"We could go to the Pizza Barn in Moorcroft?" Brandt suggested.

After the last public appearance at Dewey's, fielding a dozen questions about Landon and why she was torturing herself caring for a child that wasn't hers... Nah. Not an experience she was anxious to repeat, especially not in front of Brandt with Landon tow.

"You not wantin' to be seen in public with me?"

Her gaze caught his. "It's not about you, paranoid man. Just remembering the scream therapy I needed last time I ventured out to a restaurant. So I'd rather stay in."

Tension left Brandt's posture and he smiled. "How about if I call in an order, pick it up and we eat it here?"

"Sounds like a plan."

While Brandt was gone, Jessie fed Landon and bathed him.

She dumped out the jumbo Legos on the coffee table and they sorted the pieces by color. Landon was fascinated by how the different sized parts fit and he was pleased as punch when he figured out how to snap them together by himself. Every day at the daycare and at home, she watched Landon learn something new. And rather than getting a sense of pride, it humbled her to see how hungry he was to learn.

Jessie ate the pizza one handed because Landon demanded she hold him while he drank his bottle. Brandt returned from settling Landon in his crib with that get-nekkid look in his eye.

Good thing she'd taken the time to brush her teeth.

Tell and Dalton showed up at Jessie's around noon on Sunday. Luckily they'd called first and hadn't walked in on him and Jess going at it in the shower.

Or on the couch.

Or on the kitchen counter.

Man. They could not get enough of each other. Within a few days they'd become intimate on a level he'd never experienced. As freakin' awesome as the sex was, Brandt knew it wasn't the only reason they'd become so close. They'd let their guards down and hadn't put those walls back up.

So far.

He hadn't announced that he and Jessie had become more to each other than Landon's guardians. Would Jessie shy away the first time he showed affection in front of his brothers?

Nope. She'd gone him one better and kissed him. With tongue.

She was a natural fit to their Sunday afternoon tradition— flipping back and forth between football games and waiting for Chase to compete in a televised PBR event, knocking back a few beers. Even Landon refused to nap so he could hang out with his uncles.

But at suppertime Landon staged a crying, screaming tantrum. The thought of wrestling the crabby kid into the bathtub made him shudder, but he wouldn't pass the duty off to Jessie either. Somehow Tell and Dalton ended up bathing the ornery boy. The bath time screams Brandt expected were largely absent, replaced by giggles.

Giggles?

What the hell?

He poked his head in the bathroom door and saw Tell, on his knees in front of the tub, and Landon—with Dalton's help—was spraying Tell in the face with the hand-held shower sprayer. Tell, being even keeled Tell, just let them do it and laughed right along with them.

His brothers managed to get Landon diapered and in his pajamas without incident.

Dalton held Landon while the kid sucked down his bottle. Once he'd tucked the tyke in bed, Dalton and Tell asked if they could have Landon the following Saturday night. For the last of the McKay wild men to give up their weekend plans proved his brothers intended to be part of Landon's life.

Maybe it was a little selfish, but his first thought was that he'd have Jessie all to himself for a night.

Jessie was washing dishes two days later when Keely barged into her house, demanding, "What the hell? Luke had a kid? I hate when nobody tells me this kind of shit."

"Yes. Keely. Please. Why don't you come in?"

"Shoulda locked the door if you wanted to keep me out. As soon as I heard I had to come over here and see—"

"About adding Luke's illegitimate love child to your roster of nieces and nephews?"

"No. And wow, snippy much, Jess? I came to see if you're okay."

"I'm fine."

Keely snorted. "Yeah, and you're acting like it, lashing out at me for checking on your mental well being."

Jessie blew out a breath. "Sorry. The shock hasn't been easy, but I'm coming to terms with it."

Which it, Jess? Luke's infidelity? Or Landon's presence?

Aren't they one in the same?

"Have you?" Keely demanded. "Have you really?"

"Some days, yes. Other days I wonder what the hell I'm doing and who in the universe I pissed off to have to deal with this."

"I cannot freakin' believe Brandt expected you to help him.

139

I cannot freakin' believe you said yes." Keely paced to the kitchen and back. "Actually, I can believe you said yes."

Did Keely think she was a doormat? Only one way to find out. "Why can you believe it?"

"Because you're sweet, thoughtful, kind and generous." Keely pinned her with a look. "Damn near annoyingly perfect in that nauseating girl-next-door way, to be honest, but I like you anyway, cuz."

"Gee, thanks."

"But mostly, you said *yes* because Landon is as innocent in this whole situation as you are."

Keely's insight always surprised her. "You want a beer while I'm spilling the gory details of lost innocence?"

"No." Keely flopped on the couch. "I've got a late patient tonight so I have to head back to the clinic."

"How was the honeymoon?"

"Amazing."

"How's Jack?"

Keely smirked. "Amazing."

Jessie launched into recent events. Before she finished, Landon cried from his crib. "I'll be right back."

Landon had woken in a somber mood—not all cute smiles and sweet snuggles. Not knowing how he'd behave continued to be a struggle, so she hoped for the best and returned to the living room with Landon in her arms.

He shrank back as he spied Keely.

Keely's eyes sparked tears. "Omigod. It's like he's a clone of Luke."

"Those McKay genes are powerful stuff." Jessie grabbed Landon's cup from the fridge and a handful of animal crackers. He stayed on her lap with a wary eye on Keely.

"So you really do seem fine with all of this."

"I have my days where I'd like to leave town with no forwarding address, believe me. But I agreed to do it so it seems pointless to complain. Plus, I know it's temporary."

"Is it a possibility?" Keely kicked her boots up on the coffee table. "That it might become permanent?"

"Not for me. Maybe for Brandt."

"Were does Brandt fall in all of this?"

"He hasn't just passed the responsibility of taking care of

Landon off on me."

"Jess. That's not what I meant. I meant personally. Brandt is living with you. You're together all the time, taking care of a child. I hope you're working out some of your past issues?"

"If you mean working them out between the sheets, then yes," she said in a rush.

"And?"

"And...it's intense. But, again, that's because this is a temporary situation."

Keely gave her a calculated look. Like she was ready to call bullshit.

"What?"

"Why can't this be the start of something that will be intense for years to come?"

Jessie couldn't answer that to anyone's satisfaction, so she sidestepped the question. She brushed crumbs off Landon's shirt. "You dated Jack's brother for awhile, right?"

"Yes."

"So you and Jack haven't had any fights or discussions about the time you were with Justin?"

She sighed. "We've had huge fights, which means no rational discussion. We don't talk about the sexual aspect of it. Jack knows more about what happened between Justin and me only because Justin told him, I never would have. But my relationship with Justin happened a few years before Jack and I stopped hating each other long enough to really look at each other."

"But you weren't the source of fights between them?"

"No." Realization dawned in Keely's eyes. "Damn. You were, weren't you? The source of fights between Luke and Brandt."

"I've never told anyone this, Keely, but I overheard them. I wanted to die of embarrassment. My husband didn't love me enough to stay faithful and he made sure my brother-in-law knew it."

"Oh, Jess."

"So I'm in a different situation. It's complicated enough between me and Brandt without adding him—" she pointed at Landon, "—into the mix."

"Maybe Landon's the glue that will allow you and Brandt to be together."

Or maybe he's the wedge that will drive us apart.

"Look, it's no secret that you and Brandt spent a lot of time together after Luke died. Everyone thought—"

"That I'd just slip from one McKay bed to another without any problem whatsoever? God. Has everyone been listening to Casper talk about me?"

Keely's boots hit the carpet. "See? That's your problem. You automatically assume everyone thinks the worst of you. Casper is the exception, not the rule. What I started to say was we all hoped you'd both find happiness in what'd been a bad situation."

Landon said, "Goggie," and Lexie rose from her spot by the door and headed toward him, tail wagging.

Jessie kissed the top of Landon's head. "See? She'll come to you if you ask nice."

He reached for the dog with the hand holding the cup and almost clunked Lexie on the head with it. Lexie slunk away.

"And...that lasted thirty seconds."

The door opened and Brandt stepped in. Landon squirmed off her lap and ran to him. "Up!"

"Hey. Whoa. Watch the cup, buddy." He lifted Landon and his gaze traveled between Jessie and Keely.

Jessie knew Brandt wanted to march over and lay a big wet kiss on her like he always did after a day on the ranch. But he refrained. "Keely. You're lookin' tan. Glad to be home?"

"No. We could've used another two weeks. I told Jack next time we get married, we're taking an entire month for our honeymoon."

"Funny." Brandt stayed on the rug in his work clothes. "Jess, have you fed the animals yet?"

"No. Landon was sleeping and Keely stopped by so I haven't had a chance."

"Looks like you'n me got chores to finish, boy. Come on let's getcha suited up."

Keely didn't say anything until after Brandt and Landon were out the door. "This feels bigger than you guys just playing house. It sure as hell feels bigger than temporary."

It does to me sometimes too. "We'll see."

"Be careful."

"You afraid Brandt will break my heart?"

"No. I'm afraid you'll break his."

Jessie froze. She wasn't expecting that.

"I probably better get back." Keely leapt out of the chair and wrapped her scarf around her neck. "Anytime you need to talk, Jess, just call. I mean it. There are things..." She smiled. "Never mind. Ignore me."

"Oh, hell no. You can't just drop that into conversation and leave. What kind of things?"

"Casper... People want to believe he's just a grumpy old man, but we both know he's not. People want to believe it's not as bad as it looks in his household, but I'm telling you, it is. He wields a heavy hand with his wife and his sons, full and total control. I know Luke shielded you from a lot of what went on."

"You think Brandt will too?"

"No. But I'm telling you it won't be pretty if he ever decides to let go of the anger and resentment he's been carrying around for years. Back to that annoyingly perfect comment, you are just the type of woman he needs. You're the only woman I know who can handle anything that's thrown at you and keep standing. But that means if Brandt actually opens up to you, and you leave him, you'll do more than just break his heart. You might just break him."

Jessie stared after Keely, shocked, but not really. Brandt had a hard edge he tried very hard to hide, not only from her but from everyone. Part of her wanted him to open up that side of himself, while part of her feared it if he did.

She wondered how long before he trusted her enough to even admit it was there.

Chapter Twelve

Mark my words; Jessie is using you as much as you're using her. You'll always be a pale imitation of Luke in her eyes and everyone else's.

His father was such a jackass Brandt threw his truck in reverse and his tires spit gravel as he sped away from the machine shed.

The day had started out perfect. It was one of those times when all was right with his world. When Brandt knew he was exactly where he was supposed to be doing exactly what he'd been meant to do: be a steward of this Wyoming land he loved. Some of his cousins weren't keen on being part of the McKay cattle company, they'd moved on, but Brandt couldn't understand that mindset. He loved the ranch. He loved the day to day back breaking work. The cycle of seasons. The unpredictability of the cattle market and the weather. Working with his brothers day in and day out. The humility of being a part of something that was so much bigger than him. From the time he was a little boy, all he wanted was to look across this gorgeous hunk of earth and know it belonged to him. As he'd gotten older, he realized that he belonged to the land—it owned him, heart and soul. He couldn't imagine living anywhere else.

Naturally his father noticed his good mood and felt entitled to destroy it.

Goddamn him.

At times like this, when clouds of rage fogged rational thought, Brandt was half-tempted to keep driving until he ran out of gas. And then keep walking until he ran out of energy. What he hated most of all was the way his father could twist his love of the ranch into something ugly. Into Brandt berating himself for sticking around because he'd always be second banana to Luke. He's always be a verbal punching bag for his father.

God knows he'd tried—and failed—to protect Tell and Dalton from suffering the same fate. He'd watched his mother become a shell of a woman. Thinking that all these sacrifices and drama would mean something in the end when his father trusted him enough to turn over all the ranch operations to his oldest son.

Yeah, the McKays were just one big happy fucking family and it'd just gotten worse in the two years since Luke had died.

If the urge to physically lash out wouldn't go away, he'd head to a bar, drink until he was ten foot tall and bulletproof, and start a fight. It never made him feel better. In fact, he'd usually end up bloodied, bruised and broken. His compulsion to fight wasn't something he was proud of—the primitive need to prove himself with his fists was his deepest shame. His cousins Colt and Kane both had the same violent streak. When Colt's punching bag wasn't enough to keep his demons at bay, he and Kane mixed it up. At least they had each other to take the edge off. Brandt had no one. And Luke had taken perverse pleasure in denying Brandt a good fight.

He imagined one of those head shrinking docs would have a field day trying to analyze him, especially since the violence was never directed at anyone he knew.

Right now he wanted so badly to drive to some hole in the wall bar where no one knew who he was. He'd drink, come out swinging and after having his ass handed to him, or ending up victorious, he'd sleep off the booze and the pain in his truck. Then he'd feel calmer.

Why not go to Jessie? She has a calming influence on you.

Jessie.

Now that they were sleeping together, he couldn't get enough of her and she'd held nothing back from him in bed or out. She'd given everything of herself to him one hundred percent. He wanted her body under his the last thing before he went to sleep at night. He wanted her body beneath his first thing in the morning. He wanted her after he'd just had her. He thought about all the different ways he'd take her while he was taking her. If he thought he'd been obsessed with her before, it was nothing compared to the craving he had for her now.

Which was why he had to stay away from her right now.

He texted Jessie, letting her know he'd be late without going into detail. Then he called his mother, who was watching Landon at his house, telling her he had to finish a couple of things. She didn't complain or ask questions, but then again, she never did.

Brandt gave his mother's car a cursory glance and parked his truck behind his barn.

Too bad he didn't have backbreaking tasks like splitting wood or digging new postholes that would exhaust him. He shucked off his coat and let his anger lead him into total destruction mode. Grabbing a sledgehammer and a crowbar, he began to rip apart the last stall with the loose and broken boards. He couldn't afford to upgrade to metal and they were too damn dangerous as is.

The sledgehammer came down, the loud *thwack* followed by another *thwack thwack thwack* until he couldn't hear anything besides the blood pounding in his ears. Sweat poured down his face. When he had the boards loosened, he used his hands to break them free. The muscles in his back screamed. Slivers penetrated his holey gloves, but he didn't stop. Couldn't stop. Not until it was done. Not until this consuming fury was gone.

He finally took a break when he was down to one long board on the backside. Placing the heels of his hands above his knees, he bent over, sucking in huge gasps of air, half-wondering when he'd started heating the barn because his skin was on fire.

The hinge on the barn door squeaked and he blinked the sweat from his eyes as he glanced up.

His mother stood in the doorway.

No one he cared about should ever see him like this. Embarrassment had him snarling, "What?"

"Jessie called about thirty minutes ago when she couldn't reach you on your cell. She's on her way here."

What the fuck? "I told her I was gonna be late."

"Something tipped her off to your mood." Her gaze darted to the destroyed stall and back to him. "Which is a little destructive."

"This piece of shit needed to be torn down."

"I'm not worried about the stall, son. I'm worried about you."

"It'd be best if you went back on up to the house and let me finish this."

Her eyes focused on his cheek. "You're bleeding."

"Where?"

"Your face. Come inside with me and I'll clean it up."

Brandt shook his head. "I'm sure it's just a scratch."

"Made by a rusty nail. When was your last tetanus shot? Just let me take a quick look—"

"No," he practically bellowed. "Don't you understand? I cannot be around anyone right now."

Her face registered surprise, then hurt. "Why not?"

His entire being quaked and words poured out a stilted mess. "I hate that he still has that much power over me. I hate that he can get a reaction out of me when no one else can. I hate it's a test to see if I'm strong enough to fight this...fucking rage I inherited from him. I've tried so hard not to end up like him. So fucking hard and when I act this way, I'm exactly like him and I hate it. I hate myself."

Her eyes overflowed with pain, not tears, which was harder for him, because he suspected she'd cried herself out over the years.

"You're nothing like him, Brandt. Nothing. Don't ever give yourself an excuse to act like him by saying it's inevitable that you will end up like him, because it's not. You've chosen to be different. Even when you're like this you're different. Remember that."

For the millionth time he wondered how this caring woman had coped with Casper McKay's bitterness for so many years.

"Anyway, I thought I'd give you a heads up about Jessie, so you can, you know..."

"Get it together before I see her?"

She nodded.

"Thanks. I'll be right there. Just give me a minute."

"Don't take too long, because she will come looking for you first thing."

Not an accusation; a fact.

She left.

Despite the agony in his arm and the muscles screaming in

his back, he lifted the sledgehammer. But it was a half-hearted swing at best.

He wasn't calm, but he wasn't in that dark place either. He snagged his coat off the floor and walked outside, breathing in the fresh air to cool him down.

Jessie waited for him by the steps, wearing an anxious expression.

He couldn't muster a smile, but he went on the offensive. "Didn't you get my text?"

"Yes. That's why I'm here."

"Because I said I was gonna be late?"

"No, because I knew something was wrong."

"You got that from my text message?"

Jessie placed her hand on his chest. "I had a feeling something wasn't right, and seeing you, I see my gut instinct was dead on."

Far as he knew, no woman ever had a gut feeling about him. Certainly no woman had never cared enough to follow through with it and make sure he was all right. He held her face between his gloved hands and kissed her. "Jess. I'm fine. Now let's go inside. It's cold out here."

"Then how come you're sweating?"

Woman was too damn intuitive for her own good. Brandt pressed his lips to hers, bestowing several soft smooches. "Because you're so hot, baby, just lookin' at you makes me sweat."

She smooched him back. "I don't buy it, cowboy charmer. I'll let it slide for now, because I'm sure your mom is anxious to get home."

"I highly doubt that," Brandt said dryly. He took Jessie's hand and led her inside.

His mother put her finger to her lips. "Landon just went down a half hour ago. I know it's late for a nap, but he had so much energy today. I tried to get him to lay down with me on the couch, but he wasn't having any of it."

"I know how that goes, so no big deal," Jessie said.

"Thanks for watchin' him today, Mom."

"I enjoy him. He reminds me so much of you."

"Me? Not Luke?"

"In looks he's nearly identical to his father." Joan slipped on her coat. "But in temperament, he could be your son." She leaned over to kiss his cheek. "Take care of yourself, Brandt. If you need anything, call."

Brandt ditched his outerwear and headed to the refrigerator. Might as well have a beer if he was sticking around until Landon woke up. But he hadn't been here much the past few weeks and he was out of beer.

Whiskey?

Nah. In his mood that'd lead to trouble.

He exited the kitchen and said to Jessie, "If you wanna head home, I'll hang out until kidzilla awakens."

"You trying to get rid of me, Brandt?"

"No. But I'm not the best company right now."

She sauntered forward. "So maybe we shouldn't talk."

Brandt didn't move. "Not a good idea, Jess."

"You're tense. I have a remedy for that."

"I'm not in the mood."

Jessie lifted a brow. "Never heard *that* from you before."

And likely she wouldn't again. "Look. I appreciate the offer, but—"

"*Offer?*" she repeated. "Like you'd be doing me a favor by doing me?" Her face shuttered. "Screw that. I'm outta here." She turned so fast her coattails whapped him on the knee.

He grabbed her out of reflex. "Whoa. This is exactly what I didn't want to happen."

"Congrats. You made it happen anyway."

He hauled her against his chest, imprisoning her in his arms.

"Let me go."

"No. You started this, Jess, not me."

"What is wrong with you?"

He pressed his mouth to the shell of her ear. "I want you, okay? Fuck. I always want you. But I'm on edge in a big way today, and it'd be better if—"

"You shut me out? Wow. Like I've never dealt with *that* from a McKay man before."

Once again, she'd pushed the wrong button. In a flash, he crowded her against the living room wall. "You don't know what you're getting yourself into by taunting me."

Jessie lifted her chin. "Show me. You won't shock me."

"Don't bet on that, sweetheart."

Then she shocked him by wreathing her arms around his neck and whispering, "Trust me. Please. Don't shut me out. Let me in. I'm here for you however you need me." Her cool fingers settled on his nape.

Damn. Her touch felt good, soothing him and stirring him up. "I don't have a lot of control right now."

"So you admitting that Brandt McKay, the almighty gentleman cowboy, is showing me that he's not always as even-keeled as he projects?"

"Yes."

"That's a start." Jessie crushed her lips to his, inhaling him with a take-no-prisoners kiss and ground her pelvis against his. When he stupidly tried to pull away, she held him tighter, kissed him harder and he was done fighting her. Done fighting himself.

Brandt wrested control, frantic to touch her everywhere, her throat, her breasts, her belly, between her thighs. Letting his desire for her burn up any residual anger. Letting her help him take the edge off. Letting her in.

She writhed against him. When Jessie dropped her hand over his fly to unzip his jeans, he growled and ended all body contact.

He stepped back. "Clothes off."

Moments later, she was completely naked.

He turned her around. "Put your hands flat on the wall."

Jessie didn't hesitate.

She wasn't being obedient for his sake, because he wanted it this way. *She* wanted it this way. Her breathing had become erratic. Her body rippled with that *fuck me now* tremor that kicked his lust into the danger zone. He let his mouth tease her ear. "You sure you want this? Me fucking you, only thinkin' about how good it'll feel when I'm buried balls deep in your tight cunt? You really want me to use you hard?"

"Yes. God yes."

Brandt slipped his fingers between her thighs and found her soaked. A primitive yowl in his head had him jerking his shirttails free from his jeans. Belt unfastened, zipper undone, he removed his jeans only to the tops of his boots because he was obsessed with getting inside her and couldn't wait to get completely undressed.

"Brandt."

Please don't say stop. "What?"

"Hurry."

His cock slapped his belly before he impatiently shoved it between her legs and impaled her with one greedy push.

Her full body quiver was followed by a low-pitched, "Yes."

Brandt curled his hands over her hips and pulled her back, completely controlling her movements. His pelvis smacking her ass made a discordant *slap slap slap* sound that was almost as satisfying as Jessie's guttural moans bouncing back to him.

He reached around until his finger breached the soft nest of curls, gliding down to where their bodies were joined at the mouth of her sex. Then he slid his wet finger back up her slit to stroke her slippery nub in a gentle motion that countered the ferocity of his cock surging into her. But in this position he couldn't get deep enough. He widened his stance, but his strokes became even shallower, so he stopped moving.

Jessie turned to look at him. "Brandt? Why did you—"

"I need more of you. Lean back." She emitted a shriek when he lifted her, balancing her ass on his pelvis like she was sitting on a chair. "Tuck your feet around the outside of my boots." Soon as she did, they both groaned, because damn, that one little change immediately brought him deeper. He angled her body forward, flattening her palm on the wall, wrapping her left arm behind his neck before he slapped his left hand on the wall across from hers. With his chest plastered to her back, he gritted out, "Hang on."

Fucking her this way was a rush, not only because of the slant and position of their bodies, but because there was no finesse. No sweetness. Just desperation. Just need. His hips bucked as he kept his free hand cupped over her mound to tease her clit. He closed his eyes, losing himself in the sensation of Jessie pressing back against him as he pressed into her tight heat. Knowing there was nowhere on earth he'd rather be. Knowing her acceptance of this side of him would only cement his determination to have her as his.

He rocked into her, letting that humming greed for release amplify until they were both panting. Sweating.

When she rolled her hips side to side, he knew she teetered on the brink. For all his blustering about using her hard, he wouldn't ever deny her an orgasm.

He whispered fiercely, "Give it to me."

"Touch me. God, please..."

Brandt separated her pussy lips with his fingers and flicked his middle finger over the responsive flesh until he felt her clit expand. "Squeeze me harder. Yeah, like that—"

Before he finished speaking she unraveled. Her ass cheeks clenching against his groin, her cunt a vise-like grip around his cock, her clit pulsating beneath his finger, her nails digging into the back of his neck, her passion-dampened skin rubbing against his wherever they touched. She moaned *his* name, over and over. *His* name. No one else's.

When the word *mine* flashed behind his lids, he lost it. Fucking her with fast jabs, slamming home with every stroke. Holding his breath until he was woozy. Heart thundering, blood blazing, skin slicked with sweat, every muscle coiled tighter and tighter until that perfect moment when everything unwound.

He shouted as his cock emptied in almost violent pulses, no coherent thoughts registered beyond the words *again, again, again.* Nothing in the world existed but the connection of their bodies locked together.

Then he felt Jessie lightly scraping her teeth along the rigid line of his jaw.

His grip on her increased—mentally and physically—he never wanted to let her go. "I...Wow. I'm a little out of it."

She murmured, "No worries."

"Mmm." He nuzzled her hair, breathing her in. Filling his lungs, his heart, his soul with everything this woman freely gave him, no matter how much he asked of her. "Thank you."

"Anytime."

"Jessie, I—"

She pressed her lips to his. "You don't have to explain."

"Even if I want to explain why, after I just fucked you like a madman, I have this overwhelming urge to spin you around and fuck you face to face against the wall?" He nipped the section of skin below her earlobe just to feel her entire body shiver while he was still inside her. Just to hear that sexy little moan she made. "And then I want to take you to my bed and keep you there all goddamn night?"

"You afraid I'll say no?"

"No. I'm afraid you'll say yes."

Her purring laugh vibrated against his throat.

Then Brandt heard Landon rattling the bars on his crib.

They both froze.

He sighed. "Duty calls. At least he had good timing and didn't interrupt us again like he did last night."

The way Jessie's whole body stiffened, he realized Landon hadn't crossed her mind at all. But rather than laugh it off, chalking their oversight up to head-exploding orgasmic intensity, he knew she felt guilty. She wiggled and demanded, "Let me down. I'll get him."

Later, when they were snuggled together on the couch, watching TV, Jessie reached for his hand and he winced.

"What's wrong?"

"Ah, nothin'. Just a little sore."

"From what?"

From beating the shit out of my barn today. "From workin'. No big deal."

"Let me see."

"Jess—"

"If it's no big deal then let me see it."

Brandt held out his right hand and turned the palm side up. The glove had rubbed his skin raw. Where the glove had holes, he had slivers. Even his fingertips were scraped up.

"Oh, your poor hand. Are those wood slivers?"

"Yeah."

"Stay put. I'll be right back." She returned with tweezers, a needle, a washcloth, and a tube of anti-bacterial ointment.

"Here I was hopin' that was a bottle of lube."

"Maybe later. Right now, I'm gonna get those slivers out."

"You don't have to bother because I hardly even noticed them."

But Jessie wasn't deterred. "I noticed them and I happen to excel at sliver removal, so you're in luck." She bent her head close to his palm and started poking his skin with the needle.

As much as he didn't want to ask if she'd done this for Luke, his mouth had other ideas. "How's it that you're so good with tweezers?"

"When me'n Josie were kids, there was this really cool abandoned tree fort in the woods behind our house. We weren't supposed to go there, but we couldn't resist. Problem was, it had an old rope to climb to reach the wooden platform and we both ended up with a lot of splinters. Since the tree fort had been expressly forbidden, we couldn't tell Mom about the slivers, so me'n my little sister both got really good at picking them out."

"Where was your mom when you were sneakin' off to the woods?"

"Working."

"And your dad?"

She snorted. "Billy? Off rodeoin', where he always was."

Jessie rarely talked about her family. In fact, that was the first time he'd heard she had a sister.

She worked in silence and with such a deft touch he didn't feel a damn thing. And his hand was much more tender than he'd wanted to admit.

She said, "Almost done."

"Thanks, but you didn't have to do this for me."

"Oh, I didn't do it for you. I did it for me, for purely selfish reasons. See, I love the feel of your rough, manly hands on me, but not so much if they're swollen and pus-infected."

"Nice visual," he said wryly.

"But it's a reason you'll accept a lot easier than me admitting I can't stand to see you hurting. Not when I can do something to help you or something to stop it."

That's when Brandt knew he loved her. Not lusted after her. Not felt obligated to her. He loved her. Loved who she was, this woman who tended to him in so many ways. Who touched him in ways he was only beginning to understand.

Jessie finally looked at him. She brought his hand to her mouth and placed a tender kiss in the center of his palm. "All better."

"Now that you're done, will you let me put my hands all over you?"

"Nope. I'm thinking these need to heal up so it'd be best if I put my hands all over you." She smiled with wicked intent. "We still get to the same destination, but I hold the reins."

Brandt groaned. "You're gonna torture me, aren't you?"

"Yep. But I promise you'll love it." She gave him a thoughtful look. "Now. What did I do with those ropes?"

Chapter Thirteen

"No. That's okay. I understand." Jessie forced a laugh. "Yeah, cell service is shitty in Wyoming." She walked into the kitchen and set her empty coffee cup in the sink. "I'll check the road conditions. Uh-huh. I'll let you know. Bye, Billy."

Jessie punched the off button on her cell phone and stared at the snowy landscape out Brandt's front window. They'd finished chores as quickly as possible this morning because of the bone chilling cold. She'd looked forward to spending the whole day snuggled up with Brandt since Tell and Dalton had taken on babysitting duties.

But now...

Strong arms circled her waist. The clean scent of a freshly showered and shaved Brandt surrounded her. His warm, soft lips traveled up the side of her neck.

"Who was on the phone?" he asked.

"Billy."

"Billy...as in...your dad?"

"Yeah."

Brandt quit kissing her neck and spun her to face him. "What's wrong?"

"Nothing. He was just calling to let me know he's competing at an event in Gillette. Today."

"Today? He couldn't've told you before now?"

She shook her head. "That's how he operates, Brandt. In his own little rodeo world. Nothing else matters but chasing eight and winning that elusive gold buckle."

"So, did he call you to tell you he's just passin' through?"

"What's funny is he probably drove within ten miles of my

place and he couldn't be bothered..." Jessie extricated herself from Brandt's arms, hating the girlish, whining tone to her voice. So Billy didn't care enough to pop in and say howdy. Hell. She should be happy he remembered she lived in Wyoming. Happy. Right. The man flat out didn't give a damn about her.

Like his apathy is news, Jessie.

True. But it didn't stop the hollow feeling from expanding, a feeling she only got when she heard from her vagabond father.

But Brandt wouldn't let her shut herself off, especially not after she'd pushed him to deal with his mood the other day. "Jess. Baby, talk to me. What did he want?"

"He asked me to come to Gillette to watch him ride and he wants us to catch up. Jesus. I haven't seen him for three years. The last time was at the Niobrara Rodeo with Luke. And to say Billy and Luke didn't hit it off is putting it mildly. Luke told him a grown man should face up to his responsibilities, not run off and join the damn rodeo."

Brandt whistled. "Not that I disagree with anything Luke said, but I imagine that didn't go over well."

"Actually, Billy laughed it off. Said he'd take his judgment before God, not men." She brooded, remembering just how mortifying that conversation had been. It'd gotten worse after Luke had spouted off that being brave on the back of a bronc didn't mean shit when Billy was too much of a coward to stay with his wife and kids.

"What else did they say? Because I can tell you're holding something back."

"Billy reminded Luke that paying lip service to a sacred vow was a sin. Talk about humiliating. Billy knew Luke was cheating on me. Which made me wonder if cheaters recognize cheaters, or if Billy knew I wasn't enough to hold Luke's interest for the long haul."

Evidently Brandt had no response for that.

"So you goin' to Gillette?"

"Yes. How freakin' pathetic is that?"

"Not pathetic. Just hopeful things might change between you and your father, and darlin', that's a feeling I've been familiar with my whole life." Brandt kissed the top of her head. "I can't fault you for that hope, but I'm worried how it'll affect you if this trip ends up bein' another dose of the same old, same old. So, if you're goin', I'm goin' with you."

157

Jessie cranked her head around to look at him. "Really? You'd give up your one free weekend day to drive to Gillette and sit in an arena that smells like the barn?"

"I'm not givin' up anything. I'll be with you. That's all that matters to me." Brandt kissed her again, soundly.

Any mention of his feelings for her made her wary, but Brandt did it every chance he had. That's just the way he was.

Hands roamed, breathing became hot and heavy as the kiss heated. But she didn't break the connection, Brandt did. He muttered, "We'd better stop playin' grab ass if we're hitting the road."

She nipped his bottom lip. "We've got time for a quickie."

"No way." He slapped her butt and stepped back. "I want more than a quickie."

"We could stay here and spend the entire day in bed."

"Another time. You need to see your dad, even if it's only for a little while. Call him and tell him we're on our way." Brandt pointed at her clothes. "You gonna change?"

She glanced down at the dirt and manure stained coveralls. "You don't think I oughta meet Billy in my work clothes?"

"I don't give a damn what you wear, Jess, you know that. Just curious how soon you'll be ready. I hafta call Tell and Dalton and update them on our plans before we go."

"Give me five minutes."

In Brandt's room, she dug in her duffel bag for the extra pair of jeans. She switched out her ratty long sleeved T-shirt for a newer one, wishing she'd packed something nicer. Her gaze strayed to the closet. Maybe she'd just wear one of Brandt's shirts.

Her fingers trailed over the slim selection until she reached a shirt the color of burgundy roses, shoved in the very back of his closet. Not exactly Brandt's shade. Curious, she pulled it out and realized it was a woman's shirt.

Huh. Brandt wasn't the player his brothers were, but she doubted he'd been a monk. She heard about the on-again, off-again girlfriend. He probably wasn't aware his last squeeze had left it here.

Too bad, so sad. Finder's keepers.

She buttoned it. Nice fit. Really nice fit. This expensive brand had always been out of her price range. She stopped in the bathroom and brushed her hair before returning to the living room where Brandt waited.

"Ready? You look..." His smile dried as he noticed the rose-colored shirt.

"I hope you don't mind. I'm out of clean clothes so I borrowed it from your closet, because truthfully, this one really doesn't match your color palette."

His slow *aw shucks* grin brought out his dimples. "I forgot Lydia left it here or I'da turned it into a grease rag. Keep it if you want. It looks better on you than it ever did on her."

"Thanks."

"Let's go."

Lexie barked happily at the word *go*.

"Sorry, not today." Jessie ruffled her dog's ears. "Is it okay if she stays inside the house while we're gone?"

"Yep. I already let her out. Amazing how quick she is about her *goggie* business when it's ten below outside."

Bundling up, she followed Brandt to his truck. She loved how he held the driver's side door for her. She scooted across the bench seat, stopping in the middle. As soon as they were on the road, he set his forearm on her thigh and curled his hand around her knee. She laid her head on his shoulder, perfectly content.

Silences between them weren't unusual. So it surprised her when Brandt said, "Seems quiet without Landon babbling in the background."

"Almost makes you wish he wasn't trying so hard to talk, huh?"

He chuckled. "When I talked to Tell, he said Landon wrassled a bear last night. Granted, it was a teddy bear, but I'll bet my brothers don't make that small distinction to Landon as he's growing up. Already tryin' to make the kid tough."

"Why is it such a point of pride that the McKays are known for their toughness?"

"I don't know if it's a point of pride as much as it is proof that if you mess with one of us, you mess with all of us. So we've all gotta stand our ground because none of us wanna be considered the weakest link."

"Were your dad and your uncles like that too?"

His posture stiffened. Was Brandt aware how his body

changed whenever his dad was mentioned?

"They all had a reputation for brawlin' with each other and with any unlucky sucker who crossed them. Course, if I hadn't talked to my cousins, I never would've known any of that. If it hadn't been for Aunt Kimi, none of us—Casper's sons—would've known our grandpop. He lived with Uncle Cal and Aunt Kimi, which pissed my dad off."

"Why?" She knew little of the McKay family history because Luke never wanted to talk about it.

"Grandpop made it clear he'd rather live with the daughter of the man he hated than with his own son. I suspect that was the start of the issues between my dad and his brothers, but no one has ever confirmed that's what sparked the problems."

"Family drama. Ain't it fun?"

"Don't worry, Jess. I won't pick a fight with a random stranger or do anything to embarrass you in front of your dad."

"That's not it. I'm more worried he'll do something to embarrass *me*."

Brandt lifted her hand and kissed her knuckles.

Jessie appreciated he didn't make false promises that everything between her and Billy would be hunky-dory, sparkly rainbows and lollipops.

The roads to Gillette were icy and Brandt concentrated on driving. She must've dozed off because the next thing she knew, Brandt was shaking her awake.

"We're at the Camplex."

She stretched. "What time is it?"

"Twelve. What time does the rodeo start?"

"I'm guessing one o'clock."

"Where are you meeting him?"

"In the contestant area. Not that I have a clue where that is. I've never been to the Camplex."

Brandt frowned. "Didn't you travel around with your dad for a while?"

"You mean the summer I met you at the Devil's Tower Rodeo?"

He nodded.

"That was the third and final event I attended with him. I cramped his style." She smiled. "Which was why I ended up in the bar that night."

"Do you remember running into us—me'n Luke at the rodeo earlier that day?"

"Uh-huh. That's how I found out about the dance. Luke asked me to come."

Brandt parked. Then he turned, cupping her face to give her a tender kiss. "Any time you're ready to leave, give me a signal."

"Maybe we should have a code word," she suggested.

"Like what?"

"Hot, kinky sex?"

Brandt grinned. "I don't even wanna know how you'd work that into casual conversation with your dad sittin' right there, so maybe we oughta come up something else."

"How about slow dancing, in honor of our first meeting?"

"Deal. But I feel obligated to mention that you slow danced with my brother, not me."

She frowned. "But I know we two-stepped."

He shook his head. "Sorry. You only had eyes for Luke."

No point in arguing that one.

They paid the entrance fee to the arena and tracked down the contestant's area. No one was admitted behind the chutes, but the gatekeeper sent someone to locate Billy Reynolds.

Jessie's old fears surfaced. What if Billy had changed his mind at the last minute and had bypassed the Gillette rodeo? Wouldn't be the first time. In truth, Billy had left her hanging more times than he'd followed through with any plans they'd made. She could claim she'd outgrown that fear, but it was embarrassing that Billy Reynolds still had the ability to hurt and disappoint her.

Brandt's warm, rough, strong hand slipped into hers.

Somehow he knew. Ever since the day she hadn't walked away when he'd been hurting, things had changed between them. No declarations of love. Just a deeper level of acceptance. Even for things they didn't speak of. Like what'd happened to Brandt that day to turn him inside out. Like now, when she reverted to the young girl hanging on the corrals, hoping for attention from an absent father before he took off again.

One thing they didn't speak of? What would happen when Landon's mother got out of jail. As far as Jessie was concerned, nothing had changed on that front and Brandt knew it.

"Jessie?" came from behind her.

She turned and came face to face with Billy. Her father. Technically, her stepfather. Whenever she hadn't seen him for a while, it surprised her how short he was, especially since he'd always seemed larger than life in her younger years. He wore a different hat—black, instead of the stained gray one she remembered. His plaid shirt was pressed. His faded jeans were covered in arena dust. A championship buckle was centered between his hips and above the cinch strap on his dark brown chaps. His boots were scuffed, scarred and faded. When he tipped his hat up, revealing his face, the lines bracketing his lips and stretching across his forehead startled her. Billy had always looked at least a decade younger than his actual age, but it seemed that'd caught up with him—he hadn't aged well in the last three years. Not nice, but true.

"Billy."

He gave her an awkward hug. "Glad you could make it." He glanced over at Brandt. "Luke. Good to see you."

Both she and Brandt froze.

Billy wasn't aware he'd made a misstep.

"Luke died about two years ago, remember? This is Luke's brother, Brandt McKay. Brandt, this is Billy Reynolds."

They shook hands.

"Sorry about that," Billy said. "Sometimes I think I've landed on my head too many times and my memory is goin'."

Or you don't give a shit about what's going on in my life.

Acting like a ten-year-old, much, Jessie?

Brandt placed his palm in the small of her back. "Got time to have a Coke or something before you ride, Billy?"

"Sure." They walked to the concession area in silence.

Well, besides Billy stopping every fifteen feet to chat with someone he knew. Not once in those dozen or so times did Billy bother to introduce Jessie to his friends. So by the time they actually sat down, Jessie was wound so tight that one more snip to her tightly held control and she'd unravel.

Brandt's touch stayed steady. He held her hand, or put his arm around her shoulders, or on her back, or on her thigh beneath the table. His support was absolute.

Billy had always been a man of few words, at least around her, so Jessie was taken aback when he started a conversation without prompting. "How's your mother?"

"Good. She's living in Riverton with Roger."

He nodded. "Happy to hear it. She's a great lady. Ain't a day that goes by that I don't wish..." He offered a sheepish smile. "Anyway, it don't matter."

"Have you heard from Josie?" Jessie asked.

"Off and on. For a while it seemed I saw her all over the damn place. And in the weirdest places."

"Like she was following you or something?" she said, only half-jokingly.

"Yeah. For the life of me, I couldn't figure out why. It wasn't like she was competing or dating a professional rodeo cowboy or nothin'."

Professional rodeo cowboy. Sounded like a misnomer, but Jessie kept her mouth shut because it was probably just her bitterness about Billy considering himself a professional when he'd spent his entire adult life broke, on the road, chasing a dream. Didn't sound very professional to her.

"I shudder to think she's become one of them trashy buckle bunnies that follows the rodeo from town to town."

"Maybe Josie just wants to learn more about your life on the road," Jessie suggested.

Billy scowled. "Why? She's a grown woman. She oughta have a life of her own, not worrying about mine. Or checkin' up on me."

Rather than argue, Jessie sipped her Coke.

Brandt asked, "So isn't the rodeo season about wound down?"

"Yeah. Already been decided who's competin' in Vegas for the NFR. I came awful damn close to makin' the cut, but fell short." He shrugged. "There's always next year."

How many times had she heard that?

But Brandt wasn't easily sidelined. "What do you do in the off season?"

Billy squinted. "Off season? Ain't no off-season in rodeo. Even if some of the events ain't got a qualifying purse, there's always some place havin' an expo or a one day event. So while I'm waitin' for the season to get back into full swing, I'm tryin' to get on as many broncs as I can to improve my buck off percentage for next year. Tryin' to put a little jingle in my pocket that ain't comin' from my spurs."

The rodeo announcer tested the PA system.

Brandt stirred his soda.

Jessie fiddled with her straw.

Billy smiled. "Speakin' of jingle…"

Not a very smooth transition, Jessie thought, but subtle never fit Billy. "Yeah?"

"Any chance you could help your old dad out?"

Dad. Right. He'd insisted she call him Billy round about the time he'd left her mom. "Whatcha need?"

He leaned forward, the portrait of sincerity. "The transmission went out on my truck. It's at a repair shop here in Gillette, but I'm a couple hundred short on the repair bill."

So. This requested meet up with Billy wasn't spur of the moment. He'd called her because he wanted something. Money.

Like that's news, Jessie.

She couldn't resist poking him. "How long has it been in the repair shop?"

"Since Wednesday. Damn thing blew up right after I got to town. Luckily, I rode well Friday night and ended up in first. Last night I finished second. I'm guaranteed a top five finish today even if I get throwed on my ass. If I finish first overall, it oughta be enough cash to get my truck back. But I ain't countin' on it, because them stock contractors brought seriously rank stock for the finals today. I'd rather be safe than sorry, instead of worrying I'll have to scrub oil pans or something to get my rig outta hock, know what I mean?"

He'd been around for four days and hadn't bothered to call her. That stung worse than the fact he was hitting her up for cash.

No. That stung like hell too.

Brandt stopped caressing Jessie's leg beneath the table and reached in the back pocket of his jeans.

She didn't try to stop Brandt from opening his wallet. She didn't give a shit if her protest would've hurt Billy's feelings, but she'd never point out to Brandt that his show of generosity was for a man who didn't deserve it.

He tossed three hundred dollar bills on the table and two fifties. "I have a cousin who's on the road as a professional bull rider, so I know how tough it is when cash is tight. I'd like to think someone would help him out if he needed it."

Billy neatly folded the bills and shoved them into his threadbare wallet. "Thanks, man. I appreciate it. I really do. And I'm considering this a loan, 'cause I will pay you back. Every penny. My word is good as gold. Ask anyone 'round here."

Liar. She noticed Billy didn't tell Brandt to ask *her* if his word was good.

"I'll hold you to that," Brandt said without much conviction.

"So, what's your cousin's name?" Billy asked with feigned interest, because even as self-absorbed as he was, he understood it'd be rude to take Brandt's money and run. "Maybe I know him."

"Chase McKay. He's in the PBR."

"Never heard of him."

Another lie. With as much as Billy Reynolds lived and breathed the world of rodeo, he had to've heard of Chase, since Chase McKay ranked as one of the top fifteen bull riders in the world.

"Yeah, well, he's an up and comer," Brandt said.

They chatted politely about nothing.

Jessie tuned them out. She was too busy wondering if everyone saw *hopeful sucker* stamped on her forehead or if it was as invisible as she was.

Billy's, "Wow, look at the time," brought Jessie back to their conversation. "I gotta stretch out before my ride."

"Understood." Brandt thrust his hand across the table. "Good meetin' you, Billy."

"You too Brandt. Take good care of my girl."

God. Just stop pretending I ever meant anything to you. Stop pretending you care now. You got what you wanted.

"Will do."

"Jessie, it was great seein' you. I hope we'll cross paths again soon."

"Give 'em hell on those broncs today, Billy."

"Always." As he shuffled away, she noticed he didn't have the same spring in his step as he used to. Maybe the years beating the shit out of his body had finally begun to take its toll.

It was ironic Billy's favorite saying, *you reap what you sow,* popped into her head at that moment.

Jessie and Brandt sat side by side, in silence, for several long minutes. Watching people passing by. Inhaling the scents of popcorn, nachos, hot dogs and mini-donuts drifting from the concession stand. Feeling the anticipation in the air because rodeo kick off time neared.

When Brandt rubbed her back in a show of support, she had the overwhelming urge to bawl. Instead, she said, "Let's go home."

His hand stilled. "You don't want to stay for the performance?"

"I've just seen Billy Reynolds' best performance today, so let's call it good and get the hell out of here."

Brandt didn't say anything until they were out of the arena, in the truck and back on the road. "You okay?"

"No. I'm such a fucking idiot. I can't believe I fell for his bullshit. I should've gone with my first instinct and told him I was too busy today to drive to Gillette. Now, we've wasted a few hours and you're out four hundred bucks." She sighed. "Which I will pay you back for, of course."

"Like that's my biggest goddamn concern right now, Jessie," he snapped. "How long has this been goin' on?"

"What? A man only showing up when he needs something from me? My whole goddamn life."

His lips flattened.

Jessie didn't bother to assure Brandt he was the exception because he wasn't.

She expected he'd push her to talk, but he didn't. Not for several miles. Then he simply said, "I've been tryin' to think if you've told me anything about your childhood. About Billy."

"Not much to tell. My mom was a single parent until she met Billy. He charmed her, bedded her and wedded her. He adopted me the same year my sister Josie was born. You saw him today, Brandt. He's always been that way. Around when he wanted something, gone when he didn't."

"Have you ever met your biological father?"

What a loaded question. She knew where Brandt was going with this line of questioning. "No. My mom put 'father unknown' on my birth certificate because he'd washed his hands of her when she found out she was pregnant with me." She pressed her fingers against her burning eyes and managed a laugh. "Sounds like I have abandonment issues, huh? My 'real' dad bailed on me. Billy bailed on me. But with Luke...he mentally checked out of our relationship before he physically left. So I'll argue it was different with him. He abandoned me *before* he died."

"Not every man is like that."

"All of them in my experience have been. So that's all I know."

Another line of logic Brandt couldn't dispute.

"Jess—"

Jessie held up her hand. "Please. No more. I have a splitting headache and the glare off the snow is making it worse. I need to close my eyes for a bit."

Brandt didn't look too happy, but he said, "All right."

And she must've been more drained than she'd thought because she slept all the way to Brandt's house.

Chapter Fourteen

Brandt waited in the visitation room of the women's correctional facility in Lusk, wondering if he looked calmer than he felt. It seemed a bad sign, Samantha requesting this meeting, especially when she'd indicated that she didn't want him to bring Landon.

The door opened and Samantha shuffled in. She wasn't handcuffed or shackled, but the neon orange jumpsuit dwarfed her. No doubt Samantha Johnston was a beautiful girl—Brandt still had a hard time thinking of her as a woman. She had milk pale skin and dark brown, almost black hair. But her eyes were the palest shade of blue he'd ever seen. Her eastern European heritage was evident in her facial bone structure. With her slight frame, she looked like a good, stiff wind would knock her over. Striking as she was, she just looked so damn...young.

Samantha slid into the chair, clasping her hands in front of her on the table. "Brandt. Thanks for coming."

"No problem. Is it stupid to ask how you're doin'?"

She shrugged. "I'm doing...all right. Except I hate the food. I hate the mandatory therapy sessions. I hate we're locked down so early at night because I'm a night owl. But I don't mind working in the laundry. At least it smells clean in there. And they've got a computer in the classroom so I've been trying to figure out what to do with my life when I get outta here."

"Anything in particular jumping out at you?"

"Not yet. Since I've got my GED I'm allowed to check out the courses at the community colleges. Being's they're real big on rehabilitating us here."

A guard poked her head in. She nodded to Brandt and the door shut with an ominous thud and a series of clicking locks.

They only had so much time, and Brandt wasn't the type to make idle chitchat, especially with someone he didn't know very well. "So why didn't you want me to bring Landon along for this visitation?"

Samantha bit her lip, focusing on her ragged fingernails. "I can't believe it's been more than a month since I've seen him. Time is totally different in here."

"I imagine."

"I—I miss him. Don't get me wrong, I want to see him. I'm sure he's grown bigger and he's changed already. But I don't think if he came to visit that I could stand to give him back at the end of the hour." A tear fell on the table. "As much as he's a part of my life and being apart from him is the hardest thing I've done...it's surreal. It might sound strange, but I try *not* to think about him because without having him here, it's almost like he doesn't exist. And that's way easier."

Brandt had no idea how he was supposed to respond. On one hand, it sounded like she'd already started to phase Landon out of her life. On the other hand, it sounded like the only way she could deal with the separation was with the "out of sight, out of mind" philosophy.

When he stayed quiet too long, she said, "You think I'm horrible, don't you?"

"I honestly don't know what to think, Samantha, beyond the fact you're in a bad situation that won't improve for at least another three months."

"A bad situation of my own making," she said with a sneer.

Not touching that one.

"Sorry. That's one thing about being locked up in here. I've got all this time to think." Her smile wasn't convincing. "So tell me about what Landon's been doing."

Brandt relaxed. "He had a rough time at first, but we got a pretty good handle on it. He goes to daycare on Mondays, Wednesdays and Fridays, and my mom takes him the other two days of the week. My brothers Tell and Dalton have helped out. Landon is crazy about dogs."

"Who has a dog?"

"Jessie."

Samantha looked at him, eyes narrowed. "Jessie? As in Luke's wife, Jessie?"

"Yeah. Why?"

"You didn't tell me that Luke's wife was gonna be one of the people taking care of *my* child, Brandt."

He racked his brain, trying to remember if he'd mentioned Jessie to Samantha. No, he hadn't, because the idea hadn't occurred to him until after Samantha had gone to jail. "Last time we spoke, I didn't exactly have a firm plan in place, besides keeping Landon out of foster care. And since Landon is bein' well cared for while you're in jail, I don't see how Jessie helping out is a problem."

"Not a problem? I have a problem with it. A big problem. What if she—"

"What if she's doin' a damn good job?" Brandt supplied.

She fell back in her chair, arms folded over her chest. "Yeah. Maybe that's what I'm worried about. That she'll be a better mother than me. And between her, your parents and your brothers, they'll try to take Landon away."

He counted to ten—any outburst would send the guards in—but he wanted to shake Samantha until her teeth rattled. "You left Landon's care in my hands and my control. I promised you I'd do everything to keep that from happening."

Samantha didn't answer; she just went back to gnawing on her nails.

The need to get out of there was almost suffocating him.

Can you imagine how Samantha feels? Knowing she can't just leave whenever she wants?

"Is there anything else?" Brandt prompted. "Because we're about outta time."

"I don't suppose you've got a pack of cigarettes on you?"

"Can't help you there."

"I figured you'd be more the Copenhagen type anyhow." Samantha sighed heavily. "Thank you. I'm sure it sounds like I don't appreciate all you've done, and all you're doing, but I do. I really do. I just can't wait to get out of this place and get back to my life."

He waited for her to add that she couldn't wait to get back to her kid, but she didn't.

"As far as the next visitation?" he asked.

She met his eyes. "I'm not being melodramatic when I say skip it. I know it's a drive for you. And the holidays are coming up. I don't think I could stand to see him, knowing..." Her eyes flooded with tears and she glanced away. "Maybe after Thanksgiving and Christmas I'll be ready for him. I'll let you know. I get phone privileges soon so I can call you." Samantha stood and knocked on the glass partition. The guard let her out and she didn't look back.

Brandt wasn't sure how long he sat there, his gut churning with the thought that maybe this situation with Landon wasn't as temporary as he'd been telling everyone.

He didn't call Jessie until he was close to his house. As much as he appreciated she didn't ask questions about how it'd gone with Samantha, he needed someone to talk to.

But who? He couldn't have a rational discussion with his parents or his brothers. His married cousins with kids weren't options either. If he talked to Kane's wife, Ginger, she'd probably urge him to prepare for legal action to ensure Landon wasn't in limbo—even if his mother was.

Brandt ended up driving to his cousin Ben's place. In addition to knowing his stuff about ranching, Ben was a damn fine carpenter. It'd taken him six years, but he'd designed and built his log cabin home from the ground up. This house sparked Brandt's envy like no other house in the vast McKay family. Not only was it spacious with three bedrooms and two baths, including a master bath with a hot tub and a walk-in shower, and a kitchen that boasted every possible amenity, it was rugged, a real guy's space. Animal trophy heads lined the walls. A gigantic game room dominated the layout, with a huge big-screen TV surrounded by comfy couches, and a regulation gaming table that'd comfortably host ten card players. A fully loaded, fifteen-foot hand-carved wooden bar, a pool table, and an electronic dartboard. Just outside the garage was a detached woodshop and a metal barn. No one blamed Ben for being such a homebody when he had a home like this.

There was the rumor that his playboy cousin had never brought the same woman back to his house twice. A rumor Ben wouldn't confirm or deny, which is probably why it lived on in the annals of McKay legend.

Ben ambled out, his dogs Ace and Deuce at his heels, as always. "Brandt. Surprised to see you. What's up?"

"Nothin' much. Just drivin' by and thought I'd stop to see if you had time for a beer."

"Sure. You wanna come in? Or you wanna head into town?"

Brandt grinned. "Cuz, your bar puts any bar within a hundred miles to shame."

Ben grinned back. "That is true. I was just about to crack a cold one anyway."

The dogs followed them back inside and stretched out in front of the wood stove. Brandt parked himself on a barstool and Ben grabbed two Fat Tire beers from the fridge behind the bar. He slid one to Brandt, leaning his elbows on the counter.

"So, you wanna exchange bullshit about our families, you ask me how Quinn's new baby girl Amelia is doin', or how Chase's season is goin' in the PBR. Then I ask you if Dalton and Tell are still banging the Beaumont twins. Or how fuckin' bizarre it is that Luke fathered a kid with some teenage chick right before he died. Or do you wanna cut the crap and tell me the real reason you stopped by?"

Brandt laughed. Ben always got straight to the point, which was probably why he'd shown up here. He took a long pull off his beer. "To be honest, I ain't exactly sure why I'm here. I just got done talkin' to Samantha, Landon's mom, and she left me with a feeling I can't shake."

"Like what?"

"Like...maybe she's gotten used to bein' away from Landon and would like to continue that when they let her out of jail."

Ben whistled. "No shit?"

"That's the thing. Samantha didn't come right out and say it, I don't even know if she was hinting around or if I somehow misread it. And it ain't like I can talk to anybody in my family about it."

"What about Jessie?"

"Her stipulation was no information on Samantha for the duration of this temporary situation. So if it turns out to be a longer temporary situation than four months, and if Samantha decides she'd rather let us raise Landon..." He sighed. "Us, meaning me raising Landon with some help from Dalton, Tell and my mom." When Ben lifted a questioning brow, Brandt shook his head. "No fuckin' way will I let Landon live with my father."

"And how does Aunt Joan feel about that?"

"We're on the same page, since she's sneaking outta the house one day a week to watch Landon as it is."

"What?"

"She's takin' care of him at her house on Tuesdays, but on Thursdays she tells dad she's volunteering for some church thing when she's really at my place."

"Why the lie?"

"Because my dad..." He took a drink of beer. "Mom told me she had to go out for an hour and when she got back, Landon was screaming bloody murder in his crib to the point he threw up all over himself. Seems my dad just sat on his ass in the living room and ignored him. Dad's excuse? The kid needed to learn early on that he wasn't gonna get his way by screamin' his fool head off." His father's justification was seriously scary shit. "Jesus. Landon is barely more than a baby. And my dad's attitude is Landon is acting manipulative? At seventeen months?"

Ben pointed with his beer bottle. "How would it be bad if you ended up bein' Landon's guardian? I mean, it's obvious you care about the kid."

He didn't answer. Didn't know how to without coming across as a pansy ass whiner.

Ben whistled again. "This has to do with Jessie, doesn't it?"

"Yeah. I'd have to choose, Ben. And how the fuck do I do that? Choose between the only living part of Luke I'll ever have or the only woman I've ever..." He scowled. Way to be a pansy-ass.

"I ain't gonna point out the obvious end to that statement, but maybe you'd better tell me what's goin' on with you and Jessie? And how long has it been goin' on?"

"Since the moment I saw her." Brandt drained his beer. Ben uncapped a fresh one and set it in front of him. "Thanks."

"No problem. Keep talking."

"You sure you wanna hear this? It's old news."

"Maybe in your family it is, but I've never heard it."

"Luke and I were at the Devil's Tower Rodeo and Jessie was there. I noticed her first, something about her just...hit me. Anyway, like a total dumbass, I pointed her out to Luke. And Luke, bein' the handsome fuckin' cowboy charmer he was, got to her first, which meant I didn't stand a chance. So over the next month I had to listen to every goddamned detail of how Luke seduced her. Don't get me wrong, Luke liked her, probably because she was so different from the type of women he usually dated."

"Meaning what?"

"She wasn't trashy or wild. I think Luke saw a lot of our mom in Jessie. I also think he would've gotten tired of her, but he knocked her up. They got married, she lost the baby, and then my brother started stepping out on her."

"Fuck that. I'm sorry Brandt, but that's bullshit. If he didn't wanna be married to her, he should've asked for a divorce."

"That's what I told him. And Tell told him. And Dalton told him. Hell, my dad kept tellin' Luke to divorce Jessie, too, but Luke took extreme joy in doin' the exact opposite of what Dad wanted, as often as possible. Jessie was caught in the middle. So was I.

"Cut to me stepping in and tryin' to fill Luke's shoes after he died. So about a year later, I spilled my guts to her—yes, I was sober—and goddamn if she didn't give me the 'friend' speech. I licked my wounds and tried like hell to erase her from my memory by becoming the wild McKay I'd never been."

"But it didn't work?"

"Not even fuckin' close. After she agreed to help me take care of Landon, things have changed between us. In a good way. Now I've got her in my life and in my bed and I don't want it to be a temporary fling. But it won't happen if I become Landon's permanent guardian. So yeah, I'm fucked." Brandt swallowed a drink of beer. "Ain't ya glad you asked?"

Ben laughed. "*As the McKay World Turns*, huh?"

"Yeah. I'm just glad all this shit isn't common knowledge with our McKay relatives, although they can probably put the pieces together now that Luke's illegitimate love kid has surfaced."

"You might be freakin' out over nothin', Brandt. From what I understand, Samantha changing her mind is the worst case scenario."

"True. But in my experience? It's always the worst case scenario that plays out."

Ben returned with another beer for himself.

"So...got any advice?"

"Nope." He swigged his beer and then grinned. "That's not exactly true. I'm more of an observation type guy, so I'll tell you how I see it. You're asking yourself what you'd have to sacrifice to keep her. But why wouldn't she have to sacrifice something in order to be with you? Unless she owns up to a few things, seems you're back to being a in one-sided situation and she still has all the power."

Going round and round with this was pointless. Brandt switched gears. "What the fuck happened to Chase in Dallas?"

"You saw him getting tossed into the air and that bull dancin' the cha-cha on his back?"

Brandt nodded. "If he ain't still pissing blood after that kidney shot, he's got my vote for Iron Man of the Year."

"He's got my vote for dumbass of the year. Here he's havin' the best year of his career and he had a chance to finish in the top fifteen at the world finals. After that last wreck, the sports med doc warned him to drop out. He did, but in his free time while he's supposed to be healin' up, Chase has gotten into some...compromising positions with a couple of buckle bunnies. Naturally, their phones had cameras and they caught the whole raunchy performance on video. Which they posted on YouTube. Get this: He's already got a huge fan club, but since this happened, his PR woman can't keep up with the media requests for interviews. The women are freakin' out about seein' the almighty, bull riding great Chase McKay...buck-assed nekkid."

"First I've heard of it. What's Chase doin' about it?"

"Lapping up the media attention like the whoremonger bad boy he is. Which means the idiot is still goin' out every night, getting drunk and getting laid. I ain't upset he pissed away the world finals by getting on a bull he had no business getting on, but if he doesn't take his rehab seriously, he's gonna end up with a permanent injury."

Brandt believed Chase would get his shit together, but he also understood Ben's concern for his little brother. "Tell said you guys are headed to Vegas for the NFR?"

"Yeah. I hadn't planned on goin', but since Tell is doin' the judges course, I can stay with him. Plus, Chase is gonna be there, and he's so fucking scrambled he wants to talk to the PRCA folks about what they'll do for him if he switches to the PRCA bull riding program. Quinn can't go beat some sense into him because Libby has her hands full with Adam and Amelia, so I've been drafted."

"If Quinn needs help while you're gone, have him holler."

"Will do."

"I better head out. Thanks for the beer."

"Don't mention it. Anytime you need to bend my ear again just come on by. Quinn's preoccupied with Libby and the kids these days, and Chase is never around. I spend most of my day talkin' to the damn cattle or my dogs, so I appreciate you stopping by."

Brandt never considered that Ben might be lonely. God knew he'd be lonely if Tell and Dalton suddenly developed other interests. "Will you be around for poker night? It's at Cord's, which means we'll have good eats while he's kickin' our ass."

"That sly fucker won eighty bucks from me last time."

"Here's some advice for you, cuz. Stay away from the poker tables while you're in Vegas."

"Why's that?"

"Because your poker face is for shit."

Ben smirked. "Or maybe that's just what I want you guys to think."

Chapter Fifteen

Jessie was chopping green peppers for the batch of Spanish rice when Brandt pulled up. He'd been gone longer than she expected. But she wouldn't grill him about it because she remembered how crazy Luke got if she'd asked him too many questions.

Brandt is not Luke.

No kidding. She'd barely scratched the surface on learning what made Brandt tick.

Sex, definitely. Lots of sex. Lots of juicy, hot, mind-blowing sex.

Brandt stepped into the tiny entryway to take off his coat, boots and hat. In that order. Then he looked at her with the dimpled smile that made her belly flutter. "Hey. That smells good."

"Just Spanish rice, nothing fancy."

He looked around the living room. "Landon asleep?"

"Yeah. I know it's probably crazy to put him down this late, but he was really crabby."

"Sorry I wasn't here to help. I ended up stopping at Ben's place on the way home and we had a couple of beers."

Jessie smiled, appreciating he'd told her his whereabouts. "No need to explain, but I'm glad you did."

Brandt crossed into the kitchen, lowering his mouth to hers for a blistering kiss. He tasted of beer and need.

This sweet, hot man could wind her up in no time flat. She returned his kiss with equal fervor, loving his deep groan as she pressed her body to his and twined her arms around his neck. She felt him harden against her belly. Then Brandt clamped his hands on her butt, hoisting her up so her legs circled his hips.

He walked to the bedroom, breaking the liplock as he set her on the bed. "Damn, woman, kissing you almost makes me forget I have a splitting headache."

His face was pale. And his eyes had that squinty look she associated with pain. Any thoughts of getting nekkid with him vanished. "Would you like me to rub your neck to see if it'll help your headache?"

"Nah. That's okay. You don't have to."

"I want to." She laid her hand on his cheek. His skin seemed hotter than normal. "While you strip down to more comfy clothes, I'll throw the peppers in the pan and be right back."

"Okay."

Brandt must be in pain if he didn't argue.

In the kitchen, Jessie scooped the diced peppers into the hamburger and tomato mixture. She added a cup of rice before putting the lid on and turning the burner to low. After washing her hands, she checked on Landon and returned to the bedroom.

Oh. Lordy. Would you look at that? A half-naked, muscled cowboy hottie stretched out on her bed. Brandt had taken her strip down suggestion literally; he only wore his boxers.

He turned his head as she climbed on the bed. "I probably oughta be givin' you a neck rub."

"You've given me plenty of backrubs. It's payback." She sat on his butt, tucking her knees by his sides. "Mind if I sit like this?"

"Hell no. If you don't mind knowin' that you sittin' on me like that is gonna give me wood. Guaranteed."

She chuckled and splayed her hands across his upper shoulders. ·

"Ah, sweet Jesus, Jess, that feels so damn good."

"Close your eyes and relax, Brandt."

He muttered, "Bossy thing," and rested the side of his face on the bed.

Jessie worked his shoulders, digging her thumbs into knotted muscles. His headache probably stemmed from the tight points all over his back, not just his neck. She attempted to loosen them, paying particular attention to the area around his spine.

She let herself enjoy touching him, her hands pulling, pushing and smoothing his skin. The musculature of his back had ridges and dips and hollows, forged from hours of physical labor he did every day. Yet that same flesh was pliant. It gave way beneath her kneading fingertips. And the scent of his skin... God, she wanted to bury her nose between his shoulder blades and fill her lungs with all that masculine goodness. Rub her face against his taut flesh, wearing the scent of his skin on hers. Press her lips to his spine and follow the length with her tongue down to his tailbone, tasting his heat and sweat.

Brandt exhaled a contented sigh.

That sigh emboldened her. She gently turned his head to reach the other side of his neck, resting her hands around the base of his throat, working her thumbs from his nape to his hairline. In that position, Jessie had to squeeze her thighs against his side as she leaned over him.

She had no idea how long she'd been lost in massaging him, when a rumbling sound vibrated the fingers on his throat.

Maybe that noise was his polite way of telling her she'd been pressing too hard.

"Am I hurting you?"

"No. It feels so goddamn good. Too good if you know what I mean."

Ah. He was hard. Because she'd been touching him. A sense of feminine power arose and she nuzzled his ear. "I could work that muscle too."

Brandt chuckled. "You've already done enough."

"But I could do more." She teased his earlobe with her teeth, causing him to groan. "Let me touch you. Let me wrap my hand around your cock and get you off."

"Really?"

Why did he sound so surprised? "Really." Jessie swung her leg over his left side so she no longer straddled him. "Lift up so I can take your boxers off."

He pushed up and she slid her hand across his belly, making sure the head of his penis didn't catch in the elastic waistband.

Jessie impulsively placed a kiss on each of his butt cheeks. "My God. All that time in the saddle does amazing things for your butt. I always knew you looked good in Wranglers? But cowboy? You look even better out of them."

"How long have you been eyeing my ass?"

She shrugged. "Quite a bit in the last month, truthfully. Lay on your side. Now reach up and grab the headboard with your left hand. Good. Put your right palm flat on the mattress and brace yourself."

"Literally brace myself?"

"Yep." Jessie grabbed the lube off the dresser and liberally coated her right hand. As she stretched out behind him, she wished she'd stripped because she couldn't get enough of that delicious skin-to-skin sensation. She layered her left arm alongside his, gripping his wrist to anchor herself. Then she reached her right hand over his hip and curled her fingers around the root of his cock, while kissing the slope of his shoulder.

Brandt sucked in a quick breath.

"Tell me how you like it. Slow and teasing like this?" She slid her slippery hand from the base to the tip, sweeping the pad of her thumb under the sweet spot on the upstroke. "Or fast like this?" Keeping her hand a tight fist, she moved up and down the length rapidly.

"Jesus. That feels amazing."

"Fast it is."

He groaned, "That's it," when she found the right rhythm and speed.

Jessie kissed his nape while she stroked him, pleased how the skin on his arms broke out in goose flesh beneath her questing lips. She explored the tendons in his neck with her tongue. Her teeth grazed the ball of his shoulder and he twitched, head to toe.

"Woman you're killin' me. I'm not gonna last."

"I don't want you to last. I want you to come." She increased her tempo, and immediately his butt muscles clenched against the cradle of her hips.

"Jess—"

"Don't hold out on me, Brandt. I wanna feel your cock jerking beneath my fingers. Give it up for me."

He came with a low grunt, hips bucking as he spurted into her hand.

Jessie continued to squeeze his cock, kissing his back, wondering what to do with her sticky hand.

Brandt rolled over and handed her his boxers. "Here. Use these."

"Thank you." She discreetly wiped her hand and tossed his underwear toward the hamper. "Is your headache gone now?"

"One of them is." Brandt managed a small smile but a hint of pain lingered in his eyes. "Thanks, Jess. I should return the favor—"

Slightly annoyed, she said, "I didn't touch you because I wanted something in return, Brandt. I did it because touching you any way I please makes me happy. Very happy." Jessie placed a kiss above his heart. "Close your eyes because I can see that headache is dogging you."

Landon woke up in a better mood. He'd gotten less picky with food, and ate some of the hamburger and rice, a slice of bread and half a can of mandarin oranges. The instant he was out of his high chair, he shrieked, "Goggie!" and made a beeline for Lexie, who allowed Landon to pet and hug her...for about two minutes.

Jessie was hungry but she waited for Brandt. She did mundane things, started a load of clothes, scoured the highchair tray, let Lexie outside. Then let Lexie back inside, trying to keep Landon from opening the door and following the dog.

Thinking she had a minute to rest, Jessie sat on the couch. Right away Landon scrambled beside her, dragging his new fleece blanket from Grandma Joan and his favorite book about farm animals.

"You want me to read to you?"

Landon blinked at her.

She held up the book. "If you want me to read this, Landon, say yes."

He nodded.

She laughed. "No way, lil' buckaroo. You're not getting away with that nonverbal communication stuff so young. Say yes."

His fingers worried the fringe on the blanket and stared at

her pitifully, but he didn't utter a peep.

"Okay. Fine. If you don't wanna read the book..." Jessie set the book on the coffee table. She hated to play hardball, but Landon needed to work on his verbal skills, rather than grunting, pointing and shrieking to get what he wanted.

He yelled, "No!" and scooted off the couch, grabbing the book and shoving it at Jessie.

"We've been working on this for a while, Landon. Do you want me to read the book? Then say *yes*." She said "Yes" as she nodded her head.

Landon nodded and said, "Yef."

Jessie clapped. "Yes! Yay Landon! See? You can talk. You just need someone to force you to do it." She opened the book. Before she read a single word, Landon crawled into her lap, blanket under one arm as he cuddled against her.

Her heart turned over. Landon's unexpected sweetness and neediness had the power to undo her from her *just another daycare kid* mindset. So it seemed natural to brush her lips across the top of his dark head. She read, "Farmer George has one cow." She stopped. "Heh, he's not much of a rancher is he, with only one cow?"

"No."

She laughed and continued reading. "But Farmer George has lost his cow. Can you help him find it?" She pointed on the page to a cow hiding in the bushes. "Remember what a cow says? *Mmmoooo*." She drew out the word until it was about ten seconds long.

Landon giggled.

"Now Landon—" she poked his chest when she said his name, "—say *mmmoooo*."

"*Mmmoooo*."

Jessie clapped again. "Good job! You are gonna know all your barnyard noises in no time flat."

Usually Landon lost interest before they reached the end of a book, but tonight he stuck it out, although he was pretty squirmy at the end. When she closed the cover, Landon launched himself off the couch and ran straight to Brandt.

How long had he been lurking in the shadows? And why was she thinking it was a damn crying shame that he'd gotten dressed?

"Up!" Landon demanded.

But Brandt wasn't looking at Landon. He was looking at her with the softest expression. He broke eye contact when Landon bumped into his leg with another demanding, "Up!" and lifted the boy. "So I missed story time? Bummer."

Landon said, "*Mmmoooo.*"

Brandt grinned. "That'll come in handy when you're ridin' the range with us in a few years, trust me."

Jessie ignored Brandt's confident *in a few years* remark and asked, "Is your headache better?"

"Completely gone. Did you eat?"

"Not yet. I was waiting for you." Damn. Did that sound...needy?

Why are you so worried about Brandt's reaction? He's proven time and time again he's not like Luke.

"Thank you for waitin', Jess. I've eaten enough meals alone to last a lifetime."

There was proof of Brandt's openness. His willingness to just say what he felt. Jessie met his gaze again. "Me too. I'll dish up the plates."

Brandt strapped Landon in his high chair and poured him a sippy cup of milk. Then he set six animal crackers on the tray.

They waited to see how he'd react. Sometimes Landon calmly gummed his cookies and sipped milk. Other times he'd use the heavy bottom weight of the cup to smash the cookies into dust. If he was feeling ornery, or if he was tired, he'd slide his hand on the tray until he knocked every cookie to the floor. Then he'd usually whip the sippy cup too, and scream "No!" at the top of his lungs, arching his back, trying to throw himself out of the high chair.

Tonight Landon used both hands to drink and ignored the cookies.

Brandt tucked into his food. About five or six bites in, Jessie noticed he'd picked out all the green peppers and piled them off to the side. Feeling her curious gaze, he looked up. "What? Am I eatin' like a pig or something?"

"No, but you should've told me you didn't like green peppers." She realized she'd put green peppers in a lot of dishes. "I could've left them out of everything."

His neck flushed. "It's no big deal to eat around them. Especially when everything you fix is so good."

"Charmer. Anything else you don't like, foodwise, as long as we're on the subject?"

"Turnips, parsnips, radishes, beets, prunes, collard greens, Dijon mustard, strawberry ice cream. I could take or leave coconut. Same for cauliflower."

Jessie stared at him. "So a fall soup with root vegetables isn't a good idea?"

He smiled. "Nope. But if you made it I'd probably eat it anyway."

"Because you don't want to hurt my feelings?"

"No. Because any kind of food just seems to taste better when I'm eatin' it with you."

Sometimes the man was just so damn sweet.

Before she could formulate a decent response, Landon shrieked, "Goggie!"

Jessie attributed Lexie warming to Landon because the kid was a messy eater. The dog would park herself beside the high chair and clean up the floor as soon as Landon was done.

So why was she hearing *crunch crunch crunch* now?

Landon peered over the side of the tray at the dog and giggled. Then he grabbed another animal cracker and tossed it at Lexie.

Crunch crunch crunch and another giggle.

Brandt lifted his brows. "That's new."

"Uh-huh. Looks like Lexie will be elsewhere during meals because Landon will give *goggie* all his food in hopes she'll be his BFF."

"At least he hasn't figured out how to get the lid off his cup yet."

She jabbed her fork at him. "And you, Brandt McKay, have just jinxed us."

Landon's shrieks escalated when he ran out of cookies. Brandt ate the last bite on his plate and stood. "Okay, partner. You and me got a date with bubbles."

"No!"

"Yes." He unclipped the tray and set it on the counter.

"Yef," Landon repeated.

Brandt looked at her. "That's new too."

"I hope what I've been doing helps him. He's a little old for grunting and pointing to get what he wants."

He swung Landon onto his hip and smirked.

A smirk she recognized. "What?"

"That's what you reduced me to earlier. A grunting fool and you gave me exactly what I wanted."

"Grown men really do have the same mentality as seventeen month old toddlers."

Brandt grinned and headed to the bathroom.

Jessie cleaned up the kitchen and made four bottles. Landon was already down two bottles for the day, compared to the six he'd started with. Bath time had gotten better, but the kid really didn't like getting wet.

She heard Brandt's muffled voice and splashing as she passed by the bathroom. In her bedroom she noticed Brandt had draped his clothes over the top of the dresser, instead of leaving them piled on the floor. Another sign of his thoughtful nature—he didn't expect her to clean up after him.

She slipped on a camisole and her favorite pair of yoga pants. Granted, she hadn't attempted yoga, but she figured the pants were the best part anyway. She glanced longingly at the bed Brandt had recently occupied, rumpled sheets and the pillow held the indent of his head.

God. She'd missed having a warm male body beside her. Luke hadn't been snuggly, so it thrilled her that Brandt slept entangled with her all night. Every night. Without exception. She'd stopped wearing pajama bottoms to bed because Brandt kept her plenty warm. Plus, it was handy when he woke her up to have his wicked way with her.

Powerful stuff, how much he always wanted her. Even now, the thought of his ragged breath teasing her nape, or his mouth tasting the line of her shoulder, or his rough hands stroking her arms, her belly, and her breasts made her wet and achy. There was an odd sort of comfort in the way he touched her in the wee small hours. Almost like a compulsion. An addiction. Sometimes he'd just caress her with a feather light touch until she was ready to crawl out of her skin.

Other times he'd start kissing her neck and keep moving south until his mouth was between her thighs. Definitely erotic, feeling him sucking and licking her sex when she couldn't see his head beneath the covers and she was still floaty in that morning sleep haze.

"Jess?"

Her cheeks flamed when she looked at him, standing in the doorway with Landon on his hip. "Ah. What? I was just changing."

He smirked. He knew exactly what she'd been thinking about. And to add fuel to the fire, his gaze idly drifted over her, head to toe, with a blast of heat strong enough that she had to hold on to the dresser to keep from jumping him.

Landon grunted, breaking their connection. "Anyway, what did you need?"

"Nail clippers. Landon's fingernails and toenails are like claws."

"I'll get them." She couldn't resist kissing Landon's damp, rosy cheek as she passed by him. She couldn't resist pressing her mouth to Brandt's full lips.

Brandt's eyes held pure pleasure. "What was that for?"

She didn't say, *For turning me on in more ways than I ever dreamed possible.* Instead, she just gave him the same kind of smirk he'd given her.

Despite his late nap, Landon was tired and Brandt put him down at his usual time. She was in the kitchen, flipping through a cookbook, when Brandt moved in behind her.

"What's cookin'? Need any help heatin' things up?"

"You're funny. I'm looking for a recipe for a pear tart. I've got all these ripe pears I need to use up. And you seem to like sweet stuff."

"Mmm. I can think of one sweet thing in particular I like to eat. A lot."

Jessie blushed.

"I love it when you blush."

"I know, it gives me some color and I don't look so pasty white."

Brandt slapped her butt. "Don't say shit like that or I will spank you and turn your other cheeks red. It's sexy as hell how you'll let me do anything to your body that I want, but if I talk about it, you blush. But since you're usually dressed when I'm teasin' you, I wanna know if that blush covers your whole body." He kissed the section of skin below her ear. "So let's find out. Take your pants off."

"What? You can't possibly be—"

"Oh, I'm completely serious. And if you don't take them off, I will." He nipped her ear. "Now."

"But—"

"Huh-uh. You've got about three seconds."

Heart pounding, Jessie peeled down the yoga pants and kicked them aside.

He murmured, "Good to see you're goin' commando now."

"You're a bad influence on me, Brandt McKay."

"I beg to differ." His fingers traced the bottom edge of her lacy camisole, from the left side of her waist to the right side, causing her belly muscles to ripple inside and out. He gripped the edges and said, "Lift your arms," removing her camisole.

It was weird standing buck-ass nekkid in her kitchen, especially since Brandt was fully clothed. She started to turn around, but he boxed her in.

"Stay like this." He slid her hands to the edge of the countertop, slipping his knee between her legs in a signal to widen her stance. "Perfect."

"Brandt—"

"Trust me, Jess?"

It took about ten seconds, but she nodded.

"Good. Close your eyes. Relax."

She let her eyes drift shut, but she was in no way relaxed. His body shifted as he reached for something on the counter. Then his wonderfully rough hand glided down her bare stomach, stopping to cover her mound. His fingers stroked her cleft, teasing her folds until she felt herself growing wet, heavy with need.

His fingers vanished. Before she could protest, a cool, round object connected with her clit and she gasped, "What is that?"

"No fair peeking. Keep your eyes closed." Brandt steadily dragged it up and down her slit in a smooth glide that followed the contour of her sex from top to bottom. He whispered, "Does it feel good?"

"Yes."

His lips feathered hot, moist kisses across her neck. He circled her clit, never too hard, or too soft, exacting the ideal amount of pressure to keep her wanting more. Then he'd slide it

187

down to the juncture of her thighs, using her slick juices to slide back up.

Jessie noticed the rounded object was no longer cool, but warmed from friction against her body. It didn't feel as hard. It'd become soft, pliable.

"Imagine this is my cock riding your slit." He arced it from the opening of her body, up to the top of her pubic bone. Each stroke faster. Shorter. His breath stirred her hair and she had no problem imagining it was Brandt's cock gently driving her toward orgasm.

On the next upstroke, he brought that mysterious object up the center of her torso, between her cleavage, over the column of her throat to rest on her lips. She felt the stickiness of her juices, not only on her mouth, but in a trail from her chin to her bikini line.

Brandt growled in her ear. "Lick it."

Jessie's tongue darted out and she lapped up the taste of her own musky essence from the warm and rounded slope.

"Bite down."

Her teeth sank in, and the sweet, earthy taste of pear juice burst in her mouth. A moan escaped as she sucked at the fruit, greedily biting off a chunk of perfect ripeness. The flesh nearly melted against her tongue. The fruit flowed down her throat as she swallowed, but more juice spilled from her lips and dripped over her chin as she stole another juicy bite. And another. And another.

Brandt plucked the fruit away, spun her around and fused their mouths together. The taste of Brandt exploded on her tongue, mixing with the sweetness of the pear and the hint of her own juices. He sucked at her tongue, licking the soft depths of her mouth, guiding them to a new level of lust just with his potent kiss.

And then he gently pressed that squishy, sticky fruit to the top of her pubic bone until pear juice trickled down her cleft in a syrupy stream and dampened her thighs.

Jessie gasped at the sensation, breaking the kiss.

Brandt growled, leaving sucking kisses on the sticky trail down her body. He fell to his knees and buried his face in her pussy.

"Brandt! Oh God." Jessie's fingers scrabbled for purchase on the counter behind her as she attempted to hold on against his sensual assault.

Brandt's thumbs pulled the skin back to expose her clit. He lapped the juices—hers and the pear's—like a junkie. Thoroughly tasting every inch of her while that rumbling noise in his throat that vibrated against her swollen tissues.

When he switched to those flickering butterfly licks, she was toast. Her body shook with every orgasmic pulse. She might've gasped. Actually, she might've screamed. But she mostly couldn't hear anything over the blood pounding in ears that mimicked the throbbing goodness pounding in her groin.

It would've been embarrassing, how quickly she'd started to come after Brandt put his mouth on her, but the orgasm was so incredibly volatile that any lucid thought beyond *Yes! Yes! Yes!* didn't register at all.

Only when Brandt started kissing her quivering thighs did she float back to earth. She peeled her lids open and peered down at him.

Maybe she expected he'd be munching on the leftover chunk of pear with a gleam in his eye. But he had an even wilder look to him.

Keeping his fiery gaze on her, he ditched his sweatpants and smothered her mouth in another controlling kiss as he brought them down to the floor.

There were no sweet words. No asking permission. As Brandt scrambled her brain with savage kisses, he settled between her thighs, hiked her hips up and plunged inside her.

His lower body pumped into hers, and he attempted to pin her arms over her head, but Jessie twisted free of his grip, digging her nails into his ass as her legs circled his waist. Keeping him exactly where she wanted him.

Brandt slammed into her harder. Pushed her higher off the floor. The kiss became impossible to sustain, given the ferocity of his thrusts.

She canted her pelvis, changing his angle of entry so his every plunge brushed her clit. She hissed, "Yes. Like that."

He grunted, flexing his hips with enough velocity they skidded across the linoleum.

Jessie knew he was close, knew she needed to send him over in order to reach that pinnacle herself. She dragged her nails down his sweat-covered back, loving how the tactile sensation and the hint of pain always surprised him. Always drove him wild. Immediately his whole body shuddered as he started to come, bucking against her forcefully.

Brandt threw his head back and roared. God he was magnificent. Pure male animal.

Her interior muscles took over, tightening around his shaft, pushing her to the place where those rhythmic pulses reverberated throughout her entire being. She had the fleeting thought that this could easily become her sole reason for living—to find this sheer pleasure with this man. And she might've started speaking in tongues, because god knew she'd definitely been singing this man's praises, even if it sounded like gibberish.

His deep thrusts slowed. But didn't stop. Brandt buried his face in her neck and panted, still pumping into her. It was almost like he couldn't stop. Couldn't bear to break their connection.

Jessie ran her palms down his back of his flawlessly rounded butt cheeks. She pressed down in a silent signal for him to stop.

He lifted his head. His eyes were still wild.

She smiled. "Hey."

But Brandt didn't return her smile, nor did he bestow those yummy post-orgasm kisses she hungered for. No. A look of shock flitted through his eyes and he abruptly moved off her. So abruptly that his ass hit the floor. Hard. He jammed his hand across his scalp in a move that looked like he was adjusting his hat.

"Brandt?"

No answer.

"What's wrong?"

"Just...give me a second, okay?"

She pushed up on her elbows and let her toes slide up his shin. "You out of breath or something?"

His gaze swept over her body. Almost clinically. "Did I hurt you?"

"No. Why would you ask me that?"

Brandt looked away.

Jessie reached up and grabbed his chin, forcing his gaze back to her. "Why?"

"Why? Jesus, Jessie. Because I lost it. Completely. I took

you down and fucked you on the kitchen floor, for Christsake."

"So?" She stretched provocatively because she loved the way his focus immediately zoomed to her breasts. "You always mention my floor is clean enough to eat off of, why wouldn't it be okay to fuck on?"

He just stared at her.

Oh hell no. Was that...regret in his eyes?

"Don't piss me off, Brandt."

"Which brings up the question why aren't you pissed off at me for attacking you?"

"Because I liked it. Actually, I loved it. Not only did I love that I made you lose control, I loved the fact you were so hot to have me right then, that you didn't stop what you were doing, you didn't second guess what you were feeling, you didn't feel guilty. No. You fucked me on the floor. Hard and dirty. It was fucking spectacular and I don't regret a single second."

When he continued to wear that hangdog expression, she'd had enough. She started to get up, but Brandt brought her back down. Two hundred odd pounds of cowboy pinned her to the floor and got right in her face.

"For the record, that was the hottest sex ever. *Ever.* No regrets, Jessie. Just lookin' at you calms me. But just lookin' at you also revs me up."

She touched his face, letting the tips of her fingers follow that strong jawline. "That's good to hear even when I know it's hard for you to admit."

"I can be rough."

"You think I don't know that? I've known you for four years. I've seen that dark look in your eye and then you come back a day or two later bloody and bruised. I don't fault you for not wanting me to see that side of you, but I'm fully aware it's there."

He rested his forehead to hers. "You have no idea what it means to me to hear you say that."

"I think I do." She touched her lips to his in a gentle kiss.

"Come to bed with me, Jess," he murmured in her hair. "Let me show you my other side."

"Okay. But I think I might be stuck to the floor."

"Shit. Sorry." Brandt rolled and brought her to her feet. "Shower first."

"Deal."

Halfway down the hallway she snickered.

"What?"

"Isn't it ironic that I have pear-scented soap?"

Chapter Sixteen

"I really wish you'd reconsider and stay here for Thanksgiving, Jess. The roads in Wyoming ain't the best this time of year and I don't want you to get stranded someplace."

Jessie set her duffel bag by the door and snagged her winter coat off the coat rack. "I'll be fine. It'll be easier for everyone if I'm with my family. Besides, it's only three days." Driving to her mom's was preferable to staying by herself when Brandt took Landon to his parent's on Thanksgiving Day—since she hadn't been issued an invite. She'd spent last Thanksgiving alone, eating a microwaved turkey and dressing meal, watching reruns of holiday classics and bawling her eyes out about the pathetic state of her life. An experience she'd rather not repeat.

Brandt sighed. "Ain't no talkin' you out of this?"

"Nope." She buttoned her coat and slipped on her gloves. "Just double check that everything is shut off before you leave. I'll call you when I get there, okay?"

"Okay. But first...c'mere and give me some sugar." He curled his fingers around her lapels and tugged her closer.

Then he proceeded to turn her inside out with one of his long, drugging kisses, chock-full of passion, sweetness and heat. Boy howdy did Brandt's kisses pack a wallop. Her knees and her will went weak.

Until he chuckled against the corner of her mouth. "You sure that didn't change your mind?"

"Nope." She backed up and he released her. She reached for the duffel bag strap but Brandt firmly knocked her hand away and picked it up. She still wasn't used to all his gentlemanly quirks, but she really liked them.

But you could get used to them, couldn't you?

Yes.

She opened her truck door and whistled. Lexie's furry body was a blur as she leapt into the cab. Her tail wagged so hard it left wet prints on the passenger window.

Brandt hoisted the duffel into the truck bed. "Landon is gonna miss Lexie the next few days. Did you say goodbye to him?"

She wasn't sure how Landon would take it, given he sometimes screamed when Jessie left him with Brandt or vice versa. The last thing Brandt needed was a cranky, confused toddler. But Jessie suspected Brandt wouldn't see the logic in her decision not to give Landon an official goodbye, to tell him to be a good boy and all that parenting stuff, especially since she wasn't his parent. Yet, she didn't want Brandt to think she didn't care because she was starting to care too much and that scared the holy bejeezus out of her.

"Jess?"

Her gaze snapped to his. "Sorry. Give him a kiss for me, okay? I've gotta get on the road."

"Promise me you'll drive safe."

"I promise."

"Promise you'll call me as soon as you're at your mom's."

It was so sweet he worried about her. Had Luke ever obsessively worried about her like this? Not that she remembered. She smiled at him. "I promise."

Brandt kissed her again. "Have a Happy Thanksgiving."

"You too, Brandt." She slammed the door and backed out of her driveway. The last thing she saw as she turned the corner onto the main road was Brandt still standing on her steps, watching her go.

Luke definitely had never done that.

The drive from Moorcroft to Riverton was uneventful, with the exception of sporadic snow flurries drifting across the road. By the time she'd reached her mother's house, both she and Lexie were ready to get out of the truck. She texted Brandt rather than calling him.

When Jessie saw her mom standing in the doorway, she had the urge to run straight into her arms, like she had as a child. So it was no surprise to either of them she did exactly that.

Her mom hugged her tightly. "Jessie! It's so good to see you. I'm so glad you're here."

"Me too." No matter where they'd ended up living as she was growing up, her mom carried the scents Jessie associated with home; coffee, Aqua Net hairspray, double mint gum and Jergen's cherry-almond lotion. She inhaled deeply and sighed, happy that some things never changed.

"Come in. I've got a pot of coffee ready to go."

"Thanks, but I'm wired enough as it is." Jessie kicked off her boots, ditched her coat, hat and gloves. Then she wiped Lexie's paws. Her mom didn't mind pets in the house just as long as she didn't have to clean muddy paw prints out of her carpet.

"Where's Roger?"

"At the college. He'll be here later. He's trying to catch up on paperwork so he can have the whole weekend off."

Jessie didn't really know her mother's husband Roger Randolph very well. They'd met through the community college in Wheatland where he taught and she worked as an administrative assistant. By that time Jessie already lived on her own. Then she'd met Luke, married him and moved to the McKay ranch. About six months before Luke died, her mom and Roger had relocated to Riverton. Roger was a nice enough guy, and he seemed to make her mother happy, so that's all that mattered. "Is Josie coming?"

That gave her mother pause. "No. You haven't talked to her?"

"She doesn't exactly keep me on speed dial." Jessie's sister, Josie, had inherited her father's wanderlust. After years spent waiting for Billy to get off the road, her mother had finally divorced him the year Jessie turned twelve. The sad thing was, it hadn't affected Jessie's life because Billy hadn't been around much anyway.

But it'd affected Josie. Josie had romanticized her father and his lifestyle, so she took off right after she'd turned eighteen. It'd been a hard blow to their mother, and for that Jessie resented her younger sister. Any close relationship they shared vanished when Josie did.

"I talked to her last month," her mom said. "She's working

at a restaurant in Dallas."

No big stunner Josie was in cowboy country in Texas. Jessie couldn't muster interest in Josie's latest escapade and refused to pretend. She also refused to mention to her mother she'd seen Billy because she doubted she could be civil about him, either.

She wandered into the kitchen and snatched an oatmeal raisin cookie. Her eyes nearly bugged out at the three different kinds of pie, and cinnamon rolls, and brownies, and two different types of cookies—all homemade—that crowded the countertop.

"You want milk with that?"

Milk. Right. Jessie smiled. "Nope. I'd rather have a beer." She helped herself to one from the fridge. "Do you have time to sit down? Or are you still whipping up food for tomorrow?"

"I'm mostly done. Gotta get up and put the turkey in, glaze the hamballs and peel the potatoes, but I figured you could help me."

"Sure thing. How many people are you feeding?" She took a long pull off the Corona.

"Eight. Our friends Barb and Tim, our empty nest neighbors Rich and his wife Dawn, and Roger's new teaching assistant, Jake."

Jessie slowly lowered the bottle. "Mom. Please tell me you're not trying to fix me up with this Jake guy."

Her mother grabbed a dishrag and wiped cookie crumbs from the counter. "Not a fix up. But Jake is a really great guy. He's single, so are you. You're around the same age, I thought it'd be good for you to have someone show you around while you're here."

Regardless of what her mom claimed, this was a fix up. Although she and Brandt were exclusive while they were living together, this thing, whatever it was, was temporary.

You don't really believe that. There's more going on between you and Brandt than just hot sex. This thing could be the start of something big.

But her cynical side reminded her that there already was something very big between her and Brandt, something insurmountable: Landon's future.

"Jessie?" her mother prompted. "I see the wheels turning. What's going on?"

"Besides the fact I'm currently helping my former brother-in-law take care of my dead husband's secret love child from a jailbait jailbird? Oh, and just to make it even more interesting, I'm now sleeping with said brother in law."

After her mom picked her jaw up off the floor, she pointed to a dining room chair. "Sit and start talking. I'll get more beer."

Jessie knew her mother intended to grill her when she ditched her apron, embroidered with a big "L" for Lisa. Removal of the apron indicated the shift in parental roles from cookie and comfort giver to interrogator. She sipped her beer and waited for the barrage of questions.

It didn't take long.

"Did you end up in this situation with Brandt out of guilt?" Her mother raised her hand when Jessie began to object. "I know you're in the situation with Landon out of some obligation you feel to Luke."

Jessie ran her thumb along the edge of the sandstone coaster as she tried to figure out a way to explain it, when half the time she didn't understand it herself. "Being in such close quarters with Brandt felt different from the start. That everyday familiarity between us built pretty damn fast and in some ways, it was more intimate than sex. I missed that physical closeness, and since we were already acting like a married couple, I told him I wanted *all* of the benefits of being married."

"So you approached him?" her mother asked.

"Yes." Jessie swallowed a mouthful of beer. "Hard to believe, huh?"

"I'm happy you did. At least you're getting something you want out of this lousy situation. How you're able to handle..." She shook her head. "I don't know what I would've done if one of Billy's floozies would've shown up with a kid he'd fathered."

Her mom hadn't spoken of Billy's infidelities, but Jessie knew it'd been another reason she'd ended the marriage. Before she could answer, her mother laughed.

"See, I say that, but I probably would've done the exact same thing you did, Jessie."

"What? Caved in?"

"No." She leaned back in her chair. "In some ways hearing about Landon's mother reminded me...well, kinda like déjà vu."

"How so?"

"One day when you were about sixteen months, I was at my wit's end, with you, with my job, and this neighbor lady volunteered to take care of you for a couple of hours while I got control. At first I thought it was weird, but she told me someone helped her out when she was a young mother and she was just returning the favor. Her kindness over the next few months really changed a lot for me. For us."

Jessie was floored. "How come I never knew any of this?"

"Honestly? Because I'd forgotten about it. So many other things happened over the years. It came back to me when you said you were helping out with Luke's kid. So no, you're not a doormat, Jessie. No matter what Luke led you to believe."

She killed her beer. "Luke and I were headed for a divorce anyway."

"I know."

"I loved him. I'da done anything, let him get away with anything, been anyone he wanted me to be, just to keep him."

"I know that too, sweetie."

She held her fingers to her eyes to stem the tears. "God, Mom. I've had time to think, a lot, too much time probably, but one of the hardest parts of losing Luke was figuring out I'd lost myself too. I let him define me. And when he wasn't around to tell me who to be, I didn't know who the hell I was."

Silence fell and Jessie welcomed it.

Her mother cleared her throat. "And what about Brandt McKay? Are you letting him define you?"

Jessie shook her head. "Which might seem at odds with agreeing to help him take care of Landon. I'm not doing it for Brandt. I'm not even doing it for Luke. I'm doing it for that little boy, no matter if Landon ever knows it, no matter how hard it is. He needs me. I've already got a lot of regrets where Luke is concerned and I won't let ignoring this helpless kid be another one."

"Will you be able to let Landon go when the time comes?"

I don't know.

The door in the living room opened and Lexie started barking. Jessie grabbed her collar and issued a terse, "Stay."

"Lisa?"

"In the kitchen with Jessie, Roger."

Roger came through the door in stocking feet. Before he

acknowledged Jessie, he gave her mother a kiss on the lips. More than a peck, less than dueling tongues, but a kiss filled with warmth and affection.

"Hey, you." Her mom smiled up at him, happiness shining in her smile and her eyes. Jessie fought those stupid tears again because if anyone deserved a man who adored her, it was her mother.

Roger kissed her one more time. "Hey yourself." Then he remembered Jessie was in the room. He adjusted his glasses. "Jessie. Nice to see you. I hope the roads were all right?"

"They were fine."

Roger crouched down to pet Lexie, giving Jessie an opportunity to study him. He definitely looked like an accounting teacher with his white button up shirt, plaid cardigan, and khaki pants. Beneath his thick glasses were kind brown eyes, which were another indication of his gentle demeanor.

"Would you like a glass of wine?" her mother asked him.

"No, thanks. I'll let you get back to girl talk."

Jessie stood. "Actually, I think I'll head to bed."

"I didn't mean to chase you off, Jessie," Roger said.

"You didn't." She swiped her mother's half-full bottle of beer. "Besides, I think Mom would like that glass of wine."

"I put your stuff in your usual room."

"Thanks. Goodnight."

"See you in the morning, sweetie."

Jessie wandered into the bedroom. The first time she'd come to her mother's home after Luke had died, she'd taken one look at the twin bed—a blatant reminder of her single status—and she'd slid to the floor, weeping.

No urge to weep arose this time, but she had gotten used to sleeping with Brandt in the last few weeks, wrapping herself around his warm body after they'd made love and before they drifted off. She'd really gotten used to his unique way of waking her up.

She slipped on her pajamas. Lexie preferred tile to carpet, so she curled up on the floor in the adjoining bathroom.

Jessie slid beneath the sweet-smelling sheets and brought the down comforter under her chin. She turned on her side to get comfortable, squinting at the red numbers on the clock on the bedside table. Eleven. Was Brandt tucked in bed? Or had he fallen asleep in front of the TV?

Ten minutes ticked away. Then twenty. She heard her mom and Roger moving down the hallway, followed by the click of their bedroom door closing.

Another fifteen minutes passed. Almost midnight. She should be tired. But she was wide-awake.

Her cell phone vibrated on the nightstand. Jessie snatched it and smiled at the caller ID: "Hey. Is everything all right?"

"Yeah." Brandt cleared his throat. "Didn't mean to scare ya, I just called because I...missed you."

Her heart did a little flip. How sweet that he didn't think anything of calling her up just to tell her he missed her.

"Sorry if I woke you."

"You didn't. I was just laying here staring at the ceiling, to be honest. Did you get my text?"

"Oh, was that what the 'I'm here' meant? That you'd arrived safe and sound in Riverton?"

"Sorry."

"How's your mom?"

"Good. She's been baking and cooking all day. She's invited a few people over for dinner tomorrow."

"Anyone you know?"

Was she supposed to tell him about the single guy her mom had invited? No. Especially when she hadn't met the man yet. Not that Brandt would be jealous...would he?

Jessie had the perverse impulse to tell Brandt about her blind dinner date, just to see how he'd react.

High schoolish, Jessie.

"Jess?"

"What? Oh sorry, no, I won't know anyone."

"Well, I'm hopin' all her dinner guests are old couples and that she isn't tryin' to fix her single, hot daughter up with some guy."

Gulp.

"You're such a flatterer, Brandt McKay. Hot daughter. Right."

"You are hot. Smokin' hot," he whispered huskily. "And if you were here, I'd prove just how hot I think you are."

She rolled flat on her back and adjusted the phone. "How

would you do that?"

"I'd kiss you. And once I had your focus totally on those long, wet kisses that make you whimper, I'd start to unbutton your pajama top." He paused. "You are wearin' them long john ones you're so crazy about, aren't you?"

"Yes. Why? Would you rather I wore something sexier to bed?"

Brandt growled. "What's sexy is what's under whatever you're wearin', which is why I can't wait to peel it off you."

"Mmm. Keep going, cowboy. Then what would you do?"

"Once I had that shirt hangin' open, I'd drag my palms down your chest until I had your breasts cupped in my hands. I'd brush my thumbs across your nipples until they were tight points. Then I'd put my mouth on them. Just my lips. I'd nibble. Tease with those butterfly flicks that make you arch your back and moan. I might use my teeth. Test that edge of pain. I might get the tips wet and blow just to see hard I can get 'em. While my mouth was workin' you, my hands would be strokin' that soft curve where your heart is racing. By that time you'll be begging, grinding against me so I'd suck your nipple until I had the whole thing in my mouth."

This was actually getting her worked up.

"I heard that catch in your breath, Jessie. Is this turnin' you on?"

"Yes."

"Touch yourself. Close your eyes and do everything I tell you. Imagine my hands, my breath, my mouth on you."

Her answering, "Okay," came out in a breathy whisper.

Brandt made that low-pitched growl again. "Pinch your nipple."

Jessie switched the phone to her left hand and used the fingers on her right hand to twirl her right nipple into a tight peak.

"Is it hard?"

"Yes."

"Put your fingers in your mouth. Get them wet. Now twist the tips just to that edge of pain."

She did exactly as he asked, imagining Brandt's hands, and it shocked her that the fingers touching her nipples...didn't feel like her fingers.

"God, it's sexy as hell, listening to those noises you make. Now loosen the drawstring on your pants just enough so you can slide your hand down there. Skim your fingers over your belly. Stop and stroke that sweet, soft section of skin between your hipbones. I love how your skin gets goose bumps when I touch you there."

Her flesh rippled. "Me too."

"Now slip your finger beneath your panties. Follow the slit from the top to the bottom. Slowly."

Jessie let her index finger trace the rise of her pubic mound to the entrance to her sex.

"Tell me, Jessie. Are you wet?"

"Very wet."

"Let your fingers play in that wetness, swirling it around. Then bring the tip of your finger up those soft pink folds and touch your clit. A little, not a lot."

"But I want to touch it a lot." She let her middle finger draw circles around that hidden bit of flesh.

Brandt chuckled. "I'm sure you do. But I'm not done playin' with you. I like to drag this out because I love havin' my hands on you." His already raspy voice dropped another octave. "In you. Take your middle finger down, over your clit, separating those pussy lips and slide it inside your pussy. Slide it deep. All the way to the webbing of your hand."

Jessie jammed her fingers into her channel, arching her neck and nearly dropping the phone.

"Move that finger in and out," he said gruffly. "More. Add another one. Fuck yourself for me, Jessie."

"I am."

"Use your thumb on your clit. Find that slippery knot and start out slow, building as you're pumping your fingers in and out of that tight heat. Hold the phone down there so I can hear you fucking your hand. So I can hear how wet you are. How wet *I'm* makin' you."

She removed the phone from her ear and held it above her pelvis as she worked herself with her fingers. "Can you hear that, Brandt? So wet. So hot. Only for you. I'm so close. Send me over. Make me come. Please." Jessie heard him swear and she put the phone back by her ear.

"If I was there I'd be kissin' your neck, leaving love bruises from that spot below your ear to your collarbone. I'd feel those cunt muscles pulling my fingers in deeper with every stroke as I moved my thumb faster over your clit. Then I'd whisper, 'My sweet, sexy Jessie, come for me now' and you'd explode."

"God, Brandt," was all she got out before the spasms hit. She gasped as her clit pulsed beneath her thumb. Her fingers were wedged deep in her pussy, squeezed by the contractions so strong they robbed her of breath. The orgasm didn't last long, but it was intense enough she dropped the phone.

When she heard, "Jessie?" coming from far away, she turned, expecting to feel Brandt's warm body, because she always zoned out after she climaxed. She heard, "Jessie!" again and opened her eyes. Brandt wasn't there. She was in a single bed with her hand between her legs and her cell phone on the mattress next to her head.

"Hello? Jess? Did you hang up?"

She grabbed the phone and pushed herself up, reaching for the tissues on the nightstand. "I'm here. But, did we really just..."

"Have the most fuckin' amazing phone sex ever? Hell yeah we did, baby."

Jessie laughed softly. "You are so naughty, Brandt McKay. Making me come so hard that when I opened my eyes, it surprised me you weren't really here. But it sure felt like you were. The whole time. I especially like the way you whispered in my ear."

"You always like that," he murmured. "No matter which way we end up doin' it."

"We have given the Kama Sutra a run for its money, haven't we?"

"Don't know what that is, but I do know when you started to make those hot, sexy noises, I..."

"What? Got a hard-on?"

His rough chuckle tickled her ear. "No. I had wood from the instant you told me you were wearin' them long john pajamas. So as I was tellin' you what I wanted you to do—"

"You were taking the edge off?"

"Edge? Hell, when you started to come, I did too."

She sighed. "I guess I don't get to have my turn blowing your mind, huh?"

"You already did. But next time I'll let you take the lead."

"Tomorrow night?" she asked hopefully.

"Definitely tomorrow night."

"I can't wait." She yawned.

"You're tired. I'll let you get some sleep."

"Thanks for calling me, Brandt. Not just for the amazing phone sex, but for..." *Caring about me.*

Jessie couldn't make herself say it. She could whimper, moan and play raunchy sex games with him, but when it came to disclosing her feelings...she just couldn't. Sex? She could handle. Getting Brandt's hopes up that this might become something more than sex seemed unfair.

"Anytime sweetheart, I'm not goin' anyplace. Sweet dreams." Brandt hung up.

Before Jessie fell asleep she realized she hadn't asked about Landon at all.

Chapter Seventeen

"Only one thing puts a smile like that on a man's face," Tell said.

"And it sure as hell ain't pumpkin pie," Dalton added with a snicker.

Brandt snapped out of his flashback to the second night of steamy phone sex with Jessie—and glanced at his smartass brothers. "Maybe the smile is because I'm thinkin' about kickin' your asses."

"Nah. You'da done it yesterday when Dad pissed you off. God knows you love to rail on us when he makes you so mad. Which don't seem fair, does it, Dalton?"

"Nope. But I'm used to bein' picked on."

Tell's softly spoken, "We're all used to it," hung in the air of Brandt's truck cab like a slab of rotten meat.

Thanksgiving was supposed to be a day when family came together to eat, laugh, watch a little football, eat some more, play cards, hang out.

But that's never how Thanksgiving played out if Casper McKay had any say in it. He didn't give a shit that his wife had slaved over a hot stove creating a tasty, plentiful meal. He didn't care it was the first holiday he'd spend with his only grandson. He didn't care none of his own family ever invited him over for holiday.

No, the only thing Brandt's father cared about was if there was enough beer in the fridge. Which there hadn't been. Which sent Casper McKay rummaging through liquor cabinet during dinner.

Belligerent didn't begin to describe his behavior after a couple of belts of whiskey. For the first time since Jessie had taken off for Riverton, Brandt was glad she hadn't been around to witness the family fiasco. His dad baiting him every five minutes. His dad bellering at Dalton for something he'd done or left undone, probably a decade past. Then sneering at Tell for his pathetic attempts to keep the peace.

After three hours of pure hell, Brandt made his excuses. He and Landon hightailed it out of there. How his sainted mother put up with Casper McKay's crap for over forty years was truly a miracle. But even docile Joan McKay had snapped at her husband when he acted like an ass. Which had been frequently.

"Does that smile mean you're thinkin' about Jessie?"

Brandt gave Dalton, in the passenger seat, an annoyed look.

Tell leaned between them from the back of the quad cab. "What Dalton ain't so good at askin'—" he shoved Dalton slightly, "—is if you and Jessie are makin' plans for the future. Because you seem awful damn happy, and we'd be pissed if you were keepin' it from us."

"Yeah, because you guys have been *so* supportive when it comes to how I've felt about Jess in the past," Brandt said sarcastically.

"It's different now."

"How so?"

"Because now she feels the same way," Tell said. "She didn't before."

That jarred him. How did these two know how Jessie felt about him when he wasn't sure about it himself?

"Besides. Jessie's changed. She was pretty firmly under Luke's thumb, and it's taken her some time to figure out who she is and find herself again."

Dalton shoved Tell this time. "Jesus, Tell, what's with you spouting off all this new age, hippie, mumbo-jumbo 'finding herself' bullshit?"

"I suppose you've got a better explanation, Mr. D-minus in psychology?" Tell shot back.

"I sure do."

Brandt tuned them out as they bickered. He tuned them out so completely it took, "Whoa, Brandt, you're gonna miss the turn," to get his focus back.

At least fifteen pickups were parked at Cord and AJ's

house. Staring at Cord's big house, Brandt had that same wistful feeling he'd felt at Ben's. Not wanting a fancy place to hang his hat, but a home, his own home. His trailer wasn't much more than a place to crash every night.

His brothers were quiet and Brandt wondered if they were thinking the same thing. Landon yelled, "Up!" and drummed his feet into his carseat.

"We hear ya. I'll get him since I'm already back here," Tell said.

After he got out of his truck, Brandt was surprised to see his mother walking toward him. Did that mean his dad had decided to show up at the annual McKay post-Thanksgiving get together? "I didn't think you guys were comin' today."

"Your dad isn't. I left him at home." His mother's eyes darted to where Dalton and Tell were unloading Landon. But she didn't go over to offer them help.

"You okay?" She actually seemed nervous, which was crazy because she'd been coming to McKay family events for four decades.

Her pale blue eyes shifted to him. Her dark hair, once streaked with silver, was now all silver. Again, it struck him how much she'd aged since Luke's death. Her smiles were rare these days, too, so when she laughed, Brandt didn't know how to react.

"Honestly? I'm nervous, even when I know that's just plain stupid. It's strange showing up at a McKay family party without your father, but ain't no one gonna be cryin' in their beer Casper ain't here. Especially not his brothers."

"Which puts you in an awkward position."

"Yeah, but it's not the first time nor will it be the last. Kimi and Carolyn and Vi have always treated me well, even when they can't stand Casper." She turned and looked at the house. "Hard to believe how long your father and I have been married. But when his brothers and their wives all started havin' babies... I'd come to these things and cry for days afterward because I wanted what they had."

He knew his mother wasn't only speaking about kids.

"Then my boys came," she absentmindedly reached out and stroked Brandt's coat sleeve, "and I fit in. I could join in the discussions about toilet training, frogs in the bathtub, and the ranching responsibilities you'd all have to live up to as you grew into men.

"Then in recent years it's been about grandbabies and I've had that feeling of envy all over again. Oh, I know you boys are younger than your McKay cousins and weren't nowhere near ready to settle down, but I'd hoped Luke and Jessie might...but that never happened. And now we've got Landon..."

Feeling helpless, Brandt grabbed her hand because it was so unlike her to babble.

"After Luke died, I didn't care about anything. Especially not about them and their perfect kids and darling little grandkids and how they didn't have to deal with the unending pain of losing a child. I became bitter. As bitter as your father. I shut down and your dad got meaner yet. I ain't gonna make excuses for him, but I will apologize for myself. I haven't been much of a mother to you boys since we lost Luke, and I should've tried harder. I should've pulled you boys closer, not pushed away from all of you when we needed each other more than ever—"

"Mom. Stop." Brandt tugged her into his arms. "Just stop." She was absolutely breaking his heart.

"No," Tell said from behind him, "Let her talk if she wants to."

"We'll listen to anything she has to say," Dalton added. "She needs to know that."

Brandt hadn't heard his brothers come up behind them, but he was damn happy they were here.

She pushed back from Brandt and wiped her tears. "I've been thinking about this a lot over the last month and wanted to talk to you boys yesterday. On Thanksgiving. To let you know how thankful I am for each of you, but...well. You were there. Wasn't exactly a Norman Rockwell painting, was it?"

None of them could look at each other, which was just weird.

"Sorry." She used a lace hankie to wipe her nose. "I didn't mean to blather like a fool and get so weepy."

A moment of silence passed as they all struggled.

"It's okay, Mom. Tell cries all the damn time. It's sort of embarrassin' if you wanna know the truth," Dalton mock-whispered.

Tell probably would've shoved him, but Dalton was holding a wide-eyed Landon.

She smiled wanly, shaking her head with that "boys will be boys" look of resignation Brandt recognized. "How long have you been here?"

"An hour."

"You've been sitting in your car in the cold for an hour? Why?"

"Because I didn't want to go in there by myself." She sniffed and laughed at the same time. "Stupid, huh?"

"Not stupid. You were just waiting for us, right?"

She nodded and wiped her cheeks.

Brandt was afraid she'd start crying again, and he knew how much that'd embarrass her in front of their McKay relatives. He looked at Dalton. "How about if you let Mom carry Landon inside?"

If he thought his mother was done with tears, he was mistaken. Because for some reason, that made her cry harder.

A few hours later, the noise level in Cord and AJ's house still rivaled the floor of the New York Stock Exchange.

Kids and dogs running everywhere, inside and out. Men gathered in the den shouting at a football game on TV. Pregnant women in the kitchen. Nursing mothers and babies in the living room. Still more kids racing up and down the stairs. It was pure chaos.

Brandt loved every second of it. He wished Jessie were here because he knew she'd love it too.

"Kane?" Ginger shouted from the living room.

"I'll get him," Brandt said. He wandered to the den where his uncles were sacked out in the easy chairs, snoring, while his cousins were crouched on the floor, surrounded by kids, trying to watch the game. "Kane? Ginger's lookin' for you."

"I'm there." Immediately Kane pushed to his feet and brushed past Brandt as he lingered in the doorway.

A collective groan arose at a play on the football field.

Colby shifted his youngest son, Austin, asleep on his lap, and pointed at the TV. "That's gotta be a personal foul."

"Give it up, Colby," Cam said. "They're gonna get their butts handed to them today."

"And no pussy ref call is gonna make a damn bit of

difference," Ben said. "Shit, I mean shoot, I'm not supposed to say the 'p' word in front of the kiddos, am I?"

"Nope," Quinn said. "Ditto for the 'd' word and the 's' word."

"If poor Ben can't curse he ain't gonna have no language skills at all," Chase drawled from the other side of the room.

Ben whipped a pillow at him. "Fu—I mean funny."

Chase caught the pillow, almost without looking.

Colt whistled. "You oughta be playin' ball instead of ridin' bulls."

"I'll pass. No buckle bunnies waitin' for a hard ride after a baseball game like they are after a bull riding expo."

Tell sighed. "Dude. You have the perfect life."

Brandt looked around. This room used to seem so big, but now it couldn't hold them all. Colt was backed against the wall with Hudson on his lap. Cam was kicked back in the recliner with his two youngest boys sprawled on him. Quinn's son Adam rested his head on Quinn's thigh. Kade leaned against the recliner, his lap empty. Didn't appear his girls were the slightest bit interested in football.

A dark haired boy Brandt recognized as Carter's middle son, Spencer, was curled up in the corner. But he didn't see the kid's father. "Where's Carter?"

"Workin' on some art thing. Said he'd be by later."

Colt snorted. "So he says. But since he sent Macie over here with all the kids, what do you think the chances are that'll happen?"

"Slim to none," Colby said.

Brandt hadn't seen Keely's husband, Jack, either. "Where's Keely?"

"She and Jack went to his mom's in South Dakota for Thanksgiving."

"That's because she wants to be here on Christmas to see the looks on our faces after she gives each of her nephews a drum set," Cord said. When his youngest son, Foster, snuggled into his chest, Cord gently patted his back and lowered his voice. "If she ain't bluffin' I swear I will strangle her."

"Yeah, well, get in line. She informed me the nieces are getting tambourines," Cam pointed out. "That ain't any better."

"Keely just told you guys this?" Brandt asked.

"Yep, she doesn't want anyone to 'steal' her present ideas,

since she's dragged Jack along as her pack mule for Black Friday sales shopping."

"Poor bastard," Ben said.

"That 'b' word is off limits too," Quinn reminded him.

"I just got a text from Jack that said, *Kill me now,*" Carter said.

Everyone turned toward Carter, who stood behind Brandt.

"Hey, you are here," Kade said.

"I said I would be." Carter's gaze moved between Colt and Colby. "Thanks for the vote of confidence, guys."

"Even you gotta admit you lose track of time when you're workin' on a new sculpture," Cam said.

"What is this? Pick on Carter day?"

"Yep, gotta uphold the tradition of pickin' on the youngest since Keely ain't here," Cord said.

"Terrific."

"Grab a seat."

Carter looked around. "Where?"

"Good point."

Chase stood. "You can have my spot. I need air." As Chase passed by Brandt, he made the "wanna beer?" sign and Brandt nodded, grabbing his coat before he followed Chase out the front door.

The lid on the cooler slammed and Chase handed him a Bud Light. "Thanks."

"No prob."

Their breath came out in a misty white steam. "Damn, it's cold out here."

"Yeah, but it's quiet." Chase took a long swallow. "I'm not used to bein' around so many kids. I ain't gonna lie. It drives me insane."

Brandt didn't say anything.

"Shit. Sorry. I forgot that you're takin' care of Luke's kid for a while."

"Don't worry about it. But there's a huge difference between one kid and twenty-some kids."

"So how is it goin' with Landon?"

He shrugged. "Okay. Jessie's been workin' with him to get him to talk more. He's adjusted to bein' around kids in the daycare, but the first couple of days were sheer hell for both of us."

When Chase kept quiet, Brandt said, "You wondering how come I was such a bastard and brought Jessie into this?"

"I'd be lyin' if I didn't admit it crossed my mind." Chase looked straight ahead and drank. "So you're livin' with Jessie? At her place?"

Brandt leaned across the railing. "For now. Why?"

"Just curious. Seems everyone is pairing up and producing the next generation of McKays."

"She's already paired up with one McKay and that didn't work out so good for her."

"That's probably because she was paired with the wrong McKay to start with."

Not touching that one.

"What about you? I read all about the 'Wyoming Wild Man' in the rodeo magazines. Sounds like you've got a girl in every town and left a string of broken hearts across the country."

"You know how the media exaggerates."

"So none of it's true?"

Chase grinned. "Oh, it's completely true. The raunchier stuff don't make the trade mags." He peeped over his shoulder, then back at Brandt. "I gotta admit, I love havin' a different girl or two every night if I want. They wanna fuck a top fifteen bull rider and I let 'em. Win-win, right?"

"Right. Who's the flavor this week?"

"Flavors—plural, as in Miss Rodeo Nevada and Miss Rodeo Montana. Damn good thing the states aren't next to each other, huh?"

Brandt whistled. "You've always had a thing for them fancy types."

"What's not to love about big hair, tight jeans, high heeled boots, lots of cleavage and rhinestones? Dude. I'm so there. Not to mention them queens can ride you hard and squeeze you dry. Ain't nothin' I like better than ridin' double."

"Watch yourself, Chase. You're gonna run across one of them beauty queens whose daddy don't like his little girl bein' toyed with and he's gonna get out the shotgun."

"I can handle myself. And lookit you, B, goin' all big brother on me, worried about me getting my ass full of buckshot."

"Asshole. I'm worried about you bustin' your ass and

getting crippled up because you're too stupid to understand you ain't invincible and you ain't gonna be able to ride forever."

"True. But I'll climb on a back of a bull as long as I can." He took another drink of beer. "And the injury is healin' fine, if my nosy-assed brothers asked you to grill me about it."

"They didn't."

"Good." Chase shivered. "I forget how goddamn cold it is here."

"You're spoiled competing in all those warm climes."

"That's a fact, which is probably why I'll end up livin' someplace down south. Speakin' of... Did your dad talk to you guys about them starting to legally restructure the ranch?"

"No. Should he've been?"

"According to my dad, Uncle Carson and Uncle Cal, yes."

"Does this have to do with Keely getting a chunk of McKay land as a wedding gift?"

"Partially. But a couple of us are opting out of bein' part of the McKay land trust permanently."

Brandt froze. "What the hell are you talkin' about?"

Chase kicked back and rested his shoulders on the porch support post. "You really had no clue?"

"Nope. So who's opting out?"

"Me, for one."

Brandt looked at him curiously. "Why?"

"Because I've got my own life outside of the ranch. Even if I quit ridin' next year, chances are slim I'd move back here and be part of the McKay cattle business. Quinn and Ben always were more involved than me, they wanted this life more than I ever did, so it makes sense that my portion goes to them."

"Quinn and Ben agreed?"

Chase shrugged. "Oh, they tried to protest, but in truth, it was a relief. I have other income. They don't."

"Who else is opting out?"

"Cam. Like Keely, he's trading his stake for a chunk of land, in his case, for the fifty acres around his house, which borders the neighbor's acreage, so it'll be an easy deed transfer. Carter is still debating, but I think he'll opt out too. With his art career takin' off, not to mention he's helpin' Cash Big Crow with his ranching operation in River Bend, he's spreading himself thin driving back and forth when he doesn't have to. There are plenty of McKays to keep the cattle business goin'."

Brandt fought the surge of anger. This was the type of ranch business his father should've been telling him.

Would he have told Luke?

Yes, goddammit.

"I'm gonna kick my old man's sorry ass."

"Lemme know ahead of time. I'll sell tickets."

One thing Brandt admired about Chase; he just said what was on his mind, straight up.

Chase's cell phone rang. He dug it out of his front pocket and scowled. "It's my publicist. Excuse me." He snapped, "Sugar tits, you'd better have a goddamn good reason for calling me on Thanksgiving."

Whoa. Chase called his publicist...*sugar tits*? That didn't sound very professional.

Brandt finished his beer and returned inside. He tried to sneak past the living room where the mamas and babies were holding court, but he heard, "Brandt! Come here."

Two million pairs of eyes bored into him. Okay, it was only India, Skylar, Libby, Ginger and Macie, but it seemed like more. "What?" he said to India, who'd tucked her new baby boy Ellison so closely to her breast he only saw a blanket covered lump.

"We were just talking about you."

"Should I be worried?"

Silence.

Shit.

"Actually, we were talking about Jessie," Ginger said, shifting the baby in her lap.

Great. So now he and Jessie were permanently linked in his family's eyes? He was good with that, but he doubted Jessie would be. "What about her?"

"Have you talked to her since she left for Riverton?"

If "talked" is a euphemism for having scorching hot phone sex with her two nights running, then yes.

"Hello? Earth to Brandt."

He cleared his throat. "Yeah, I've talked to her. She's havin' a good time."

"I'm glad. She deserved a break."

Was it his imagination, or did the room turn a little hostile?

Were they blaming him for Jessie needing a break?

Of course they are, dumbass.

"Jessie is great with all the kids at Sky Blue." Skylar tucked the pink blanket around Ginger and Kane's baby girl Maddie, nestled in her arms. "We'd be lost without her."

"No argument from me." Dammit. That wasn't what he'd meant.

Or was it?

Again, those two million eyes pinned him in place.

Quick. Change the subject and get out before they pounce. "Look, have you seen—"

"Your mom and Landon?" Macie supplied. "Yes, she's changing him. Said she'll be right back so you might as well stick around and chat with us."

Chat. Right. They planned to hold his boots to the fire.

The baby pressed to Macie's shoulder let out a huge burp. Macie rubbed her back. "Good girl, Poppy."

"So what's Jessie been doing while she's staying at her mom's?"

"I dunno. We haven't talked about it."

Skylar and India exchanged a look.

A look Brandt didn't like at all. "Why? What's goin' on?"

"Nothing, probably," Skylar said.

"Sky," India said gently, "it won't hurt to ask him."

"Ask me what?"

"If Jessie mentioned anything to you about looking for a job while she was in Riverton?"

Surprised, Brandt said, "No."

"See? I told you, sis. You're worried for nothing."

"Why would she look for a job there?" Brandt asked.

"She misses her mom, among other things."

Sky gave India a sharp look, which indicated there was something else going on, but India clammed up.

Brandt half listened as the women chatted about daycare, but his brain had gotten stuck on one thing: the possibility of Jessie leaving.

The logical portion of his brain pointed out that she loved her job. The nasty part of his brain pointed out that if Landon became a fixture in the McKay family, she'd put distance between them in a helluva hurry. And to be honest, how could he blame her?

His gut twisted. He considered the women in this room, all happily married to his cousins, wondering if they had any advice on how to keep Jessie here, in his life, forever.

But they weren't paying attention to him.

When Amelia fussed, Libby lifted her shirt.

When Paulson fussed, Ginger lifted her shirt.

When Ellison fussed, India lifted her shirt.

Skylar laughed when Maddie started bumping her head into her chest. "Huh-uh, girlie, I've got nothing in there for you. Let's get you back to mama."

Ginger sighed and lifted up the other side of her shirt.

Dear God. Were all these women just whipping out their breasts like it was no big deal?

Don't look. Your cousins will beat your ass for gawking at their wives' bared breasts.

This was so freakin' weird. Yeah, he knew that breastfeeding was natural and all that jazz, but he had brothers for Christsake, not sisters, and he'd never actually seen a live pair of breasts until he was sixteen. He'd never seen woman nurse a baby. Ever. And it sure as hell didn't look as clinical and messy as a cow standing around chewing her cud while a calf noisily sucked on her teats.

"Brandt? You okay?" India asked.

"Um, I gotta go." He raced out so fast he nearly tripped over his own feet.

Feminine laughter chased him out of the room.

Brandt slipped into the den and heaved a sigh of relief. All men in here, burping, farting, scratching themselves, arguing, being guys. Guys, he understood. Women, not so much.

And maybe that was his biggest problem.

Before he left Cord and AJ's, Skylar took him aside. "I'll be honest, Brandt. This is a confusing time for you and Jessie both. But you need to remember one thing."

"What's that?"

"If you give her a reason to stay here, she will."

"And how do I do that, Skylar?"

Her gaze flicked to Landon, sleeping on his shoulder, and then back to him. "By not giving her an excuse to leave."

Well, that cleared things up a whole helluva lot.

Not.

He smiled tightly. "Thanks for the advice."

Later that night he lay in bed and waited for Jessie to call. But she didn't.

Nor did she call the next night.

Would he seem too fucking needy if he called her?

Or would it seem like he didn't give a shit if he *didn't* call?

Man, he sucked at this relationship stuff.

Finally he called and left a message on her voice mail.

But she didn't call him back.

Chapter Eighteen

Good. He was home.

Jessie left Lexie outside to run off her extra energy after being cooped up inside the truck for the last five hours. She tried to be quiet as she snuck up the steps, wanting to maintain the surprise.

It worked. After she opened the door and slipped inside Brandt's trailer, she glanced at the man who sat on the couch, remote in hand, completely goggle-eyed.

Then his sly, sexy smile appeared. "Damn girl. It's great to see you, but you had me worried since I haven't heard from you the last two days."

Jessie kicked off her boots. Unwrapped the scarf. Peeled off her gloves and unbuttoned her long wool coat. "Sorry about that. I lost my cell phone Friday afternoon in the Tetons when we were snowshoeing. By the time I realized it and activated a new phone, and charged it up, it was time to head home. So here I am."

"I'm glad you're here." He set the remote on the coffee table, next to a full bottle of Corona. "Did you have a good time at your mom's?"

Brandt? Making idle chitchat? Which would be sweet if his hungry eyes weren't already stripping her bare. Not a sweet thing about those midnight blue eyes right now.

She skirted the coffee table. "Is Landon sleeping?"

"Yep. He's been down about a half hour."

"Good. Then I timed it perfectly."

His eyebrows lifted. "Timed what perfectly?"

"This." She straddled his lap, held his face in her hands

and kissed him. She tried to keep it easy, a deep, slow, wet reunion kiss. But the sensation of his full warm lips beneath hers, the glide of his tongue against hers, his taste and his scent made her wild, and she inhaled him in a blazing kiss of pure need.

Heady stuff, how he met her kiss for kiss, touch for touch, breath for breath.

She moved her lips along the line of his jaw to his ear. "God, Brandt. I'm dying for you. Phone sex was hot, but I want real sex. Lots of it. Right now." She slid off his lap.

Keeping her eyes on his, she circled her fingers around his wrists, tugging him to his feet. While gorging herself on his addictive kisses, she herded him down the hallway to his bedroom. After locking the bedroom door, Jessie jerked Brandt's shirt off. She made short work of his jeans, yanking the denim and his boxers to the floor.

Then she pushed him on the bed.

Brandt propped himself on his elbows, not the least bit bothered by his nakedness. Or his full-blown hard-on. And he shouldn't be. His rockin' body should always be naked.

"What are you grinning at, Miss Jessie?"

"The thought of you being naked twenty-four/seven."

"Wouldn't be much fun if I was nekkid alone. Speaking of nekkid..." His predatory gaze moved over her in a sensual caress. "You have way too many clothes on."

"Do I? I might be inclined to take them all off, but there is one little condition."

He said, "Name it," without hesitation.

"I get to have my wicked way with you and you just have to lay there and take it."

"Deal."

There was that smile of his, the smile that promised he'd keep his word, but also guaranteed delicious payback.

Jessie disrobed and crawled over him, loving how his body heat warmed her skin. She tucked her knees by his hips and bent down, letting her hair fall in a curtain around their faces. She savored the give and take of mouths, as they both took a turn at leading the kiss.

Brandt's arms were casually thrown above his head, but before too long, those rough-skinned hands were sliding up her arms, gliding down her back, stopping to cup her butt cheeks. He whispered, "Jess. Before we... I need..."

"What?"

"To put my mouth on you. I know you're wet. I can smell that hot sweetness between your thighs. The need to taste you is makin' me crazy." He nuzzled her temple. "You can do anything you want to me after, but first, I wanna feel you come against my tongue."

Ah. What was she supposed to say? No way? When her clit was doing the wave in anticipation of Brandt's mouth? "You drive a hard bargain, but...okay."

He laughed.

Jessie pushed back to balance on her knees as she straddled Brandt's thighs.

"Sexy girl. Stay just like that. Don't move." He wiggled his body down until his head was between her knees. "Goddammit my mouth is watering and I can't reach you. Fall forward on your elbows and hands. That's it." His palms pushed on the inside of her thighs, sliding her legs out farther and then his fingers gripped her ass.

She couldn't see what he was doing, but a second after she felt the first wet swipe of his tongue, she nearly went blind with pleasure anyway.

Brandt didn't tease. He lapped at her slit. Licked and mapped every inch of her folds with absolute gusto. Buried his tongue in her channel and fucked her with it.

"This isn't gonna take long," she gasped.

"Then I can do this again later." He did a twirly, swirly maneuver from her clit to her anus. Using his lips and his tongue in such raunchy ways.

"Brandt." So close. She rolled her hips back, wanting that continual attention to her pleasure point.

He growled and brought her down, so she straddled his face. She had no idea how he was breathing, but when he fastened his mouth to her top of her sex and did a sexy rhythmic, slurping thing directly on her clit, she didn't care. "Yes. Please. Don't stop."

Her hands grabbed fistfuls of the quilt as Brandt kept pushing her higher. Each lick. Each suck. Each incredible flicker of his tongue and she was sure her body would simply ignite.

And it did. Jessie pressed her face into the mattress and bit back a scream as her clit pulsed against Brandt's hot mouth. Despite the blood pounding in her groin, her ears and her throat, she still heard the sexy sounds of him swallowing. Drinking her down.

That set her off again.

When she floated back from that head rushing, body buzzing happy place, she pushed herself back up on her knees. She smoothed back her tangled hair and scooted down Brandt's upper torso so she could see his face.

His look of cockiness was totally justified. He licked his lips and said, "Mmm. Tasty."

Jessie fastened her mouth to his, surprising him with an openmouthed kiss, sucking her taste from his tongue, rubbing her face through the sticky glaze on his cheeks, nipping and biting and enjoying his shock. She said, "Move up and spread out."

"Jess—"

"No arguments, buster. You agreed. Me. In charge."

Brandt sighed, but it wasn't a sigh of frustration.

She pinned his arms above his head and allowed her hands to track the muscles from his wrists down the sinew defining in his forearms, over the bulge of his biceps to the cup of his shoulders. "I never get to touch you enough."

"Anytime you want, all you want."

"You're usually so busy touching me. It makes me lose my mind and I sort of get lost." She snared her gaze. "That's not fair to you."

"If you knew how long I'd dreamed of getting my hands all over you, Jess, you'd know how untrue that statement really is."

Her belly fluttered. She ducked her head from the intensity in his eyes and let her palms drift over his pectorals. God. There was just something so wholly masculine about a guy with chest hair. This part of his body always smelled good. Not musky like his groin, but earthy. Soap and sweat. She rubbed her lips down the delineated line between his pecs, loving how the crisp hair tickled her chin and cheek. She rubbed her face all over his chest, practically purring.

Brandt's hand landed on the side of her head and he brushed the hair from her cheek.

She looked up at him. "Did I say you could touch me?"

"No. But I like watchin' you touchin' me. It's sexy as hell."

"Mmm. So you wanna watch me do this?" Jessie used the tip of her tongue to trace the outline of his right nipple.

His arms broke out in goose flesh. "Christ."

"I guess you like that." Jessie closed her eyes and sucked the flat disk until the center drew up into a rigid point. She let her tongue flick back and forth before she sucked hard again. Then she used her teeth. She felt his cock jumping between their bodies and she curled her hand around the shaft, pumping it while she tongued his nipple.

"Fuck. Oh fuck."

Reducing Brandt's vocabulary to curse words was a good sign. Her lips skimmed his skin as she blindly sought the nipple on the other side. Her mouth enclosed the tiny nub and she got those same hot, sexy noises when she worked it relentlessly.

His hips pumped up, which meant he was ready for the next phase of seduction. She slowly kissed her way down the trail of dark hair running along the center of his belly.

"Jess. Fuck."

"No fucking yet. I want you in my mouth for a little while first."

He groaned.

She smiled. She let her breath tease the purple crown of his cock before she swallowed him to where her right gripped the thick base. She didn't move, concentrating on the heat and the hardness and the taste of this intimate part of him.

Brandt didn't buck his pelvis, or grab her head, or ask for her to finish him. He allowed her to do what she wanted, despite the rapid beat of his pulse in the vein running up the length of his dick, a vein that pulsed so sweetly against her tongue.

Jessie took her time, using all the tricks she'd learned about him that made him moan or twitch or curse. She stopped teasing him and lifted her head. "I'm giving you two choices."

"Which are?"

"I suck you off. Or..."

Just a tad impatiently he demanded, "Or what?"

"We do something new."

He waited.

"What's your dirty girl fantasy, Brandt?"

"What do you mean?"

"What's something you've always wanted to do to a woman but you've never tried?"

His gaze skittered away and then back. "Why are you askin' me this?"

"Because I wanna fulfill that dirty girl fantasy, Brandt. I wanna do the one thing for you that you've never had the guts to ask any other woman." She suckled the head of his cock while keeping her gaze firmly on his. "Tell me. Anything you want."

"Anything?"

"Yes." When Brandt squirmed, she knew this was stepping far outside his comfort zone.

Good.

"Tell me," she repeated.

He reached down and traced her jawline, from the front of her temple down to the tip of her chin. Then he swept the rough pad of his thumb across her bottom lip. "I wanna come on your face. I wanna see my come coating your lips before you lick it off and swallow it all."

Holy crap that was a hot request. Really hot. Especially coming from a cowboy gentleman such as Brandt McKay. She smiled and licked another pearl of pre-come from the slit in his dick.

"Okay."

"Just like that? You'd say yes?"

"Yep. So where do you want me? On my knees between your legs, sitting on the floor? You'd probably have better aim if I was on the floor."

Brandt looked stricken for half a second, then he laughed softly. "God. You're killin' me, woman. Yes. On your knees on the floor."

Jessie slithered down his body purposely letting her hair drift across his groin, his thighs and the tops of his feet, because she knew how ticklish he was.

"Playin' with fire, Jessie." Brandt sat up and pressed the creases of his knees into the edge of the bed.

Setting her hands on his thighs, she bowed her head over him, taking his cock into her mouth completely. Keeping her lips suctioned tight didn't keep the saliva in her mouth. She used the wetness to move faster, letting it trickle out of her mouth and coat his shaft.

"Fuck, I love it when your mouth gets me so wet I can feel it dripping down my balls."

The husky way he dirty talked made the inside of her thighs sticky. Jessie slid her hand down to fondle his sac. So tight. So ready.

Then the skin on his shaft seemed to tighten even more.

Brandt eased out of her mouth and she looked at him.

"Enough." He fisted his cock in his hand and was beating off with more force that she'd dare try. He rasped, "Watch me."

As if she could tear her gaze away from the eroticism of him masturbating.

"Put your hands on my thighs. Lean closer but arch your back. Yeah, like that. You're so goddamn hot, Jess, I can't believe you're..." He groaned. "Close your eyes and part your lips."

The slapping sounds increased as did his moans and the first spurt landed on her cheek. The next on her chin. The next on her chest. Followed by warm drops hitting her upper lip. Several droplets slid down the center of her lip and dripped into her mouth. The salty tang made her want to swallow the full taste of him, but she stayed still.

The flesh slapping noises stopped and Brandt's strenuous breathing filled the room. She could feel his eyes, drinking her in, as she kneeled before him, her body bearing the marks of his passion.

She felt his pleasure even when he didn't utter a word.

Softly, he said, "Don't move."

The droplets had cooled. Brandt swept his thumb over the stickiness on her lips and said, "Lick it."

She did.

Brandt swiped a wet spot on her jaw and pressed his thumb into her mouth. "Suck it."

How different his come tasted on his hand instead of directly from the source.

He continued to wipe every drop of come from her chest, her neck, her face. She sucked and licked his fingers. His slow, deliberate means of drawing out the connection set her skin to tingling. Her focus dimmed to just fulfilling Brandt's needs. There was incredible power in surrendering to this man because she knew he wouldn't abuse it.

His lips grazed her ear, sending a shudder from her neck to her toes. "Sexy, nasty Jessie. Are you my dirty girl now?"

"Yes. God yes."

"If I reach between your thighs will I find you wet?"

She could come just from him whispering in her ear. "Yes."

"And just what should I do about that wetness?"

"Anything you want. Just touch me."

"Look at me'."

Jessie opened her eyes.

Brandt's cheeks were rosy. His eyes were brimming with lust and his cock was fully erect again. He took her hands in his with a forceful, "C'mere," and he moved them into the center of the bed. Then he flipped them so Jessie was on her back. He eased into her bit by bit, watching her eyes with the possessive gleam that caused her stomach to somersault. The instant he began to stroke inside her, she brought her legs up and circled his waist.

This was what she wanted. Needed. Him. This closeness. This tight fit. This perfect friction. This bond she only got from being with him.

He joined their hands and slid them above their heads, bringing their bodies in full contact from chest to legs.

"I like that."

"Me too." Brandt kissed her.

When he kissed her, everything fell into place. She brushed her lips over the spot below his ear that made him shudder. "I missed you," she said softly.

"I can tell." He stroked her hair. "I missed you too, Jess. A lot."

And rather than taking an afternoon to prove how much he missed her, Brandt took the entire week.

Not every instance was sexual. He made her coffee. He shoveled out her truck after it snowed. He got up early and fed the animals so they could have a long shower together before starting their workday. All thoughtful things that showed

Brandt really listened to her. He cared that she was happy. That was the sweetest feeling of all because she'd never had that before.

He made love to her every night before they went to sleep. Sometimes hard and urgent. Sometimes slowly and tenderly. Every night after he'd rocked her body and her world, he'd spooned behind her in her bed and held her all night long.

With every touch, every laugh, every new inside joke, Jessie knew this was moving out of the realm of a temporary situation, into something permanent.

Chapter Nineteen

Jessie had forgotten how much she loved the holidays.

It wasn't because Landon brought out her childish glee. The kid was still too young to understand what the hustle and bustle was about. But he loved the sparkly lights, the excitement in the air. The cookies. Her little man was as much a cookie monster as her big man.

Her happiness stemmed from having someone like Brandt to share simple things with. They'd done no Christmas shopping. They hadn't decorated much. They hadn't attended a single holiday party.

The Sunday trip into the woods with Landon to chop down the perfect pine tree hadn't started on a fun note. Lexie had taken off after a deer and knocked Landon over with enough force he'd rolled down a small hill and landed face first in a snowbank. With snow inside his jacket, snow down his pants and snow in his boots, he'd screamed bloody murder. Then Brandt fell into a shallow stream hidden beneath icy layers of snow, soaking both his boots and his pants up to his knees. When they'd gotten back to the truck, wet and miserable, Jessie realized she'd forgotten Landon's bottle, but she'd remembered the thermos of coffee. Too bad she hadn't remembered to screw the lid on tight because the coffee had spilled, creating a puddle on the passenger side floorboard of Brandt's truck.

But after they'd returned to Jessie's place, cleaned up and warmed up, the three of them snuggled on the couch to watch cartoon Christmas classics. They'd gorged themselves on sugar cookies, loaded with colored sprinkles, and warm, chocolatey milk. Then after Brandt tucked a sticky, sugary, exhausted

Landon in bed, they'd curled up together on the couch, talking, laughing, making out like teenagers. Indulging in long, candy-flavored kisses, cold hands straying beneath wool sweaters, rubbing noses, creating static electricity from rubbing their fully clothed bodies together, drifting off in front of the soft glow of the Christmas tree lights.

It'd truly been one of the best days Jessie remembered.

"Jess?"

She glanced at Brandt. "Sorry. What?"

"Do we need peanut butter?"

"Yes. Jelly too. Here's the list. I'm going to grab some tater tots."

As they passed the junk food aisle, Landon said, "Cookie!"

"No way, lil' buckaroo."

"Yef!"

"Nope. You've eaten your weight in cookies this week. We're all boarding the veggie train. Carrots. Broccoli. Snow peas. Yum."

She slowed in the frozen food section after passing two hundred kinds of frozen pizza. She'd just tossed a bag of tater tots and a bag of chicken nuggets into the cart when she heard, "Is that Landon?"

Jessie looked at the woman blocking her cart. Around forty, she had dyed red hair with two inches of brown root showing. She reeked of cigarettes. Her pale face was pinched as if she'd been sucking on a sour pickle.

This couldn't be good.

The woman leaned to squint at Landon. "That is him." She focused on Jessie. "Is the boy's name still Landon or did you change it?"

"Excuse me?"

"Samantha did the right thing and finally gave that kid up for adoption. That girl had no business being a mother. When my son told me some of the shit she pulled...well, it's a wonder she stayed out of jail as long as she did."

"Who are you?" fell out of Jessie's mouth.

"I'm Drexel's mom."

Who was Drexel? And who in their right mind would name

their kid Drexel?

"Samantha moved in with Drex after her aunt kicked her out. She took off about six months later. I wasn't surprised. Drex had gotten tired of her bullshit and lies anyway." She jerked her chin toward Landon. "He's a cute kid. Lucky to have the chance to overcome his bad start in life."

Jessie frowned.

"I hope you had him tested for mental problems. If not, you should because Drex was pretty sure Samantha drank like a fish and smoked pot when she was pregnant."

"I don't see how that's any business of yours."

Those bloodshot eyes drew together. "Well excuse the fuck outta me for tryin' to help you. I doubt you knew what you were getting into when you agreed to adopt him."

"What's goin' on?"

The woman turned. Then her calculating gaze winged between Brandt and Jessie. "You're the adoptive father? I was just telling your wife about some of the issues you might have with the kid."

Brandt bit off, "Not that it's any of your business, but we're Landon's guardians, not his adoptive parents."

The clicking noise of the woman's acrylic fingernails against the glass doors sounded like one of those killer insects about to sting. "So she really did it, huh? Dumped the kid off with his father's family."

Landon's mother had told this freak she intended to contact the McKays?

"I don't know who you are, lady, but you don't know squat."

"I know more than you do. When Samantha lived with Drex, she talked about turning the boy over to his father's family so she could be free. Most the time she was so wasted she didn't remember she even had a kid, let alone knowing how to take care of him. Get used to him being around permanently, because she won't want him back."

"That's enough." Brandt didn't look away from the woman when he spoke to Jessie. "Jess. Go."

A million thoughts spun in her head as she reached the checkout line. Obviously the woman knew Landon. But not as well as she knew Landon's mother. How much of what she'd said was true? Had Samantha just been biding her time?

Brandt hadn't said anything about his jail visit with Samantha, but Jessie knew the visit had upset him. Had Samantha already told Brandt she didn't intend to take Landon back?

It'd been easy to forget these fears when everything had been going along so smoothly. She cared about Landon, but she had no desire to be the kid's mother. Because she never really would be his mother. No matter what she did for him, he'd always be affected by his mother abandoning him. He'd always have that kernel of hope that someday his biological mother would come to her senses and connect with him.

Jessie could spend her life loving him and it wouldn't be enough. And it had nothing to do with him being a McKay.

"Miss? You have to unload the cart yourself," the checker said to her.

"I'll do it," Brandt said from behind her. When he set his hands on her shoulders, she shrugged him off.

Brandt was smart enough to not push the issue as they drove back to her house. He readied Landon for bed and for once Landon didn't insist Jessie read him a bedtime story.

Jessie was grateful for the busy work of putting away groceries. Once she had that done, she decided she'd scour the kitchen and the bathroom. If that didn't allow her brain to shut off, she'd go into the barn and find some project to keep her energy and thoughts focused elsewhere.

Brandt came into the kitchen. "We need to talk about what happened at the grocery store."

"No, we don't." She squirted the cleaning solution on the countertop and scrubbed furiously, her rubber gloves squeaking with each stroke.

"Jess—"

She spun around and aimed the spray bottle at him. "Don't push me. Leave me alone."

Brandt snatched the plastic bottle out of her hand. "No. Now give me the goddamn gloves and sit on the couch so we can talk about this like rational adults because we're not gonna shove this under the rug."

"You don't get to order me around."

"Fine." He exhaled slowly. "Jessie, will you sit on the couch with me so we can hash this out?"

Say no.

Scream no.

He said, "Please."

Looking at him, she stripped off her gloves. "Give me back my spray bottle."

"When we're done talkin'. Do you want a beer?"

"I'd rather have whiskey."

"Two shots comin' up."

Jessie chose to sit in the easy chair, which didn't make Brandt happy. But she needed to keep a clear head, and whenever Brandt touched her, she pretty much went mindless.

He set the bottle of Maker's Mark whiskey and two shot glasses on the coffee table. He poured. He knocked one back and refilled it again, holding the shot out to her.

She gulped it, welcoming the burn.

"I know you said you didn't want to hear anything about Samantha, but in light of what happened, there are a few things you need to know. First off, that woman we saw tonight? According to Samantha, she's psycho. She's the mother of the guy Samantha lived with for a while. This woman used to show up, all hours of the night and day, looking for drugs, booze or money. She gave Samantha parenting advice, usually along the lines of give the kid up for adoption, your life will be better."

"The woman said that stuff about adoption in front of her grown son?"

"Apparently. She badgered Samantha about Landon's father, if he was paying child support. Between that and the issues with the boyfriend, it got bad enough Samantha left. And no matter what that psycho bitch claimed, Samantha didn't drink or do drugs during her pregnancy. I believe that."

"Why? Samantha could be feeding you full of shit, Brandt."

"True. But I talked to her aunt and she said Samantha was really sick the entire pregnancy. And Samantha was embarrassed. She barely left the house. As far as what happened after she gave birth to Landon, who knows? She racked up two DUIs. As far as her dumping him off with us for the long haul? Nothin's been decided because she's still incarcerated."

Jessie poured another shot. "There is no 'us' in that context. You do understand that, right?"

"As a matter of fact, no. I don't understand it."

"Where is Samantha right now?"

Brandt looked at her skeptically for dodging the question. "In the halfway house. Why?"

"How long has she been out of jail?"

"A week."

"And in that week has she asked to see her son at all?"

The muscle in his jaw flexed. "No."

"So after being locked up and away from him for months, she's not chomping at the bit to see how he's doing? Especially since she left him in the care of virtual strangers?"

He swallowed the whiskey in his shot glass.

"And since it's a halfway house, she could have him overnight at some point. Couldn't she?"

"I guess."

"Has she asked you if she can have him over Christmas?"

"No. But I'm sure she has a—"

"Valid excuse?" Jessie supplied. "What? She's afraid she won't have time to buy him a Santa gift? No. The reason she hasn't asked for him is because she doesn't want him."

"That's not true. The halfway house is just that, a place halfway between jail and normalcy. She's adjusting. She's got two more months before we should even be talkin' about this."

"Agreed." Jessie lifted her glass in a mock toast but didn't drink. "I will uphold my end of sticking out the full four months. But it will end at four months, Brandt. I have not changed my mind. I like Landon, but he's not my child. If this whole thing heads south, like I suspect it will, if you want to file for permanent guardianship, fine. You can do that on your own. You don't need me."

"Why is this so different from if Luke had a kid from a previous relationship and that kid lived with you?" Brandt demanded. "Would you've kicked him to the curb after Luke died?"

She shook her finger at him. "Not the same thing. If I knew that kid, if I'd been raising him, I'd continue raising him because chances would be good that kid would have no other alternative and he'd probably consider me his mother. But Landon already has a mother."

"You are impossible to reason with."

"No. I'm right and you know it."

"As long as we're supposing, what if it comes down to Landon needing a permanent home and I become his legal guardian?"

"I'd be happy for Landon because you'd be good for him."

"That's it? You wouldn't be a part of either of our lives?"

A sharp pain stabbed at her, thinking about walking away from Brandt forever. But unless she wanted to live her life waiting for the other boot to drop, she'd have no choice. "No."

The bitterness and pain in Brandt's eyes was like another hot poker to her heart.

"Look. I care about him. But he's not mine, Brandt. He never will be. Even if I pour all my love, my heart and my soul into raising that boy, I'll never be his real mother. And if Samantha signed off on him as a toddler and had a change of heart or changed her life, ten or so years later? What then? Landon would need to give his mother a chance to be part of his life. I would have to encourage him to forgive her. I would have to let him go. So it's easier for me to let him go now and save myself years of heartache."

"But aren't you forgetting the years of joy Landon might bring to your life?"

Jessie knew she wasn't getting through to him. Didn't know if she ever could. "Might doesn't make right.

"That's bullshit. You don't know—"

"I do too! You have no freakin' clue what I went through as a kid."

"Then explain it to me."

She slammed the remainder of the whiskey. "You met Billy Reynolds. He adopted me, but I still wondered about the man who'd fathered me. I still wished he'd come to his senses and search me out, especially when things were bad at home. I can't tell you how many hours I spent imagining my 'real' father would show up and rescue me. He'd admit he'd been searching for me for years, he'd tell me how much he loved me and then he'd take me away. I had those stupid daydreams even when I resented the hell out of him for abandoning me."

Brandt stared into the bottom of his empty shot glass. "Don't you think there were times when I was growing up that I fantasized there'd been some mix up at the hospital and I went home with the wrong people? All kids feel like that at some point in there lives."

"Or they feel like that all the time because it's not a fantasy, but reality. So you can't tell me I don't know how Landon will feel a few years down the road, because I have a pretty good idea. Better than you do."

"Protecting yourself at all costs?" he asked.

"Yes, maybe for the first time in my life. And even you can't fault me for that."

The pointlessness of the conversation prompted her to retreat. Brandt didn't attempt to stop her.

In her bedroom, she stripped, slipped on her long johns and crawled in bed, burrowing under the covers because she couldn't seem to get warm.

A while later, Brandt entered the bedroom. She heard his clothes hitting the floor and felt the mattress dip. Then his warm body connected with hers. He wrapped one arm around her waist, one arm stretched under her pillow, tangling their legs together so they were touching from head to toe.

As Brandt toyed with her hair, so sweetly, so soothingly, Jessie released some of her tension.

"We will figure this out, Jessie," he said softly.

She had figured it out. He just needed to accept it.

Later, when he thought she'd fallen asleep, and he whispered, "Don't make me choose, Jessie, please don't make me choose," she feared he already had.

They both had.

"It's only for a few hours. I promise."

Jessie scowled at him. "Why do I have to go?"

Brandt couldn't resist kissing her scowling mouth. "Because I don't wanna leave you alone on Christmas Day. In and out quickly, I promise. Landon will open his gifts from my mom, we'll eat dinner and then we're gone."

"Will your dad be there?"

Brandt rolled his eyes. "What do you think?"

"I think you've already broken two of my original stipulations," she muttered.

And the morning had been going so well.

Jessie sighed. "Fine. Am I supposed to buy a gift for your mom?"

"No. Why?"

"Don't you guys open presents on Christmas Day?"

"Yeah, but we don't give each other gifts."

"Why not?"

"To be honest, we never really did."

She frowned. "But the year I was there, you guys exchanged gifts."

"With you," he pointed out. "Not with each other. Luke told us we'd better get you something since you intended to give each of us a gift. Luke wanted to pretend, for your sake, that we had the same type of normal Christmas everyone else did."

"You didn't celebrate Christmas at all? Ever?"

"We must've for a while when we were kids. I think Luke broke the news to Dalton that Santa wasn't real when Dalton was around five. Dalton asked Dad if it was true and that was the end of presents on Christmas morning."

Jessie turned back toward the sink. "That's sad. Now I really don't want to go."

"But my mom loved it the year you were there. Gave her an excuse to put up a tree and do the holiday stuff she hadn't done in years."

"And gave your father another reason to resent me. Which is all the more reason to be thankful, I guess." She sighed and sank her hands all the way into the dishwater.

"Thankful for what?"

"Thankful I didn't end up like your mom, because God knows I was headed that direction. Luke McKay's mouse-like wife who wouldn't rock the boat even if it was about to go sail a waterfall."

"I never saw you that way, Jess."

"You're the only one."

Brandt curled his hands around her hips and bent his head to taste that sweet section of skin below her ear. "As far as I'm concerned, I'm the only one who matters."

She murmured, "Brandt," but she didn't attempt to pull away.

"So..." His lips moved up to nibble on her earlobe, "Landon is napping. Wanna get nekkid and wild?"

"Maybe when I finish the dishes."

He growled, "That's it," and yanked her hands out of the

water, spinning her to face him. "I haven't been paying enough attention to you if you'd rather do the dishes than do me."

Jessie laughed. "I *am* feeling neglected. We only had sex once yesterday."

"Couch." He kissed her hard. "Now."

A trail of clothes littered the floor from the kitchen to where they were naked on the couch.

Brandt was ready to be inside her the instant his bare ass hit the cushion and he had a naked, wiggling Jessie on his lap. But he forced himself to slow down. To take the time to marvel that this gorgeous, sexy, spontaneous woman wanted him. That she was his.

But for how long?

Forever, if he had his way, but he knew Jessie wasn't ready to hear that from him yet. He didn't believe if it came right down to it she'd walk away from him and Landon, no matter what she said.

Focus on the nekkid woman in front of you, man.

He kissed down the delectable arch of her neck. Once his mouth reached the upper swell of her breasts, he urged, "Lean back."

Jessie placed her hands on his thighs above his knees, and let her head fall back, giving her body the most beautiful curve, from the tip of her chin down to the angle of her hips.

Sometimes the woman took his breath away.

Brandt cupped her breasts in his hand, using his thumb and index finger to tug the right nipple into a tight point. He latched onto the left nipple and sucked. As he switched sides, he rubbed his face on her chest. He loved the sensation of her soft, warm skin against his cheeks. Loved leaving tiny red marks from his razor stubble on her tender flesh.

She moaned, pressing her chest against his mouth.

He suckled, nipped and caressed every inch of her pretty tits until he felt her short nails biting into his thighs. Until he caught a whiff of her sweet cream.

Brandt took her hand and put it on his cock, murmuring, "Take me in, Jess."

She drew the tip across her wet folds, catching the rim of his cockhead on her clit, stopping to rub it over and over. When he growled, she splayed her knees, lowered her pelvis and sheathed him completely.

"That's good. Goddamn that's good."

"Better than dishes."

"Definitely."

His greedy hands were all over her skin. Down the softly rounded globes of her ass. The outside contour of her thighs. He reached between them, letting his finger trace the pliant skin stretching to accommodate his dick. Then his finger moved back a fraction of an inch, brushing over the pucker of her ass.

Immediately Jessie stiffened.

Brandt kept kissing her neck, stroking the sensitive ring, pressing against the resistance. Using the wetness from her body, Brandt pushed his finger inside her anal passage, up to the second knuckle. He let her body get used to the intrusion before he began to move his finger. Fucking that tight hole in the same rhythm she was fucking him. The muscle clamped down on his finger and he groaned, imagining his cock being squeezed so forcefully.

"Brandt, what are you doing?"

"Playin'. Seein' how far you'll let me go."

"That's far enough."

He lightly scraped his teeth down her throat. "Okay. But I'll point out that you like my finger teasin' your ass while I'm licking your pussy. You like my tongue teasin' it while I'm licking your pussy too. Makes me wanna watch this sweet little hole stretching to take my cock. Don't you want that?" He pumped his finger in and out, stopping to tease that ring, now that his finger had brought blood to those nerve endings.

"No. I'm, ah, not fond of anal sex. It hurts."

It surprised him she and Luke had experimented with it, since Luke bragged he'd gone elsewhere to satisfy what he called his carnal needs.

"Doesn't have to hurt. We could go slow. I bet I could make you like it."

Jessie groaned as he flexed his hips and drove his cock in deeper. "You probably could, but right now I'm liking this a whole bunch. I'm close, but I need it harder."

He did too. He slapped her butt. "Get up for a second and turn around."

The pleasure fog in her eyes cleared and she frowned at

him. "I don't think—"

Brandt laid a smacking kiss on her lips. "Don't worry. I'm not gonna plow into your ass right now. If we switch to reverse cowgirl, I'll be able to move better." He kissed her again. "Faster." One more soft smooch. "Harder."

"God yes." She scrambled off his dick so fast he laughed.

Scooting to the very edge of the couch, he repositioned her on his lap, facing forward, her knees by his hips. "Reach for the edge of the coffee table." He pressed his hand over her mound, keeping her pelvis tilted so he could toy with her clit.

She pushed back into him as he drove forward. "This position should be called frogger with my legs like this," she panted. "And I don't like how my ass is in the air."

"I love your ass in the air. It's sexy."

"It's weird.

But Jessie's tense body supported her statement. He stroked his thumb side to side on her clit in the way that made her forget everything but how good he could make her feel. "Come on, Jess. Let go. Let it take you."

"I can't. This feels too much like...we're trying to be circus performers."

Her words had the intended effect. He stopped moving. She pushed up to look at him. The uncertainty in her eyes was his undoing. As much as he loved to test their boundaries, their flexibility, there came a point when it wasn't necessary, like now.

Somehow he got her turned around. Somehow in the mix of arms and legs and strangely angled bodies, and the tightly pulled thread of need tethering them together, they ended up on the floor. Face to face, skin to skin. He put his lips by her ear and breathed, "Jessie McKay, you own me," and slid inside her.

Brandt rocked into her. Their pelvises moving in tandem. In opposition. In perfect synchronicity.

A rush of wetness coated his cock and her cunt contracted around his shaft. He held still, letting her body drag him over the edge. He closed his eyes to lose himself in the moment. To lose himself in this woman he loved.

As soon as Brandt's cock quit pulsing and her contractions tapered off, Brandt lifted his head from where he'd buried it in the sweet spot of her neck.

She grinned. Wickedly. "On the floor beneath the tree on Christmas Eve afternoon, Mr. McKay? Mmm. I feel so very naughty. Probably means Santa's not coming tonight, huh?"

"Oh, I wouldn't say that. I have a feeling Santa is coming a lot of times tonight."

Chapter Twenty

"Merry Christmas," Brandt whispered, nuzzling the back of Jessie's head.

"Merry Christmas to you too." She yawned. "What time is it?"

"Eight."

She groaned and rolled away from his tempting body. "I told you not to wake me up until noon."

"But somebody woke me up, so I wanted to spread the love."

"Landon is up?"

"Yep." Brandt scooted closer. "Which is a shame because I had great plans involving me tasting your sugar plum first thing this morning." He whapped her on the rump and she yelped. "Get up. I already fed the animals. I made coffee. And a coffee cake."

She whipped around so fast they almost bumped noses. "Excuse me? I must've had the covers over my ears. I thought I heard you say you made cake."

Brandt smooched her chin. "I did."

"You? Made...cake?"

"I have been cookin' for myself for years, Jess, so I'm not totally helpless in the kitchen."

"I didn't say you were. I would've expected you to whip up scrambled eggs. Or oatmeal. But coffee cake?" Did he know how much she loved coffee cake? "What kind?"

"Caramel. It's warm and gooey, because you know how much I love warm and gooey first thing in the mornin'."

Jessie threw the covers back. "If you're lyin' to me Brandt

McKay, so help me..."

"I'm not." He tossed her a robe. "Come on. The boy is anxious to open his presents."

"Which boy?" she asked his retreating back.

He turned around and grinned. "Both of 'em."

Landon raced over and slammed into her knees. He had two speeds, full throttle and idle. She swooped him up. "Merry Christmas, lil' buckaroo. Should we see if Uncle Brandt's cake is edible?"

"Yef."

"So agreeable." She couldn't resist nuzzling him. He smelled like baby shampoo, orange juice and little boy.

Breakfast was fast. Jessie inhaled two pieces of coffee cake and settled in the living room with her new mug that Santa had left for her by the coffee pot.

Brandt demonstrated how to rip into wrapping paper and it was over. Landon shrieked while shredding every last inch of Christmas paper from his gifts. Brandt had gone a little overboard buying presents, but he had almost as much fun watching Landon rip the paper as Landon did shredding it.

"See? That fire truck has a working siren." Brandt pushed the button and a really obnoxious *whoop whoop whoop* erupted.

Jessie stared at Brandt until he said, "What?"

"*You* picked that out?"

"Yeah. Why?"

"Because it's annoying, that's why."

"All boys love fire trucks. It's a right of passage. Besides, if you think this one is noisy? You oughta see what Keely bought him."

She shuddered.

Landon hit excitement overload, ignoring his gifts and sitting in the pile of wrapping paper, throwing it in the air, or at Lexie, or tearing it into smaller pieces.

Two unopened gifts remained under the tree. "Aren't you going to open your present from me, Brandt?"

"Don't you wanna go first?"

"Nope. I'm comfy drinking my coffee. You go ahead."

Brandt snagged the box from beneath the tree. When Landon saw another paper ripping opportunity, he loped to Brandt's side. Brandt said, "I suppose you can help me," as

241

Landon tore away a chunk of paper.

Jessie's stomach knotted. Maybe Brandt would think her gift was stupid. She hid behind her coffee cup as he lifted the lid on the box.

When Brandt froze, her heart fell to her toes. She prepared for a polite look of interest on his face when he finally glanced up. But all she saw was astonishment. "Jess. I can't believe you—"

"I still use the wallet you made me. It was one of the best gifts I've ever gotten." She dropped her gaze to her coffee cup but she couldn't keep from babbling. "I don't know if you still do leatherwork, which you should, because it'd be a damn crying shame to let that talent go to waste. I'm not sure if you have punches like those, but I thought they were cool and if you don't like them I can take them back—"

Then Brandt's hands were on her face, his mouth was on hers and he was kissing her with such gentleness and gratitude she could scarcely breathe. He pulled away to rest his forehead to hers. "No one has ever...you are...Jess. Thank you. It's perfect." He groaned. "And now I'm wishing I could take yours back because it's nowhere near as—"

"Brandt. I'm sure it's fine."

"I guess we'll see, won't we?" Brandt pushed the box to her with his foot and sat on the opposite end of the couch.

Landon bulled his way over to help. Jessie lifted the box onto the coffee table and waited as Landon's next strategic rip revealed...a machine that shampooed carpets. "Wow. Is this really what's in the box?"

"Yeah. I remembered one night we were watching TV and an infomercial came on and you said you always wanted one. But it's kind of lame, isn't it?"

Jessie had zero expectations when it came to receiving gifts. She must've waited too long to respond because Brandt swooped down and picked it up off the table.

"Never mind, no biggie, I'll return it."

She stood and tried to snatch the box out of his hands. "Hey, that's mine. You gave it to me, so you don't get to take it back."

"You don't have to pretend you like it, Jess, just to spare my stupid feelings. It was a dumb gift idea."

She jerked the box away from him and set it aside so she

could get right in his face. "It's not dumb. It's thoughtful and I'm sorry I wasn't jumping up and down screaming with joy. But I'm not really a scream-and-jump-up-and-down type of woman."

His cheeks were red with embarrassment. "You don't have to explain."

"Yes, I do. Because you know what buying that carpet cleaner proved? That you listen to me. That you pay attention to me. So in my mind, the gift is perfect. Thank you." She brushed her lips across his. One, two, three, four times. By kiss five he was fully on board, kissing her back.

"Up, up!" Landon said, trying to worm between their legs.

"So sorry we weren't payin' enough attention to you," Brandt said. "How about if we look at some of the toys you're ignoring?"

After Jessie listened to Landon beat on the drums for ten solid minutes, she vowed to get even with Keely. She ducked into the bedroom to get dressed for the McKay family feud. She reminded herself she was doing this for Brandt.

With Landon's things loaded in the diaper bag, she smooched Brandt on the chin. "No offense, but I'll take my own truck. That way if you and Landon wanna stay and hang out after the meal, you can."

"That way you won't get stuck there."

"True."

"Maybe Casper will be on his best behavior," Brandt offered.

Jessie said, "Wanna make a bet?"

Good thing they didn't bet on it.

Casper was a nightmare. Brandt figured his father had been drinking for several hours before they arrived.

It was the Christmas dinner from hell.

Casper ranted about everything under the sun from the stupidity of the government, to inflated cattle prices, to his brothers' idiotic decisions with running the ranch. He wasn't blatant in calling his sons brown-nosing, suck ups, when it came to their uncles and cousins, but it was heavily implied.

Dalton and Tell stuffed their faces rather than engage him.

His mother was up and down throughout dinner, getting this and that. If he hadn't known better, he'd suspect she was hitting the bottle in between refilling the gravy boat and the bread basket.

However, for some reason, Casper ignored Jessie completely. He didn't look at her, didn't talk to her. It was as if she was beneath his notice. Brandt comforted himself with the knowledge Jessie was better off being invisible than in Casper's line of fire.

But no, Casper was just sneakier and waited to approach Jessie until Brandt wasn't around. He'd cornered her by the bathroom. Casper leaned back with a smug smile when Brandt appeared and grabbed Jessie's hand. "Come on. Mom is dishing up pie."

Jessie left immediately following dessert.

Brandt wished he could've left, too, but he stayed to watch Landon rip open more presents. He was glad when Landon had a total screaming fit, because it gave him a valid excuse to leave.

The long day had taken its toll, and Landon was down for the count early. Brandt bided his time, waiting to talk to Jessie until after they cleaned up the wrapping paper mess.

She tied the garbage bag and headed outside to dump it.

He followed her. She hadn't worn a coat and it was freezing out, so she'd be anxious to get the conversation over fast.

"What did my father say to you?"

She tried to sidestep him, but he blocked her. "I don't want to talk about it."

"Tough. What he said upset you."

"Like that's news, Brandt. Just drop it."

Brandt grabbed her biceps and ran his palms up and down her arms to warm her. "Please. If you don't tell me it'll just drive a wedge between us, which is exactly what he wants."

"He said that you'd taken that old bible verse about a man's responsibility in taking care of his brother's widow literally and all I am to you is an obligation. That you'd tire of me soon, just like Luke had."

Goddamn good thing he was freezing his ass off, it was probably the only thing keeping his blood from boiling. "That bastard. You know that's not true. That I—"

"Yeah, I do. But it still stings. It pisses me off that he can cut me so deeply so quickly."

"He's always had that uncanny ability to know just where to put that knife. I'm sorry."

Jessie looked up at him. "Please don't confront him about this. It'll just make it worse."

"I won't. In fact, let's just forget all about it." He kissed her cold cheeks. "Because I believe you'n me have a date with the couch, a bowl of popcorn and a whole pile of westerns."

The shadows cleared from her eyes. "Sounds good. I need to change into something more comfortable first." She started toward the house.

"Comfortable? Like what?"

"Well, I was thinking my pajamas because I'm freezing my ass off, but I might be convinced to wear something else."

"Like what?"

She sent him a *come and get it* smile over her shoulder. "Like...just my skin."

Immediate erection.

He chased her inside, down the hallway and tackled her to the bed. "Great idea. Let's have intermission first."

"Just make sure you and Landon are bundled up really good. I'll be right back."

Jessie glanced at the clock. Granted it was only ten on New Year's Eve, but it was two and a half hours past Landon's bedtime. He was holding up pretty well, showing no signs of an impending meltdown, which was in itself a miracle given the rough week they'd had.

Since Sky Blue closed over the holidays, Jessie had been home with Landon every day, much to Landon's disappointment. Because ranch work needed done regardless of the holiday season, Brandt's schedule hadn't changed and he hadn't been around. Plus, Joan McKay had caught a terrible cold and didn't want to expose Landon to it, so Jessie didn't get a break until Brandt came home.

One thing the week had taught her? She wasn't cut out to be a fulltime stay at home mom if she was blessed with children of her own. During her short pregnancy she'd imagined her days filled with holding and admiring her cherubic babe. Oddly enough, she'd never seen past that idyllic image to the sacrifices that parenting demanded.

Now that she'd worked in daycare, she appreciated not only the structure and activity it provided, but the chance for the kids to interact with other kids of different ages. Her charges had become enthralled when Ginger and Kane's babies became part of the daycare. The fact Skylar helped out on the days the twins came really proved to Jessie how much she'd come to consider the people she worked with at Sky Blue her family. Yet, she admired the satisfaction Skylar, Ginger, and India received from having a career outside of parenthood. Not that Jessie faulted those women who chose to stay at home with their children, but it'd moved something inside her, interacting with the women she worked with after she'd started taking care of Landon. Most of them had been in less than ideal situations at some point. It amazed her how they'd been able to turn their lives around.

Which always led her to thinking about Landon's mother. Had she reached that tipping point in her life yet? Or would she need a few more years to pull herself together? Brandt never mentioned his conversations with Samantha, but Jessie sensed when he'd had contact with her, because his mood was subdued. Or more likely, his mood reflected that he'd attempted to contact Samantha and she hadn't been available or responded. Jessie overheard a conversation between Brandt and Tell, where Brandt expressed his frustration with Samantha's lack of communication since landing in the halfway house.

Even Skylar had asked what would happen if Samantha wanted to waive Landon's responsibilities after her release. Jessie didn't answer, mostly because she wasn't sure how to answer.

Fortunately, she had six weeks left to figure it out.

A rumbling noise sounded and Jessie realized she'd been so lost in thought she hadn't gotten ready for Brandt's mystery outdoor excursion. New Year's Eve hadn't ever ranked in her top five favorite holidays; actually it was at the very bottom of the list. She was glad Brandt declined the party invite from his cousin Colby. Evidently Keely decided to host a massive slumber party for all of her nephews and nieces and her cousin's kids, so her brothers, cousins and their wives could have an adult night. She wondered how Jack was faring after his wife *volunteered* him to help with twenty-some kids under the age of ten.

By the time Brandt came inside and stomped the snow from his boots, both Jessie and Landon were bundled up. He grinned. "Grab some extra blankets and let's go."

The side-by-side Yamaha ATV idled by the steps. Lexie jumped in the back. Landon clapped his mitten-clad hands, shouting, "Yef! Yef!" The kid loved riding in the four-wheeler, and having Lexie along was like Christmas for him all over again.

Jessie asked, "Where are we going?"

"To my favorite spot on the ranch. It's a full moon tonight and it's so cold the sky is completely clear of clouds. I thought it'd be fun to take a moonlight ride."

Damn. He'd gone the extra mile to set aside time just for them after she'd spent all day taking care of Landon. His thoughtfulness—without expecting anything in return—was just one of the many reasons she loved him.

Yes, she'd finally come to terms with the fact she'd fallen for him. It felt right. She loved him. She'd said it out loud a few times, practicing how it sounded. Natural? Fake? Desperate? It'd been years since she'd used those particular words and never to any man except Luke. She'd loved Luke and it hadn't been enough. So she couldn't help fear history was about to repeat itself. She loved Brandt, but once again, she wasn't sure if love was enough.

The wind blown snow crust was solid enough the ATV rolled over the top of the snowdrifts without problem. Brandt tried to follow the tire tracks made from feeding cattle, but the four-wheeler bogged down, so he forged a new path. He was mindful of speed and angle of the dips and rises since Landon sat on her lap. Even so, the somewhat bumpy ride had lulled Landon to sleep.

The night, though cold, was magical. Due to the brilliance of the moon, the sky wasn't a solid black backdrop, but a dark gray swath punctuated with silvery stars. Moonbeams bounced off the snow, making the icy crystals dangling from sage plants look like rhinestones. The snow itself sparkled as if the wind had swirled glitter across the land. In all the years she'd lived in

Wyoming she'd never seen the harsh beauty appear so enchanted. Dreamlike. With no other sounds or noises or lights, it was as if they were the only ones in the world.

The ATV scaled a steep rise and they were on top of a plateau. Brandt cut the engine. With the cloudless night, visibility in all directions was unobstructed and they could see for miles.

"Breathtaking, ain't it?"

"Yes. I...I don't even know what to say."

"I've been comin' here my whole life and I'm still not used to how this view just knocks me flat." Brandt put his arm behind her on the seat. "It's humbling."

"It is." She'd always known the ranch meant a lot to Brandt. But in that moment, she knew that he was as much a part of this Wyoming land as the soil and the sage.

"Thanks for sharing this with me, Brandt."

"No one else in the world that I'd rather be with or share it with, Jessie, you know that, right?"

She nodded.

"I brought something to help us celebrate the New Year in style." He reached back in the storage compartment and pulled out a bottle of champagne.

Jessie laughed. "You're crazy. That'll be all kinds of shook up after our trek across the frozen tundra."

"Yeah, but it'll be nice and cold." He took off his glove and twisted the wire cage holding the cork. Then he slowly eased the cork out and not a single drop foamed out the top.

She said, "I'm impressed with your pop topping technique. In more ways than one."

"But in true redneck style, I didn't bring glasses. We're drinkin' it straight outta the bottle."

"Works for me."

Brandt held the bottle to her lips and she drank carefully, enjoying the cold tang of the champagne bubbles bursting on her tongue.

Then Brandt drank. They watched the moon move across the sky as they finished the bottle. When she shivered, Brandt pressed his warm lips to hers and murmured, "Happy New Year, Jess."

"Happy New Year, Brandt."

She snuggled close to him on the drive home, still taking it all in. The moonlit ride. The majesty of the place he called home. That simple kiss that held more emotion than any words he could've said. A feeling of peace, of rightness drifted over her.

But life was never that easy and she should've known her sense of peace wouldn't last.

Chapter Twenty-One

When Brandt excused himself after answering his cell phone, Jessie knew something was up.

He'd been outside for almost a half hour and she began to worry something bad had happened. Phone sex with her not withstanding, Brandt hated to talk on the phone. His conversations where short and to the point.

Landon smacked his mini dump truck on the coffee table, culling her attention. "Careful, lil' buckaroo, you might smash your fingers."

He pushed the dump truck to her; she pushed it back. It'd become one of his favorite games, seeing how hard he could push a wheeled vehicle before it sailed off the table. And any time it went flying, he giggled.

She told Brandt that meant Landon was testing his boundaries.

Brandt told her that meant Landon was being a boy.

The truck made the trek over the flat surface eight times before Landon sent it careening over the edge on top of a sleeping Lexie.

The dog slunk away and now that she was awake, Landon decided it was time to play. He patted her head. Her belly. Lexie put up with Landon hugging her neck, but when Landon tried ride her like a bull, she balked and darted away.

Brandt returned from outside and Lexie shot out the door. Landon attempted to chase her, but Brandt caught him around his midsection with one hand. "Whoa, it's cold and dark out there. And if Lexie's runnin' from you, she's got good reason, so you need to stay put."

"Goggie!"

"How about if we have that bath?"

"No!" Landon became as limp as a worm.

But Brandt was wise to his tricks. "Nice try, but you're getting in the tub."

"No! No! No!" echoed down the hallway until the bathroom door shut.

Jessie told herself if it'd been really bad news, Brandt would've told her instead of allowing Landon to distract him. She tidied up the toys, folded up the blankets, swept the floor. By the time she'd finished, a scrubbed Landon barreled toward her and didn't stop until he'd hit her knees.

"That was a fast bath tonight."

"Up!"

She perched him on her hip and he curled into her, nestling his head on front of her shoulder. "I swear when you're such a sweet-smelling, sweet-acting boy I can almost forgive how you torture my poor dog." She smooched his crown.

"Are you gonna read to him?"

Jessie looked up and saw Brandt leaning in the doorjamb, wearing a pensive expression. "I'd planned to. Why?"

"No reason." Brandt smiled. "He just loves it."

A snuggly, attentive Landon was a treat after dealing with his rambunctious ways all day. She settled in the easy chair and grabbed the book on the top of the stack—a book about dinosaurs.

Brandt draped Landon's blanket over him and retreated to the kitchen.

Landon's eyes were drooping by the time she finished the story. She tucked him in his crib and he didn't fuss about not having a bottle.

She debated whether to crawl in the shower or find out what Brandt's phone call was about. No contest.

Brandt sat in the middle of the couch and patted his lap. "C'mere and give me some sugar."

"In a second. I need a drink." She poured a glass of water and brought it back to the living room with her. "So you gonna tell me about the phone call? Or just distract me with sex?"

His humor vanished.

"Who was it?"

"Samantha."

Jessie remained standing. "What did she want?"

"To tell me she'd been released from the halfway house in Casper."

"When?"

The muscle in Brandt's jaw flexed.

"When?" she repeated.

"Five days ago."

"And she's just calling you now?"

"Evidently she had some stuff—"

"I don't want to hear you make excuses for her, Brandt."

"I'm not." Brandt rubbed the line of his forehead where his hat usually rested. "It wasn't her choice, it was a court thing. Anyway, she wants to meet with us. Specifically...you."

Jessie had the sensation of falling. Air rushing in her ears, her body bracing for that bone jarring impact. Everything blurred.

"Jess?"

She jumped. "What does she want?"

"I don't know."

She didn't believe him, but picking a fight to get him to come clean wouldn't be wise. "Where and when will this meeting take place?"

"At the Pizza Barn in Moorcroft at noon." He paused. "The day after tomorrow."

"She can take five fucking days to get her shit together and she gives us thirty-six hours?"

"We knew this day was coming. It came more than month earlier than we expected, but it's not a surprise."

"We're just supposed to pack his stuff and hand him over?"

Brandt's inquisitive eyes trapped hers. "Yes. Isn't that what you wanted?"

No.

I don't know.

I have no clue what I want anymore.

Jessie fought a feeling of panic. However her hand remained steady as she drained the glass of water. "Yes, I suppose it is."

Silence.

"Well, I'm gonna hit the hay. Night."

"Night, Jess. I'll come to bed in a bit."

In her bedroom her fingers were numb as they worked the buttons on her western shirt. Somehow she stripped. Somehow she crawled in bed. Somehow she found the energy to berate herself for her emotional investment with the pesky kid when she'd sworn she wouldn't let that happen.

Yet, for the first time in her life, somehow she found the strength not to cry.

Jessie, girl, you're such a liar.

Brandt had tried to remain neutral, to see if she would be honest and admit her once hard stance toward long term care involving Landon had softened. But she'd thrust out that stubborn chin, denied it and run away.

But she couldn't deny what he'd seen tonight. What he'd seen the last few months. Jessie's patience, kindness, firmness and amusement regarding Landon. She loved him.

Jessie had been exactly right. Landon would break her heart and there wasn't a damn thing he could do about it. Because it was his fault. He'd brought that heartache right to her.

Would she ever forgive him?

He slipped into bed and spooned in behind her. He appreciated she didn't feign sleep. "You wanna talk?"

"Nope."

"You wanna fuck?"

"Nope."

You want me to tell you I love you, I've loved you forever and I'm relieved I don't have to choose between you and my nephew?

Her answer would be nope to that too.

Brandt hadn't told Jessie that Samantha insisted all of Landon's stuff be boxed up and ready to go. Maybe Samantha was proving she had the power. Maybe she was ready to become a parent to her son. He knew Jessie well enough that if he told her about Samantha's request, she'd obsess about what it meant.

He called his brothers and asked if they could take Landon tomorrow night, as they'd planned. It might be easier for everyone.

That was a total fucking lie. This wouldn't be easy on any of them.

When Brandt informed her Landon would spend the night with Dalton and Tell, rather than them, Jessie fought her urge to lash out at him.

We knew this day was coming.

They'd watched TV like any other night. In bed, Brandt reached for her, like he did every night. His way of dealing with her melancholy wasn't to match it with sweetness, but to counter it with heat. Lots of heat.

Brandt hadn't been content to stick with the tried and true. After whipping her into a frenzy by making her come three times, once with his fingers, once with his mouth and once with her vibrator, he pushed her on her back. While remaining on his knees, he hooked her right leg over his right shoulder. He turned her lower body sideways so he could imprison her left thigh between the back of his left thigh and his calf. Then he fucked her. He controlled everything. The depth of his thrusts. The spread of her pussy, and the contact point where her clit abraded his groin.

Oh, it was breathtaking, watching this ferocious man master her. Teach her. Pleasure her. Mesmerized by the fire in his eyes, Jessie had just held on, as her body became his playground. He watched her breasts bounce with every deep thrust. He watched her bring herself to orgasm. He watched his cock shuttling in and out of her pussy. When Brandt started to come, he turned, sinking his teeth into the outside of her thigh right by his head, giving her the sexiest love bite she'd ever had. They'd both collapsed.

He'd tucked her against his naked body, like he did every night, and drifted off.

She slept for maybe an hour or two and then she'd lain in his arms, restless. She disentangled from his embrace and snuck out to the kitchen.

A cup of hot herbal tea didn't induce sleepiness. She didn't dare clean or she'd wake Brandt. So she sat on the couch and tried to process everything that'd gone on the last three months.

Jessie wasn't sure why Samantha had insisted on talking to her face to face. Was Samantha gauging her fitness as

Landon's temporary guardian before she dropped the bomb she wasn't ready to resume fulltime parenting responsibilities yet?

For the past day, Jessie wrestled with the situation regarding Landon, the facts, the fears, the promises given and the promises broken. Mostly she weighed the promises she'd made to herself to keep an almost clinical detachment for the boy, to set a time limit for how long she'd allow herself to care for him. It was laughable now, thinking she could ever protect her heart from such a sweet soul, from Luke's son.

It was pitiful that she'd ever even tried.

Since she'd insisted Brandt didn't discuss anything involving Landon's mother, she couldn't bring up the fact she'd changed her mind about everything. Not until tomorrow.

Chapter Twenty-Two

Jessie loitered outside the Pizza Barn in Moorcroft. She kept her phone to her ear, pretending to be in the middle of an important conversation.

Stop stalling.

She pocketed her cell and entered the restaurant. Normally she took a second to breathe in the tangy scents of oregano, tomato sauce, spicy meat and cheese, and the earthy aroma of baking crust. But today, she didn't smell a thing.

Probably because you're holding your breath.

Two tables had customers. One booth held an older couple chowing down on pizza. A petite woman sat in the other booth, stirring a glass of soda. Had to be Samantha.

Jessie's heart galloped as she slowly crossed the room and stopped in front of the booth. "Samantha?"

"Yes?"

"I'm Jessie." She slid into the opposite seat without being asked, and scrutinized the woman without apology.

Samantha Johnston looked young now, so Jessie couldn't fathom how young she must've looked two and a half years ago. Her body type was slight. Not busty. An air of fragility surrounded her. A feature Jessie recognized because she'd had that same trait when she'd met Luke McKay.

"So if you're done inspecting me..."

She shrugged. "You had to expect that."

"Yes, I did. Thanks for coming early. I worried Brandt wouldn't pass along the message that I wanted to meet you."

Jessie frowned. "Why wouldn't Brandt—"

"Because he's very protective of you." Samantha leaned

back into the booth seat and crossed her arms over her chest, almost defiantly.

The waitress took Jessie's order and neither she nor Samantha said another word, nor did they look at each other until the waitress dropped off the soda and left.

"So why the summons, Samantha? I'll admit I wasn't sure this was the best idea."

"First of all, I really wanted to thank you in person for all you've done for Landon. I...it's so far above and beyond..."

Please don't get weepy.

"Plus, I feel I owe you an explanation about a couple of things regarding Luke."

Jessie held up her hand. "Not necessary. I don't need the down-and-dirty details about what went on between you two. Landon is proof enough for me. In fact, I'd rather not know."

"Part of my A.A. program and rehab assignment is owning up to my past behavior."

"Apologizing for it?" Jessie asked sharply.

"Would you accept an apology from me?"

I don't know.

Samantha blurted, "The truth is I wasn't in love with Luke and he wasn't in love with me. We weren't star-crossed lovers consumed with overpowering lust or any of that romantic movie bullshit."

That caught her attention.

"For about a month after we met, we hooked up when he came into the bar where I waitressed. Since it was bar, he thought I was older than I was and I didn't bother to tell him differently." Samantha looked away. "And I honestly didn't give a rat's ass he was married. Sounds terrible, doesn't it."

Not a question. Jessie reached for her soda to try and wash away the sour taste in her mouth. So Luke hadn't hidden his marital status. Was he hoping she'd get wind of this affair and leave him?

Would you have? If you'd known about this young woman, would you have left him?

No. Not then. Now? Yes. It hurt like a bitch to admit that to herself, but she was done lying to herself.

"Bottom line: I was convenient after closing time and so was he." She blatantly studied Jessie. "You surprised?"

"To be honest, I don't know what I am. Hurt and mad mostly. During that time I suspected Luke was seeing someone." *But I didn't have the balls to confront him about it.*

"We were only together a couple months. I was exclusive with him, even knowing he was going home to his wife after we..." She cleared her throat. "I never begged him to leave you, never wanted anything permanent with him. I broke it off with him a week before he died. No fuss, no muss. When I heard he died, I was sad, but not devastated. Probably not like you were.

"After I found out I was pregnant, I didn't know what to do. Especially when some of Luke's bar friends gossiped about how his family shut you out and cut you off completely. I figured they wouldn't believe me about being pregnant, and I thought they'd do the same to me."

"That's where you're wrong."

"Didn't matter at the time because I wasn't sure if I was gonna keep the baby. I'd contacted a couple of adoption places, but they didn't want to talk to me until the baby was born and I had a better grasp on my plans. I couldn't even work in the bar because I didn't want anyone to know I was pregnant."

"When did you decide to keep the baby?"

"The minute I pushed him out of my body. I never knew I could love like that. I'd never felt anything like it." She paused to take another sip of her soda. "Anyway, my old boyfriend showed up when Landon was two months old and living with my judgmental aunt was making me crazy, so we moved in with him. Mistake. Not only was his mother certifiable, within four months I'd gotten a DUI. When I got my second...Talk about a serious wake up call. I was just lucky Landon wasn't in the car with me. As I sat in county lockup, I realized I was headed down the same stupid path my mom had taken, drinking too much, relying on random men, leaving my kid with strangers so I could..." Samantha paused, keeping her face pointed at the table, not meeting Jessie's eyes.

It was difficult to watch her struggle because Jessie's first impulse was to comfort and reassure her. She squeezed her hands into fists beneath the table and kept her mouth firmly closed.

"I ain't gonna play the 'my childhood sucked' card. It sucked getting dumped off whenever my mom got tired of me, but I know I'm not the only one who had a shitty go of it growing up. I know I shouldn't use it as an excuse to be a shitty mother to my own kid. He deserves better."

Was this where Samantha confessed she still wasn't ready to take on that role? Jessie braced herself, but she couldn't stop her heart from racing.

"So I left Drex and crawled back to my aunt to prove to her I was gonna change. But she refused to believe it, refused to agree to take care of Landon when I went to jail. I panicked. I mean, what was I gonna do? My only option was to tell Luke's family about his son and hope they could take him in for a while."

"So you wouldn't've told them about Landon if you'd had another option?"

"I don't know. The risk of the McKays taking him away was better than Social Services getting a hold of him and making me prove for the next sixteen years that I'm a fit mother. So when I met Brandt...I trusted him. Immediately. I knew Landon would have family, no matter what happened to me." Samantha glanced up and locked her teary-eyed gaze to Jessie's. "Now that I've told you the ugly truth, can you be honest with me about something?"

Somehow she worked up enough spit to speak. "I'll try."

"Did you come here today because you were hoping you'd get to have Landon a little longer?"

Jessie was too stunned to answer.

But Samantha wouldn't let it go. "Or were you scared you and Brandt might be stuck with Landon permanently?"

Inwardly Jessie squirmed. But she supposed the questions weren't any harder to answer than they were for Samantha to ask. "I had no freakin' clue. I suspected you'd need time to get your life back together after being in jail and I wasn't sure how long it'd take. But I know Brandt never would use the word 'stuck' when it comes to taking care of his nephew. He loves Landon. Unconditionally. He would've done what needed done."

"What about you?"

Brandt's words, *Don't make me choose, Jessie, please, don't make me choose,* stuck with her. Haunted her.

"Landon is a sweet boy and I liked taking care of him and being a part of his life."

"But?"

Being totally open with Samantha about her change of heart, when she hadn't told Brandt about it yet felt like a breach of trust. Jessie looked at her. "But I'm glad you're stepping up to your responsibilities."

"I know it won't be easy. I made some mistakes. And it might sound like I've been brainwashed or something, but being in jail was good for me. Being away from Landon was good for me too. Because now, I understand what's important in my life, when before..." Her voice wavered. "I love him so much and I want him to know it every day. I want to be the mom who tucks him in every night and reads him bedtime stories. I want to teach him how to do stuff like ride a bike. I want to take him to the park. I want to sign him up for little league when he's bigger. I want him to have friends. And family. I want to make sure he's got more to eat for supper than a bag of Cheetos. I want be the kind of mother I never had. I can do it. I know I can do it. I *want* to do it. Learning to take care of myself and my son is all that matters to me now."

That's when Jessie knew. This woman, given another chance, would be a good mother. She'd be a good person. She'd paid for her mistakes and now she had a chance to make her life right, to move on and to put her past behind her. She deserved the chance to prove it to herself and to Landon. She needed Jessie's support. Not her scorn. Not her skepticism.

Keep it light or you will lose it completely. "You're in luck because in the last couple months Landon discovered he loves having stories read to him."

Samantha wiped her eyes. "Really? I never had extra money to buy him books."

"He's got a box full of them now. And there's always the library when he gets bored with them." Jessie smiled. "I had extras from the daycare, and Brandt...well, he and Tell and Dalton had such a great time buying Landon boy toys. I'm afraid you'll have a whole bunch of stuff to pack."

"Trust me. I don't mind. I can't wait."

She noticed that Samantha's focus kept drifting to the door. "What are your plans?"

"I'll start my education rehab at the community college in Casper in a couple weeks. They've got housing and daycare and I can do work-study during the day, so I can be with Landon at night and on weekends. Since that's where the halfway house was, I've gotten involved with a local A.A. program. My sponsor introduced me to a counselor and he's really encouraging about making *positive forward progress*, which is a first in my life, to be honest."

All of a sudden Samantha's face lit up. She made a soft gasp and hopped out of the booth and then seemed frozen in place, as she waited. Was she afraid her son wouldn't recognize her? Was she afraid Landon would come to Jessie first?

A dark head streaked past and Jessie heard a shrieked, "Mama mama mama!"

Samantha lifted Landon in her arms, hugging him tight, sobbing, "Omigod, baby, I missed you so so much. I swear I'm never gonna..."

"Mama mama mama!"

She held him and cried buckets. Through her gasping cries, Samantha babbled, making Landon incoherent promises. Kissing his cheeks. Rubbing his back. Touching him as if his presence might be a dream. Just holding him like she'd never let him get away from her again.

That softened the knife's edge of pain a little.

Samantha's eyes drank in every nuance of his face. "Lookit you. You're such a big boy now."

"Yef."

She laughed, even though she was still crying. "And you're talking too. I'm in for it now, huh?"

"Yef."

Jessie slipped from the booth, desperate to escape because this was goodbye she'd been dreading since the day she'd first set eyes on him. With her feelings in such turmoil, she was as afraid she'd break down as she was afraid she wouldn't break down.

Landon finally looked at her and those big blue eyes lit up.

"Hey, lil' buckaroo," she said softly.

He said, "Down," and wiggled until his mother released him. He ran to Jessie hell bent for leather. His contact with her was more of a body check than a hug, which made her laugh. She squeezed him with one arm and placed a kiss on top of his head. "I'm gonna miss you, sweet boy."

Jessie expected him to squirm away, because even at nineteen months the kid had a time limit on hugs, especially when his uncles were around. God forbid if a McKay—of any age—appeared too girly.

But Landon didn't race away. He heaved a contented sigh against her neck. Then he moved back and placed a sticky hand on each of her cheeks. He locked his serious gaze to hers and gave her a kiss, square on the mouth. He emitted a noise deep in his throat, then he raced back to his mother.

It took about ten seconds to sink in.

Landon had acted exactly like Brandt. Holding her face. Kissing her. Making that possessive growl.

Her heart absolutely turned over. Landon had just told her, in his little boy way, that he loved her.

Good thing she'd crouched down because she didn't think her knees would hold her.

But Brandt was already helping her up, giving her his full support.

Tell said to Samantha, "We loaded all the stuff in your car so you're good to go."

So Brandt had known Samantha planned to take Landon with her. He had to've known packing up Landon's things would cause her pain and anxiety, so he simply hadn't mentioned it to spare her. Would she ever get used to the way he put her needs first?

"Thanks." Samantha buttoned her coat. Then she picked Landon up and held him very close. "I can't thank you guys enough for what you've done for us. I'll never be able to repay you."

"Takin' good care of him from here on out will be payment enough," Brandt said.

"That I can promise. I'll keep in touch about visitation and stuff." She fastened the Velcro under Landon's chin, securing his hood. "We'd better hit the road, huh, buddy?"

"Yef."

Brandt said, "Drive safe."

"I will."

And with that, Samantha and Landon walked away.

Jessie couldn't move. She was frozen in mind. In body. In spirit.

Brandt turned her around, trapping her face in his hands, wiping her tears, kissing her lips, her cheeks, the corners of her eyes.

How long they stood there, Jessie didn't know. At least until the server asked if there was a problem. Brandt grabbed Jessie's hand and led her outside to take her home.

Jessie stared out the window and Brandt didn't push her to talk. However, he wouldn't let go of her hand. He needed that constant connection to her.

She mumbled something about chores as soon as he shut the truck off. Her distraction could be dangerous so he followed her into the barn. When she slipped on a pair of coveralls, he did too. They worked side by side in silence, spreading hay to feed the horses and the llamas. She checked the stock tank to make sure it hadn't frozen since this morning. She did everything on autopilot. Brandt wondered how long before she'd crash.

Inside her trailer, neither she nor Brandt remarked how bare the living room was without Landon's toys strewn all over the rug. Without his bottles clogging the fridge. Without his trucks, cars, trains and books scattered across the coffee table. Even Lexie seemed out of sorts. She'd wander to the door, to Landon's room, then make a pitiful whine before she curled up in the kitchen in the spot where his high chair stood.

Brandt finally forced her to look at him. "Are you okay?"

"I don't know. Seeing her...Samantha. She's not what I expected. I sort of felt sorry for her. Then I realized I shouldn't feel sorry for her. She might not have much but she's got what I always wanted from Luke."

"A child."

"Yes. But that's not all I've been thinking about...I'm having such a hard time getting the words to make sense. And you need to know, Brandt. You deserve to know." Tears shimmered in her eyes and she looked so...lost.

"God. Jess. You're breakin' my heart. What can I do?"

"Let's do something. Anything. Go to a movie, or go out dancing, or go play pool, just get me out of this house and out of my head for a few hours."

That's when Brandt understood Jessie would be okay. For the first time all day the tight feeling in his chest loosened a little. "Great idea. We'll hit Applebee's in Spearfish for supper first and then we'll slip on our dancin' shoes at the Rockin' R outside Beulah."

"That sounds perfect."

"It's my lucky night, finding Brandt McKay at the bar first thing."

"Hello, Lydia."

"Howdy, stranger. I haven't seen you in ages."

He shrugged, keeping his eye on the door and not on Lydia's display of cleavage. "I've been busy."

"I'm glad you're here," she cooed. "I worried you might've found Jesus and were shunning honkytonks and temptations of the flesh or something noble."

"Not hardly." He'd given into the temptations of Jessie's flesh more times than he could count. In more ways than he could count. That thought brought a smile to his face.

"Lord, that sexy grin of yours still makes me weak kneed." Lydia leaned in, toying with the buttons on his shirt. "I remember putting a smile like that on your face a time or ten."

"Old news, Lydia."

"You know what they say...everything old can be new again."

Brandt laughed. Hard to believe he used to find this type of hardcore desperation attractive. He finished his beer and set the empty on the bar. "Nice talkin' to you. See you around." He started to leave.

But Lydia wrapped her arms around his waist. "Don't run off. Lemme buy you another beer for old times' sake."

"I don't think—"

"Fine. Then dance with me. Please? None of these guys dance as good as you. You could go for hours without getting tired."

Lydia could be very persuasive and sadly, Brandt wasn't immune to her flattery. Besides, Jessie had just stepped outside to take a call from her mom about what'd happened with Landon today. "Okay, one dance. That's it."

They zigzagged through the crowd on the dance floor. Lydia spun into his arms, like she'd done dozens of times when they'd been dating, but the flirty move annoyed him. He clasped her hand and started two-stepping. At least the fast tune would keep them from talking.

Unfortunately, Lydia wasn't deterred by the music's pace. "So whatcha been up to?"

"Ranch work." He twirled her, resetting the distance between their bodies.

"Aren't you gonna ask me what I've been up to?"

"No good, probably," he muttered and twirled her again.

"Bein' bad feels so good, doesn't it. You used to think so, too, cowboy." She spun herself and brushed her ass against his groin. "Or do you need a little reminder?"

This had been a mistake. Lydia had gone from persuasive to conniving. He managed a curt, "Behave."

Another laugh. "With the uptight way you're acting, I believe you might've found religion after all."

No. He'd found something better. Jessie.

Brandt tuned out Lydia's suggestive comments, maintaining a bland expression as his eyes kept darting toward the exit. What could be taking Jessie so long?

Thank God the song ended. Brandt immediately dropped Lydia's hands and attempted to retreat as the dance floor cleared.

But Lydia wasn't having any of it. She herded him backward even as he tried to dodge her. When the creases of his thighs hit the stage, he caught the edge to keep from falling on his ass. Lydia took advantage, slithering between his legs. She wound her arms around his neck like twin anacondas, unhinged her jaw and swallowed his face.

Jesus. Brandt felt like he was choking she'd jammed her tongue so far down his throat. He stood abruptly, expecting that'd dislodge her, but she clung to him like a deranged monkey.

Goddammit. Enough. He put his hands on her hips, intending to shove her away as he tried to dislodge his mouth from her fangs.

They were roughly pulled apart. "What the hell is goin' on here?"

His gaze flew to Jessie. Holy fuck was she pissed off. Brandt immediately got to his feet.

Lydia coyly wiped her mouth. When she sidled closer to

Brandt, Jessie inserted herself between them and snapped, "Answer the question."

"Me'n Brandt just got carried away, didn't we, honey?"

"Shut your mouth, Lydia."

"Sorry," Lydia pouted, without an ounce of remorse. "I was just trying to explain."

"Don't," he snapped.

Jessie's fury-darkened eyes never looked away from his. "Is it true, Brandt? Did you and Lydia get *carried away*?"

"No."

Her expression shifted. She whirled to face Lydia. "You get your kicks out of kissing an unwilling man?"

"Oh, sugar, don't kid yourself for a second he was unwilling."

"Bullshit."

Lydia smiled cagily. "What are you gonna believe? What you saw with your own eyes? Or what he tells you? 'Cause, you're awful damn naïve if you don't think he'll lie about what just happened to spare your feelings."

Direct hit. Brandt needed to get Jessie out of here now. "Jessie—"

Jessie's laughter cut him off. "You want proof?" She pointed to Brandt's groin. "He doesn't have a hard-on. If anything you did even turned him on a little, he'd be sporting wood. Trust me, I know. So, *sugar*, take your desperation to some other man because Brandt is not interested in you."

But Lydia wouldn't let it go. "So you're Jessie. The poor little widow whose husband couldn't keep it in his pants." She gave Jessie a derisive head-to-toe inspection. "No wonder he wandered. Looks like you're trying—and failing—to prove you can keep the interest of another McKay man."

"Shut your stupid mouth. You don't know a goddamned thing about Brandt."

"Hit a nerve, did I?"

"I'll show you hitting a nerve." Jessie leapt at Lydia.

Lydia screamed as they hit the floor, Jessie's fists flailed as she tried to connect with every part of Lydia's body she could reach. Then Lydia bucked and sent Jessie sprawling. But that didn't stop Jessie from crawling back and pouncing on her.

Brandt had never seen Jessie enraged. She'd wind up in

jail for assault if any of her punches actually landed. He crouched down, wrapped both arms around her middle and lifted her off Lydia.

"Let me go! I'm gonna beat her ass."

"I think you made your point."

"No, I'm not done. She doesn't understand that she doesn't get to say shit like that about you. I'm gonna make her understand if it takes all goddamn night!"

He held her, hugging her back to his chest, attempting to contain her. "Jess. Baby. Calm down."

"That fucking bitch attacked me," Lydia said as she picked herself up off the floor. "You all saw it."

Everyone who'd gotten closer to watch the catfight walked away. Not a single person stuck around to back up Lydia's claims.

Brandt figured they'd best leave too. He loosened his hold on his surprising hellcat.

Mistake.

Jessie broke free and loomed over Lydia, who finally had the good sense to cower like a whipped pup. "Stay away from him, do you hear me? I will fuck you up if I ever see you looking at him again. And if you ever touch him, I swear to God I will—"

"And...we're done." Brandt picked Jessie up, snagged their coats off the chairs and carried her out of the bar.

As soon as they were outside, she thrashed and said, "Let me down."

"Only if you promise me you ain't gonna make a break for it and go back inside."

"Bitch would deserve it," she muttered.

Brandt didn't release her until they reached his truck. He tossed her the long duster and slipped on his jacket. "Get in."

"No. I'm too fucking mad."

"If you wanna try scream therapy again, we need to get out of town first."

"I just wanna punch something. Or someone. But since you won't let me do that..." She kicked a clump of dirt. Tracked down another and kicked it too.

Brandt watched her, unruffled by this violent side of his sweet Jessie, mostly because he understood it. "Why did you go after her like that?"

"Because she had her hands on you. Because she was kissing you. God. She had no right. Are all women so desperate? Didn't she know better than to throw herself at another woman's man? In public, no less."

He froze. His brain backtracked. Wait a second. Jessie hadn't gotten pissed off because of what Lydia had said about her or Luke, she'd gotten pissed off over Lydia lumping *him* in with all other cheating men in the world. Hope like he'd never experienced filled his chest. Somehow he managed to keep his tone even when he asked, "So do you make a habit of this?"

Jessie snorted. "Fighting? Not hardly. I've never wanted to kill anyone with my bare hands as much as I did the second I saw her plastered to you."

"That's interesting."

"Why?"

"Because I've never had a woman fight over me."

"Well, I've never had a man worth fighting for."

Brandt erased the five feet between them, forcing her to look at him. "Run that by me one more time."

Jessie, his sweet fiery Jessie, didn't stay passive. She slapped her hands on the sides of his face and locked her gaze to his. "You are the one man in the world I will fight for, Brandt McKay, because I love you."

"You do?"

"Yes. Before you jump to the conclusion that I'm telling you this now when Landon isn't in the picture, you'd be partially right. What I didn't say earlier today before Landon left with his mother was that I'd never make you choose. But now that he's gone I was afraid that you don't need me anymore—"

"Since all I wanted you for was Landon's childcare?" he demanded. "And all you wanted me for was sex?"

Her eyes searched his. "No. But did the high emotions and intensity of the situation and the hottest freakin' sex on the planet heighten everything between us?"

The knot of fear in his belly tightened. Oh hell no. He was *not* losing her now. "Let me make this clear, Jessie. I love you. I've loved you for a long goddamn time, even when I shouldn't have loved you. I know you love me—even when you were too stubborn or scared to admit it. I see it whenever you look at me. I feel it when you're touchin' me. So I cannot for the life of me understand why you're questioning this now. Now when we have no obstacles and a lifetime ahead of us."

"Because I want a clean slate about everything. That includes the big 'what if' scenario that's been hanging between us for three months."

"So what are you sayin'?"

"If Samantha had shown up today and asked you to continue as Landon's guardian without specifying how long, I would've pulled up my big girl panties and stayed by your side where I belong. I would've found a way to deal with it."

This woman...goddamn, she could knock him to his knees.

"I want you in my life, Brandt. So if part of your life is caring for your brother's son, then that makes it part of my life too. Whatever black and white view I had of this situation with Landon in the beginning changed over the past few months. I care about him. I care what happens to him." Her eyes filled with tears. "I'm happy we had him for as long as we did. But seeing how much Samantha loves him and how happy he was to see her...I know he belongs with his mother."

"This is why I asked you to help me. Because you've got a big heart and you're willing to put it out there, even if there's a chance you might get it stomped on. Jessie—"

She placed her thumbs over his lips. "Us being together won't be an easy road. There will be people like Lydia, like your father, who will want us to fail. So you should know I fell in love with you not because you're Luke's brother, but in spite of it.

"You've become everything to me in ways Luke never was. I never imagined I'd find a man like you, who's sweet, sexy, funny, thoughtful, kind. A man who makes me feel like I'm enough for him. A man I can trust without question. A man I will fight anyone for." Her eyes filled with tears and she whispered, "God. I feel like such an idiot because you've been here the whole time."

"Hey." Brandt wiped her cheeks. "You weren't ready to see me in any of those roles in your life."

"Yet you waited until I was."

"After you were so shocked when I told you I wanted more than a family type relationship, I realized too late you still needed more time. Come to find out time was good for me too."

"Meaning what?"

"The years you were married to Luke, it hurt me to see how he treated you. After Luke died, I made myself available, hopin' you'd see me as the man who could heal you. And you took what I offered, but gave me nothin' in return."

"I'm sorry."

Brandt kissed the inside of her wrist. "I know you are. I also know it wasn't intentional. In the last few months, I've gotten to know you, the real Jessie, not the idealized version I'd built up as the woman I was determined to save. Not the woman who needed me only as her handyman and grief counselor. Not the woman I lusted after. I realized what I felt before wasn't love. Because now? Now I understand what real love is. It's this." He lowered his mouth and kissed her, loving how she wrapped herself around him as if she'd never let him go. He broke the kiss with a laugh.

"What?"

"Never thought I'd be confessing my love to you in the damn parking lot of a bar."

"I never thought it'd take a hair pulling fight to prompt me to tell you how I felt about you." Jessie rubbed her lips across his and whispered, "Promise you won't stomp on my heart, Brandt McKay. I swear it would crush me in a way I'd never recover from."

"I promise. I love you. So will you marry me?"

Her mouth opened. But something stopped her from answering.

"You do understand that I won't be like Luke? I promise to be faithful to you forever. I don't see fidelity as an option clause in marriage vows."

Jessie bit her lip and stared at him with those wide eyes.

"Don't leave me hangin' now," he half-snarled.

"What about your family? I think Dalton and Tell will be okay with us being together. But your dad? He hates me. Can you—"

"What's the worst he can do? Say no?" Brandt kissed her. "Nothin' would be worse than not havin' you in my life, Jess. Nothin'."

"Then if you're sure...Yes. I'll marry you."

He whooped and spun her around, not noticing the cold, or anything else except the look of happiness in Jessie's beautiful eyes that he knew mirrored the happiness in his soul.

Chapter Twenty-Three

Brandt would rather have a root canal without anesthesia than talk to his father.

He knocked on the front door of the house he'd grown up in.

His mother answered, dishtowel in hand, as usual. "Brandt. Sweetie, it's good to see you. You don't need to knock. Come in. What's up?"

"I have something I wanna talk to you guys about."

She kept her expression neutral. "Go into the dining room. Your dad's in there. I'll be right in with coffee."

Brandt rounded the corner and saw his dad sprawled in his padded captain's chair at the end of the big oak table. He stopped out of habit to gauge his father's mood.

If Casper McKay was happy he'd push back in his chair and tip his hat up to meet your gaze. If Casper was out of sorts, he wouldn't acknowledge your presence at all.

Brandt studied him. In the last two years he'd aged ten. His black hair was mostly gray. The deep blue of his eyes had faded into the hue of old denim. His eyebrows were still black, still drawn together in a frown. The firm set to his mouth gave the appearance of a permanent scowl. His lean face and long neck flowed into a hard, tight frame, a body weathered on the wide-open spaces of Wyoming. A mindset that was as cold, hard and unforgiving as the land that'd forged him.

No smile. No "How are you?" just a calculating stare and a curt, "Brandt."

Definitely in a piss poor mood.

Brandt left his hat on and he grabbed the back of the dining room chair in front of him. "Dad."

"You here for a reason?"

"Yeah."

"Well, spit it out."

His mother brought Brandt cup of coffee and refilled Casper's cup before attempting to hightail it out of the room. Brandt snagged her elbow. "Stay. I want you to hear this too."

She nodded and slipped into the chair on her husband's right side.

"Well?"

"Landon's mother picked him up yesterday and they're gonna be livin' in Casper. After they get settled she wants to talk about visitation rights."

"Oughta be the other way around. She oughta be here askin' *us* for visitation. That boy belongs with his family. If you'd hired a decent lawyer that specializes in these cases—"

"You mean that ambulance chasin' bozo from Cheyenne? Wrong. Besides, Landon belongs with his mother." Brandt glanced at his mom, but she was busy studying the floral pattern on the placemat.

"So you here to gloat that you got what you wanted? My only grandson taken away from me?"

Like Casper had paid any attention to Landon while he was here. He didn't want him, but he didn't want anyone else to have him either. "No. I'm here to tell you that I'm marryin' Jessie."

Silence.

His dad slowly stood. "Is this some kind of goddamn joke?"

"No."

"What the hell is wrong with you, Brandt? It ain't enough that she made your brother miserable, and that misery got him killed?"

He retorted, "She had nothin' to do with Luke's car accident. And I ain't gonna argue with you about who was more miserable in their marriage because neither you nor I lived with them. But that's all in the past now."

"Past? Sounds like you're not putting her in the past where she belongs."

"That's because she belongs with me. Her future is with me."

"That right? So she spread her legs for you. Big fuckin'

deal. Don't mean you gotta tie yourself—and us—to her again. The only good thing to come outta Luke's death was her leaving."

This was a fucking nightmare, way worse than he'd anticipated. "She didn't leave voluntarily. You forced her out. Which was the shittiest thing you've ever done."

He shrugged. "So you say. And you ain't exactly unbiased, are you?"

Count to ten.

"I'm marryin' her and there's nothin' you can do about it."

His dad moved closer, a sidewinder about to strike. "Oh, don't be too sure about that, son. Don't forget who owns this ranch and who pays your wages."

Brandt's fingers tightened on the back of the chair. "Is that a threat?"

"Just stating the facts. Everything you've got, except that pitiful chunk of land you and your brothers bought, comes from me. And I can take it back any goddamn time I want. Your name ain't on the papers, boy, mine is."

Before Brandt could say a word, his mother stood. "Casper. Don't do this."

The mean glint intensified. "I'll do anything I damn well please, and it's time this boy really understood that. So if you insist on tyin' yourself to that woman in any way, you won't inherit a single inch of McKay land. And you know I don't bluff."

At that moment his dislike for his father bloomed into full-blown hatred. The next thing Brandt knew, he'd pushed the smarmy son of a bitch into the wall and pressed his arm across his father's windpipe, holding him in place.

He vaguely heard his mother say, "Brandt, stop," but the rage had overtaken him.

"Let me tell you something, you mean goddamn bastard, I'm done. I'm done puttin' up with your bullshit excuses for why you haven't turned the ranch over to your sons. I'm done with you lording it over us. We've been runnin' this ranch since before Luke died, not you."

Casper choked on his own spit as he tried to say something.

But Brandt wasn't about to let him speak before he said his piece. "So if you think you've got it in you, old man, to do everything yourself, then by God, I'd like to see you try. But we both know that won't happen, will it?"

When his father didn't respond, Brandt eased up on his chokehold. "Answer me, goddammit."

"You think you're so fuckin' smart."

"I know it don't take a rocket scientist to figure out that you've got *no one* in your life to help you if I walk away from the ranch. Tell and Dalton won't stick around. And you'd rather let this place fall into ruin and let the cattle starve before you'll ask your brothers for help, wouldn't you? So yeah, chase me off. You go on out there in the bitter fuckin' cold and deal with feeding twice a goddamn day. Good luck with calving season and everything else that it takes to run this ranch, since you haven't done a goddamned thing for close to ten years. Ain't that right?"

"You think I owe you something? I don't. I owe you nothin'."

Brandt got right in his dad's face. "I've busted my ass for years even when nothin' I ever did pleased you. I've put up with your bullshit. I've watched you prefer the company of a twelve pack to the company of your wife. I've watched you destroy any chance of a relationship with me, Tell and Dalton, because you're pissed off at God and the universe that we're here and Luke isn't."

"He shouldn't have died."

"But he did. And it's no one's fault, least of all Jessie's."

"If she woulda made him happy, he wouldn't've been lookin' for it all over the goddamn county. That little bitch made him miserable from the day he married her. And she'll make you miserable too. Mark my words."

Brandt shoved him again, hard. "I'm so fuckin' sick and tired of you running off at the mouth about her. You don't know a thing about Jessie. You never have."

"And I never will."

"Brandt. Let him go."

He felt rather than saw Tell and Dalton move in behind him. But he couldn't make his hand release his father's shirt. He couldn't move his arm.

"Come on, bro. This isn't helping."

A beat passed and Brandt finally let go and stepped back.

A smirk twisted his father's face. "Felt good, didn't it? To give in to that anger? I saw it in your eyes. No matter what you say, no matter how hard you try, you know the truth. You're just like me."

Infuriated, Brandt lunged for him again, but he got there too late.

Tell had pinned their father against the wall. "Shut it, old man. Brandt may've gotten the hair trigger temper from you, but my anger has been smoldering for years and I guarantee you don't want me to give in to it. Ever." Tell shoved him once and stepped back.

Their dad's eyes slid to Dalton. "What? You ain't gonna tell me how long you've been gunning for me? Waitin' for the day to beat the crap out of your old man?"

Dalton said nothing.

He laughed cruelly. "Still actin' like a boy, letting our brothers do all the talking, taking all the punishments to save your precious hide. How long before they realize you ain't worth it?"

"Stop it. All of you," his mother said, sobbing. "Stop it right now."

Silence.

Brandt glared at his father, his rage a living thing.

"You can have her or a stake in the ranch, Brandt, but not both. You choose."

He didn't look at his brothers or his mother as he picked up his hat and left.

Jessie had just gotten back from feeding the animals when she noticed Brandt's truck was parked in front of her trailer. No sign of him. He'd probably gone inside.

Without saying anything to her? That was strange. Brandt always searched her out when she did chores. Always.

Maybe he was tired. Yesterday was long and emotionally trying for both of them. Not to mention he'd kept her up half the night, making love to her until they fell asleep still joined—which had been a first for her, and more romantic than she'd imagined. Draped across Brandt's warm body, her head nestled under his chin, her knees curled by his hips with his cock still embedded inside her, his hands cupping her ass. She'd woken up a couple hours later when he hardened inside her. He rolled her over and made love to her again, whispering words of devotion. Declaring his undying, never-ending love for her. Making promises she actually believed.

It'd been the greatest night of her life.

Smiling, she dropped the bucket and the pitchfork next to the gate and raced to the house. She burst inside. "Brandt?"

No answer.

Lexie lifted her head and gave her a crabby look for disturbing her nap.

Huh. That was weird. Brandt's boots weren't on the rug. His clothes weren't hung up on the coat tree. She kicked off her overshoes and walked down the hallway. "Brandt? You okay?"

No answer.

He wasn't in the bathroom.

He wasn't in the bedroom.

Maybe she'd just missed him and he was in the barn.

As Jessie was slipping her boots back on, she heard her cell phone beep, indicating she had a voice mail. She snatched the phone off the coffee table and checked the missed calls. Tell had called. Four times in the last hour.

Her stomach sank to her toes. She dialed her voice mail and listened to the first of two messages.

"Jessie. Brandt is on his way there. Or I assume he's on his way. He's not answering any phone calls from me or Dalton and...Jesus. We're freaked out. It didn't go well with Dad today and...Just call me, okay?"

Didn't go well? What the hell did that mean? The next message started to play.

"Jess, I know I already left you a message, but it's really important you get back to me right away and let me know you're okay. I've never seen Brandt like this."

Never seem him like this. Like what? Why would Tell be worried that Brandt would hurt her? Brandt would never ever hurt her.

Maybe he's worried that Brandt will hurt himself.

Oh God. No.

Fear spiked her pulse. Jessie tore down the steps and sprinted to the barn. But when she reached the side barn door, which had been left ajar, she skidded to a stop. Busting in on him was a bad idea.

She slipped inside as quietly as possible. The familiar scents of hay, manure, dirt, grain and grease didn't offer the usual comfort, especially when she heard harsh grunts and the hard and fast *thud thud thud* of one object striking another.

The sound of a chain rattling echoed from the tack room. A sound she recognized. The heavy bag.

She crept to the back of the barn and froze.

Any relief that Brandt was taking out his aggressions on the punching bag fled when she saw all the blood. Spattered on his face. On his bare chest and arms. Bloody streaks smeared on the canvas cover of the bag. His knuckles were raw. His forearms were scraped from elbow to wrist. Bloody scrapes spread across both his shoulders.

He'd taken off his shirt to inflict the most possible damage to his body. His neck and chest and abs were coated with a mixture of sweat and blood. When Jessie found the guts to look at his face, she couldn't withhold a gasp. His hair was plastered to his head. His face was bright red, the muscles in his jaw flexed with every punch he threw. The veins in his neck bulged to the point she could see his pulse pounding. His forehead and cheeks and chin were wet, but she couldn't tell if it was from sweat or tears. But it was his eyes that stopped her. She recognized the rage and grief. She didn't recognize the feral light that made him look like a wild animal, incapable of rational thought.

He's hurting himself. Stop him.

But Jessie was frozen in that place between logic and fear. What if she stepped in and he was so far gone he somehow hurt her? Without knowing what he was doing? Brandt would never forgive himself.

Can you forgive yourself if he has an aneurysm and you stood by and let it happen?

No. That snapped her out of her trance, watching Brandt beat the heavy bag and himself to a pulp.

"Brandt."

No response.

She said it louder. "Brandt."

Still no response.

Jessie moved closer. "Brandt. Stop. You're hurting

yourself."

Without missing a punch, he said, "Go away. You don't want to be around me right now."

Left punch, right punch, left jab, right jab. She stood there long enough to memorize the pattern. Her gut tightened into a knot when she noticed the skin peeling back from his knuckles. "I'm not going anywhere. Talk to me."

He grunted and nailed the heavy bag harder. "Get the fuck out of here, Jessie. Now."

"Why should I leave?"

"Because I'm pissed off."

"You think I haven't dealt with a pissed off man before?"

"Not like me. Never when I'm like this."

"So? I can handle—"

"I'm not Landon, throwing a little boy tantrum."

"You sure?" she shot back.

"Don't fuckin' push me."

"Don't fuckin' shut me out."

Brandt made a roaring noise and started whacking his forearms into the bag. Left, right, left, right each blow harder than the last. His need to grit his teeth to deal with the new pain he was imposing upon himself was the last straw.

Jessie lost it. Angry tears, frustrated tears, scared tears all poured out at once and she screamed at him, pulling the canvas bag away from him. "Goddammit Brandt, stop! Stop it! You're hurting yourself. You're hurting yourself and it's killing me. My God. Please. Just stop."

The flying arms slowed, then stopped. Brandt leaned forward, chest heaving with every ragged breath, his body shaking as he rested his forehead to the heavy bag and wrapped his arms around it to keep himself upright.

She stumbled behind him, pressing her face into his sweaty back, molding her body to his. Holding him as he vibrated with rage, holding him as he bled, trying to hold them both together.

Brandt's voice was a whisper of pain. "I hate him. I fucking hate him. I never…" His voice broke and once again they were locked in hellish silence. "I never wanted you to see me like this."

Jessie understood him not wanting to show weakness to others, but she thought they'd gone beyond that. "So why did you come here, Brandt? To my house?"

Another long silence. Then his soft, "Because I had no place else to go."

Angry tears formed and she released him. "So I'm a last resort now?"

He whirled around so fast he bumped into her, knocking her off balance and sideways. In super slow-mo she crashed into the wooden slats, hissing as a splinter sliced her cheek, gasping as she twisted her body to land on her hands and knees, sucking in a harsh breath as gravel and hay dug into her palms and her knees skidded out from underneath her.

Then Brandt was roughly hauling her upright. His grip on her biceps hurt, but she sucked up the pain. The little sting was nothing compared to the damage he'd exacted on himself. She looked at him.

The agony in his eyes stole her breath. "Oh God, look at you. You're bleeding. I did that. I hurt you."

"I'm okay."

Brandt recoiled in horror. "I have to go."

"Go where? Brandt, you don't even have a shirt on—"

He stumbled back, turned and walked out.

Don't let him go. Not like this.

Jessie snatched up his clothes and chased him down, planting herself right in front of him. "At least put your goddamn clothes on if you're leaving me."

He ducked his head and grabbed the bundle. But he didn't deny he was leaving her.

"Talk to me. I deserve that much."

"You deserve much better than a man who lashes out in anger and hurts you."

"You didn't do it on purpose."

"But it still happened. It can happen again."

"That's bullshit and you know it. Tell me what the hell happened with your dad today."

Wincing, he yanked his shirt on, then his coat. He finally looked at her. "I need some time."

Oh God. She went dizzy. Her legs, her world threatened to go out from under her. Gritting her teeth, she locked her knees to keep them from buckling. "Time for what?"

"Time to think." He gently moved her aside from blocking

the driver's side door. "Go inside before you freeze to death."

But she couldn't seem to make her feet move. She watched him drive away.

She stood there until the wind picked up and snow swirled around her. Until Lexie's barks roused her and she trudged inside, absolutely numb.

Her entire body shook. She stripped down and stayed under the shower spray until she drained the water heater of every drop of hot water. She dressed in her warmest flannel pajamas before she started a pot of coffee. But she couldn't get warm. She put a healthy dollop of whiskey in it before she dialed.

He picked up on the second ring. "Jessie? What the hell is goin' on? I've called you like a dozen times. Have you seen Brandt?"

"He left."

A pause, then, "He left?"

"Yeah. After he beat the shit out of my heavy bag and himself—"

"Goddammit, did he hurt you?" Tell demanded.

"Intentionally? No. But he thinks he did."

"What the fuck did he say to you?"

"Nothing. I have no idea what's going on. He said he needed some time and he took off."

"That's it?"

"Yes. So maybe you oughta tell me what happened today."

Seemed a full hour passed before Tell spoke. "Some of this I heard from Mom, some of this I saw firsthand. Brandt told Dad you two were getting married. Dad, bein' Dad, spewed bullshit. Told Brandt he'd have to choose between you and his portion of the McKay ranch, because he couldn't have both."

Her Irish coffee threatened to come back up.

"Then Brandt threw Dad against the wall and that's when me'n Dalton came in. After that, Brandt left."

"So you don't know if he's decided—"

"Don't say it, Jessie, don't even fucking think it. Brandt loves you. He always has."

She tipped her head back and closed her eyes. "But he loves that ranch too. That's all he's known. That's all he's ever wanted was to take over running it."

"And you think our Dad don't know that?"

"I know that once Casper has drawn the line in the sand, he won't erase it, he won't move it, and he sure as hell won't back down from it. Brandt will have to choose."

A muttered curse, followed by, "Yeah, it sucks, but he will."

Poor Brandt hadn't wanted to choose between her and Landon. He'd dodged that bullet only to have the gun waved in his face again. As much as she wanted to be the one he'd pick, as much as she wanted to plead her case and offer him assurances that their life together would be worth giving up his heritage, she couldn't. She wouldn't. She had to give him the time to decide, even if it damn near killed her, so he wouldn't have regrets about his choice.

Even if she did.

Chapter Twenty-Four

Brandt couldn't go to his trailer, couldn't go to Tell's place or Dalton's place, couldn't go to Ben's. Definitely couldn't go back to Jessie's.

His entire body burned with shame. After he'd left his folk's house, he'd driven to Jessie's on autopilot. But once there, he realized he didn't want her to see him in such an extreme state of anger. So he thought he'd take the edge off by using her heavy bag.

Everything was a blur after that. Until he saw Jessie watching him. Every ounce of shame surfaced.

It defied logic when she'd wrapped herself around him, offering him comfort when he should've been reassuring her that he wasn't an animal.

An animal that'd hurt her.

His beautiful, sweet, kind, loving Jessie had blood on her face. Blood he'd brought forth in anger. It'd made him absolutely sick.

He'd had to get out of there.

He needed a place to think things through.

He'd ended up at the bunkhouse. It sat empty for most of the year, only used during calving and haying season. Or when one of his cousins and their wives needed alone time, hence the nickname the *nookie shack*.

It wasn't easy to get to, especially not in a snowstorm. Equipped with food, water and a bunkbed, Brandt figured he could crash a couple days before anyone thought to look here.

He fired up the wood stove and set a pan of snow on the top to melt. He'd need to clean himself up since his wounds were starting to sting. But his adrenaline rush was history and he crashed. He hit the bed with his boots on, his clothes on, his gloves on, in too much pain to do anything but groan before he passed out cold.

Brandt dreamed of Luke.

The old Luke. The brother he'd laughed with and worked with and worshipped his whole life. The brother he'd mourned more than anyone other than Jessie had ever known.

They sat around a campfire, drinking icy cold Fat Tire, staring at the black sky overloaded with stars. The silence between them wasn't awkward, as it'd been the last few years.

Brandt sipped his beer, taking in the wide-open space. It wasn't anywhere he and Luke had ever been. Everything about it seemed...too perfect. He looked at his brother. "So, is this heaven? Or hell?"

Luke shrugged. "Neither, really. I guess you'd call it neutral ground."

"Why are we here?"

"You tell me. It's your dream, bro. I'm dead."

Brandt winced. He wondered how much this dream brother knew about what'd happened in the past few months.

"I know about you and Jessie," he said softly.

"Then you know I love her."

"You've always loved her."

"Did you really hate me for that, Luke?"

"No. I felt guilty. I should've let you have her that first night. I shouldn't have tried so damn hard to prove that I was the better man. When it's always been obvious that you are the better man. In all respects. It kinda pisses me off." Luke smirked, and flicked the cap of his beer bottle at Brandt, like he always used to.

"Hey! What was that for?"

"Old times' sake." Luke's intense gaze didn't waver. "None of that past stuff matters anymore. You are doin' the right thing by her?"

Brandt kept his cool since he'd already lost his temper once today. Granted, he doubted this dream embodiment of Luke could swing back. "Do you really think I'd pick a chunk of dirt over Jessie? Do you really think I'd walk away from her now when I've got everything I've ever wanted?"

Luke shrugged again. "I figured it wouldn't hurt to ask."

"I know what's important. I won't be like you, Luke."

"Good."

"What? No excuses?"

"There wasn't any excuse for what I did. I just wanted to—"

"Give me your blessing?" Brandt poked in the fire with a long stick, close enough he felt the heat burning his knuckles.

"You don't need that from me. Just havin' her in your life will be blessing enough."

When Brandt looked up from the fiery red embers, Luke was gone.

He woke up gasping, coughing from the campfire smoke, his knuckles smarting from being too close to the fire.

But as he pushed himself upright, he remembered where he was. In the bunkhouse, which accounted for the smell of smoke. He glanced down at his hands, hot because they were still encased in gloves.

That explained it.

But still...What a weird fucking dream.

Brandt tossed another log on the fire, downed four aspirin and returned to the bunk. His clothes were stuck to his body with a mixture of blood and sweat, but he couldn't muster the energy to clean himself up. He managed to toe off his boots. As he took off his coat, something pinged on the wooden floor. Despite the shooting pain in his arms, he reached down and caught the circular object on the tip of his finger.

A metal cap from a bottle of Fat Tire beer.

No. It couldn't be.

He spun around the room, half-expecting to still be in that alternate reality, praying everything today had been some kind of twisted dream. His father gleefully cutting him out of his heritage. Losing his mind in a fit of rage in front of Jessie and hurting her. Hoping the walls of the bunkhouse would disappear and he'd see his brother, sitting by the campfire, drinking beer and grinning at him. Just like old times.

But nothing changed.

Took Brandt really long time to fall asleep after that.

Chapter Twenty-Five

Day 1
Brandt hadn't stopped by. He hadn't called. Jessie went about her Sunday routine as usual. Cleaning. Washing clothes. Paying bills. Feeding the animals. Cooking a pot roast with all the trimmings—enough food for two.

Day 2
Brandt hadn't stopped by. He hadn't called. Jessie took advantage of the Monday holiday to work with her horses. Then she fed the animals. She drove to the store for ice cream. She watched TV. She called her mother. She fell into bed alone.

Day 3
Brandt hadn't stopped by. He hadn't called. Jessie couldn't face going into work at Sky Blue so she called in sick. And she was heartsick. She curled up on the couch with Lexie. She drank tea and ate toast. Between the bouts of sniffles, she checked her phone to make sure the damn thing was working. She fed the animals. She heated up a can of soup and shuffled off to bed alone.

Day 4
Brandt hadn't stopped by. He hadn't called. Just how much time did the man need? But Jessie couldn't face Skylar or India or Kade or Kane or Ginger or Simone without breaking down completely. She needed another day. Despite the guilt, she called in sick.

Jessie assumed the person rapping on her door at ten a.m. would be Skylar. Jessie considered ignoring it, but it'd be easier to 'fess up here, rather than in an official capacity at Skylar's office. She shushed Lexie and opened the door.

Joan McKay stood on her porch. She looked different but Jessie couldn't put her finger on what it was about her that was off.

It hit her. Jessie grabbed Joan's arm. "Has something happened to Brandt?"

Joan shook her head. "As far as I know Brandt is fine."

She sagged against the doorframe. "Thank God."

"Haven't you heard from him?"

"Not at all."

Sorrow flickered in Joan's eyes. "Can I come in?"

"Ah sure." Jessie poured two cups of coffee while Joan took off her coat and settled on the couch. She handed her a cup. Did she sit next to her former mother-in-law? Or keep her distance, like she always had?

"I imagine you're wondering why I'm here."

Jessie sat beside Joan on the couch. "You never were one just to stop by to chat."

"How sad is that? Anyway, I wanted to clear a couple of things up before I..." She set her cup down on the coffee table with a resounding thud. "Actually, I want to apologize."

"For what?"

"For not standing up to Casper after Luke died. I've convinced myself I was so lost in grief I wasn't thinking straight. But the truth is, making waves wouldn't have changed anything, Casper does what he wants and to hell with everybody else. That was how I justified my 'head in the sand' behavior when it came to you and everything else in that situation. I'm sorry."

Jessie didn't know what to say. She watched Joan struggle, this woman she'd always seen as torn between her duty as a wife and as a mother.

"And I should've tried harder to have some kind of relationship with you, Jessie, after you and Luke got married. Casper didn't like you, and I figured after you lost the baby early on, he'd do everything to break you and Luke up." She distractedly rubbed the center of her forehead. "I felt bad for you, but us being friends would've just pissed Casper off even more and he would've taken it out on both of us. And Luke. Trust me."

"Know what I never understood? Why Casper hated me so much in the first place."

Joan drained her coffee and walked to the kitchen. Almost on automatic, she poured herself another cup, but it sat cooling untouched on the counter for several excruciating minutes while she stared out the front window.

Jessie followed her, a feeling of dread settling in her bones. "Joan? Is everything all right?"

"No. I can't even begin to tell you how wrong it is. All of this." She braced her hands on the counter in front of the sink. "Casper hated you because your bun-in-the-oven marriage to Luke reminded him of me. Of us."

Okay. That was news. Luke had ever mentioned it. Or maybe Luke hadn't known. "Yours was a shotgun wedding?"

"Yes. Are you shocked?"

Jessie had to tread lightly. This was the most Joan had ever opened up to her. "Yes. I am."

"Because Casper ended up with someone like me?" Joan asked, not bothering to hide her petulance.

"No. The opposite. I can't fathom how a woman like you ended up with a man like him."

"You really are sweet," Joan murmured. Then she sighed. "The truth is, at one time, Casper was considered quite a catch. He came from a good family. His future was set as part of the ranching McKays. He was good-looking, charming, fun, wild as hell, but that bad boy side is always so appealing, isn't it? Why do women have this overwhelming desire to tame a bad boy? Then we're shocked when that taming doesn't happen. Or worse, when it does stick we lament the man they used to be."

Joan seemed lost in thought so Jessie stayed quiet. But she hadn't seen Luke as the bad boy to tame. Brandt was the polar opposite of a bad boy, so it wasn't a female mindset she understood, but she'd seen friends drawn to that type of man again and again and it rarely ended well.

"Anyway, I wasn't particularly pretty. I wasn't particularly charming. I wasn't particularly clever. I was actually pretty plain. I knew plain, shy and boring would never catch the eye of a dynamic man like him. And I wanted him more than anything on earth."

As hard as she tried, Jessie couldn't make the connection between that man Joan was describing and the Casper she knew.

"Casper had half a dozen girls on the string at any given time. So I became the type of girl he couldn't resist." She paused for effect. "Easy. He'd come to me after his pretty, clever, charming little girlfriends wouldn't put out. He came to me often because I'd do anything in bed he wanted. Any time, any place.

"This went on for about six months. At first I believed I could get him to fall for me. That our bedroom romps would make him like me. Would make him willing to have me on his arm in public, instead of just his dirty little bedroom secret. I dreamed he'd take me dancing. Or out for dinner. But like most nineteen-year-old girls, I was naïve. I'd heard a rumor from my friends that Casper was getting serious with a woman from Spearfish. One night I snuck into his favorite bar and watched them. She was one of those beautiful blondes, curvy body, perfect face, life of the party. She was everything I wasn't. I knew Casper was head over heels in love with her. I knew after the first time he took her to bed I'd never see him again."

Jessie held her breath.

"So I lied. I told my father I was pregnant. Told him I'd been sneaking around with Casper McKay for months. My father went directly to Jed McKay and demanded his son do the right thing and marry me."

"And he did."

"Yes. I was happy. Obviously Casper was not. I'd hoped I'd get pregnant for real right away and ours wouldn't be a relationship based on a lie. When four months passed and I wasn't showing, I faked a miscarriage. It was a lot easier to do in those days. Ten years passed before I got pregnant and by year five Casper figured out I'd tricked him."

She felt sick. Everything was clicking into place but it didn't make it easier to accept or understand.

Joan reached for her coffee and drank before continuing. "He flew into a rage and said I'd ruined his life, which was probably true. It was the only time he ever hit me. He left and didn't come back for a week. And when he came back, he was a different man entirely.

"I was so...grateful he hadn't thrown me out and so relieved he still wanted to bed me, that I lived solely for him to make up for the lie and the trouble I'd caused. Like any man, he got used to using me doing everything for him, never questioning him. By the time we started having the boys, he'd turned bitter. He took out his frustration with how his life turned out on them—as a punishment to me, not to them, because he knew how much I loved our sons. He ostracized his brothers. And I was still too afraid that he'd leave me, proving every fear I'd ever had about my worth, so I did nothing. I kept my mouth shut. For years."

"What changed?"

"Luke died. And Casper has become more bitter, if that's possible. When we found out about Landon..." Joan turned around but she wouldn't look Jessie in the eye. "It sliced me to the quick to discover that Brandt didn't trust me with Luke's child. Not because I'd be cruel to the boy, but because I wouldn't stop Casper from being the same way to Landon that he'd been to his own sons."

God. This was so ugly. So unnecessary.

"These are my mistakes, Jessie, and I've owned up to them. But the final straw? When Casper told Brandt to choose between the ranch and you. When he told me that our child would never be welcome in our home again. When he told me he never wanted to see Brandt again." Joan lifted her head and met Jessie's gaze. "I won't lose another son. I won't lose Tell or Dalton either. I can't do this anymore."

Was Joan looking for a place to stay? Or just moral support? Jessie wasn't sure and didn't want to make a misstep with Brandt's mother after she'd reached out to her. "What are you going to do?"

"I've already done it. I've left my husband."

Jessie's mouth fell open in shock. "What?"

"I should've done it long ago. So when he raced over to talk to his brothers after cutting Brandt off, I packed up and lit out."

"Where did you go?"

"I've been bouncing between Carolyn's, Kimi's and Vi's. They've rallied around me, which has been nice. But..." She sighed. "It's time I moved on. We've been miserable together for so long, maybe we have a chance to find happiness if we're apart."

"But where will you go now?"

"I'm going to Casper." Joan expelled a nervous laugh. "Funny, huh? That I'm leaving Casper to go to Casper? After I found out about Samantha and Landon, I visited Samantha in jail a few times. Poor thing doesn't have anyone in her life she can rely on. She needs help and she's accepted my offer to be there for her and Landon. He's such an unexpected joy. I haven't had much joy in my life lately. At sixty-two years old I feel I'm due."

"Will you be living with them?"

She shook her head. "Close by. I've got a cousin who's agreed to let me stay with her temporarily. I don't know how long I'll be staying there. Luckily I won't need to get a job, not that I'm qualified for more than cookin' and cleanin' anyway, because I've got the 'mad' money I've been saving."

"Mad money?" Was that like...egg money or something?

"Every time Casper got mad about something, I put a dollar in the jar. You can imagine I've got a tidy pile after forty years."

That did cause Jessie to smile. Until she realized she might be the first one Joan had confided in. "Does Brandt know you're leaving?"

"Yes. I talked to Dalton and Tell last night and I stopped at Brandt's house right before I came over here."

Her heart leapt at the mention of Brandt's name. "Oh. So he's home then? Not at the ranch?"

"Why would he be at the ranch?"

"Because...hasn't Brandt...I mean—" *spit it out, Jessie,* "—he hasn't...Fine. I haven't seen or heard from him so I thought he'd already made his choice."

Joan placed her hand on Jessie's forearm in such an uncharacteristically loving gesture Jessie's heart stalled. This couldn't be good. "Jessie. Brandt loves you. There never was any question in anyone's mind who he'd choose. Including his father's."

Before relief swept through her fully, she demanded, "Then why haven't I seen him for four days?"

"Maybe you oughta be asking him that, instead of me."

Jessie realized Joan was exactly right. No more of this giving him time, waiting around for him to come his senses bullshit. The old Jessie would stand around and wring her hands and wait for him to come to her. The new Jessie, the Jessie who'd found the man of her heart and soul, needed to go to him first. As soon as humanly possible. "Thank you."

"No. Thank you for listening to me babble. It actually felt good to get that off my chest." She frowned. "But I'd appreciate it if you didn't tell Brandt or his brothers."

"I won't. It'll be just between us girls."

Joan did the oddest thing: she tugged Jessie against her for a fierce hug. She whispered, "I'm sorry. I hope you'll give me another chance to be part of your lives. I like you, Jessie. I'd like to get to know you. I'd like to put all that bullshit from the past aside and start fresh."

Jessie said, "That sounds like a great plan, Joan," and really meant it.

As Joan McKay drove off, Jessie finally realized what was different about the woman. She actually looked...happy for a change.

Jessie wanted that same happiness for herself. Dammit. She deserved it.

And the only way to get it was to take it.

After she changed into work clothes, she hitched the empty horse trailer to her truck and headed out.

Butterflies danced in her belly as she drove down the long driveway leading to Brandt's house. By the time she reached the banks of snow piled by the deck, Brandt stood on the steps, waiting for her.

"Jess? What are you doin' here with a horse trailer?"

She scaled the stairs in one step and got right in his face. "Did you mean what you said? When you told me you loved me and wanted to marry me?"

"Yes. But—"

"Did you tell your dad to take a flyin' leap as far as the ranch is concerned?"

"Yes. But—"

"In the past four days when you haven't contacted me *at all*," she lightly cuffed him in the arm, "have you had any regrets about anything that's been going on between us in the last few months?"

"No. But—"

"Good. Then what are you waiting for? Let's get your stuff packed up and loaded in the trailer so we can take it back to my place."

Brandt circled her biceps, stopping her. "Whoa. Wait a second. Do you know what's happened? I've lost my identity, my job, and I've got a limited skill set in the world outside ranching, I'm damn close to destitute and you're..." His eyes narrowed. "Chipper as a damn squirrel about that."

Jessie laughed. "Of course I am."

"Why?"

"Because—"

"Why would you want me?"

"Because—"

"I can't offer you anything."

She knocked free of his hold and grabbed him by the lapels to get nose to nose with him. "Now you listen to me, Brandt McKay. I love you. *You.* Not your ranch, not your station in life as part of the McKay ranching dynasty. You've already offered me everything I want."

"Which is?"

"A lifetime with you."

His eyes softened. "Jess."

"Don't you dare back out on me now. So we've hit yet *another* rough spot. So? Ain't the first time and I doubt it'll be the last. But I have every faith we'll overcome it. Together."

"But—"

"You're the best man I've ever known. You are worth fighting for. *We* are worth fighting for. I love you. I love you so freakin' much. Don't give up. Please." She moved even closer, completely invading his space. "Say something, dammit."

"I would if you'd left me get a word in edgewise." He brushed his lips across hers. "I missed you." He kissed her. "I love you." He kissed her again. "God, do I ever love you." One last smooch to her mouth. "But you're too late."

Her heart damn near stopped. "Too late for what?"

"To help me pack. Everything is already loaded in the back of my truck."

Then she kissed him. Jessie wanted to kiss him with all he hunger and passion he always gave her, but it was hard to keep their lips attached when all she could do was smile.

"I can't believe you're here," he murmured against her mouth, much later, as they were twined together in his bed. "What prompted you to come after me?"

"The fear that you changed your mind and decided I wasn't worth all the hassle."

"What hassle?"

She gave him a light head butt. "Oh, a little thing like your dad making you choose between the ranch and me." Her eyes searched his. "Why didn't you tell me that the day you showed up and killed my poor heavy bag?"

That flash of shame appeared, heating his cheeks. "I get in these...rages, Jess. They're ugly and I'm mean. I come out swinging and don't stop until everything and everybody in front of me is leveled. Or until someone hands me my ass or I pass out. Fun stuff." He sighed. "I'm so goddamn sorry that I hurt you—"

"You didn't mean to. And it hurt me a helluva lot worse when you walked out."

"There was some stuff I needed to work out." Maybe someday he'd tell Jessie about the bizarre dream he'd had about Luke.

"So you really picked me? Over the ranch?"

"No contest."

Brandt and Jessie had started loading tack into the horse trailer when a pickup pulled up. Jessie tensed. The pickup looked exactly like Casper's but Brandt knew the pickup belonged to his Uncle Carson.

He watched as all three of his McKay uncles climbed out of Carson's truck. Carson and Cal were twins, not identical, but that wasn't obvious at first glance. Charlie had the same look about him as his brothers did, but he was shorter, stockier. As far as McKay family dynamics, Charlie should've been last on the pecking order as the youngest son. But it'd always been Casper, the oldest of Jed McKay's sons, at the bottom of the heap.

Strange, seeing his uncles here. They rarely ventured to this part of the ranch, and never to Brandt's house. So they must've gotten wind of Casper's ultimatum. Brandt's pride appeared, reminding him he didn't need his uncles' charity.

He told pride to shut the fuck up.

"Brandt." Carson removed his glove, thrust out his hand and Brandt shook it, then he shook Calvin and Charlie's hands in kind.

"I don't gotta ask why you guys are here," Brandt said. "But I do wanna know who called you."

Carson shoved his hands in the front pocket of his Carhartt coat. "Actually Casper contacted us."

"That surprises me."

"Surprised the hell out of me too," Charlie said. "Jesus. The man showed up at my place out of his mind."

Brandt frowned. "Your place?"

"Yeah, guess he considers me the weakest link in the McKay chain of command." Charlie shot his brothers a sideways glance. "But that's always been Casper's problem. We've never had the 'me' versus 'them' mentality."

"But he has."

Charlie nodded. "As soon as he showed up Vi called Carson and Cal."

"Did he…" How could he ask his uncles if his dad had told them he'd attacked his father?

Cal clapped Brandt on the shoulder. "Son, we know what he's like. Which is why we all needed to be there. Been brewing for a long goddamn time. It's time we dealt with it." He looked at Jessie with that trademark charming McKay smile. "Darlin', if you wouldn't mind givin' us some time with Brandt—"

"Sorry. Brandt and I are a package deal now. Whatever you intend to discuss with him can be said in front of me. Rest assured, I'll never repeat what I hear, but Brandt and I have had too many family things between us, keeping us apart for too long."

Brandt had such a fierce sense of pride, such an overpowering feeling of love for this woman. He reached for Jessie's hand. Right then he knew he'd never have to worry where he stood with her, because she'd always stand beside him.

Jessie said, "It's too damn cold out here. Let's head inside."

After outerwear was removed, Brandt passed around beer. He sat in the easy chair with Jessie perched on the arm beside him. "So I guess I'd like to hear what my dad said to you before I tell you what really happened."

"It ain't pretty, Brandt. Just figured I oughta be up front with you about that," Cal warned.

"Understood."

"Casper said things'd gone to hell in a hand basket since Luke died. He'd entrusted you with the ranch and you'd make some piss poor decisions and he no longer trusted your judgment."

Jessie threaded her fingers through his.

"When we pressed him for solid facts, Casper sputtered something about you convincing your brothers to buy more land, when the three of you couldn't take care of what you already had." Charlie grunted. "Course, that's when we pointed out for the last two years, since you've taken over, your calves had a higher weight ratio than ever. Then I told him you boys buying that grazing land, even when you had to put yourselves in hock for it, was one of the smarter decisions anyone's made."

"Casper didn't wanna hear that," Carson pointed out. "He also didn't wanna hear us tellin' him that he hadn't been pullin' his weight for damn near a decade. And that if it hadn't been for his sons bustin' ass, we would've redistributed his parcel amongst the three of us and our sons."

A feeling of pride and dread surfaced simultaneously. Brandt and his brothers had done everything to make their part of the McKay ranch as successful as the others. But with their dad overruling them, they'd lost some of what they'd gained. "What was his response?"

"Typical Casper blustering. Told us if we thought we could do a better job, then we could go ahead and buy him out."

Brandt went motionless. Not only would Casper McKay cut him out, he'd cut out Tell and Dalton from their heritage too. He took a long swallow of beer and met his Uncle Carson's gaze, managing to keep his voice steady. "What did you say?"

"We took him up on it."

Silence.

Brandt felt as if he'd been sliced in two.

"Now before you go getting that look on your face, son, hear us out. You know we've been restructuring several aspects of the ranch over the last few months."

"Chase mentioned it, so did Kade, but I'll admit Casper kept us in the dark. Whenever we asked, he refused to talk about it."

Charlie nodded. "Chase said as much. Which let us know that anything we were doin' had to be completely above board. It also forced us to look very closely at the past legal documentation for the ranch. And what Dash Paulson found sort of shocked us."

"What's that?"

"We were under the impression that if just one of us wanted to sell our portion of the ranch, the other three owners would be forced to sell theirs too. Which is how Casper tried to control us, or at least got away with a lot more shit than we would've let him, had we known the real legalities of the matter."

Carson pointed with his beer bottle. "It entails lots of legal gibberish that took us slow readin' ranchers some time to understand, but the bottom line is we were wrong. Casper never had the power to force us to sell."

Brandt held up his hand. "Wait a second. My dad threatened to sell his portion of the ranch?"

"Several times over the years. To be honest, he even went as far as to have it appraised about six months after Luke died."

That son of a bitch. "Why?"

"So he could point out what idiots we were for keepin' it, when we could have more money in our pockets than we could ever spend."

"How much money we talkin'?"

The three brothers exchanged a look. Then Carson met his gaze. "On paper? Over eighty million dollars."

"Holy fucking shit."

"So yeah, Casper thought he had the ace in the hole, thinkin' if we wanted to buy out his portion of the ranch, it'd cost us over twenty million dollars each. Which none of us have in cash obviously."

Brandt looked at Cal. "What is the legal discrepancy the lawyer found?"

"I'll tell you, my daughter in law is one smart cookie. Ginger and her dad pored over the paperwork the last couple days and discovered a clause written into the original trust that'd been forgotten."

"What's that?"

"Majority rules," Charlie said. "We'd intended to talk to Casper about it, but he's been such a prick..." He looked at Jessie. "Sorry, Jess."

"If anyone knows how much of a prick Casper can be, it's Jessie." Brandt kissed her hand. "I'm assuming he told you the choice he gave me?"

"Yeah. He said he wanted you off the payroll and to treat your departure the same as we had when Chase, Carter, Cam and Keely opted out of the land trust."

Seemed his father really did want to leave him destitute.

"'Course, we said no." Carson grinned. "Then we sprang the 'majority rules' clause on him. Which means we all have a say in what happens to his portion of the ranch, but only as it relates to naming his successors."

"I don't understand."

"We can't take over or sell his portion of the ranch, but we can give control to his descendents. So you, Tell and Dalton now call the shots. Your father has officially been retired from ranching. He'll still receive a portion of the profits, but as far as the day-to-day operations and decision makin'? You and your brothers are in charge."

Brandt couldn't keep his jaw from dropping. "Are you serious?"

"Completely. But we should also point out in doin' this we couldn't single out your father. So me'n Cal and Charlie all officially retired too. The fourth generation of McKays are now one hundred percent in charge of the McKay cattle company and the ranch."

"So...you knew this all when my dad came to see you?"

"No. We listened to him, told him we'd hafta wait until Monday to talk to the attorney. Then Tuesday we met up and told him what we'd decided."

"How'd he take it?"

They exchanged another look and Cal spoke. "He didn't say a lot, Brandt, bein's that he was dealin' with your mother leavin' him."

"We couldn't tell him where Joan's been stayin'," Carson said. "Caro and Kimi and Vi have spent the last few days helpin' her...hell, I don't know what the four of 'em have been doin'."

A minute or so of awkward silence hung in the air.

"Do you have any questions?" Carson asked.

"About a million. But they'll keep. Wait, there is one, since I went off her grid for a few days." He sent Jessie an apologetic look. "Did you talk to Tell or Dalton about any of this?"

Charlie shook his head. "As a matter of fact, we haven't told our sons about it yet. Wanted to let you know first, since it changes everything for you and your brothers."

That floored him. He'd gone from flipping through the classifieds to find work to finding out he had a bigger stake in the ranch than before.

"No doubt our boys will be on board, happy to be kickin' the old men to the curb," Carson said dryly. "Little do they know we're gonna be watchin' them closer than ever."

"Yeah, only thing that'll change is we ain't haulin' our asses outta bed to do chores at the crack of nothin' any more," Cal said.

"A benefit of bein' retired," Charlie added. "Effective immediately."

All three men laughed. Then they stood.

"We'd best get on our way so we can have this same conversation again. Luckily, all the boys will be together later this afternoon so we'll only have to do it once."

Boys. Brandt wondered if these guys would still be calling them boys when they were in their sixties. "I'd like to be a part of the conversation, if you don't mind. Me'n Tell and Dalton."

"Thinkin' of makin' some changes already?" Carson asked.

"We'll see, but it'll nice to be involved in the decision makin' process for once."

"Agreed."

Brandt slipped his arm around Jessie's waist and pulled her close. "Anything else?"

"Just one." Carson looked between Brandt and Jessie. "We're all happy for you two."

He waited for Carson to add something, like Luke would be happy for them, too, or advise them to start having McKay babies, but he turned away and spoke to Cal as they put on their winter wear.

"Did you hear what Liesl did the other day?"

"Yeah, Eliza told me."

"Was she in on it?"

"No, but I swear them two girls are gonna be more trouble than all their male cousins combined."

"Probably more than their uncles and fathers combined," Charlie offered.

All three men groaned on their way out the door.

Brandt tugged Jessie on his lap and just held her, trying to process everything. And she rested her head into that spot on his body that'd been made for her.

"What're you thinkin' about?"

"How it's sad your uncles' wives are finally offering Joan support now, when she doesn't need it. She needed it years ago."

Brandt kissed her forehead. "It's sweet of you to stand up for her, Jess, but my mom should've asked for support years ago. Plus, it just goes to show you that it's never too late to change."

"True. Do you think Joan just needs time away? That she and Casper will get back together down the road?"

"I don't know. I plan on keeping my nose out of their marriage and I hope they extend us the same courtesy."

Jessie wrapped her arms around his neck. "Speaking of marriage...when are we making it official?"

"Within the week, Jess. I'm not givin' you time to change your mind. So pick a day."

"You're serious?"

"I've never been more serious in my life. Let's do it as soon as possible."

"But what about—"

Brandt smothered her protest with a kiss. A kiss that heated rapidly, as kisses between them were prone to do. He kept kissing her, pouring everything of himself, everything he was feeling into her. He rested his forehead to hers. "I want to spend my life with you, Jessie. Every day. With you as my wife. I don't want to wait because my feelings ain't ever gonna change."

"I feel the same." Jessie laughed. "Okay. Let's do it."

"How about Friday?"

"Oh. Wait. It's not Friday the thirteenth, is it?"

He laughed. "Knowing our luck, it probably is. But I can't help but think our luck is about to change."

About the Author

To learn more about Lorelei James, please visit www.loreleijames.com. Send an email to lorelei@loreleijames.com or join her Yahoo! group to join in the fun with other readers as well as Lorelei:
http://groups.yahoo.com/group/LoreleiJamesGang

She surrendered the reins. Now he's raising the stakes.

Raising Kane
© *2010 Lorelei James*
Rough Riders, Book 9

When a patch of ice sends attorney Ginger Paulson head-over-high-heels down a flight of stairs, she has no one to care for her young son and her invalid father—until lethally sexy Kane McKay shows up at the hospital, determined to prove his cowboy chivalry. Past experience has inoculated her against take-charge men, but even Ginger isn't immune to Kane's invasive charm and Built Ford Tough body.

For two years rancher Kane McKay has followed the Little Buddies mentoring program's cardinal rule—hands off his Little Buddy Hayden's mama. But one look at Ginger's bruised body and Kane is through watching the stubborn woman take care of everyone but herself. The feisty, curvy redhead needs his help, and he'll give her the hands-on type whether she likes it or not.

After Kane throws out doctor's orders and issues his own demands—her full sexual submission—Ginger realizes Kane's caring nature extends beyond just fulfilling her physical needs.

Can the former hell-raiser convince the gun-shy single mom to look beyond his past...toward a shared future?

Warning: Contains one sweet and hot hunk of cowboy manflesh who uses every sexual trick in the book to render a sassy, fast-talking attorney speechless and put a new twist on the term "binding arbitration".

Available now in ebook and print from Samhain Publishing.